Since 2004, internationally bestselling author **Sherrilyn Kenyon** has placed over sixty novels on the *New York Times* bestseller list; in the past three years alone, she has claimed the No.1 spot seventeen times. This extraordinary bestseller continues to top every genre she writes within.

Proclaimed the pre-eminent voice in paranormal fiction by critics, Kenyon has helped pioneer – and define – the current paranormal trend that has captivated the world and continues to blaze new trails that blur traditional genre lines.

With more than 25 million copies of her books in print in over 100 countries, her current series include: The Dark-Hunters, League, Lords of Avalon, Chronicles of Nick, and Belador Code.

Visit Sherrilyn Kenyon online:

www.sherrilynkenyon.co.uk
www.facebook.com/AuthorSherrilynKenyon
@KenyonSherrilyn

Praise for Sherrilyn Kenyon:

'A publishing phenomenon ... [Sherrilyn Kenyon] is the reigning queen of the wildly successful paranormal scene'
Publishers Weekly

'Kenyon's writing is brisk, ironic and relentlessly imaginative. These are not your mother's vampire novels'
Boston Globe

'Whether writing as Sherrilyn Kenyon or Kinley MacGregor, this author delivers great romantic fantasy!'
New York Times bestselling author Elizabeth Lowell

Esse
301

D0270127

SHERRILYN
KENYON

DEADMEN
WALKING

piatkus

PIATKUS

First published in the US in 2017 by Tor Books, New York
First published in Great Britain in 2017 by Piatkus
This paperback edition published in 2018 by Piatkus

1 3 5 7 9 10 8 6 4 2

Copyright © 2017 by Sherrilyn Kenyon

The moral right of the author has been asserted.

*All characters and events in this publication, other than those
clearly in the public domain, are fictitious and any resemblance
to real persons, living or dead, is purely coincidental.*

All rights reserved.
No part of this publication may be reproduced, stored in a
retrieval system, or transmitted in any form or by any means, without
the prior permission in writing of the publisher, nor be otherwise circulated
in any form of binding or cover other than that in which it is published
and without a similar condition including this condition
being imposed on the subsequent purchaser.

A CIP catalogue record for this book
is available from the British Library.

ISBN 978-0-349-41218-4

Printed and bound by CPI Group (UK) Ltd, Croydon, CR0 4YY

Papers used by Piatkus are from well-managed forests
and other responsible sources.

Piatkus
An imprint of
Little, Brown Book Group
Carmelite House
50 Victoria Embankment
London EC4Y 0DZ

An Hachette UK Company
www.hachette.co.uk

www.littlebrown.co.uk

As always, to my husband and boys for being the light in every day of my life and showing me that real heroes exist, and that they're funny to boot. To my friends who keep me sane. My readers who take these trips of fantasy with me and who never fail to make me smile. And a special thank-you to Claire, Linda, and Robert for giving me the chance to do something I've been wanting to do for a long time and for not clipping my wings when I finally took the leap over the edge.

Most of all, for my big brother, who never once rolled his eyes at my stories when I was a girl, and for all the crayons you gave me so that I could draw my characters and leave you in peace. I miss you every day of my life and wish you could have seen the series you loved so much reach even higher than that pirate kite you saved for me from the mean, angry tree that tried to eat it. You were and shall always be my greatest hero. The monster slayer who battled the closet demons of my mind and kept me sage through the darkest nights and storms that seemed to go on without stalling. I don't know where I'd be had you not been my brother. I love you, Buddy. This book is for you.

Acknowledgments

To my grandfathers, who introduced me to the world of demons and angry spirits, and who taught me to see beyond the veil and showed me how to protect myself and to fight for others. And for all those spiritual warriors in my life who continue the fight and who've aided me so many times when I needed you. Thank you, Tish, Bill, Leanna, and Marianne. Most of all, my Grandmother Moon, who taught me to read signs, pay attention to nature, and to see the unseen. There is magick all around us. We just have to stop and open our eyes.

DEADMEN
WALKING

PROLOGUE

In the Year of Our Lord 1715, July 31
Off the Shores of Cape Canaveral, Florida

"Well, we learned a vital lesson here today, me mateys. You canna keelhaul a demon no matter how hard you try for it. The rotten crafty beastie bastard won't be having none of it."

Half the crew turned to stare agape at Captain Paden Jack. The other half rolled their eyes and cursed him, then questioned his saintly mother's impeccable reputation, as well as the legitimacy of his parentage and all his intelligence.

If they weren't about to die, he'd take a mite more

offense to their sordid insults. But right here, right now, as he looked past them and saw the great, heinous monster what was rising up from the darkest swirling depths off their port bow, insubordination seemed like a wee bit of a petty concern.

Never in all his years at sea had Paden beheld anything like its twisted, inhuman form, and he'd seen quite a lot. Its leathery skin literally boiled and caused the water 'round it to bubble with the same noxious fumes—a fetid sulphuric stench that exploded the moment it contacted the fire left from all the attempts they'd made to lay the beast low.

Nothing had worked. Not a single trick.

His quartermaster staggered back. "The sea is the devil and that wicked bitch takes pity on none."

Aye, Paden couldn't agree more. They were done for. To the watery locker they be headed, with every last man-jack here.

At least those who weren't headed straight for hell.

Strange how he felt no fear, what with his assured damnation looming. And he should. You'd think what given the sins of his past and all the things he'd done in this life, they'd be haunting him now. Yet all Paden felt was an untoward kind of peace with it all.

This was the way of it. He'd known this day would come for him—sooner, rather than later—the heartbeat he'd accepted his destiny by taking up his mother's sword and embracing the blood that flowed within him. It always did for ones such as he. His only regret was that he'd be taking his crew with him for the journey down.

And that he'd be breaking his promise to marry Letty on his

return. But the greatest burn of all was that his poor baby sister would be left alone in this world, with none more to look after her.

That his great, horrific burdens would now fall to her tiny shoulders.

Damn shame, that. Cammy deserved better than what the fates had dealt the lass. They'd be coming after her now to pick up the mantle their ancestors had cursed them with. But there was no use lamenting for it. God and all His saints had turned a deaf ear to his pleas and prayers long ago.

His quartermaster, Edmond, passed a sorry stare to him before crossing himself. "What be your orders, Captain Jack?"

"Abandon ship, Mr. Symmes. Save as many as you can."

It wasn't until after Symmes had relayed those orders that he realized Paden had no intention of joining them in their escape.

Safety wasn't his calling this day.

Instead of trying to find room on a dinghy with the others, Paden was rolling barrels of gunpowder closer to the port bow, where the beast still tried its best to devour them whole.

"Captain? What are you about, man?"

Paden handed his quartermaster his cutlass and flintlocks. "This fine ship be me ladylove—me one true mistress and owner of me hell-bound soul. It's me duty and honor to escort her to her final destination. And be damned if I'm letting that bastard there have her without taking a piece of him with us. Get yourselves safe. Think naught of me anymore, Mr. Symmes. God be with you as I know He's never been with me."

His gaze sad, Ed hesitated. But a moment was all he had, as the demon slammed against the ship, knocking her sideways and causing her to list. "It's been me privilege, Captain." He held his arm out to Paden.

"Mine as well." He shook Ed's hand. "Now off with you, quick."

Ed ran as the ship tipped dangerously, spilling more men over her side.

Retrieving the linstock from the deck where one of their powder monkeys had abandoned it as he fled for the dinghies, Paden waited until the last of the boats had dropped. He pulled a striker and flint from his pocket and lit the cord so that he could ignite the powder.

The demon started after his fleeing crew.

"Hey now!" he shouted at the beast. "Where do you think you be headed, you filthy, odiferous bung!" He waved the linstock over his head to get the demon's attention back on him as he struck the side of the ship with the end of it, making as much racket as he could.

It worked.

Snarling, the demon turned and, with a hell-born cry, made straight for Paden.

His heart pounding in anticipation of what was to come, he waited for their inevitable confrontation.

This time, the beast dared to climb aboard.

That's it, ye filthy bastard. Come get some of me. Leave me crew in peace.

With no real form, the gelatinous mess slithered across the deck and rose up before him with dark, soulless eyes.

Refusing to show his fear, as it would only make the beast

stronger, or to back down before it, Paden stood his ground with every bit of grit he possessed. "Aye, you want me, don't you? You know what I am, and I know ye for the evil in your heart."

Possessed of great bulbous eyes, it slobbered and drooled and reached with one taloned hand.

Just as it would have slashed him open, Patrick Michel Alister Jack lowered his linstock to the keg of gunpowder that lay between them and set the barrel ablaze.

The last sound he heard was deafening, and it ended with a bright flash and one massive explosion of pain.

1

In the Year of Our Lord 1716
Jamaica

"Way I hear tell it, that one's so bad, he whups his own arse thrice a week."

Eyes wide, Cameron Amelia Maire Jack burst out laughing at the unexpected, dry comment she overheard above the raucous tavern voices and music. Until she caught sight of the man it was directed toward. *That* sobered her quick enough.

Holy mother of God . . .

There was no way to miss that giant mass of

human male as he swept into the crowded room like the living embodiment of some ancient hero.

Nay, not a hero.

A pagan god.

At least six and a half feet tall, he towered over everyone else there, and had a shoulder width so great he was forced to turn to the side to come through the doorway, and stoop down lest he decapitate himself with the thick, low-hanging beam. A feat he accomplished with a masculine grace and swagger that said he'd done it enough that it was habit from years of experience.

Which made her wonder how many times as a boy he must have whacked his head afore he learned to instinctively duck like that.

With a quick swipe of his massive hand, he removed his black tricorne hat and tucked it beneath his muscled arm, exposing a thick mane of unbound, wavy sable hair that gleamed in the dull candlelight. He held a set of rugged features that appeared chiseled from stone—in perfect masculine proportions.

Never in her life had she beheld his equal in form, strength, or grace, but it wasn't just the unexpected sight of him. He possessed that raw, commanding presence that was unrivaled by king or commander. An air of noble refinement that was offset by an aura of bloodthirsty intolerance, cool indifference, and utter ennui.

He was lethal, no doubts there. Beguiling. More than that, he was an enigmatic study of warring contradictions that quickened her heart a lot more than she wanted to admit to anyone, especially herself.

In a festering den of inhospitable inequity and evil, this man reigned as its supreme emperor. And while his two companions were dressed in brightly colored brocades—like the other vain occupants of the room—this one, in stark contradiction, wore a somber black wool coat, breeches with plain brass buttons, and an unremarkable dark brown waistcoat. Even his cotton shirt and neckerchief were as black as his hair and boots. Like a Quaker . . . and yet his demeanor and weaponry said he didn't partake of their religion or peaceful ways.

The only color on his body was the bloodred hilt of a barbarian-styled cutlass. And a flashing ruby signet ring on his pinky that caught the light.

But for his fierce stance, deadly demeanor, and the firm hand that stayed planted on the hilt of that sword, he could easily pass for a respectable man. Nobleman even.

Until one met that cold, dark, intelligent gaze that saw everything around him to the most microscopic detail.

She could literally feel him tallying the strengths of everyone in the tavern and sizing them up for their every weakness of character and physical flaw. . . .

As well as their caskets.

He was exactly the kind of unnerving male that caused her and Lettice to draw straws on his entrance back home in the Black Swan to see which of them would be stuck for the night waiting on his table.

And Cameron always cheated to make sure *she* wasn't the one left with it. Something that would bother her conscience a lot more but for the fact that it was Lettice's father who owned the Swan, and while Nathaniel Harrison would guard his daughter's reputation and well-being, he wasn't nearly as circumspect when it came to hers. Especially when placed against his need for profit. He'd sell all *but* his daughter for that.

Even his own mother, and probably his wife to boot.

Not wanting to think about that, Cameron scowled at the men flanking the newcomer. His companions were much more the typical pirate or privateer fare one would expect to find in such a sordid place. The one to his right had a mane of long brown hair he wore tied back in an impeccable queue, along with a well-trimmed beard, and eyes so light and merry a blue they glowed in the dim light. Each of that man's fingers held an ornate ring—no doubt plunder from some unwary ship he'd raided—if not some unfortunate corpse. Still, he seemed amicable enough.

While many Caribbean pirates had a tendency to pierce their earlobes, this one had chosen to place a small gold hoop in his left eyebrow, just off its arch. His elaborate burgundy and black coat was widely cut at the waist—in the latest fashion craze. And where the beguiling and dangerous captain had chosen a plain black neckerchief to wear, this pirate's cravat was stark white silk, and trimmed in layers of decadent lace.

The man on the left was dressed in a peacock blue silk coat that covered an insanely ornate gold waistcoat. One so fine a silk that it shimmered in the light like water. He wore a small white wig that concealed his hair color, but judging from his skin tone, dark eyebrows, and the careless whiskers that dusted his well-sculpted cheeks and jawline, she assumed his hair was as dark as his captain's. Yet where the captain had a set of coal black eyes, his were a deep shade of hazel blue.

While his mood and countenance weren't as dark and sinister as his captain's, he was nowhere near as jovial as their companion, either. She'd guess him as the quartermaster.

Or a hangman.

The three of them swept past her without so much as a glance in her general direction, letting her know they saw her as no threat whatsoever—which was fine by her. Last thing she wanted was to be crossed up with such terrifying and deadly men.

They made their way to the back of the tavern to an empty table. The large, burly guard who'd been keeping it reserved for them inclined his head, then went to fetch their drinks.

Something he returned with so quickly that it no doubt set a speed record for the inn. From her years of working in such an establishment, she knew it said much about his fear of angering the three newcomers, and even more about their temperaments and personalities. These men did not like to be kept waiting, nor did they want to be interrupted once settled.

For the first time, Cameron's courage faltered as she watched the men begin a private and intense whispered conversation.

What are you doing, Cam?

This was what she'd come for—to speak to Captain Devyl Bane and enlist his aid.

Maybe it's not him.

She knew better. He was just as he'd been described. Darker than sin and more dangerous than dancing with the devil's favored handmaiden. There was no one else it could be. The witch-woman had told her to look for a captain who'd take her breath and leave no doubt in her mind that he was the bane of the devil himself.

That definitely described the man in the center of the other two. No one could be deadlier or more sinister.

"Greetings, governor. You be wanting some company, like?"

Cameron winced as an attractive prostitute plunked herself down on her lap. Because Cameron was dressed as a man and passing herself off as one so that she could travel unmolested and with ease, the prostitute had no idea she was wasting her time there.

Grinding her teeth, Cameron caught the woman's hand before it drifted to a part of her body that would scandalize them both. Cameron shook her head sharply.

"What? You mute?" She reached to touch Cameron's face and smiled wide. "That's all right, love. Don't be needing no words for what I do best, no ways. Fact is you be getting more your money's worth if'n we don't be speaking no how."

Cameron caught the woman's wrist again and reminded herself to toughen her voice and lower it an octave. "Not interested, me sweet. You're not me type." She cast her gaze meaningfully toward the three men.

The prostitute laughed. "Ah . . . can't says I blame you there. They each be so fine you can't help but crave a bite of those backsides and pray for lockjaw." With another winsome smile, she sighed. "Best of luck to you, mate. Way I hear tell it, though, you don't got a chance with none of them."

And with that, she left Cameron's lap to pursue another, more probable client.

Taking a deep breath, Cameron debated the sanity of seeing this mission through. It was obvious that the three men had no desire to be approached by a stranger.

In fact, they appeared to be arguing.

Heatedly.

This is all kinds of insanity. . . .

But Cameron Jack was not a coward.

Maybe a little?

She shushed the voice of reason in her head that told her to run for the door before they gutted her. *Jacks aren't craven. Now get in there, me girl.*

Scared and breathless, she forced herself to her feet and crossed the room, trying to exude a confidence she definitely didn't feel. Her legs trembled as sweat beaded on her forehead and upper lip.

For a moment, she feared she'd faint.

You can do this. Don't you dare back out now. Patrick needs you. You're all he has in this world. . . .

The moment she neared them, they fell silent and all three pairs of eyes pierced her with a malevolent glare she was sure had turned lesser beings into stone.

Or, at the very least, caused them to soil their breeches.

Captain Bane took a drink of his ale before he spoke in a voice so deep, it rolled out like thunder over a dark, stormy cove. "May I help you?"

She took a nervous step forward.

The brown-haired man pulled his sword and angled it at her neck. "That be close enough, lad. Declare yourself."

She cleared her throat and met the captain's gaze levelly. "I was told that you're Captain Bane?"

Without confirming it, the one she was sure was he brushed his thumb over his bottom lip. "Why do you seek the good captain?"

"I was told that he . . . or you, rather, were part of the salvage for the Plate Fleet that went down?"

His mate stood and, with his sword, forced her to step back. "We know nothing of what you speak."

Too late, she realized that they probably mistook her for one of the king's pirate hunters who'd been tasked with going after the raiders of the sunken ships and their cargos. "It's not what you're thinking. Me brother was on one of the ships."

Bane reached out to touch the man's hand and force the point of his companion's sword toward the floor. "And?"

"I was told he went down with his ship." She choked on her tears that threatened to overwhelm her. Ever since she'd heard about her brother's fate, she'd been unable to cope. Unable to breathe. Not after all the two of them had been through together. "Please. I have to know the truth."

The wigged man spoke with a degree of sympathy in his voice. "Only one ship made it out."

"Aye," she whispered. "The *Griffon*. He wasn't on that one. His ship was the *San Miguel*. He was the captain of it . . . Patrick Jack."

Bane's gaze softened. "Sorry. The captain didn't make it out."

As they began to ignore her, it angered her to be dismissed so casually, and Cameron stepped forward again. "If what you say is true, then can you explain *this* to me." She tossed the bit of salvage that had been delivered to her door with a note from her brother.

It skidded across the table to land beneath the candle in front of Bane.

He and his companions froze for a full minute as she held her breath, waiting.

It was a worthless trinket that made no sense whatsoever. A strange bit of a charm designed in the shape of an ornate cup, with a pair of wings rising over the rim and a stake with ribbons that fell from the bottom of it. And marked with a fleur-de-lis in the center of its bowl. While it was pretty enough, she had no idea why her brother would have sent such to her. Why he would even bother.

Never mind anyone else. It would be all kinds of cruel were it a hoax.

The captain scowled at the necklace charm, but made no move to touch it. "Is this supposed to mean something to me?"

She shrugged. "No idea." Slowly, she approached the table and held out the note that had been wrapped and sealed around the item. "This was what he used to hold it and send it to me."

Bane took the crumpled parchment from her hand and read it. The letter was simple and heartbreaking. One she'd committed to memory.

Cam,

Forgive me for leaving you as I have. Know that me loyalty is with you. Always. Listen not to anyone. Keep your weather eye to the horizon and this to your bosom. Tell no one that you have it. Not even Lettice. Trust none at your back.

Ever yours,
P.J.

With a gruff countenance, Bane returned it to her. Again without touching her or the necklace charm. "And so what's the first thing you do with this?" he mocked.

He was right. She'd done exactly what her brother had instructed her not to do—she'd handed it over to someone she didn't know. "True, but I have to find me brother, sir." She turned the letter around and pointed to the top of it. "Note the date. It's months after they went down, and he supposedly drowned by all accounts. Yet if he drowned, how did he send it to me?"

A peculiar light flickered in Bane's dark eyes. One that made them appear almost red in the candlelight. Surely an optical illusion of some kind. "Who told you to come here?"

"A witch-woman named Menyara. She said that you'd be able to help me find me brother."

He let out a fetid curse under his breath. It was so foul and guttural that it caused the man on his left to snap to his feet and step away from him, as if fearing an imminent attack of some sort from his captain.

"Who's Menyara?" the man asked.

A tic started in Bane's jaw. "Don't ask questions you don't want answered, Will. And pray to your God that you never meet that bitch." With a dark, deadly grimace, he finally took her trinket into his hand to examine it more closely.

His expression unreadable, Bane met her gaze. "Did *she* see this?"

"Nay. Only the letter."

"Why did you show it to me, then?"

"I . . . I'm not sure."

He flipped the trinket through his fingers several times while Will slowly returned to his seat.

"What are you thinking, Captain?" the one in the wig asked.

"All kinds of folly." He paused to meet the man's curious gaze. "I commend her to you, Mr. Meers. Take her to the ship."

"Beg pardon?" He scowled fiercely. "What *she* be this?"

The captain screwed his face up at him. "Are you dafter than a doornail, son? Our little Cameron Jack here be a lass as sure as I be your devil's bastard seed."

Both of his companions gaped at him, then her.

And she returned their slack-jawed stares without blinking or flinching. "How did you know that?" No one could ever tell she was female whenever she disguised herself as a lad. It was a ploy she'd been using ever since her parents had orphaned them when she was a small girl. A ruse Patrick had insisted on to keep her safe from harm, and under his nose so that he could watch after her.

Bane scoffed as he reached for his ale. "Never try to fool the devil, love. I can see right through you. Besides, no man has an ass that fine. If he did, he'd serve to be changing my religion on certain things." He took a deep drink, then inclined his head to his companion. "See her to the ship, Bart."

Bart hesitated. "Are you *sure* about that?"

"Aye, and settle her in private quarters for now. Make sure the others know to leave her in peace or face my full wrath."

Bart saluted him. "Aye, sir."

"And Mr. Meers?"

He paused to look back with an arched brow.

"I expect on my arrival to the ship to find the lass as virginal after parting your company as she is on leaving mine right now."

Bart let out an irritated growl. "I hate you, Bane. You live only to suck all the joy out of me death, don't you?"

He snorted. "Pray that joy is the only thing I ever strive to divest from you, my friend. The day I seek greater entertainment than that is the day you should live in absolute terror of."

"Duly noted, and me testicles have adequately shriveled back into me body so as to pose positively no threat whatsoever to the fair maiden in boy's clothing."

"Good man."

"Eunuch, you mean."

"And well you should remain, lest I make that condition a permanent one."

"Aye, aye, Captain."

Terrified by the thought of being alone with them and their crew, but too desperate to let her fear interfere with her need to find her brother, Cameron reached for her letter and medallion, praying with everything she had that this wasn't a mistake.

Please God, protect me.

Swallowing in nervous apprehension, she nodded, tucked away her possessions, then followed the captain's mate.

Devyl sat back to watch them leave. He cut his gaze toward his quartermaster. "What?" he snapped at Will.

"As I value me own testicles . . . not saying a single word, Captain. Just sitting here, nursing me rum." He held it up pointedly before he took a swig.

Devyl snorted at him. "Hope you find more courage than that for the task we have ahead of us."

"No fear there. Have more than me fair share. But you forget that I've seen you in a fight. And I'm neither fool nor drunk enough to think I can take you. Besides, you cheat and bite."

Those words pulled a rare laugh from Devyl. It was one of the reasons why he'd chosen Will as his quartermaster. Unlike the rest of his crew, Will was unflappable and bolder than he should be. He maintained his composure, good nature, and calm rationale under even the most harrowing of events. And he did so with a biting sense of sarcasm and gallows humor.

More than that, Will was as courageous as stated. Courage mitigated only by a sound ability to reason and measure the merits of confrontation.

Aye, William Death was one of the best men Devyl had ever fought with. It would be an honor to die by his side instead of the way Devyl had been gutted before. . . .

"Permission to speak freely, Captain?"

Crossing his arms over his chest, he leaned back to pin a sinister glare on Will. "If you've the backbone for it. Go on. . . ."

"Just wondering what mind you have to be bringing a human on board our bewitched ship."

"Did you get a look at what her brother sent her?"

"The meaningless bauble?"

Devyl scoffed. "And you're the one who claims to be the faithful religious man between us."

"Meaning?"

"That bauble, as you claim it, Mr. Death—"

"Deeth," Will corrected under his breath. It was ever his pet peeve that they didn't pronounce his name with a long *e* as opposed to the way it was spelled. Though why his ancestor had chosen to be so antagonistic with either the spelling or pronunciation was anyone's guess.

"Death," Devyl repeated incorrectly, as he was ever a cantankerous bastard, "is from the sword of St. Michael."

"Which one?"

He reached to flip at the silver medallion that hung off a leather cord Will had wound about his left wrist. "That winged bastard creature you believe protects and watches over you."

"I don't understand."

"Neither do I. But until I do, I thought it prudent to put her under our guard lest something foul decide to make her its next supper."

"And if that something foul proves to be a member of our crew?"

Devyl allowed his eyes to flash to their natural red state. "They would have a bad day, indeed. . . . My mood, however, would be vastly improved by their act of blatant stupidity that would result in my natural retaliatory act of extreme and unholy violence."

And speaking of . . .

The hairs on the back of his neck rose as he felt the hand of unsavory evil prowling toward the tavern.

Scowling, Will glanced about. "Do you feel that?"

"Aye. It's come ashore as I said it would." And headed for the largest gathering of victims . . . just as Devyl had also predicted.

Meanwhile, the humans in the tavern went on, oblivious to the malignant force that was headed for them.

Devyl rose, intending to keep them in their ignorance. But he only made it halfway to the door before it opened and three plat-eyes came in, wearing the skin of regular sailors.

Will pulled up short behind him. "Sailors from the downed fleet?" he whispered in Devyl's ear.

Devyl gave a subtle nod as he debated how best to deal with the unholy bastards who'd come to feast on the innocent and take their souls back to feed their mistress. Part of being a bound Hell-chaser was to let no one know that neither he nor Will had come to battle these demons.

Unfortunately, the plat-eyes didn't have a Code they were tied to. They passed an evil grin to one another, then went on a vicious attack that resulted in the three humans closest to them being ripped to shreds.

Utter chaos exploded as the humans sought cover and escape.

Devyl cursed as he was forced against the wall by the tidal wave of terrified humans who were hysterical over being trapped inside by inhuman predators. With their preternatural abilities, the plat-eyes had sealed the door so that no one could flee them.

They thought to feast tonight.

Groaning and shoving at a drunken male who was trying to reach a window, Will made it back to his side. "What do we do, sir? I can't get near them for the crowd."

Devyl pulled his coat off with a flourish, then handed it to his quartermaster. "Have I ever said how much I detest the sound of screaming humanity?"

"Really? Rumor has it, it was once your most cherished melody."

Hitting the release for his sling bow, Devyl passed an annoyed grimace to him. "Nay, the sweetest music to my ears has always been the death gurgle of an enemy slain at my feet as he gasps his last breath." Completely calm, he loaded the small bolt and released it straight into the skull of the nearest plat-eye.

The beast fell back and exploded into a black cloud.

Stunned, the other two turned to gape at Devyl. Then they must have realized who and what they faced.

Their eyes widened in unison before they shifted into wolf form and ran for the door.

But Devyl's power was greater than theirs and he held them inside.

Will grinned. "That got their attention, Captain."

As soon as the plat-eyes realized they couldn't escape, they shifted into their true hideous demonic bodies. Then they each split into three more beasts to attack.

Will cursed. "Vulnerable spot?"

"Between the eyes. Decapitation." Devyl caught the first one to reach him and twisted his head off. "But it won't kill them."

"Pardon?" Will visibly paled.

He took out two more before he turned to face the man. "Creatures of vengeance and lapdogs. These are shadow manifestations." He caught a fourth one with his knife and drove it straight through its skull. "To kill them for good, we have to find the bodies they assumed when they entered this realm and destroy them."

Will growled before he drew his sword and dispatched the one that came at his back. "I hate me job, Captain."

Devyl finished off the last, then quickly spread a compound of yew, salt, and ground jasper over the doorframe. That would keep more plat-eyes from coming inside to prey here again.

Will retrieved Devyl's coat and rushed to join him as the crowd began to realize the danger had passed. Now, they wanted answers neither of them was at liberty to give. And before the crowd could compose themselves further, Devyl and Will made a fast exit.

Outside the tavern, the moon had turned an eerie bloodred, and clouds hung thick in the sky, making it even darker.

Handing the coat to Devyl, Will grimaced. "So those are not the beasts we seek either?"

Devyl shook his head as he shrugged his coat on. "They're merely servants."

Will winced. "In our last few months together, I have seen unbelievable things that appear to have been spat out of hell itself. And I can't help but wonder just what exactly does the Carian Gate hold back from this world, if we haven't seen *it* yet?"

Fastening his cuff, Devyl met his worried stare with a knowing smirk. "The most corrupt, horrifying evil that ever gurgled up from the farting arse of the cosmos."

"Lucifer?"

He snorted and clapped Will on the back. "We should be so lucky. Nay, Mr. Death . . . what's coming up from the sea makes Lucifer look like a petulant, harmless child."

Will crossed himself. "What exactly is it, then?"

Devyl sobered at the memory as a wave of bitterness and fury washed over him and burned him to the core of his blackened and withered soul. "In short, Mr. Death . . . my ex-wife."

2

Cameron had to struggle to keep up with Bart's long, forceful strides that she was beginning to suspect he did apurpose just to wind her. "So how long have you served on Captain Bane's crew?"

He cursed her under his breath.

Again.

Honestly, she was beginning to develop a mental disorder over it. And an extreme case of paranoia.

"How many of these questions do you plan to assault me with, lass?"

"I know not. But I should like to have an answer to at least one of them . . . eventually. And before I die of frustration from it."

He ground his teeth so furiously that she could actually hear them gnashing together. "Would it perchance stop this aggravating deluge?"

"Might quell it some."

Clasping his hands behind his back, Bart slowed as they finally approached the docks and gave her a sideways glare. While not as breathtaking as the captain, he was exceptionally handsome with those piercing eyes. "All of us are new to the ill-tempered captain's company.

He assembled our crew a few months ago."

"What happened to his old crew?"

The moonlight cast spooky shadows over his sharp features, turning them sinister and cold. "There are many questions that are best left unasked, my lady. And that particular one definitely tops the list."

Perhaps, but it wasn't in her nature to let things rest. "Did pirates kill them?"

He gave her a sardonic smile.

"They say he *ate* them."

Cameron jumped as a thickly accented French voice came out of the shadows next to her. With an undignified squeak, she rushed to the other side of Bart, who laughed at her actions.

"Leave off the lass, Roach. Captain's orders."

"Lass?"

"Roach?" she asked in perfect synchronization with his question as the man stepped into the light so that she could see that he was a few years older than Bart. And quite a bit shorter.

Nowhere near as fashionable in his dress, he had a simple linen cap and a shirt with the sleeves rolled up to his elbows, held there by a bit of leather cord. And while he had a neckerchief, the collar of his shirt had been left unbuttoned and open so that the cloth was wound about his neck and not his shirt. His brown gloves were as worn as the dark red waistcoat he left unbuttoned. But the most curious thing was the whip he had around his tan-colored breeches in place of a belt.

Nor did he carry a sword. Rather, he had a baldric that secured a small double-headed hand-axe to his left hip. And now that he was closer, she realized he had flesh-colored vambraces. . . .

Nay, not vambraces. They were cleverly disguised dagger sheaths, which was why his shirt was tied up at the sleeves. That allowed him access to the hilts that were on the inside of his forearm and tucked into the crook of his elbow.

Very, *very* peculiar.

Bart rubbed at his brow. "Milady Cameron Jack, meet our resident cockroach, so named for the shadows he calls home and the way he scutters about them and sneaks up on everyone. Some claim so that he can cut their throats for profit and theft."

The Frenchman made a rude sound of disgust. "Ignore the mannerless, motherless snipe. Armand de la Roche at your service, madame." He clicked his heels together and gave her a proper court bow that was completely at odds with his shabby, careless clothing. *"Enchanté."*

"Merci, monsieur. Ravi de vous rencontrer."

Covering his heart, he acted as if he savored every syllable. "You speak beautifully and yet I detect a hint of an Irish lilt in your voice."

"Me mother was French and me father Irish. They brought us to Virginia when I was a small child."

"Us?"

"Her brother." There was a note of ice in Bart's tone that Cameron didn't quite understand. "Now, Roach, if you don't mind . . ."

He stepped in front of them to cut off their path. *"Pardon, Monsieur Meers . . . mais* you do not want to be doing that."

"Why ever not?"

"There is a bit of a calamity onboard. It would appear as if *le soul* has gone a-missing . . . again."

"Ah, dear God." Bart appeared sick to his stomach.

"Oui! Exactement!"

Cameron scowled at them. "Soul?"

Bart let out a long-suffering sigh. "Not even sure how to begin to explain this . . . one of our crew—"

"Absalon *le lune*—"

Bart grimaced at Armand. "He's not crazy. Per se."

"Ja, he is!"

Armand's use of German amused her.

"Anyway," Bart said between clenched teeth, ignoring him. "Sallie is under the stupidity that his soul was somehow sucked out of him and trapped inside an old rum bottle by a malicious witch."

Cameron gaped incredulously at the utter travesty of that belief. "What? Why?"

Bart gestured helplessly. "We've learned not to ask these questions, as they lead us into a realm of madness from which there's no escape. And let's face it, reason and logic abandoned this crew long ago. Therefore, we don't judge each other over the insanity, for there's not a member here who isn't a bit . . . touched in the head and peculiar in the ways."

"That is also true," Armand agreed. "But more so than any other, Absalon is . . . how do you say? A moonbug?"

She arched a brow. "Moonbug?"

"Lunatic," Bart said with a grimace. "Roach screws up about half of everything he attempts to say. English is not his native tongue. Stupidity is."

Roach made a sound of supreme irritation. And an extremely vulgar gesture that left Cameron wide-eyed and gaping—and she'd grown up an orphan, working in one of the most dangerous taverns in Williamsburg, frequented by scoundrels, pirates, and known rabble-rousers. In fact, she prided herself on being jaded and worldly for her age. Yet these men made her feel rather naïve and prudish.

Suddenly, she heard a loud whooping sound that was followed by cackles of raucous laughter.

"Ach, now! Ye faithless, motherless dogs! Give me back me soul! What's wrong with the sorry lot of you! What kind of cretin bastards be stealing a man's soul now, I ask you?"

Bart groaned out loud and slapped himself across the forehead. "I can't believe I died painfully in order to deal with this shite. I think I'd have rather stayed in hell. At least there, I only had Lucifer and *his* demons to contend with, and not the Devyl's bane and his idiots. No offense, but our Devyl scares me a whole whopping more than Old Scratch. Bastard's deadlier too, and more cantankerous. Never do you know what's going to set him off. Or how he'll react to anything."

Laughing, Roach clapped him on the back. "There, there, *mon ami, ca c'est bon*! 'Tis better than hell, anyway."

The look on Bart's face contradicted that as he rushed forward to deal with the thunderous voices.

Cameron stayed back, unsure of what exactly she was getting herself into on this quest to find her brother and return him home for Lettice, and her own personal sanity and safety. Time was running out, quickly, for the lot of them. Paden had left them all in a bad situation, and he had no idea of it.

Nathaniel had taken ill a few weeks back—as had Lettice, yet Lettice's illness had turned out to be an unexpected pregnancy only she and Cameron knew about. The girl was to have Paden's baby, and if he didn't return in the next few months to make an honest woman of her, there would be hell to pay for the whole lot of them. No doubt, Nathaniel would take his anger over his daughter's un-wed pregnancy out on Cameron's head if he couldn't locate her brother. There was no telling what the surly man might do to her in retaliation.

Nor did she wish to find out. Nathaniel barely tolerated her presence in his inn and tavern as it was. Only his fear of Paden kept him in check.

If he learned Paden was dead and that her brother had left Let-tice in a bad way . . .

Nathaniel would pull his protection of her, and Cameron would be penniless, homeless, without friend or family. Alone in a world that didn't look favorably upon anyone without means, references, or prospects.

Those thoughts scattering, Cameron slowed as she neared the

ship and saw the extent of the crew's utter madness. Men, and women who were dressed as men—so much for *her* being original—were chasing each other around the deck of the ship as they tossed an old amber bottle among themselves to keep it from the hands of a middle-aged seaman who stood an inch or two shorter than Cameron.

With a scruffy dark beard that was liberally laced with gray, he appeared affable enough. Why they sought to torture him, she had no idea.

Bart let out a fiercely loud whistle. "What manner of blatant stupidity be this? Are ye all daft? Or just wanting your enemies to sneak up and cut your throats while you're all distracted and screaming about like a bunch of weak-kneed trollops?"

Strangely amused and equally terrified of this group, Cameron stayed on the dock and watched as Bart slowly subdued them and collected the poor sailor's "soul" from a large Maasai warrior before returning it to the distressed man.

"Zumari!" Bart chided the warrior. "I can't believe you of all the ones on board would partake of such cruelty."

"I'd have never, had he not started in on me first!" Zumari's voice was as deep and lyrical as Bane's. But his mood was much lighter, in spite of the fact that she held no doubt he was every bit as lethal in a fight.

Cameron was just about to head onboard the ship to join them when she became aware of a small group of soldiers nearing her.

Grim-faced and heavily armed, they stalked past her with a determined stride that didn't bode well for whatever target they had in mind.

It froze her instantly.

A good thing, too, since that target turned out to be Bane's crew.

Stepping to the side so as not to be in the middle of whatever mal intent they had, she caught the feral grimace on Bart's and Zumari's faces the moment they saw them that said they were both a bit put out at the way fate had decided to treat them this night.

With his legs braced wide apart and his arms crossed over his chest, Bart met them at the top of the gangway and refused to allow them access to the deck of the ship. "What can I do for you, gentlemen?" The icy tone of his voice undermined the cordial words. As did the number of crewmen who came to stand behind him as reinforcements.

The soldiers didn't flinch, especially not their leader, a dark-haired bloke who bore a jagged scar over his left eye that said he was lucky to still have it. Unlike the others, he wasn't dressed in uniform. Rather, he wore the clothes of a well-dressed port official, or another privateer captain. "It was brought to our attention that you came into port earlier this day without colors or jack. We're here to inspect your papers and whatever cargo you might be carrying."

Bart curled his lip. "On whose authority?"

Their leader didn't flinch or back down. "Are you refusing to show your papers?"

"I don't bow to a common pirate hunter, if that's what you be asking, Barnet. You can take your men now and begone from this ship. There are no pirates among us. You're wasting your time and ours with this useless endeavor."

"If you know me, then you know I won't be leaving here until I see that paperwork."

A slow, insidious smile spread over Bart's face as Zumari stepped closer to back him. "Wouldn't be taking that wager, were I you. But I'll be taking odds on your leaving with disappointment in your heart, any day. Thrice on it today."

Just as the notorious pirate hunter Jonathan Barnet began to bluster in argument, a deep, resonant voice came out of the shadows. "There a problem? And the correct answer is nay, Devyl, there is not."

The color faded from Barnet's face as he turned slowly to see Devyl Bane and William Death parting from the fog on the docks. They walked past Cameron without acknowledging her in the least—which was fine by her since she didn't want to be under anyone's scrutiny while they were embroiled in this bit of heated controversy. Best to keep a low profile—that was the first lesson she'd learned as a girl after the death of her parents.

And how Captain Bane's voice traveled so effortlessly without his raising it, she had no idea. Yet it held that chilling, commanding tone and hung in the air like the voice of some ancient war god.

"Captain Bane," Barnet greeted with the smallest hint of a quiver in his own throat. "This be your ship?"

"Don't make a habit of trespassing on other men's vessels." The way he said that conveyed an insinuation that he wasn't talking strictly about boats. "Now get your mud-laden boots off her boards, as your mere presence here offends me to the core of my being, before I seek to teach you the manners your mother should have."

He didn't pause to even look at Captain Barnet. Rather, he kept walking straight past the entire group as if they were of no consequence or concern whatsoever.

Barnet took a step forward, but Bart and Zumari blocked his path to prevent him from following after their captain. "You have a new crew . . . ," Barnet said.

Bane didn't so much as glance back at the infamous pirate hunter. Instead he made his way straight to his cabin.

William, on the other hand, paused at Bart's side and turned to smile at Captain Barnet and his men. He fussed at the cuff of his jacket in the manner of a jolly fop. "Greetings, Johnny. Catch any *scary* pirates lately?"

Color returned to the pirate hunter's cheeks to darken them with a sudden rage. "Looking for Captain Cross. Heard he'd made his way into our waters. Him *and* Jean St. Noir."

William *tsk*ed. "Does this look like the *Fickle Bitch* or the *Soucouyant*? Barnet . . ." he chided. "I'm highly offended. Our lady ship's offended." He *tsk*ed at the group with Captain Barnet. "Best you go on before Bane hears of this and takes a sword to you for the insult to our lady's honor. This be a first-rate man-o'-war here, not some half-rigged sloop or frigate. He won't like that slight . . . not at all."

Grimacing, Barnet swept his gaze across the silent crew who stood around to back their quartermaster. "There's something not right about the lot of you."

William winked at him. "There's something not right about the lot of the world, mate. We just embrace our natural differences with gusto."

And with that, Captain Barnet and his soldiers finally departed the gangway.

William followed them down to the dock as if to ensure they left the area and didn't double back in an attempt to sneak aboard some other way.

Cameron didn't move until after Captain Barnet and his men had vanished into the night.

"Did they scare you, *ma petite*?"

Cameron let out a startled shriek at the voice that manifested right beside her ear. Jumping away from it, she turned to see a peculiar man standing so close that she could feel his breath on her flesh.

His skin was a rich caramel color, stretched tight over a body that rippled with defined muscles the likes of which she'd seldom seen on any male—Captain Bane notwithstanding. And that wasn't the only peculiarity he possessed. His black hair was cut short and worn spiked atop his head in a strange, unique style.

And those eyes . . .

Merciful heaven!

They were unlike any shade she'd ever beheld in her life, especially with the rest of his coloring. A cool, steely blue, they had a deep grayish cast, and yet . . .

The color truly defied explanation. More like a silvery storm on a dark, sinister sea. In a weird way, it reminded her of how the parson and his scriptures described the color of the pale horse that Death rode in the Apocalypse.

Stranger still, the sleeves of his black linen shirt were rolled up to his elbows, displaying that both his forearms were covered with scrolling black tattoos that appeared more akin to a second skin color than actual ink.

He quirked one finely arched eyebrow at her continued silence. "Devil got your tongue?"

She shivered at the sound of his voice. "That is an incredible accent you have there. Wherever are you from?"

His smile turned warm and charming. "A place I know you've never heard of. Wyñeria. The accent's a form of Igñeri . . . Island Carib."

He was right about that—she'd never heard of his homeland before. But over the years, she'd learned of many different towns and small islands in the Caribbean. "Which island?"

"Let's just say it's between Trinidad and Tobago, and keep it at that."

"Leave off our new crew member, Kalder. Captain's orders," William said as he joined them.

His tone wistful, he spoke to Mr. Death in a lyrical language Cameron had never heard before, then he headed for the ship.

She scowled as she realized Kalder was barefoot, with no stockings. As with his arms, his legs from the knees down held peculiar scrolling tattoo marks.

"What did he say?" she asked William.

"Not fit for repeating to a lady, me love. Afraid you'll find the majority of our crew isn't the most refined of creatures. Kalder Dupree is one you'll be wanting to give a bit of a berth to."

"Why? He seemed cordial enough." If not a bit unnerving with his silent movements and piercing stare.

He winced. "If you keep going on what things seem to be, child, rather than what they really are, you're in for a long haul with this group."

A sudden whistle rent the air.

Before she could ask about it, William took her arm and ran with her for the gangway. He all but dragged her onboard while the crew scrambled as if they were making sail in the dark.

William didn't slow until they reached the mainmast, where Kalder stood next to an even more peculiar-looking man. This one was tall and lean, with a bare chest decorated by animal bones, beads, and feathers strung together to form the kind of adornment she'd only seen worn by certain Powhatan tribal elders who came to trade with merchants in Virginia or meet with town officials. Yet that and the feathers strung to his staff and beaded armbands seemed at odds with his long, dark blond dreadlocks that were favored by some of the islanders she'd met on this latest quest. And he'd painted his face like no one she'd ever seen. Not shaman or warrior. Meanwhile, he wore the breeches and boots of a fine European nobleman and the sword of a Saracen nomad. Truly the man had a style unique unto himself.

"What is it?" William asked them as he let go of her arm and moved to stand beside the strange man.

"There's an ill breeze blowing off the port bow." The man glanced to Kalder. "Reeks of what we're charged with policing."

Kalder rolled his eyes. "I think the fetid bitch just wants to make sure none of us sleep tonight."

He snorted at Kalder's rude words. "I'm not the one you need to fear, brother." He jerked his chin at something behind Cameron. "Sancha appears to have been ass-up in Nelson's Folly a bit early tonight."

Cameron turned to see an exceptionally tall and gracefully lanky woman headed for them. Her long, curly black wig was askew as she weaved across the deck, making her way for the steering wheel. Without a word, the woman clapped a hand to Kalder's shoulder as she attempted to step around them, fell against him, then righted herself. With a kiss to his cheek, she pushed herself away and fell against Bart, who then helped her stand upright. How the woman could make her drunken dance appear so beautiful, Cameron had no idea. Yet Sancha was elegant while tipsy.

But when the men actually allowed the woman to take her place at the helm, Cameron gaped at them. "What the hell, man?" The curse was out before she could stop it. "You're planning to let her steer the ship while drunk?"

The strangely mismatched man laughed. "Of course. We only fear her when she's sober. Then Sancha's a nasty tart with a wicked twist of the whip . . . and a tongue that lets even more blood, ever quicker."

That only confused her more. "Then why did you say you feared her?"

"Everyone fears her, love. I merely commented on the fact that, second to the captain, she's the scariest thing on this ship, and that she's imbibed quite a bit tonight . . . even for her." He winked at Cameron. "Name's Rosenkranz, or Rosie, and what be the name of such a sweet tender morsel as you?"

As she opened her mouth to answer, a cry sounded for Kalder

to duck. Yet before he could oblige the call, a bucket of water ended up being slung against him.

She expected him to explode into anger.

He didn't.

Rather, he groaned as his entire body changed instantly . . . his skin became slick and silvery like a fish's iridescent scales. Gills opened at his neck, while his teeth elongated to fangs. What she'd mistaken for tattoos became fins that protruded from his arms and legs.

Choking, he sputtered and coughed, then turned to glare at the sailor who'd doused him. "Careful! You lousy bilger! Watch where you be tossing that or I'll be making you drink it through your nose!"

"Sorry, Kal, it slipped from me hands. Won't happen again."

"See that it don't. Or else I'll be plaguing and poxing a piece of your anatomy you're going to miss using."

"Here, Mr. Dupree."

Cameron bit back a scream as Captain Bane literally appeared out of nowhere to stand beside Kalder with a towel for him. He handed it off, then began to help shout orders as they cast off for the open seas.

Too stunned to speak, she watched as Kalder's skin and coloring returned to normal, though "normal" was beginning to take on a whole new meaning with this particular group.

Kalder cast an amused grimace toward her. "You handled that well, for an air-breather. Surely, you have questions about *it* . . . and me?"

Aye, she did—of course she did. But the more she looked at this crew . . .

She didn't know where to begin as her head spun from the madness of it all. The riggers moved along the masts and lines with inhuman skill. It was terrifying to watch the way they scaled the spiny wood and thick ropes to drop sails, without fear or hesitation. The way all of them rushed about, displaying talents that hadn't been born of this world or of a typical woman. Surely, they were demons all.

This is a crew of the damned.

And she'd walked right onboard. Voluntarily.

With both feet.

What have I done? She'd given no real thought to joining them. Not really. Rather, she'd placed her trust in total strangers she knew nothing about. And that wasn't like her. Ever. Cameron Maire Jack trusted no one. Never in her life had she done such as this.

Was she really *that* desperate?

Of course I am.

Without Paden, she had nothing in this world. She had no one. Even before her parents had died, she'd worshiped her older brother. He'd been everything to her. Her best friend and protector. Her confidant and playmate.

While her parents' deaths had been hard to bear, news of his had devastated her to a level she'd never known existed. The pain had been unimaginable. Indescribable. Sent her reeling into a despair she had yet to recover from.

Since the day she'd learned what death meant when she was a girl at age five and her favorite pup had perished after tangling with a fox, she'd known that her parents would precede her to the grave. That was to be expected, as it was the way of things. The natural order that children outlived their parents and carried on their lineage.

But Paden . . .

Five years her elder, he was to always be here. Always. No matter what, he wasn't to leave her alone in this miserable world. He'd sworn that to her. That he would be forever by her side to keep her safe. He wouldn't fail her or his word. Not for anything. Not for anyone. It would always be the two of them. Thick and thin, and all that lay in between. Not even the devil and all his demons would keep her brother from her.

That had been his vow every night of her life when he'd tucked her into bed. . . .

Have no fear.
Keep your cheer.
It'll always be
You and me.
Thick and thin
To the end.
Neither heaven nor hell
Will keep me from me Cammy-belle.

How could Paden have broken her heart so? Did he not know that it wasn't his life he'd lost at sea?

It was *hers*.

But worse than that, he'd taken her faith and hopes with him to the grave. Her heart. Her belief in God Himself. Truly, she was now a hollowed-out shell with nothing inside except a profound, unending pain, and a sense of loss so deep she feared she'd never feel anything else ever again.

"I think we've sent her into shock."

Cameron turned at the high-pitched feminine voice to find . . .

Well, she wasn't quite sure what *this* newcomer was. Only an inch taller, she was dressed in a high-fashion *robe à l'anglais,* yet it was made of sackcloth. Her skin didn't appear human, but rather was made of straw. . . .

She smiled at Cameron. "You have *that* look, dearest."

Cameron blinked in confusion. "What look is that?"

The woman sighed in that odd voice of hers as she cast her gaze toward Bart. "It's the look, isn't it?"

"Aye. But you can't fault her for it, really."

"Suppose." She let out another heartfelt sigh. "Still, I'd like to meet someone and not have it anymore."

"Have what?" Cameron asked with a frown.

"The look that says I'm a freak," she whispered in an ominous tone. "Name's Valynda. And yes, I'm not human . . . though I was at one time. 'Til a love spell went awry and this became the consequences of it."

Cameron paled. "What?"

She held her hands up in helpless despair. "Wasn't my spell, mind you. Rather, the idiot who wanted to make *me* love *him*. He bought a lwa from a witch, and this is what it did to me because he knew naught what he was doing. Sucked my soul straight into the doll and there was nothing to be done for it."

"Nothing?" Cameron asked, aghast at what she was hearing. Was this even real? Was any of this possible? Surely she was dreaming. . . .

No one could be turned into a living rag doll. Could they?

By accident? Truly it was a horrifying thought.

William shook his head. "Superstitious preacher burned her body. Left her in a bit of a pickle, indeed."

Valynda nodded. "But for Lady Belle, I'd have been trapped in between forever."

In between what?

Cameron wasn't sure she wanted to know that answer, so she asked the other question that plagued her. "Belle?"

"Our doctor," Bart said, jerking his chin toward one of the riggers. "Belle Morte's one you don't want to run afoul of. She's a powerful maven who can give the strongest hell beasties a run for their money."

Cameron scowled at the sight of a beautiful dark-skinned woman who seemed harmless enough—until she pulled out a large machete to slash expertly at the ties of a sail before flipping down to land on the deck with the skill of a master assassin. In one fluid, graceful movement, she sheathed her weapon then shimmied up another rope. Aye, the deadliest objects were often the most beautiful. "An Obia?"

"Nay, love. Something much, much darker. We don't speak of it, lest we offend her and she curse us for it."

Cameron crossed herself. *What have you gotten me into, brother?* She'd come here seeking help and salvation for the two of them. Yet there was no salvation on this ship. Never had she seen a more damned lot in all her life. If ever there was a crew bound to Lucifer's lowest pit, this had to be it.

And she was sailing in the midst of them all, straight for hell's domain.

Stark cold terror seized her as a rotten feeling crept through her very soul. "Question, Mr. Death?"

"Aye, lass?"

"Am I the only human on board this ship?"

To her deepest chagrin, he hesitated. And when he finally answered, it wasn't what she wanted to hear and gave her no comfort whatsoever. "Define the word 'human.'"

HELLCHASER

3

"Am I the only human on board this ship?"

Devyl didn't so much as blink at Cameron's question as she came to rest right in front of him where he was issuing orders to the riggers on deck. If anything, the good captain appeared bored by her while they left the port behind and broke into open sea. "Suppose it depends on the definition one uses for 'human.'"

She gave him an irritated, droll stare as he repeated

his quartermaster's words in a bland mumble. "I am unamused by your hedging, Captain."

He arched a sardonic black brow with a look that caused a chill to run down her spine. "Who says I'm hedging?"

It was a titanic effort not to roll her eyes at a man—or perhaps infernal beast would be more accurate—who she was quite certain might very well suck out her immortal soul and feast upon it. "Can you at least tell me why I was brought on board this ship, then?"

"For your protection."

Why did she have such a hard time believing that? Probably because she couldn't imagine a more dangerous group in existence than the one rushing around her.

"From?"

Forget the crew, she was beginning to doubt if there could be anything more lethal or terrifying than the creatures who called this ship home.

He let out a long, slow breath as if seeking some sort of patience. "We are not your enemies, Miss Jack. Of that much you can rest assured. While we might be an unsavory, untoward, and uncivilized group, we are not without our honor."

"Meaning?"

"Meaning we reserve our venom for those who've earned it."

And those words failed to comfort her. "You'll have to forgive me if your benediction causes me alarm."

"No need to apologize. You've every right to fear us. As I said, we are an unsavory lot." He turned those dark, soulless eyes toward her, and this time, she saw for a fact that they did indeed turn red as blood.

They glowed in the darkness with an unholy light.

"And an acquired taste."

Yelping at his sinister tone, she jumped back on the deck and crossed herself as true, unmitigated horror engulfed her. This was not what she'd meant to sign on with when she'd promised herself and Lettice that she'd find her brother no matter what and bring him home. She had already been gone longer on this quest than she'd ever anticipated. Longer than Nathaniel Harrison would forgive her for.

Nor had she meant to find the devil's ship and his crew to sail with. No doubt to hell itself they were bound!

Dear heaven, I've consigned myself to Perdition. . . .

Everything had seemed so simple when she'd opened her brother's letter and first set out to locate him. She was to come to Port Royal and ask a few questions. Find out why Paden hadn't come home after the shipwreck that he'd obviously survived. Take him to task for being so cryptic in his missive, then return home to her life with her wayward brother in tow, and let Lettice beat him sideways for his thoughtlessness and the worry he'd given them.

This was never supposed to be part of it. And the horrifying captain in front of her was definitely not part of the bargain.

Bane froze as he witnessed the absolute stark terror inside Cameron. She literally quivered by his side to such an extent he was amazed she didn't wet the planks beneath her feet.

There had been a time once when he'd lived to instill that amount of fear and intimidation in others. When the sight of petrified men had been mother's milk to his cold, dead heart. Compassion and tenderness had been virtually unknown to his warring people.

And yet . . .

In the flash of one single heartbeat, his mind took him back to the days when he hadn't been the leader of his race. To the time before he'd first taken a life in battle and had been nothing more than the beloved older brother of his younger sister.

No longer on this ship, he was again in the green meadows where he'd run as a boy. And as was his wont, he was off to join his friends to hunt for game and play for a rare afternoon of freedom—something he'd worked and suffered hard for.

And as was typical of his sister, Elyzabel was hot on his heels, annoying the very piss from him. Five years his junior, she was a tiny wisp of a thing, yet she thought herself his equal in size and abilities.

"What are you about, Du? Why are you carrying Ta's spear? Does he know you have it?"

"Aye, he knows. Why are you bothering me now with your inane prattle? Off with you! Isn't there someone else you can annoy for once besides me? We have a sister, you know. Surely, she's more suited to your tastes than I."

But she'd never preferred Edyth's company over his. And not that he blamed her that. Edyth was a futtocking handful on her best day.

"Are you off to hunt? Can I come? Please, please!"

"Nay!" Turning on his heels, he'd growled at Elyzabel. Then froze as he saw the tangles in her brown hair and the dirt on her freckled cheeks. More than that, he noted that, beneath the dirt, a bruise had started to form that deepened the shade of her amber eyes, and there was a tear in her dress.

Though scarce more than tick-size, she was ever ready to stand toe to toe with him, never flinching in her temerity whenever he'd said or done anything that displeased her. She would even dare to shove at him when no man save their father would so much as meet his gaze in anger.

Shout in his face whenever she was mad at him.

She even stood up to their father during his most drunken rages.

Her guts and fire had always amused and amazed him, even when he'd wanted to put her through a wall for not listening to him, or refusing to hide when it was the more prudent thing to do. In all his life, he'd never loved anyone as much as he'd loved his little sister.

Not even Vine.

But while he might have verbally fought with his sister whenever she pushed the boundaries of his patience and all common sense, by the very gods, no one else was allowed to do such and no one was *ever* to lay hands to her.

No one.

Not even their father. And he had the scars to prove it.

"What's all this about?" he asked, indicating her cheek.

Elyzabel glanced away. "'Tis naught. Can I come with you?"

"Elf . . ." he'd chided, cupping her chin and gentling his tone with her. "Tell me what happened to you, lass."

She let out a long sigh before she finally screwed her face up and confessed it. "'Twas the beast!"

"Derphin?"

"Nay. The other hairy one I hate most of all."

"Ilex?"

"Aye! He said a girl wasn't fit to climb a tree and that I should get back to me mum's breast before I got hurt. So I climbed the tree to show him what a girl could do, and then he shoved me down and we fought about it."

Those words had ignited his fuse. "He hit you?"

She nodded.

That had been the first time Devyl had met the part of himself that had made him famous on the battlefield. That cold, unreasoning beast that wouldn't stop until he had his enemy lying in pieces at his feet, either dead or begging for a mercy he'd never shown anyone save his precious Elyzabel.

Only Elf had ever stayed his furious hand. Only her tears had ever moved him to mercy or compassion.

Until today.

Something about Cameron reminded him of his precious sister, and this tiny chit touched the last shred of a humanity he'd thought had gone to the grave with his Elf.

Sink me. . . .

Cameron swallowed hard as she met Bane's fierce, bloody gaze. For the first time, she saw the slightest softening of his demonic countenance. The merest glimpse of a soul beneath the evil.

His grimace lightened as he held one large hand out toward her. "There's no need in that, lass."

Refusing to give in to her terror, she forced herself to her feet and fell back on the strength Paden had taught her to stand on after the death of their parents.

Let no one see your weakness, Cam. Ever. We are Jacks, by God. And Jacks don't buckle or fold.

In it for a half-pence. In it for a pound.

For that matter, she was in this whole matter way over her head. No way out now. Hell, or high water.

Or damnation itself.

Whatever it took. She had no choice, except to see it through.

"I still don't understand why it is you brought me here, Captain."

"Truth? Neither do I. Other than I fear something quite unholy has taken control of your brother. My experience with such things is that when they happen and the poor bastard who's held in thrall reaches out to an innocent such as yourself . . . the consequences are always dire to said innocent, especially when it involves something as important as the trinket in your pocket."

"It's not a worthless bauble, then?"

The wind whipped at his wavy black hair while his eyes faded back to their ebony color. He glanced across the stormy sea surrounding them. "Quite the contrary, Miss Jack. Wars have been waged for that bit of gold you keep, and countless throats cut. Tell no one else you carry it. Ever." He glowered at her. "How your brother managed to get that to you is what puzzles me most."

"It came in the post."

He gaped at her as he found that the most incredulous bit of all. As if it defied all reason.

She held her hand up in solemn testimony. "I swear it. I thought it nothing more than a letter that must have been sent before he left on his voyage. I kept it nigh on a fortnight before I could bring myself to open it to read it, and then when I did . . ."

"Did anything strange happen to you around the time you received it?"

"Other than meeting all of you and the lady Menyara?"

His dark grimace said that he didn't appreciate her humor.

She softened her own expression to let him know she was teasing. "Nay, Captain. Nothing untoward." In fact, she'd not had so much as a nightmare since receiving it, which was strange given that she'd had a number of them before it came.

"Very peculiar, indeed."

Cameron narrowed her gaze on him as he continued to watch the dark waters around them, as if seeking something only he could detect. "What is it that you're not telling me?"

The red returned to his eyes an instant before he dropped his coat from his shoulders in one fast, graceful shrug and unsheathed his cutlass. "Kalder! Off to port! Sancha, bring a spring upon her cable! They're coming up our stern!" He took Cameron's arm and gently nudged her toward William while Kalder jumped over the side, into the sea below. "Seal her to my quarters for the fight."

"Aye, aye, Captain." William grabbed her fast and hauled her away.

But not before she saw what was rising up from the bowels of the stygian waves to engage them.

Holy mother and all her saints . . . !

Cameron couldn't breathe at the sight of what had to be Lucifer's own prized pet shark he'd crossbred with an octopus. Scaly, huge, and tentacled like nothing she'd ever seen or heard of, it came after them while the crew took aim and fired cannons at it. The deck beneath her feet vibrated from the recoil of it all. Her ears rang from the sharp percussion.

William shoved her into Bane's quarters and slammed the door tight.

Gaping and terrified, Cameron stumbled toward the windows to watch the creature that was after them. One who appeared to have brought even more sinister friends with it. Her heart pounding in her chest, her ears filled with the sound of rushing blood and more cannon fire, along with shouts and gusting wind. The smell of gunpowder and sea nauseated her. Never, never had she seen or heard such. This was the stuff of nightmares and horror.

From where she stood, she could see Kalder fighting against the beast that dwarfed him as they tangled in the water. The merman stabbed it with a long spear while Captain Bane sent balls of fire from his fists into its scaly hide. The creature screamed and arched its back, reaching for them both with its thorny tentacles.

Until the beast met her gaze through the lead glass as if it sensed her watching it.

Time hung still for a long minute until it let out a piercing cry unlike anything she'd ever heard. It was so shrill, it shattered the glass between them, raining pieces of it over her.

Closing her eyes, she raised her arms to protect her face until the shrapnel settled. The ship rocked from the fierce waves the creature caused. Nauseated by the rolling sensation, she staggered back against Captain Bane's desk. Winds from the sea whipped against her, tearing pieces of her hair free from her queue.

With a deep growl, the creature dove for her, heading straight toward the cabin. She gripped the desk so tightly that the wood bruised the palms of her hands.

In that moment of sheer, utter terror and unbelievable horror that reminded her she was without weapon or protection, Cameron reached for the medallion in her pocket and remembered the prayer her mother had taught her as a girl. The one that Paden had always recited with her whenever she was scared . . .

"Thou shalt not be afraid for the terror by night, nor for the arrow that flieth by day. Nor for the pestilence that walketh in darkness, nor for the destruction that wasteth at noonday. No evil shall befall thee, and neither shall any plague come nigh thy dwelling. For He shall give his angels charge over thee, to keep thee in all thy ways. They shall bear thee up in their hands, lest thou dash thy foot against a stone. Thou shalt tread upon the lion and adder, the young lion and the dragon shalt thou trample under feet. Because He hath set his love upon me, therefore will I deliver him. I will set Him on high, because He hath known my name. He shall call upon me, and I will answer Him. I will be with Him in trouble. I will deliver Him, and honor Him. With long life will I satisfy him, and shew him my salvation."

No sooner had she finished those words than her pocket and hand began to heat up—the pocket where she held the stashed talisman Paden had sent her for her protection should she need it.

Devyl staggered back as he saw the shimmering veil fall over the ship and every member of his crew. It even covered Kalder in the water. A gossamer light rained down like a spring shower. Only, instead of leaving them wet, it cast their skin in an ethereal glow, like that of coal that held fire inside its darkness.

William and Bart stared at each other with slack jaws. Then they turned toward him for an explanation he couldn't even begin to give them.

"Captain?" Belle asked as she shimmied from the rigging and moved to stand beside him.

He had no answer for her, either. Not for *this*.

And definitely not for whatever caused the beast and its compatriots in the water to splinter into a fine gleaming mist that settled over the waves only to vanish in the blink of an eye.

What the hell?

If that wasn't shocking enough, a huge wave lifted Kalder from the sea and set him down on the deck near the prow, as if to make sure he was safe, along with the rest of them.

His own jaw agape, Devyl handed his sword off to Belle before he made his way toward the only source for this he could imagine.

Cameron Jack.

He found her in his cabin, on her knees, clutching at the medallion her brother had sent her. Her eyes had lost all color. Her lips were as pale as her body as she whispered a barely audible prayer. Even her hair had turned a bitter white.

The stark red, bleeding cuts caused by the shattered windows provided the only color anywhere on her body. Yet the strangest part?

Glass hovered in the air around her, forming the illusion of glittering wings jutting out from her back.

William drew up short behind him and cursed. "What manner of creature is she?"

When Bart stepped around them with a raised sword to attack her, Devyl stopped and disarmed him. "She's not our enemy, Mr. Meers." He returned the sword.

"What is she?" He repeated William's question.

"Something that would piss down the leg of those what don't think much of us if they knew she was among our crew. And it explains much about what happened to her brother and why the Plate Fleet be sunk as it was."

William scowled. "You've lost me, Captain."

Devyl carefully closed the distance between them before he took the medallion from Cameron's hand. The moment he had it pried loose from her fierce grip, her hair returned to its natural chestnut shade and her eyes to their blue-green color.

The glass fell to the floor, where it struck and let out a small, tinkling sound reminiscent of jester bells.

Cameron blinked twice as if waking from a deep slumber. With a fierce grimace, she glanced among them. "Is the fighting over?"

Bitterly amused, Devyl released a tired breath as he rubbed his thumb against the searing medallion. The ancient power and the soul of the warrior it contained thrummed from the metal, similar to a heartbeat. No wonder Menyara had sent her to them.

Damn that interfering bitch for it.

"Aye." He glanced to his men over his shoulder. "It appears we needs amend our earlier answer to the lass, Mr. Death."

"Deeth . . . and what answer be that, Captain?"

"There are no humans aboard this ship, at all."

Cameron gaped at him. "P-p-pardon?"

64

He held the medallion up in front of her face so that she could see the remnants of the faint glow it contained from having been activated by the evil that had come up against them. "Do you remember anything from the last few minutes?"

Her scowl deepened as she cast her gaze around as if seeking an answer before she shook her head.

Handing the medallion back to her, he closed her fingers over it. "You are born of a Seraph's bloodline, lass. And this trinket of your brother's is the proof of it. I'd been hoping I was wrong with my earlier assessment. Sadly, I wasn't." He stepped back as he contemplated what it all meant. "The good news is, since you had no idea of your family's origins . . . unless you have a sibling your parents failed to speak of, your brother's still alive somewhere—you were right with your assertions. They didn't kill him, after all."

Cameron gasped as hope finally filled her. "You're sure about that?"

Bane nodded before he dipped his chin toward her fisted hand. "As we've all just seen, the medallion reacts to your blood when you're under demonic threat. Had Captain Jack died, you'd have been approached by those he serves about replacing him in this fight. Since no one's come for you, he's alive without a doubt. And that medallion is from his own sword, which I'm sure he inherited from one of your parents."

Cameron's breath caught as she opened her hand to study the emblem more closely. Never had she seen it in her parents' possession. "Me mother had a sword that belonged to her father before he died, but we were never allowed near the locked chest where she

kept it. She always said that it would pass to Paden on her death."
She bit her lip as she remembered something she hadn't thought
about in years. "After her death, he never let me see it, either. I never
thought anything about that, until now. Like her, he guarded it with
the strictest care."

"Because of the power it contains, a vile beacon it be. One that
draws evil to it like a flame summons moths. Unless it's kept shielded
and enclosed, it would be a threat to any nearby innocent unaware
of what it actually is." Devyl crossed his arms over his chest. "Your
brother must have sent the Seraph medallion to you to keep his
enemies from using his sword or destroying the soul of your ancestor. And to keep you safe in his absence."

"What is this Seraph you keep mentioning?" William asked.

Before Devyl could speak, a pale, shimmering woman appeared
in the center of the cabin.

Gasping, Cameron shrank away from her. The men, however,
didn't blink. They acted as if her ghostly presence among them was
normal and expected.

More beautiful than a fairy queen, she stood eye to eye with
Devyl and had hair unlike anything Cameron had ever seen before.
Pale golden-brown, it was laced with strands of ice white—not gray
or any facsimile of gray. It was a silvery, gleaming white . . . like
fey-locks that fell in unadorned waves to her waist. Her black-and-
white-striped silk gown was plain, yet richly cut and elegant. A
white lace kerchief encircled her neck, and as with her hair, it had
shimmery silver threads laced through it—the same lace decorated
the edges of her sleeves and hem.

Yet the most peculiar bit was that she stood barefoot even while she held the bearing of some grand empress. Obviously she didn't fear splinters from the ship boards.

And her eyes . . .

Almond-shaped, they were a deep amber brown. She turned to face Cameron and offered her a kind smile. "No need to fear me, child. I mean you no harm."

Devyl stepped forward. "Cameron Jack, may I present you to our lady ship, Marcelina?"

Cameron bowed to the noblewoman. "It's a pleasure to meet you, my lady."

Marcelina smiled. "I'm not a lady, child. You misunderstood Du's words, as was no doubt his intention." She passed a chiding grimace toward Captain Bane.

Confused by that, Cameron waited for an explanation. William laughed while Bart bit back a smile.

Devyl gave each of the men a chilling glare before he explained the lady's comment. "Mara is this ship we sail upon, Miss Jack. Our warden—in all senses of that word—for this grand misadventure."

"Pardon?"

"Perhaps this will help?" Marcelina posed herself like the ship's figurehead. Before Cameron's eyes, she turned into the wooden piece from head to toe.

"Holy mother of God!" Cameron crossed herself.

Marcelina returned to flesh. "No need to panic, child. As Du said, I'm the guardian for all who reside here. So long as you fall under my protection, I will do anything to keep you safe."

"And ensure you have no fun whatsoever," Bart mumbled under his breath.

The captain elbowed him in the stomach hard enough that he doubled over.

Shaking her head, Cameron did her best to absorb all of this, but . . . "How is this possible? How can *she* be the boat?"

The smile returned to Marcelina's face. "I come from an ancient race. We are the wood and the wood is us."

"They were the gods and guardians of the forest," Devyl said. "Ever lurking among humanity and causing problems for them and us."

"I don't follow."

Marcelina glared at Devyl. "We are the protectors—"

"My ass cheeks."

"Du, please! Watch your language!"

"Watch your lies! Are you really going to stand there and preach that as if I wasn't there?"

Marcelina grimaced at him. "And what of yours? How many fell to your race and army? Need I remind you how we met?"

"Need I remind you how we parted? Blood soaks us both!"

"And you're an unreasoning beast!"

"Better than being an unreasoning—"

"Don't you dare!" Marcelina shrieked, cutting him off before he could insult her.

A fierce tic started in Devyl's jaw as his eyes glowed a deep, dark red in the dim light.

Her breathing ragged, Marcelina turned toward Cameron. "Anyway, my race predates the existence of mankind by centuries."

Cameron frowned as she tried to understand what they were

telling her. "Then why have we never seen you? How is it that I've never heard of your people?"

Marcelina turned another hostile grimace toward the captain. "War thinned our numbers to virtual extinction. While there were millions of us centuries ago, there are but a handful now." She gestured at the captain. "Du and I had our destinies bound together long before the world you would recognize came into being. So when he accepted this task, I was forced to it, as well."

"Payback's a bitch," he mumbled under his breath.

Cameron didn't understand his hostility, but at least she was beginning to figure out his peculiar relationship with his crew and boat, and why they spoke of things the way they did. As William had warned her, things here were not as they seemed, in any sense of the word.

She inclined her head respectfully to Marcelina. "So you're the captain's wife, then?"

Captain Bane snorted rudely. "Hardly. I'd have slit my own throat first."

"As would I," Marcelina said in the same scoffing tone. "Neither of us had a real say in our fates or misbegotten whatever this travesty burden we share is." She swept a less than flattering grimace over his body. "I can't imagine a more horrid fate than what you speak."

Captain Bane laughed bitterly. "I can . . . being husbanded to *you*."

William cleared his throat as the captain and Marcelina began to escalate their verbal conflict. "Ancient ones? You have children present and it upsets us when our parents fight."

"Speak for yourself, Will," Bart said with a smirk. "I find it highly entertaining. Especially when they begin to launch things about, and throw fire at one another."

Without so much as glancing in his direction, the captain let fly a dagger at Bart that seemed to have appeared from thin air.

William caught it and *tsk*ed. "Best be careful with that sudden flailing, Captain. Could put out someone's eye with this."

"Was rather hoping to put out someone's life with it."

"Och now, that's just mean."

"Do they always fight like this?" Cameron whispered to Bart.

He screwed his face up in thought. "Actually, this is rather tame for them. Thinking it must be because you're new to our company that they're tamping it down a bit."

"Anyway," Marcelina said again, returning her attention to Cameron. "My race—Deruvian—was all but destroyed by the very ones we're after. Our goal is to keep the same fate from befalling mankind."

Marcelina moved to stand near William. "And to answer your question, Mr. Death"—she spoke his name correctly—"Seraphs were chosen from an elite group of fighters who once battled beside my race for the survival of this world. After the war ended, the Cimmerian forces refused to stop preying on the innocent. And they proved more resourceful and resilient than the gates made by our side that held them back from your realm. Even worse, they found ways to beat back the Seraphim until there were only thirty-seven of them left out of their once great army. As a last resort, and to keep the balance intact, the Sarim council made a dark bargain and used forbidden magick to make those last thirty and seven souls immortal—with the help of my people, they bound them to medallions like the one in your hand."

Devyl let out a heavy sigh. "It was a desperate but necessary act, as those last thirty-seven possessed unique skills and powers that take years to master and learn . . . provided an apt pupil could be located for the instruction. But rather than start from the beginning, the medallion allows the soul of the Seraph to temporarily take over the body of their descendent to battle their enemies."

Marcelina nodded. "Aye, and it must be a member of their direct bloodline to fully access their powers. Otherwise, the Seraph becomes tainted and an easy tool for evil."

"So each soul must be carefully watched over and guarded to ensure no other finds it, corrupts, and bonds with it," Devyl said. "Along with the sword the soul controls." The captain picked up Cameron's hand that held her medallion. "The bad news is that now that you've tapped the power of your bloodline, you've sent out a signal to those who seek to destroy all of the remaining Seraphim. They won't stop until *you're* dead and they have your medallion."

Cameron winced at the last thing she wanted to hear. But that left her with another question. "Are you a Seraph, too?"

Stepping away from her, Devyl scoffed bitterly. "Nay, lass. I was the very thing they gave their lives fighting against."

"I don't understand."

The red returned to his eyes as his expression became sinister. "Never mistake that I'm anything more than a damned soul, gal. I'm here only for vengeance and blood. I leave redemption and kindness for better folks than I, as I've no use whatsoever for any of it. To hell with anything save blood and violence." And with those chilling words hanging in the air, he left them.

When William started after Bane, Marcelina stopped him. "Let Du go, Mr. Death. He's in no mood for comfort and won't welcome anything more than bloodshed in his current state of mind. Trust me, you don't want to be on the receiving end of it."

"As you say, mum." He inclined his head to her, then left in the opposite direction the captain had gone.

Bart hesitated. "Should I show Miss Jack to her quarters?"

"I'll see her settled. Take the helm from Sancha and make sure Kalder takes the watch."

"Aye, aye, mum." And with that, he departed.

Marcelina offered Cameron a kind, benevolent smile. "The men were right. For a woman with no experience in such matters, you are taking all this rather well. Should I be worried?"

Cameron slid the medallion into her pocket. "Sadly, hard knocks are rather the norm for me life. Though, to be honest, these have left me reeling quite a bit. I think I'm rather drunk from the punches here of late."

She laughed. "I can imagine."

Cameron rubbed the sudden chill from her arms as she tried to come to grips with all the new information she'd been run over with. Honestly, it had her staggering as she tried her best to get some bearings with everything she'd heard and seen. "May I ask you something?"

"Of course."

"Why do you call the captain Du?"

" 'Tis his real name. Dón-Dueli. Du or Duel for short."

Dón-Dueli . . . that name sent another shiver down her spine. It denoted a sense of evil even darker than the name Devyl Bane, and reminded her of the tales her father had once spun of his Irish homeland. Of the sinister fey and the dark bean sidhe who stalked the night and preyed upon the weak. "I've never heard of a name like that before."

"Like me, he comes from an ancient race. Only, where my people sought tranquil peace, his sought war and domination."

"Is he a demon?"

"Nay, child. That would be an easy excuse for him and his kind, when there is no reason for the brutality he embraced in his mortal lifetime. He reveled in the misery of those around him, and drank it in like mother's milk."

"Then why is he helping you and the others now?"

"I assure you, it's not by any real choice or out of any sense of noble obligation. He was forced to this task against his will to right a wrong he once committed."

"Against?"

"A girl like you. Sweet. Innocent. Until she met him and made the mistake of commending her heart to his most callous hands."

There was no missing the bitter undertones in her voice.

Or the hatred.

"You?"

"Nay, child. My younger sister."

Did you sink that damnable ship?"

The lusca paused as he noted the anger in his lady's voice. More grateful than ever that she had yet to breach the barriers that kept her locked from the world of man—and from reaching him—he swallowed hard. "Nay, my lady. They carry a Seraph with them now. When I tried to break the hull, it activated a shield of some sort around them all and the ship, and almost killed me."

Vine shrieked in frustrated rage as she slammed her hand against the portal that kept her shielded from the world she was desperate to enter. And from the creature she wanted to disembowel.

The shield cracked more.

But not enough.

Only a mere fraction, teasing her like the merciless bastard who had trapped her here while the world of man loomed just beyond her reach.

Damn you, Dón-Dueli!

And damn Marcelina for her interference.

Sister or not, she wanted Mara's heart in her fist every bit as much as she wanted his. Wanted to feel both of their organs beating against her fingers while their blood coated her flesh, until her need for vengeance was quenched.

And the world of man bowed to her feet and licked them clean.

Gathering her layered skirts, Vine turned to glare at the pathetic bastard her servants had managed to drag through the portal for her amusement a few months ago.

Weak and bleeding, he was barely recognizable as human now. While his strength had been formidable in the beginning, he was starting to fade beneath the barrage of their endless feedings from him.

Still, he refused to give them the location of the key they needed to open this damnable doorway so that she could walk the human realm again.

But the Seraph would break eventually.

They always did. No matter who or what had shat them out into this universe.

And that begged a very important question. "A Seraph sails with them, you said?" she asked the lusca.

"Aye, dearest lady. There was no doubt about it. I saw the transition myself."

That could not be a coincidence.

She toyed with a crimson seam along the edge of her veined skirt. "Did you perchance catch a scent of its bloodline?"

"Nay, Lady Vine. I couldn't get close enough for that."

Growling, she flung her hand out and used her powers to drag the lusca closer to the barrier.

Its tentacles left a slimy smear across the earthen floor that smelled even worse than the sea monster itself. Or perhaps it was the piss the creature let loose in fear of her intentions for it and its realization that, though Duel's magick kept Vine locked in, it didn't completely protect those near the barrier from her wrath or powers.

Not that it mattered. It was good for them to fear her. Fear kept the lesser creatures in line. And they should be afraid. For, sooner or later, she would be free again and once she was . . .

She would rain down her wrath on all those who'd participated in locking her in here. And then she'd finish what she'd begun.

A new world order, where she reigned as queen and blood flowed freely to feed her and her blode sisters.

"Gather whatever it takes to sink that ship, and bring me the heart of the bitch it's carved from. Do you understand? Or it'll be your soul I drink next!"

She used her powers to knock the creature away.

Furious and determined, she returned to the man hunched on the floor. His breathing was shallow and ragged. Pain filled. They'd made good use of the Seraph bastard and still he wouldn't give them what they asked.

His resolve and strength reminded her much of another man she'd known once. He, too, had resisted and fought against her. In the beginning, at least. To this day, she'd never met his equal. Not in face, form, or strength.

Only he had ever had the ability to fully resist her.

Only he had ever had the ability to defeat her.

It was why she'd been forced to cut out his black heart and feed it to him before he turned on her completely.

Damn you, Dón-Dueli of the Dumnonii!

But she wouldn't think of her ex-husband. She'd deal with that devil later. Right now . . .

Right now, she had a Seraph to torture and a gate to crack. She was done with these games. Her patience was through.

4

"Nah! None of that, now. You'll be bunking with us."

Cameron paused as Valynda and Belle practically kidnapped her from her assigned cabin and dragged her off to their quarters, which they shared with Sancha and an affable Trini named Janice Smith.

Valynda twirled Cameron toward a low-lying bunk that was covered with a dark blue quilt. The peculiar design of the bed was more like a crib, so that it would keep her from being tossed about in a storm. "You can sleep between me and Janny."

With a wealth of long, wavy black hair flowing over her shoulders, Janice looked up from the Tarot cards she had spread out across her bed to smile at Cameron. "Welcome aboard, Miss Jack. Nice to have another woman in the mix. There be too few of us here as it is. We need to stick together in this testosterone stew where we've been tossed."

Cameron opened her mouth to thank her for the welcome, then scowled as she saw the Death card in her spread. "Is that not a bad omen?"

Janice wrinkled her nose, which somehow made her even more beautiful. "Bah! Nay! Only to those who don't know the cards. Only means a change is coming. Death to one thing is the birth of another. The cards to fear are not so obvious in their meaning, and it takes more than one bad card to make a bad fate."

"That's good to know, and applies to more than just a reading, eh?"

Janice winked at her. "Truth to that, me girl." She held her hand out to her. "Be nice meeting you, Miss Jack."

She shook her hand. "And you, Miss Smith. What brings such an elegant lady to this rowdy bunch of miscreants?"

"Janny be our necromancer," Sancha said as she offered Cameron a mug of rum. "Like Lady Belle, she has powers that are frightening beyond belief. The kind they burn the witches for."

As Cameron took the mug, she noted the burn mark on Sancha's wrist that was identical to the ones they all bore—a strange

Celtic cross ribbon, with a circle in the center that held a skull and crossbones.

Inclining her head to the mark, Cameron scowled at it. "Might I inquire about the source of *that*?"

Sancha pulled her sleeve back to expose more of the mark. "Sure you want to know?"

They all seemed to hold their breath in expectation of her answer.

But Cameron wanted to understand this new place she seemed fated to call home. "Aye."

Sancha pulled the dark wig from her head, showing that her hair beneath was snow white. The color most wore wigs or heavily powdered their hair to achieve. Cameron had never seen a human being with hair that pale before. Especially not a young person, nor one whose skin and eyes were so dark. Sancha couldn't be more than three-and-twenty, or five-and-twenty at most.

She tossed the wig down on her own bunk before she drained her mug and spoke again. "That be the Deadman's Cross we bear."

"Pardon?"

"We are the dead, Miss Jack. And the damned. Every jack and molly here." She fell against her bunk and let her insanely long legs fly up. "It's why all who sail on this ship are known as Deadmen. The Deadman's Cross be the mark of our bondage to a beast they say is the son of the devil himself."

"The captain?" It would make sense, given his name.

Sancha laughed. "Nay, love. The real and true Lucifer, who sits on a fiery throne in hell and rains down his wrath on those poor souls he's taken in."

Cameron glanced at each woman in the room. Belle, Valynda, Janice, and Sancha. "I'm not sure I follow."

Belle answered in her own lyrical accent. "You know about me Valynda there, and how she died her death. Sancha and I lived less than auspicious lives. Unlike poor Valynda, we earned our damnation with both fists, brawling every step of the way to our deaths. As did the rest of the men on this ship. Hell-bound from crib to grave we all were."

"But each of us committed at least one decent act that brought us to the attention of a . . ." Sancha screwed her face up as she reached for more rum. "How would you describe the beast?" she asked Belle.

"The devil is the beast," Belle said blankly. "And the beast is the devil."

Cameron cocked her head at the casual way Belle spoke, trying to make sense of it all. "Captain Bane or the other?"

Belle let out a low, evil laugh. "The other." She reached for Sancha's rum to drink it. "This one gives our fair dark captain a run for his money when it comes to his evil aura and badassery."

"Thorn be this beastie's name, though." Valynda picked up the tale. "As Sancha noted, they say he's the son of Satan himself. For true. As in Lucifer's very spawn. And it's a story I believe. He has the air of it. And the power to pull souls from hell itself—which would make sense if he is the son of Old Scratch. 'Tis how some of us have come to be here. The Deadman mark is what allows us to stay on this side of things and not be sucked back to whatever dark realm he pulled us from. It's a binding spell that holds us on this side of the barrier."

Sancha lifted her cup. "And to keep other creatures from returning us to whatever dimension we came out of until either Thorn wills it or we earn back our freedom."

"Aye, and he has the power to remove the Deadman's mark at will should we do something wrong and fall from his favor." Belle took a swig from the bottle. "It's the bargain Thorn made with the lot of us. We serve his needs. Police his demons back to their respective cages. And should we survive our trials and battle, we'll earn our salvation and be returned to the land of the living as full mortal beings."

Cameron suppressed the chill that ran down her spine at the very thought of what they described. "If you fail?"

A shadow darkened Sancha's gaze. "We're cast back to the demons that were torturing us when he saved us."

"That hardly seems fair."

Belle scoffed at Cameron's puerility. "Fair's got nothing to do with our sorry lot. Never did. Never will."

Sancha nodded. "Truth be to that." They clanked mugs.

Cameron paused to consider everything they'd told her. Which made her wonder one particular thing . . . "So how many demons does it take to redeem yourselves, anyway?"

"Depends on the severity of the deed what got us damned and our remorse for it. Each has his or her own path to follow." Sancha pulled back her sleeve to show her emblem to Cameron. "The mark lightens as we get closer to earning our freedom. When it's gone completely, so are we."

"How do you mean?"

Sancha reached for her drink. "We're set free and given a chance to screw up anew."

"Even Valynda?"

Valynda nodded. "That's what Thorn promised me. A brand-new body as a woman, once more. I pray he's not lying. I would love to be human again." She closed her eyes and smiled. "To have a real human body!"

"And Janice?" Cameron asked. "Did you earn your freedom already?" Unlike the others, she didn't bear the Deadman's mark on her wrist.

Janice shook her head as she gathered together her cards. "I be a little different from them, me lovey." She pulled her shirt up to show a double bow mark on her hip. "I was not damned, per se. Me mistress be a Greek goddess, and me soul be held by her for *all* eternity, under an entirely different set of rules and conditions."

What the blue devil? Cameron gaped at the last thing she'd expected to hear. Even among these preposterous tales. While her father, who had been enamored of the Classics, had taught her and Paden much about ancient Greeks and Romans and their beliefs, she'd never believed any of it to be real. "Come again?"

"I gave up me soul for vengeance over a wrong what was done to me and mine. Technically, I shouldn't be here with the Deadmen, as it's not really allowed for a Dark-Huntress to mingle with them."

"Which tells you how dangerous our mission is that Acheron would allow her to live and work among our crew," Valynda whispered. "Even the Dark-Hunters have a vested interest in our success."

"The Dark-Hunters?"

"Be the term for what I am, Miss Jack. Acheron be me boss man." Janice covered her mark. "Deadmen pursue demons who've escaped their prisons or who be preying on humanity and return them to their place of origin. Dark-Hunters are a band of warriors what hunt demons known as Daimons."

"There's a difference, then?"

"Oh, aye to that. Our demons be born of an ancient race, cursed by the Greek god Apollo."

"Cursed why?"

" 'Tis said their queen was once a beloved of Apollo's and that she lost his favor, after her miscarriage of Apollo's child, to a beautiful Greek princess who bore him a son. So jealous was she that the queen ordered her soldiers out to slaughter Apollo's mistress and son, in the most brutal of ways. She wanted them ripped apart as if an animal had done it."

Cameron cringed at the horror. No wonder the god had cursed them. She'd have wanted revenge herself had someone dared take the life of her child. But only on the ones who'd done it. She certainly wouldn't have gone after other innocents over it.

As her mother had so often said, two wrongs never made a right. Especially in a tragedy of this magnitude.

Janice placed her cards aside. "To thwart his curse, some of them Apollites done learned to steal souls so that they could feed from them to elongate their own lives. But the problem is, when they do that, they destroy the soul forever. Our goal is to kill those Daimons and free the stolen souls so that they can restore themselves and go on to their eternal rest. If we fail, those souls vanish forever."

Cameron crossed herself at what Janice described. "Was it Apollo who made the Dark-Hunters, too?"

Belle shook her head. "It was Apollo's sister, Artemis, who used her own blood to create the first Dark-Hunter to hunt the Daimons and kill them. That original Dark-Hunter, Acheron, is now their leader, and he's the one what trains them whenever Artemis makes a new Hunter."

"That's why Janny has fangs and we don't . . . different Hunters, different abilities." Sancha winked at Janice.

Cameron let out a nervous laugh, hoping that was a jest. Surely the woman didn't really have fangs.

Did she?

"W-w-what?"

" 'Tis true." Janice opened her mouth to show off her unique dental features.

Holy mother of God!

Cameron shot off her bed to move closer to Belle, who laughed at her overreaction.

"There now, girl! No fear of our Janny. She only bites male posteriors."

Janice grinned. "Truth be to that. And that I do with great relish. In particular, wouldn't mind me a piece of a few of the ones what be sailing on this very ship, or me boss, Acheron. Oh, that one . . ." She sucked her breath in sharply between her teeth—or fangs, rather. "He's got the finest backside what's ever graced a man. If ever there be a one you want to sink teeth to . . ."

"And pray for lockjaw?" Cameron added, remembering what the prostitute had said to her earlier.

"Hear, hear," Sancha laughed. "Wouldn't mind a romp in the sheets with Acheron meself. Can you imagine the skills he must have after all these centuries?"

"Or Bane?" Belle said with a laugh. "I'd lay money he's not one to be shy or timid. Rather, he'd no doubt set fire to the bed, what with his passions."

Janice grinned wider. "Or our dear William or Kalder."

"Or Bart." Sancha purred. "Hell, sign me up for a piece of that Wild Kat or Zumari! Would love to offer up a salutation to their flagpoles and change their religions." She winked.

"Aye!" Belle and Janice agreed in unison.

Sancha took a deep quaff of rum and sighed. "One day, me ladies, we've got to find some way around the captain's ban on crew fraternizations. Even if it means all of us seducing our good captain at once to change his mind on that particular law that chafes me all the way to me nether quarters."

Valynda laughed. "Stop it now, you're scandalizing our Miss Cameron. Look at the poor thing! She's as red as a British officer's jacket."

"I've heard worse." She cleared her throat, even though her cheeks were scalding hot. "Work in a bawdy tavern at home." Cameron returned to sit on her bed before she spoke to Janice. "So how is it that you've come to live among the crew if you're not supposed to be here?"

Janice let out a tired sigh as she propped up her pillow and leaned back against it. "Evil Apollite bastards thought it funny to set me out to sea to die. I'd have burst into flames had Bane not seen me boat and known me for what I was. Caught me right before dawn, he did, and barely saved me hide."

That made no sense whatsoever to Cameron. "How do you mean?"

"Apollites are the race Apollo first created, then cursed," Belle explained. "Just like the Dark-Hunters can't kill humans, they can't kill Apollites until they begin taking souls, as they're considered innocent until they take a human life. The Hunters, like we Deadmen, have a strict code they must follow that dictates what they can and can't do and who they're allowed to hunt and when."

Janice nodded. "So there I was, adrift at sea in a tiny dinghy, helpless as a newborn babe. No oar and no way of getting back to shore on me own, since I know not how to swim. Cursing every line of Acheron's Dark-Hunter manual he forces us to read and live by. Thought I be a goner for sure . . . even after I was seeing this fine ship pulling up alongside me. Couldn't imagine how to explain me predicament to a normal crew of folks. Lucky I was it turned out to be this group of miscreants what knew who and what I was. They rushed me under cover just a mere heartbeat before I'd have burst into flames."

Cameron arched a brow at her dire tone. "Burst into flames? That a metaphor?"

"Oh . . ." Janice flashed a grin. "Nay, lovey. That be an important detail, indeed. Never open a port window and be letting daylight in whenever I be down here, as it be quite lethal to me health."

"Really?"

"Aye!" they said in unison.

Valynda poured more rum for Cameron. "All Apollites, Daimons, and Dark-Hunters are forbidden by Apollo to be in his domain. A single ray of sunshine will instantly cause their skin to blister and burn. Full exposure incinerates them. Part of their curse from the evil sun god who hates the sorry lot of them."

"How awful!" Cameron shuddered in sympathy as she tried to imagine having to live her life without daylight.

For eternity, no less.

She could imagine no worse existence.

"'Deed!" Janice sighed. "Honestly, I feel bad for the buggers. The Apollites, not the Daimons, mind you. Can you think of being cursed to die at age twenty-seven for an act your ancestors done committed that you had nothing to do with? Tragic, really."

Belle snorted. "Feel bad if *you* want, but few in life are innocent past their walking knickers. Most are out only for themselves, Janny. Hence your unfortunate past what caused you to be in our company."

Sighing, Janice nodded glumly.

Before Cameron could ask her to elaborate, Valynda moved to sit beside her. "So what about you, Miss Jack? Have you a beau or a belle at home?"

She scowled at the exceptionally bold and scandalous way these women talked. While she was used to some bawdy ways from the patrons of the Black Swan, this group put even the rowdiest men there to shame. "Neither, I'm afraid. Paden and I had been making plans for him to purchase the Black Swan once he returned from this latest voyage. The current owner has been looking for a buyer and they had an unofficial agreement for it. We'd planned for me—and the girl he was to marry on his return— to run it for him while he sailed. Because of that, I wanted no entanglements from any man to distract me or turn me head from business."

"Wise woman." Belle leaned back on her bed. "Men are ever a distraction."

"Aye to that," Sancha agreed. "But they're oft the best kind of distraction. At least for a few minutes." She wagged her eyebrows, which caused Belle and Janice to laugh and Valynda to groan and shake her head.

While Cameron understood the insinuation, she chose not to comment, as it was apparent that she was the only one in the cabin without direct experience in this matter.

Something the others quickly picked up on.

Sancha *tsk*ed at her. "I take it from your silence that you've never sampled the dangling fruit of the bull, Miss Jack."

More heat crept over her face. "I have not. Though I've heard quite a lot about it in my time."

"Working in a tavern with the reputation of the Black Swan, I imagine you have," Belle said with a laugh.

"Probably seen a few, too." Janice snickered.

"More than I care to think about." Cameron cleared her throat as more embarrassment filled her. "Some are not as circumspect as they should be."

"Yet you've never been curious?" Valynda arched a straw brow.

"Not with what's walked through the door of me tavern. They were all welcome to keep their fruits and nuts planted firmly in their breeches."

They all burst into laughter.

Still, Cameron couldn't refrain from allowing her thoughts to wander toward a couple of the men sailing aboard this ship that the others had mentioned earlier. Unlike the patrons of the Black Swan, the crew here were a different breed.

A much finer, more handsome group she'd never seen confined in one place. The ladies were right about that. The Deadmen definitely stood out as if hand-selected for their exceptional forms.

Which made her curious about something else. . . .

"Are all of you really dead?"

"Aye," Belle said, sobering. "Every last one of us. The only living creatures here are you and the ship, herself. To our knowledge, Lady Marcelina never perished. She alone retains her lifeblood."

"Even Kalder?"

Sancha nodded. "He was gutted. There's a vicious scar on his belly what shows where his enemies slit him good."

"But it be the scar on his soul that continues to bleed."

Belle scoffed at Janice's words. " 'Tis the scars on all our souls that continue to bleed, sister." She turned her dark gaze to Cameron. "Even our fair Miss Jack. I feel her pain. It reaches out to me and twists like a dagger in me heart. She has her own secrets that she keeps, and it's not just her brother what haunts her."

Cameron's jaw dropped that the woman would guess something that she'd have sworn she was keeping quite private. "How do you know that?"

An esoteric smile curved her lips. "No one hides from me, love. I see everything. Even the fact that you haven't been completely honest with the captain."

"What?"

"Are you going to deny it?"

Cameron wasn't sure what to say. "I'm not hiding anything." But even as she spoke, she knew it was a lie.

Worse? So did Belle.

Devyl listened to the creaking of the boards and to the whispers of things he wished he couldn't hear. To the voices of the aether that never left him alone.

Ironic really, since he'd sold his soul long ago for the ability and powers to tap into the very things that now irritated him.

Or perhaps it was justice that he was tortured by them.

"You dared to call for me?"

He looked up from the book he was reading to the shadowed corner where his old enemy peered at him. "You dare take that tone?"

Thorn scoffed as he stepped into the light. Though he wasn't quite as tall as Devyl, he was still a well-muscled bastard who would intimidate most. But then, Devyl wasn't most, and the two of them had never been particularly friendly.

Indeed, they'd once battled hard against each other. Their armies had waged a bloody, devastating war on opposite ends of an intestine-laden field. It was so odd to peer into those frigid green eyes without a battle helm framing them. To sit peacefully in the presence of a being he'd once sworn to see dead at his feet.

Much had changed. Instead of ancient ringed armor, Thorn was dressed in a fashionable brocade coat and buckled shoes. Hell, he even wore a powdered wig over his brown hair.

How fucking off.

But then, Devyl was a long way from his warrior's cloaked armor, too. His braids were gone, as was his thick black beard and philosopher's paint. Nor did he brandish his twisted runic staff.

Nay, they were not the same barbaric enemies they'd been.

Neither were they friends. Certainly not family. Probably the best term for them was bitter strangers.

Thorn crossed the cabin to stand before him. In a move that was as audacious as it was foolhardy, he knocked Devyl's feet from the chair where they rested and took a seat on it. Leaning back, he folded his arms over his chest and cocked one arrogant brow as if daring Devyl to take him to task for his brave stupidity.

"You are a cheeky bastard."

Thorn smirked at him. "And you're a bullish one. Now can we dispense with the insults and you tell me why you rang my bell?"

Closing his book, Devyl scratched at the whiskers on his cheek. "We have a bit of a problem."

"Demons proving too much for you?"

He cast the bastard a menacing glare for that dig when Thorn knew better. Not even the mighty Thorn and all his army had been able to take Devyl down. Had it not been for Vine's treachery, they'd all be paying homage to him under his eternal reign as evil overlord. Damn shame the bitch had gotten greedy and he'd gotten stupid.

"Hardly. Nay, there's a bit of a fluff you need to know about."

Thorn arched his brow even higher. "What fluff is this?"

"I've stashed it belowdecks with the Dark-Huntress I dredged from the sea."

"Pardon? What Dark-Huntress?"

Devyl *tsk*ed at him. "You've fallen way behind, Leucious. How unlike you to not know everything I've been up to."

"Well, as cute and adorable as you are, Duel, I do have other, much more appealing asses to stay on top of. Now, would you like to catch me up? Or should we continue this game?"

He let out an annoyed "heh" before he spoke again. "Appears your friend Menyara has sent a Seraph to my door."

Thorn actually choked. Pity it wasn't fatal for him.

Devyl handed his mug to him to help clear his throat of the gall that had gagged him.

He took it and drank deeply, then spat the contents out and cursed Devyl for everything he'd never been worth. "Blood? You're drinking futtocking blood and you handed it to me without warning? Seriously? When you know what blood does to me?"

Devyl didn't react to the fact that such a beverage could turn both of them into mindless killing animals who would commit any atrocity to taste more of it. "Since when do you discriminate? Besides, it's demon blood. Not human. Pity, that. But I knew you'd get your tits in a wad if I chose a more fulfilling libation."

"You evil excuse for a sentient being. I can't *believe*"—Thorn stressed the word—"I let Savitar talk me into bringing you back."

Devyl snorted. "As you said on my resurrection, to destroy evil of this magnitude you don't send out choirboys, unless you want to feed your enemies lunch."

Thorn sighed irritably as he wiped his hand over his mouth. "Is there anything in this place to drink that didn't once filter through internal organs?"

"When did you become such a prissy quim?"

"Careful, Duel, lest I don my armor and we take up where we once left off."

"That would be fine by me. We never did settle that last fight, as I recall. You turned tail and ran."

The expression on Thorn's face could have frozen fire in August on the equator. "I advanced in a new direction."

Yeah, right.

Scoffing at the bullshit answer, Devyl cast his gaze to the corner where he kept his alcohol. "Cabinet behind you. Serve yourself."

Thorn got up to peruse the meager potent potables Devyl kept on hand for his visiting crew, who would be even more horrified by his preferred beverage than Thorn. "Not by my choice. I'd have gladly sent you to your precious Annwn that day, had it been up to me."

"You'd have tried. 'Twould have been your heart I'd have delivered to your father for my reward, rather. Quite the price he places on you."

Thorn went ramrod still.

"Fear not, Leucious," Devyl said, using Thorn's real name. "I have no intention of telling anyone who your true father is. Or the truth of your birth. A bastard I might be, but I'm not a scabbing piece of shit. Your family trauma be no business of mine. Have my own to deal with."

Relaxing, Thorn chose a hearty wine to pour. "Appreciate your discretion."

Devyl snorted. "Don't. As you know, I settle my issues on a battlefield, as the gods intended. I've no use or respect for sneaky treachery, or those who participate in it."

"That's the one thing I've always respected about you, Duel.

Even when we were enemies. Always knew where we stood." He returned to sit. "So tell me of this Seraph."

"It's not her, per se. Rather, it's her brother, who seems to be in Vine's custody. Somehow he managed to smuggle out his medallion to his sister, who in turn was sent here by way of Menyara."

"How did he manage to get his medallion separated from his sword?"

"That be the question, don't it? But then, he's of Michael's bloodline."

Thorn released a low whistle. "Powerful blood, that."

"Indeed. I never knew he had issue. Other than rumors, of course. Did you?"

"I don't delve into those places or ask those questions. I'm no more welcomed among my brethren than you'd be. For that matter, I'm trusted even less, given what fathered me . . . and how."

"Never mind the why of it."

"Exactly." Thorn nursed his wine as he considered the matter. "If Vine has a Seraph in her custody—"

"A powerful one . . ."

"She could open the gate."

"Could open more than that. Michael's blood is a most potent tonic. And if she has custody of his sword to boot . . ."

Thorn winced. "You're sure the sister holds the medallion?"

"Saw it myself. And it activated under threat. There's no missing that spectacular light show. Lit up the sky for leagues. Surprised you missed it." Devyl set his book aside. "Is Michael still among the Sarim?"

"No idea. As I said, they don't exactly talk to me. We're Hell-chasers. The Hell-Hunters are a different breed entirely, and they don't trust me or like *us* as a rule. The Necrodemians have always been prissy assholes when it comes to our demonic ranks."

Because they expected treachery from Thorn. Born of two powerful, cunning demons who'd betrayed them all and a weak human mother's greed, Thorn was likely to turn on them—at least that was what they assumed. It didn't matter that for thousands upon thousands of years Thorn had served the same side as they. They still refused to trust him completely.

Devyl couldn't blame them for that. It was a rare dog indeed that didn't return to its vomit.

Only the strongest of the strong could resist the urge.

Of course, he'd never met any creature stronger than Thorn, and while he'd never admit it aloud, it was what he respected about the beast. Thorn possessed a rare integrity that he knew would never be tempted by the darkness that Devyl willingly gave in to.

But then he didn't have the tethers to the light that Thorn did. There was nothing for him to hold on to. Nothing he craved or wanted past Vine's head on his wall.

At this point he didn't even care if he returned to his infernal pit of eternal torture or not. He'd endured it for so long that it no longer held any deterrent to him whatsoever. Indeed, a part of him had even learned to derive a bit of masochistic pleasure from the pain of it all. Sick though it was.

Thorn pinned him with a probing stare. "You're taking this awfully well. Should I ask why?"

"Unlike you, I don't fear the gate opening. 'Deed, I hope it does."

"Since yours is the first ass Vine will be after, might I ask why you're so eager for it?"

"As you said, mine is the first ass she'll seek. This time, when I go to my grave, I won't be headed there alone. I plan to take her and all her sisters along with me."

"Including Marcelina?"

"If she gets in my way."

"What happened between the two of you, anyway? Why does she hate you so much?"

Devyl fell silent at the question that took him back to a time and place he hated. Back to a boy who'd died a harsh, painful death long before Vine had carved out his heart, fed it to him, and ended his mortal life. "She blames me for corrupting her sister."

"Did you?"

"What difference does it make? The past is done with. Blame is nothing more than a waste at this point. Besides, we're all guilty of something."

Thorn knew that look in Duel's eyes. A pain so profound and deep that you dared not speak of it because no amount of time could dull the way it lacerated your soul and left it bleeding and raw. It was a turmoil he lived with himself. Guilt. Anguish. And a self-hatred that overrode all other feelings to the point you wondered at times how you managed to remain sane.

Or maybe you didn't.

Maybe you were insane. That would at least explain the horror that was life. The travesty of it all.

Denial was the easiest way to cope. You ignored it as much as you could and prayed it stayed in the dark recesses where you locked it away tight and prayed it never got out again.

Yet no matter how great the seal—how carefully you guarded that door—sooner or later some stupid bastard always had to open it and force you to look inside. Face the very thing you didn't want to see.

Today, he was that stupid bastard.

It was almost enough to make him feel sorry for Duel. Perhaps there was some semblance of a soul left in this vicious blighter after all.

Then again, given some of their nastier battles, he wondered if there'd ever been a soul in Dón-Dueli of the Dumnonii. They hadn't called him the Dark One or Black Soul because of his hair color.

A knock sounded on the door.

"Enter."

Thorn was ever impressed with the way Duel could command his voice to such a threatening intensity without actually raising it to a shout. As a warlord himself, he'd never quite perfected that shit-in-your-breeches growl to the same extent.

William drew up short as he saw Thorn in the cabin. "Beg pardon for the interruption, but we've got a bit of a situation and wanted your input, Captain."

Devyl let out a weary sigh. "Who has Sallie's soul now?"

"Not that. There's a ship approaching fast off the starboard aft. She just hoisted her colors."

He arched a questioning brow.

William swallowed hard before he answered. "Red jack."

A pirate flag. Take no prisoners. Show no mercy. Death to all. No prey. No pay.

A slow smile spread across Devyl's lips. "Slow her down, Mr. Death. Swing her about and, by all means, let the bitches catch up."

5

Devyl stood on deck with his telescope, eyeing the approaching ship, while Thorn moved in to rest just behind him. Something the demon knew made the hairs on Devyl's neck rise—along with his hackles. He'd never been one to stomach a friend at his back.

Never mind a former enemy who'd once lifted his sword in battle against him.

Though allies they might be today, it still didn't erase the years they'd fought viciously to destroy each other. Nor did it lend itself to the formation of any kind of trusting bond between them.

It never would.

Devyl used his powers to check the *Sea Witch*'s defenses. Cannons had been rolled into position and stood ready to rain down iron hell on the approaching group. To keep his crew from spooking, he lifted his telescope to survey the sloop that was gaining on them, even though he didn't really need it to inspect them.

With or without it, he'd have been able to catch the name of the ship that was painted next to the green mermaid figurehead.

Soucouyant.

"Avast!" he ordered Will. There was no need to blast this particular crew of pirates from the waters.

At least not quite yet.

Confused, William arched a disbelieving brow, but passed the order along without hesitation. Though it was obvious the man didn't quite agree with it.

Devyl's hesitation proved to be prudent when one of the *Soucouyant*'s crew members waved a white flag of truce over his head at the same time they lowered Captain Cross's red jack and replaced it with a plain white flag for parlay.

Not quite trusting them, as Rafael Santiago and his pirates weren't exactly known for their honest ways, Devyl kept his men in position, then tapped his powers again to determine the *Soucouyant*'s threat level. He didn't pick up any treachery. They had yet to roll their cannons into place. And no one seemed to be scurrying about in subterfuge.

But then, one never knew for sure, and he wasn't about to risk his ship or crew for any reason. Especially since he knew Santiago had other means of attack no one, other than he, Thorn, or Belle would see coming. Attacks his crew wouldn't be able to defend against with traditional weaponry.

Glancing at Thorn over his shoulder, he caught the older demon's eye. "What do you think?"

"That Santiago knows you too well to try it."

Thorn was right about that. Firing on the *Sea Witch* never ended well for anyone. "Hoist the truce back, Mr. Death! Stay your positions."

And if the pirates tried anything, he'd be feasting on more than demon blood tonight.

The thought brought a rare smile to his lips.

Please try something. He would relish a good fight.

True to his nature, the *Soucouyant*'s captain, Rafael Santiago, came forward to stand on top of the rail until they'd pulled up close enough that he could swing from his deck to Devyl's.

The moment Rafael's black boots touched their boards, Bart and Zumari flanked him. He laughed at their threatening bluster and clapped them each in turn on the back as they brought him closer to Devyl.

Even in height to Zumari, Rafael was broad shouldered and well muscled. His dark skin was covered with scrolling tattoos on both arms, his neck, and even his shaved head.

Devyl was one of the few who knew the true origins of Captain Cross, or Rafael Christoph Santiago, as he'd been named at birth. The son of Masika, a freed Ethiopian slave, and a "merchant" father, Cristóbal Cruz Gabriel Santiago, Rafe had learned the buccaneer trade aboard Captain Cris Cruz's pirate ship at the loving hand of his beloved father. And much to his mother's horror, it was a proud family tradition Rafe carried on, in spite of land law and common sense.

Fearless, and bold in the manner of any second-generation pirate, Rafe ignored his escorts and approached Devyl. "I knew the red jack would work to slow you down." He winked. "You're way too predictable, mate."

Snorting, Devyl crossed his arms over his chest. "Hell of a gamble you made."

"That's what life's all about, my friend. No risk. No reward."

Devyl shook his head at the ever-jovial marauder, who had more bullocks than brains. "So what brought you on this suicidal quest?"

"Heard you were in these waters. Been looking for you for days now. You're a hard crew to find." He flashed another grin at Devyl and William. "Anyway, took something a sennight ago . . . Am thinking you need to see it, Devyl. It's got your Belle written all over it. We could definitely use her expertise on this bit of cargo. *And* yours."

Even more curious, he passed a questioning brow to Thorn. "Want to join us for this inspection?"

"Why not? I'm here. Better than nursing curiosity."

Now it was Rafe's turn to appear perplexed.

"Rafael Santiago, may I present Thorn?" Devyl stepped back so that Thorn could offer his hand to the pirate legend.

"Friend?" Rafe asked.

"More like brethren." The snide smirk on Thorn's face made Devyl want to knock the expression into oblivion. Especially since the bastard was currently in possession of his soul and held full control over him—two things that rankled every last bit of Devyl's core.

Brethren, my ass. More like pox or plague on his private anatomy.

Rafe shook Thorn's hand and stepped back. "No surname? Or is Thorn it?"

"Thorn is all anyone needs to know about me."

"As in thorn up all our collective nether regions," Devyl muttered.

Rafe laughed. "Understood." He gestured toward his ship. "Gentlemen, after you."

Devyl snorted at the invitation that could still be a trap. "I'll pull the rear."

Rafael gave him an exaggerated innocent stare. "What? Don't you trust me?"

"After you took a shot at me outside that tavern last time? Nay. But don't take it personally. I never trusted my own mother, either."

Rafe feigned indignation. " 'Twas a drunken misfire at someone else. How many times do I have to tell you that?"

"Until I believe you, which will be never."

Thorn shook his head and sighed before he swung himself over to Rafe's ship. He sent the line back for Rafe, who followed suit.

Refusing to have his hands that far away from his weapons, Devyl ignored the line when Rafe slung it to him and, with a running start and Herculean feat, jumped from his ship to Rafe's. Something that caused an echoing gasp and ripple of stunned awe to rush through Rafe's pirate crew.

And Devyl's.

Especially as he rose slowly from his crouch like the predator he was and swept a weather eye around the entire group to make sure that if any treachery existed in their hearts, they rethought it fast. He was, after all, a motherless bastard who wouldn't hesitate to lay an attacker low.

Rafe snorted with an amused smirk on his handsome face. "Always one for the grand entrance, eh, mate?"

"Benefits of a heartless reputation, and quick sword arm."

Thorn laughed at Devyl's surly tone as he crossed the deck to stand by his side. Though he'd never admit it out loud, he actually held a lot of respect and affinity for the giant beast of a warrior. "Heartless for you is a step up, my brother."

And yet there had been a time in his past when Thorn would have slit his own mother's throat to have commanded a general as cold-blooded and ruthless as Devyl Bane. Even a warrior with half this demon's incomparable skill set in battle. It was a good thing the boy hadn't been born until long after Thorn had turned against his father and abandoned his cause for a far more nobler and kinder goal.

As united warlords, they would have brought this world to its bloody knees and ruled every part of terra firma.

In retrospect, a terrifying thought. So thank God Bane had been born centuries later and none of Thorn's original generals had been this fierce or capable. Or willing to slit a throat to win a battle or hold their lands.

Devyl glanced about the top deck as a strange sensation went down his spine. And this time it wasn't from Thorn's presence here.

Nay, there was another powerful entity here. One trying not to let him sense it and yet unable to remain hidden from him.

"So what's this about, Santiago?"

Rafe motioned for them to follow him below.

Wary and highly suspicious, Devyl cast another jaundiced gaze around the ship and its crew before he climbed down, with Thorn right behind him.

Irritating bastard that he was.

It only took a moment for Devyl's eyes to adjust to the darkness. But the scent down here was unmistakable.

Unique and revolting to any beast who was familiar with it.

Like dried musk, mixed with something soured. It sent a chill down his spine. He instinctively moved his hand to his sword and prepared to confront something that should be dead and buried.

Or better yet, burned beyond all recognition and scattered to the four winds so as never to rise again.

Rafe lit a lantern. "At first, we thought it a jumbie."

"It is a jumbie." Only this one didn't live in a silk-cotton tree.

It was a Blackthorn. One of the deadliest of its breed.

"Dón-Dueli . . ." The creature's voice was low and husky, and filled with malevolence. "Free me, my lord, and I will serve you again."

He felt his eyes begin to turn. Something verified by the crew, who scrambled madly for the ladders to escape being belowdecks with him.

Only Rafe held his ground. "Should I ask about *that*?" He jutted his chin toward Devyl's eyes.

"Not really." Devyl paused to glance around. "Did you find anyone around *it*?" He inclined his head toward the demon in the cage. A demon that swayed like a tree in a breeze only it could see or feel.

"Nay. We discovered her on a ghost ship. No one was on board and no traces of the crew remained. Not even a bone fragment. We assumed they'd abandoned ship to escape her."

They'd most likely been eaten before they had a chance to flee. Devyl winced at the poor, unsuspecting bastards' fates.

"She seemed friendly enough at first. Told us sickness had claimed the others. Then she went for my throat . . . with fangs bared."

Of course she did.

Devyl folded his arms over his chest. "How did you capture her?"

Rafe pointed to the talisman he wore on a black cord around his neck. "My mother's protection. When she came for me, my mother's spell knocked her out. Thank God for that. We bound her here, and haven't gone near the cage since, except to toss food and water at her."

Too bad that wasn't what the creature needed to sustain her illbegotten form.

Devyl cast his gaze to Rafael. "How is your mother?" He'd only seen her once, when Rafael had been transporting her to his home so that she could meet the pirate's intended. And yet, she'd been a woman of extreme kindness and grace. One of the purest, gentlest souls he'd ever known.

Sadness darkened his eyes. "She took ill last winter and passed."

Damn shame, that. The world could use more people with the integrity and decency of Santiago's mother. "My deepest condolences."

"Thank you."

"Aye," Thorn said earnestly. "Sorry for your loss."

Rafe rubbed at his necklace. "At least I was with her at the end. And my father, as well. And it was peaceful. There are worse things in life, and I like to think she was watching over me and my crew when we came upon this creature."

No doubt. Something exceptionally powerful had to have been protecting them. It was a rare, rare beast who encountered a hostile Deruvian and survived.

Especially when they didn't know what they were facing and the creature had gone Winter on them—a term Devyl's race had coined for anyone who embraced the dark ways of Marcelina's people. Judging by this one, she'd been Winter for quite some time, too.

And having been married and bonded to one, Devyl had more experience with one in Winter than most. His stomach pitching with disgust and anger, he neared the cage where she watched him from a pair of hate-filled whisky-colored eyes. She lay in chains. Her black hair gnarled and greasy. Malnourished from her captivity, she held a grayish tint to her skin, and her veins appeared black beneath it. Thorny.

Yet even with that, her lips were a vibrant, unnatural shade of red.

"Blackthorn . . . where's your partner?"

Sinister laughter answered his question. "Where is yours?"

Hissing, he rushed toward the bars, wanting to rip out her heart and eat it raw until he was whole again himself. Like her, it'd been too long since he'd fed on what sustained him, and he was starving for what he really needed.

Still, she offered him a cold smile. "Anger you, did I, Majesty?"

"Don't play this game with me. I could use a good bonfire." He raked her with a meaningful glare as he imagined her being consumed by the flames. That form of a death sentence for her race was what had led to the burning of witches in mankind's history. Not knowing about the Deruvians, Christians had taken up the punishment Devyl's people had once reserved solely for hers and used it against innocent humans. Even the test to see if witches floated in water came from the fact that Deruvian bones were made of wood, and it was how earlier human tribes had once identified her species when they didn't have access to his people to help them determine Deruvian threat.

Foolish humans. They had no idea what they were dealing with. No idea that the only way to kill a Deruvian was to burn them completely and then scatter the charred ashes over water so that they couldn't take root and regenerate.

Otherwise, the bastards returned even angrier and more vicious and vengeful as enemies. Not human sorcerers. Rather, preternatural creatures with powers far beyond mortal comprehension.

And if they regenerated a third time, they came back petrified as a supreme power unlike anything imaginable.

That was the last thing anyone wanted to fight or encounter. An unholy hell-beast that only those well trained could stand against or kill.

Her eyes glowing softly in the dim light, she laughed again. Until her gaze went past his shoulder to focus on the other "Thorn" in the room. That sobered her quick. "Well, well. Bedding with your enemies these days, I see. How fast the mighty do fall."

Fuck this. He had no tolerance for her or her insults.

Stepping back with a sneer, Devyl turned to Rafael. "Take her topside and set her ass on fire. Scatter her charred and besalted ashes over the waves, far out to sea."

With those words, he headed for the ladder.

"Druid! Wait!"

Devyl froze as she let out the one tidbit of his past he *never* spoke about.

To anyone.

And it sucked every bit of oxygen from the room. Only Thorn and Marcelina knew about the days he'd donned the black robes of a pagan leader and counselor.

Only they knew the cost of *that* particular stupidity.

He took a deep breath to control his rage, then continued on for the exit.

"Wait!" she screamed again. "I can help you!"

"Can and will are two entirely different things," he shot over his shoulder.

"I *will* help you! Duel, I swear it. Please!"

He paused to look back at her. "I should believe you . . . why?"

"Because the Carian Gate is cracking even as we speak. More of us are being unleashed. I know you want to find it and reseal it before *she* is released."

Hardly. The bitch had no real, true idea how badly he wanted

Vine's neck within his grasp. However . . . "I don't need you for that."

"But you need me to find the Seraph she holds, if you're to free him. You'll never find him without me. Not alive or before she turns him."

He steeled himself to show no emotions whatsoever. To give nothing away. It was the only way when dealing with a species so treacherous and cold. "What Seraph?"

"Surely the great Dón-Dueli knows about the Seraph Vine captured." She cackled with laughter. "Is that not what brings the great Forneus here, too?"

At the mention of Thorn's one true demonic summoning name, Rafael crossed himself and stepped back. He paled considerably from his sudden fear of who and what Thorn really was.

Thorn went completely stiff, while Devyl held his breath at something not even *he* had the bullocks to do. The use of his Leucious birthname was ballsy enough and as far as he dared take insulting the demon.

After all, in life, there were some actions just not worth the gamble.

Jumping from a cliff that overlooked a raging sea and sharp rocks. Eating glass. Throwing yourself into a raging inferno inside a volcano.

Touching the Dark-Hunter Acheron on the back of his neck.

Trespassing on the Chthonian Savitar's island without his permission.

Telling the demon Simi *no* when she didn't want to hear it.

And using Thorn's summoning name.

"Your lack of discretion is foolish," Devyl warned her. "Were I you, I'd stop before I lose more ground and my head."

"Is what she says true?" Rafe asked Thorn. "Are you the demon Forneus?"

Thorn passed an irritated grimace toward the pirate. "No one can help who they're born as. But we all have a choice as to who we become, and especially in who we are. The demon Forneus died an excruciatingly long time ago, as Captain Bane can attest. I'm not the same beast who led his army of demons over the lands of man to conquer this world for his father. I'm here to make sure creatures like her mistress pay for their crimes and harm no innocent."

Rafe arched a quizzical brow at Devyl.

He met Thorn's cold green gaze before he answered with the truth. "Thorn isn't Forneus." At least not anymore. Though to be honest, Devyl would have liked to have met *that* warlord. They could have been friends.

Better still, they could have been allies.

But the curse of this world was that it was ever changing. Friends today. Enemies tomorrow. And, as was presently true, even enemies could become friendly.

Life was ever peculiar that way, as it kept everyone on their toes. You never knew where it was going to land you, or how quickly.

Sinner to saint. Hero to villain. A person's role could reverse itself in the blink of an eye. All it took was one good deed for redemption.

Or one misplaced lie by another that others were too quick to grab on to and hold close to their hearts, even though they knew it for the fabrication it was. In that one single heartbeat, your whole life was ruined. For no other reason than people didn't want to do their own thinking or learn their own facts. Rather, all too many were willing to follow along like mindless sheep to the slaughter.

Or the lynching.

He'd never understand the human mind. Especially the hypocrisy of it all. Just as he'd never understand why Thorn had given him this chance to earn back his soul when they both knew he didn't deserve it.

Thorn wasn't the one Rafe should be cringing from.

He was. In his day, he'd made a mockery of the vile, evil creature Rafe had caged before them.

And with that knowledge firing deep in his gullet, Devyl turned on Mona and bared his fangs at the Blackthorn bitchtress. He let his eyes glow their true bloody color so that she could see he was through with her games. "Tell what you know, Mona! Where is she?"

"So you do care, don't you now? Och, Du." She *tsk*ed at him with her blackened teeth. "The truth comes out. Dark lord you might be, but me lady always held your nubby heart, such as it is. You should have been there when we fell, my lord. Vine herself lamented your death over it. She said that, had she not killed you, we wouldn't have been taken. None to blame for it but herself, she said."

He scowled at her nonsense. "Stop the riddles!" He blasted the cage with his powers.

The force of it knocked her from her feet and sent her straight to the ground, where she slammed against the side of the ship.

From the floor, she wiped one pale, black-veined hand across her bleeding nose and laughed. "Poor Du!"

When he went to blast her again, Thorn caught his arm. "Don't bother."

Growling deep in his throat, he curled his lip at Thorn's compassion. "What are we to do with her? We can't leave her here. Sooner or later, she'll feast on them all, and well you know it. You banish her to return to her prison and she'll only escape and be back to bother us all the more and wreak who knows what harm on the humans. She's naught but a disease to plague and eat away at anything that she sets her roots to."

An insidious smile curved Thorn's lips. "I'll plant her in a place from which there's no escape."

Bitter amusement swept through Devyl as he realized that Thorn intended to take her into his home realm of Azmodea. He was right. It would be the one place from which she could never again escape. But what a hellish nightmare that would be, especially if Thorn planted her in his garden. . . .

Devyl smirked. "You are an evil bastard."

"Indeed." As Thorn headed to her cage, she shrank away from him.

"I'll take you to the gate, Du! Please, lord! Mercy! Mercy!"

Devyl met Thorn's gaze and let out a tired breath, as he actually felt sorry for the bitch and the fate that would await her in that hole.

This was a bad idea. Every instinct he possessed told him he was a fool to even consider it.

She was lying about helping them. He knew it without fail or doubt.

And yet . . .

What if she wasn't?

It would be a lot easier to have a map to the gate than to play the guessing game they'd been doing by following the trail of the plat-eyes and other creatures released from it. Save them time. More than that, it would save human lives, and that was what Thorn wanted him to do.

They might actually make it to the Seraph before Vine killed him and absorbed his blood and its power. Or, as the Blackthorn had pointed out, Vine converted him into a tool they could use against them—which was the last thing any of them needed.

"Well?" Devyl asked him, even though it wasn't in his nature to confer with anyone.

Thorn released an equally agitated breath. "I leave it up to you. Feel free to gut or burn her later, I suppose."

Rafe let out a low whistle. "And they call *me* heartless?"

"Aye, well, you might want to stand back as I release her, or she might make that a literal statement instead of a figurative one." Devyl headed for the cage.

He hesitated as he swept his gaze over her fragile appearance. She looked so harmless and weak, and yet she was one of the deadliest of creatures.

Like a rabbit possessed of a cobra's venom and razor-sharp teeth.

She brushed at her dark, matted hair. Licking her lips, she reminded him of a street beggar. "I need sustenance, Majesty."

"We have pig blood on the ship."

Curling her lips to expose her fangs, she groaned in protest.

"There's no living person there for you to feast on. We're all Deadmen."

She screwed her face up into a perfect expression of absolute horror. "What?"

"'Tis true. There's not a living creature among us." He didn't make mention of Cameron, since the last thing the girl needed was to be singled out by this beast.

She groaned even louder. "Then leave me here."

"Never." Mona would only escape her cage and destroy Rafael and all his crew. "You go with me or Thorn. Your choice."

Glancing to Thorn, she shook her head. "I'll take me chances with you, Du."

"Why do I feel so insulted?" Thorn asked.

"You? I think I'm the one most slighted by her choice." Devyl was definitely the one most offended by her stench. Holding his breath, he opened the cage and tried not to think about the fact that she seemed to be rotting.

From the inside out. Gah, the bowels of hell had reeked less.

Mona smiled up at him as she followed Thorn toward the ladder. While this wasn't the most ideal situation, at least she was getting off this ship and away from the crew that had captured her. Sooner or later, Du would have to make port and then she could feed. But first . . .

First she would find the Seraph medallion Vine had sent her

after. Then she would tear the heart from the fetid beast and deliver them both to her mistress for reward.

Along with the souls of every member of Devyl Bane's damned crew. And then they would all have their just rewards, and the world would finally be their playground.

MICHAEL'S
KEY

6

"You know this is a trap and that creature is a liar?"

Devyl passed a smirk to Thorn. "Of course I do."

Shaking his head, Thorn snorted. "Still letting the bitches catch up?"

"Best way to keep an eye on your enemy is to have them under your thumb. Learned *that* from you."

"And here I thought you weren't paying attention." There was a light of respect in Thorn's eyes as he watched Rafe's men escorting Mona up the ladder.

"You sure you're ready to take her?" Rafe hesitated before they completely released her.

"I'd much rather she be among my crew than yours." His Deadmen—and, more to the point, Mara—could handle the beast and put her down if needs be.

Santiago's sailors were nothing more than a walking banquet for the hag. They were all lucky that, given Rafe's mother's extreme powers and knowledge about such things, the pirate captain had known and wasn't taken aback by the fact that Devyl wasn't quite human. That Rafe had recognized the fact that Mona was highly dangerous when they'd found her, and his mother's spell had protected them all. Anyone else would have been killed instantly and their crew sacrificed.

In fact, Santiago was among the tiny few who knew Bane and his men were not of this world, but belonged to another species entirely.

Rafe clapped him on the arm. "No offense, my friend. But I feel better with her in your custody myself."

Devyl snorted at his misplaced humor. "Before we go, I should warn you that Barnet has moved into our waters and is hard pressing for information as to your whereabouts. He's determined to collect the bounty on your hide."

"Wonderful," Rafael said drily. "Appreciate the heads-up. I'll be sure to warn St. Noir and Bonny about it when next I see them, as well."

Devyl almost smiled at the mention of the female pirate. Anne Bonny was a unique piece of work. "Give Rackham my best."

A strange look came over Rafael's face. "You know Anne isn't with Jack anymore, right?"

That news stunned him. Jack Rackham, Anne Bonny, and Mary Reade were so tight that he'd assumed the three had magically melded into a single life form. "Since when?"

Rafael let out a nervous laugh. "Since she conceived Jean-Luc St. Noir's child and Rackham found out about it. The three of them have been at each other's throats ever since."

Wow. That was indeed impressive news. Devyl shook his head. Pirate drama. They could get into more shyte than anyone he'd ever known. "What of Reade?"

"She and Anne have both taken up with St. Noir's crew for the time being. While Mary was fond of Rackham, her loyalty will always be to Bonny."

"Well then, give them all three my congratulations."

Rafael appeared bemused. "All three?"

"Aye. Jean-Luc and Anne for the baby. Jack for escaping the hell known as matrimony and fatherhood."

Rafe laughed. "Ah." Then he sobered as the demon was hauled past him and taken topside. The look in Mona's eyes promised Devyl a *merry* time to be sure.

Little did she know, such challenges only fired his resolve. And they *never* boded well for his enemies.

Thorn had the scars to prove it.

Looking forward to the challenge, Devyl said his good-byes to Rafael, then returned to his own ship with Thorn in tow.

By the time he was on deck again, William and Bart already had Mona in custody.

"What do you want us to do with *this*?" William gestured at their newest "guest."

Devyl pondered his options. In truth, he still wanted to set fire to her and scatter her ashes.

The glimmer in Thorn's eyes said he concurred.

But for now . . .

"Put her under Belle's guard and have Miss Jack moved to my quarters."

William's jaw went slack as Bart's eyebrows shot northward.

"Pardon?" William's voice cracked on the question.

"Have you lost your hearing, man? Those be your orders. See about them and be quick on your way."

"Aye, aye, Captain." They hurried away while a slow smile curled Mona's lips.

Devyl was tempted to blast her. Yet somehow he managed restraint. Though it was one of the rare times in his life that he'd ever done so.

Thorn slid a knowing smirk toward him. "I take it Miss Jack is the Seraph's sister?"

"Aye. She is."

Thorn paused as if considering that for some reason. Though why it warranted such stern attention, Devyl had no idea. Cameron Jack was the last woman he was interested in. His heart had been claimed long ago by a callous lady who still held it with an iron-taloned fist.

"And you offer her your *direct* protection?"

He pinned a murderous glare to Thorn at the insinuation in his snide tone. The boots on his feet were older than the girl. "She's an innocent *child*."

Thorn had to keep his own jaw from dropping at the defensiveness that lay beneath those deeply growled words. Dón-Dueli . . . the Dark One . . . the World-King who'd slaughtered any and *every*-thing that got in his way, was protecting someone?

*Any*one.

No fucking way.

It was unprecedented.

Thorn couldn't get his mind to wrap around this inconceivable concept. For the first time in his insanely long life, Thorn's treatment at the hands of the higher Sarim council made sense.

Aye . . . now, I get it.

Because *this* . . . this made no sense whatsoever. It was so far out of character for the vicious beast he knew Devyl to be. There was a better chance of Lucifer becoming a virginal choir girl than Devyl Bane sheltering someone without it benefitting him.

Yet those thoughts vaporized as soon as he saw the woman nearing them on deck.

At first glance, Thorn thought her a very slender teen boy or young man like Devyl's rigger Katashi—Wild Kat as the crew had dubbed him. Until Thorn noted the delicate arch of her brows and the line of her cheeks. Though her thick chestnut brown hair was pulled back into a queue and she wore the coat and breeches of a man, it was still obvious that those hips and that posture and walk belonged solely to a woman.

One with a nice, well-rounded ass.

And her hazel blue-green eyes were absolutely mesmerizing.

But none of that should induce a cruel, heartless bastard like Duel to protect her.

Nay. Her features were too average and pretty. Her guile lacking all sophistication. She was nothing like Duel's ex-wife. Possessed of vibrant titian hair, and goddess curves, Vine was exquisitely formed. Breathtakingly beautiful. The kind of woman who left all women lurking in her shadow in a jealous rage, and men gaping and speechless, fully erect and incapable of any coherent thought other than how to entice her into a bed as fast as possible.

He'd never had any trouble figuring out how Duel had lost his heart or his soul, never mind his life, to that bitch. Any man who favored female companionship would have gladly done whatever Vine asked and abandoned all conscience and reason for her.

But this one . . .

The only part of her that was remarkable was just how woefully average she appeared.

"That's Michael's bloodline?" Thorn whispered to Duel. "You're sure?"

"Aye."

Incredible. Normally, those born to Michael's blood were hard to miss. They were blond, as a rule, tall, and exceptionally handsome.

This one . . .

Well, she did have one thing in common with the ancient being.

Her eyes stewed with venom as she planted herself firmly in front of them. "I'm not sleeping in your cabin, Captain. Have you *any* idea how inappropriate that is?"

"Aye, and I couldn't care less. There's not a soul here who would dare defy me or speak ill of my intentions. You will sleep where I say, Miss Jack."

She laughed incredulously. "You would be wrong." She sobered to glare up at him with an audacity that was as stupid as it was commendable. "*Most* wrong."

Devyl actually felt a smile tugging at the edges of his lips as she started in the opposite direction of his cabin. "Miss Jack?"

She paused to look back at him with an arched, defiant brow.

"My cabin, or we leave you adrift in the sea . . . without an oar . . . or boat. I believe the term is 'walking the plank.' "

"I beg your pardon?"

"Beg all you want, but it changes naught. You heard me, lass, and I meant it. Those be the terms of your stay here. Now hie thyself off to where you're supposed to be headed."

"You can't be serious."

Devyl arched a brow at the cheeky lass. "I can and am."

With a foolish stride, she returned to stand in front of him. "You *will* regret this, Captain Bane."

Doubtful. The only thing he regretted was the stunned look on Thorn's face that made him want to slap the bugger.

Thorn finally managed to shut his gaping mouth. "Can I see her medallion?"

She paled at Thorn's question. "You told him about it?" she whispered to Devyl.

"Aye," he whispered back. "And the low tone is useless, as his hearing is without equal."

A deep red stain crept over her cheeks.

Thorn laughed. "No fears, child. I'm the last one who would harm you for the token. I only want to see it for myself to make sure Devyl doesn't have a head injury that's causing him to imagine things."

Devyl felt another impulse to give *him* one, but didn't move as she reluctantly pulled it out and handed it to the repugnant oaf who made his current living death even more unbearable than his time spent in hell.

The moment Thorn saw the medallion, his eyes shot to the same hue of red as Devyl's natural state. He turned the medallion over in his hand. It glowed a deep, vibrant green in protest of Thorn's demonic grasp. It even hummed as if screaming in agony. Devyl definitely knew that feeling, as he felt the same compunction himself.

"You're right. No doubting the origins of *this*."

Devyl crossed his arms over his chest. "Told you. I'm not the one with a head injury."

Thorn locked gazes with him, and if he didn't know better, Devyl might think there was actual panic there. "We have to get to her brother. Sooner rather than later. Otherwise, there's no telling what Vine will do to him."

"Well aware of that fact."

Thorn clenched the medallion in his hand. "Mind if I keep this for a bit?"

Cameron was aghast at his question. "Of course I mind. Me brother entrusted it to me care."

"I know, but I really need it for a little while so that I can use this to hopefully find him."

She glanced to Devyl. "Can I trust him?"

"*You* probably can."

"What does that mean?"

"That *I* would never trust him. For anything. Not even to clean spit from my boots. But you shouldn't have any problems, as he doesn't virulently hate you."

Jerking her head back, she scowled up at him. "I thought he was your friend?"

Thorn let out a hysterical laugh. "Devyl has no friends. He doesn't believe in them."

She gaped. "Truly?"

Devyl snorted at the innocent question and stepped back toward Death's location. "William? Tell our innocent guest here what friendship gets you in this life."

Will didn't hesitate or pause over his standard motto. "A conviction and a noose."

Devyl lifted a smug, taunting brow at Cameron, who gaped at them both, especially given how flat and dry William's tone had been.

"You can't really believe that?" she asked them.

"Believe it?" William challenged as he drew near her. "Know it as truth." He pulled his cravat down to show her the obvious imprint of where he'd been hung. There was no mistaking or denying the mark of where the rope had torn through his flesh and left him with a bitter, awful scar.

Gasping, she reached for it, then caught herself, as she must have realized how inappropriate it would be to touch him so intimately. "I-I-I-I'm sorry."

"So was I when the executioner dropped the floor from beneath me feet, then waited an eternity before he yanked me legs to finish the job. Bloody plague-ridden bastard." William straightened his collar. "Sorry I ever made the mistake of calling anyone me friend. Sorriest of all that I put such a rotten piece of dung at me back." He cut a seething glare toward Thorn. "Swore to meself when Thorn brought me back that it was the one mistake I'd not make again. Put no one and nothing to your shadow unless you're prepared for a blade to be sliding between your shoulders when you least expect it."

The captain moved to stand shoulder to shoulder with Will. "And that's why we get along so well. Mutual understanding."

William smirked. "And mutual mistrust."

"Exactly."

"That just makes me sad for the both of you." She stepped forward to hug William and then the captain.

Devyl froze at the sensation of her arms around his waist. Of her body pressed so intimately against his. For a full minute, he couldn't breathe as a wave of fire erupted through his veins and awoke a peculiar feeling inside him he would have never believed possible.

No one had touched him like this since the day he'd buried his Elf. Not a sexual embrace, or one intended to lead to such. This was an innocent hug meant to give comfort. One offered out of kindness and true compassion for another.

It was true caring and innocence.

And it awakened something. He couldn't even name this feeling because it'd been far too long since he'd last felt even an inkling of . . .

Words failed him utterly.

What the hell, man?

She gently rubbed her hand against his arm, offering him a compassionate smile before she turned to face Thorn. "I'm trusting you, Mr. Thorn. Please return me brother's trinket to me as soon as you can."

As she walked away, Devyl realized he was gaping now, too. Snapping his mouth shut, he cleared his throat. Then saw red as it dawned on him that she was heading back to her quarters, where he'd stashed the Deruvian bitchington.

"Fetch the lass, Will!" He shoved at his quartermaster. "See her to my quarters!"

"Aye, Captain." He ran to obey.

Turning, he caught the look on Thorn's face. "Don't start with me, demon. In the mood I'm in, I'm likely to stock up on my favored beverage supply, and *your* blood would be a most special and welcomed vintage."

Thorn held his hands up in surrender. "All I'm thinking is that it's her Seraph's blood you're reacting to. Nothing more."

"How so?"

"That unnatural attraction you feel inside you has nothing to do with any real feelings you have. You know it as well as I do. When you're born in darkness, you seek the light. We crave it. It's how they destroy us in the end. We're so helpless against its lure that we dive into it even when we know we're headed for our ultimate doom."

He scoffed at the older demon's wisdom. "What do you know of it?"

Sadness darkened Thorn's green eyes. "More than you can fathom. And I loved mine in a way I wouldn't have believed possible. She alone tamed the angry fury inside my heart. She's the only reason I'm human now."

Those words shocked Devyl most of all. "You're confiding in me?"

"Nay, brother. I'm warning you. The moment she learned what I really was . . . saw the truth? My lady never believed another word from my lips. How could she, given what I've done and who my parents are? She never once thought me capable of any kind of love. To this day, I can't blame her for that. Some days, I'm just as sure as she is that I'm incapable of it, too." He glanced away. "That's our curse. To seek the light and to always be banished back to the darkness that birthed us. We are the damned and hopeless. Maybe that's all bastards like us deserve."

And with that, Thorn vanished.

Devyl stood there, ruminating on what Thorn had said. While he recognized the truth the demon spoke, there was one vast difference.

Cameron had seen the beast in him. She knew what he really was.

Still she'd hugged him.

Hugged. Him.

It defied all reason.

"Captain!"

Blinking to clear his thoughts, he walked toward the prow, where Sallie was rushing back and forth between the muscled mountain that was their striker, Simon Dewing, and Katashi, who barely cleared five feet in height. Wiry and lean, Kat had black hair and deep hazel-brown eyes. Because of his proclivity for pranks and harassing any sailor not doing their part, half of Bane's crew was convinced the Japanese sailor was part namahage. A fear Kat played into by the way he dressed and wore his hair in feathered knots around his head.

But Devyl suspected a lot of it came from the fact that Kat had been the youngest of five boys. Something that tended to make him rambunctious and forever into things he should leave alone.

Like a hungry rat ferreting.

Hence his nickname. It was both a play on the fact that Kat was mouselike, and therefore they called him by a rodent's mortal enemy. And he was curious to a level that Devyl didn't doubt for an instant Kat would sacrifice nine lives to uncover one truth.

Likewise, Simon, as a former priest of Exú—like the African spirit he served—was an innate trickster capable of being a fierce protector or a vengeful enemy.

Almost even in height to Devyl, Simon wore his hair in a short black Greek style that softened the sharp, angular lines of his handsome features. And while Devyl's eyes became red under stress or threat, Simon's dark brown eyes would turn a vibrant gold serpentine whenever he communed with his spirits.

"What mischief are you about?" He eyed them as he saw how distraught Sallie was.

"They've stolen me soul again, Captain. Make them hand it back!"

"Si . . . Kat . . . where is it?" he growled at them.

"Captain," Simon chided. "It's ridiculous for you to humor him so. The man needs to learn his soul's not in a bottle."

Devyl felt his eyes turning at their cruelty toward their older mate. "And what harm is it to you if he chooses to carry his soul in a bottle or not? Were you once frightened as a small child by a bottled soul?"

Kat laughed.

Simon's nostrils flared, but he knew better than to show his anger to Devyl. "I can't believe a grown man is so ridiculous. You should shatter it now, Captain, and show him how foolish he's being."

"And you should both be ashamed of yourselves for tormenting the poor lad over his soul in this manner. Now hand it over and let him have his peace."

Kat pulled it out of his pocket with a grimace. "It does seem a bit off, Captain. He nurses it like a child with a poppet. I've even seen him talking to it."

"Again, I ask, what's the harm to you if he does? Would you rather he be talking to you or nursing *you*?" He gave a pointed stare to each of them. "And I'd like to think the two of you, of all the members of this crew, would be the least likely to torment another over *any* matter."

Simon grimaced. "That's just a low blow, Captain."

"And so's stealing a man's soul."

"We were just having a bit of fun." Kat moved to stand closer to Simon.

"Fun at the expense of another's suffering isn't fun, Mr. Mori.

That bitch is known as cruelty, and her mantle is lasting anguish. It's the inalienable right of all sentient creatures to sleep in peace. To live lives of dignity and free of torment. To pursue whatever courses they, themselves, choose of their own volition. And no one should ever be beholden to another. Not for their necessities, and damn sure not for their liberty nor for their lives. And never for their immortal souls. Now hand the man his soul that you took before I aid in sending yours back to hell!" Those last words came out as a deep growl that caused them to scamper away the instant they handed it over.

Devyl returned the bottle to its owner.

When he started to leave, Sallie stopped him. "Thank you for understanding about me soul, Captain."

Devyl inclined his head to the physically older male. However, he had been born long before the man in front of him, or even Sallie's great-grandparents. "No worries, Mr. Lucas. Though might I suggest in the future that you find a smaller bottle or safer place to be keeping such a precious commodity?"

Absalon grimaced. "I tried a smaller bottle once. Damn thing's too big to fit in one. Caused all manner of ruckus over it. Sad to say, this is the smallest I could manage and keep him happy."

Devyl bit back a smile. " 'Tis a mighty large rum bottle."

"He likes the rum the best. Gives it a nip, every now and again. For good health, you know?"

"Take a nip myself, for the same reasons."

"Well, me thanks again, Captain." Cradling the bottle like an infant in his arms, he wandered off to tend to his duties.

Devyl took a moment to visually check where his men were and listen to the sea and the aether that stirred around him. A million voices screamed out in it, letting him know that Vine was awake and on the move again.

So close that he could almost smell the scent of her skin, and yet he couldn't reach her.

He needed that gate's location. How ironic that he couldn't find it, given that he was the one who'd sold his soul to lock her there. But then, that had been part of it. She'd been imprisoned after his death, so that he hadn't had the pleasure of seeing her downfall and imprisonment that he'd caused.

Damn her for it. Yet how he'd have loved to have seen her expression the moment she learned his powers had been so great that he'd been able to reach out from the grave to extract his revenge on her and trap her in her hellhole so that she couldn't enjoy her success over him. It was the one thing she'd never imagined.

Marcelina either.

No one had held any idea of just how incredibly powerful he'd been as a mortal being.

He'd always been a creature of secrets. One who never let anyone know anything about him. Not even his own wife.

And this was far from over.

I will find you, you bitch. You're not safe, even in your prison.

One way or another, he would get to her and seal that gate and make sure that she stayed locked in her hole for all eternity. Even if it meant returning to hell himself.

Or he'd have spare lumber for his ship and new blood for his cup.

Aye, he'd win either way.

And mount Vine's head upon his mantel.

7

"Why did you never tell me about your sister?"

Devyl froze at the barely whispered words. Words that drove a bitter wave of agony through his heart. Ignoring Mara's question, he kept working.

Until she manifested in front of him and pulled the rope he was knotting from his hands. "Answer me, Du."

"There's nothing to say."

Sadness darkened her pale eyes to a vibrant shade

of blue. "She was the reason you attacked my village that day, wasn't she?"

He felt his own eyes turning red as he met her gaze. "I don't talk about Elf . . . with anyone."

Marcelina flinched as he brushed rudely past her, no doubt to join his crew outside, away from her. Closing her eyes, she saw the day they'd met so clearly in her mind.

Dón-Dueli had sat in his saddle as tall as a mountain. A giant, muscled mass of rage who'd ridden into her forest like an avenging spirit from the very bowels of hell itself, dressed in his black leather armor, with a full black beard and long, braided hair. Even his horse had seemed more like a demon than a flesh-and-bone animal. Painted to appear as a skeleton, the beast had been given fairy hair to make it seem even more fierce and supernatural.

Like his rider. A creature of supreme and unholy malice and wrath.

Never had she witnessed that level of carnage or fury from any man or creature. Dón-Dueli had come alone and burned her sisters and brothers to the ground in their nemeton as he sought information about a rival clan they protected.

Or so she'd thought.

Not once had she had an inkling of what had truly driven him to viciously slaughter three dozen of her people that day. The savage brutality of his crazed fury had chilled her to her very bones. No one had been able to slow him down or defeat him. Anyone who tried fell fast and hard to his ruthless battle skills.

Combining their powers, the Sylphs and Deruvians had tried

their best to fight him off and drive him from their forest, while he demanded the heads of the ones who'd gone after . . .

"Elf!" He'd shouted that name to the heavens. A fierce, anguished cry that had sent animals scrambling through the brush and birds into flight. "Give me the ones who attacked my Elf! I want them, and I will kill every fucking one of you until I get to the culprits and pull their intestines out through their arses! So help me, Dagda! I will not leave before I taste their blood and feast on their desecrated corpses!"

She'd stupidly thought that the possessive way he used "Elf" had meant he was there over a pet or his servant. It was an unheard-of name for a human.

Calling out that name as a battle cry, he'd cut them down or used his sorcerer's fire to scorch them to ashes. But given what she'd heard him tell Thorn earlier . . .

It all made sense.

He'd been there that day to avenge his younger sister. Something Mara could definitely relate to.

Pain choked her as she remembered Dón-Dueli grabbing her while she'd sought to distract him from her own sisters who'd fled to safety. With hell-born fury in his eyes, he'd forced her at sword point to her knees. Shaking in terror, she'd waited for the killing blow she was sure would come.

A blow he'd hesitated to take. At the time, she'd assumed it was because he wanted information and she was the only one of her people who'd been stupid enough to transform into a human body that he'd seen. The only one dumb enough to fall into his hands, because she was intentionally distracting him to save the others.

But as their gazes locked, and his eyes flared to their unholy red, she'd seen his desire to strike her down. Seen the anguish and torment that burned so deep inside his soul.

And in that instant of his hesitation, she'd reached up and cradled his sword hand in hers. Then, she'd whispered the sacred, binding words.

It'd been a desperate gamble to join them in an unholy alliance. One she'd spent ten thousand lifetimes regretting, as Dón-Dueli recognized the fact that she'd bound their life forces together. Her intent had been to take him with her to the grave.

Then, as now, he'd proven an uncooperative beast. But how could she have known that he'd have knowledge of her people and their ways? That he'd instantly realize her spell and what its consequences were?

He'd cursed her for everything she was worth. "Undo your sorcery, Deruvian!"

"I cannot. Once spoken, it's everlasting. We are one. Kill me now and you die with me."

She'd expected that to end it. That he'd be so insane as to slay them both in his anger.

Instead, Dón-Dueli had captured her and forced her to watch as he continued the slaughtering for days on end.

By the time his wrath had cooled and his rampage ended—only after he'd done unspeakable things to the ones who'd harmed his Elf—she'd lost count of the lives he'd ruthlessly taken. Lost count of the days. Ceased to see him as a human, or even a basic sentient life form. He'd become an unfeeling animal to her. The very epitome of the Aesir her people had hated so vehemently, and a prime example as to why they'd warred against them, trying for generations to eradicate his kind from existence.

And still the Dumnonii branch of the Aesir had bred and spread like a plague upon the earth. Sowing destruction and war everywhere they went. Pillaging. Looting. Raping.

Barbarians all.

Though to be fair, while Du had seldom spared anyone his sword, she'd never known him to rape a woman. Not that he needed to. Even the conquered women had fought and clawed for a place in his bed.

It'd sickened her, especially when his men would pit poor women against each other to fight it out and then offer up the victor to their leader as a trophy.

She'd hated absolutely everything about Du and his people. Had cursed every day she'd been forced to endure his detestable company. Hated herself for the spell that had united them even more tightly than marriage.

For his part, he'd ignored her and only summoned her to a human body whenever he wanted to feed on her blood for his own spells.

Until the day Vine had come to her. Broken and bleeding, her sister had been near death from a separate group of barbarians who'd attacked her husband's nemeton.

Terrified of losing her last family member, Marcelina had done her best to keep Vine hidden from the Aesir and, in particular, Du. To make sure none of Du's men saw her or that Du discovered her presence, lest they harm Vine, either because of her beauty or because she was Deruvian.

Mara still didn't know how Du had finally met Vine. One day, Mara had been summoned away to protect a family she was bound to, and on her return, she'd found the two of them in bed.

That image of him rutting with her sister was forever seared into her memory. He'd only stopped when he realized she was watching them in horror.

Instead of being embarrassed, he'd given her an insolent smile. "Care to join us?"

Blushing, and chiding him for his jibe at her, Vine had grabbed a fur to cover herself. "It's not what you think, Mara!"

Without any remorse or modesty, Du had rolled over onto his back and propped himself on his elbows to watch them. His obscene display had caused Mara untold discomfort as she sought to glance anywhere else in the room.

Though, to be honest, he'd held one of the best physiques she'd ever seen on any male. Rippling with muscles, his tawny skin could beckon even the most chaste. And he was exceptionally well endowed. Something she'd *really* tried her best to ignore.

But it hadn't been easy.

Worse? Du had known it. He'd always known how women coveted his body, and that devilish smirk on his face confirmed it as he cut a glance toward her sister. "Actually, it's exactly what she's thinking, love. I was buried to me hilt inside you when she arrived to disturb us. Damn shame she couldn't have tarried a bit longer."

Vine had blushed an even a darker shade of red than Marcelina. "Why are you being so cruel as to taunt her?"

Refusing to answer, he'd let out a deep sigh, then gotten up to wash himself off without dressing or covering any part of his anatomy.

He was a shameless barbarian, after all.

But it was only then that she'd seen the horrendous scars on his back and across his buttocks. Deep and ridged, they'd made her jaw go slack as she tried to imagine the horrendous beatings he must have endured to be marred so grievously.

Vine pulled her dress over her head, then rushed to Marcelina's side. "He's not so awful, sister."

As if! She knew better than what Vine proclaimed. "You weren't there. You didn't see—"

Vine had cut her words off by placing her fingers over Marcelina's lips before she led her into a dark corner. "You are the one who told me that no one is beyond redemption or unworthy of forgiveness."

Mara had choked on those words being thrown in her face. While she believed that where others were concerned . . . "He's a different beast!" Most assuredly!

Those whispered words had caused him to glance at her with a sneer that had chilled her all the way to her soul. Snatching at his black robe that had been cast to the floor with careless abandon, he'd thrown it over his head, and left them to speak in private.

But not before he'd given her a look so cold and malevolent that it had rattled her all the way to the marrow of her bones.

"What were you thinking?" She'd scowled at Vine.

"That an enemy leashed is better than one who wanders, unwatched."

"Meaning?"

"We have no one to protect us. You are bound to him. Forever.

Since you can't leave and I have nowhere else to go, I was trying to woo said beast and tame him."

Marcelina had gaped in horror at the very thought. "Are you mad? There are some beasts beyond taming. And I'd plant him firmly at the top of said list."

"You don't know him."

"Neither do you."

Vine shrugged and stepped back. "Maybe, but he's the best chance we have at survival. You know it as well as I do."

She'd rolled her eyes at Vine's naiveté. How could her sister be so stupid?

So blind?

And against all her protestations and rationale, Vine had pursued Dón-Dueli until he'd convinced them both that he was harmless and in love with her sister. Like Vine herself, Marcelina had bought into those lies.

Though he'd never been overly affectionate toward Vine, he hadn't been cruel to her. Which for him was a miracle, as he was a bastard animal to everyone else.

Everyone.

Even fiercely trained, massive warriors had scuttled away like terrified rodents at his approach.

But to her and Vine, at least, he'd practiced restraint. So long as Marcelina had lived in his home, he'd treated her with deference and had gutted anyone who showed her anything less than their best behavior. His protection over Vine had been even more extreme. To the point that some of his savagery still haunted her.

Honestly, Mara didn't know what had finally happened to tear his marriage apart. Or why her sister had chosen to kill him. Vine had never explained herself. While Vine had been high-strung and at times overemotional, she hadn't normally been *that* extreme, reckless, or cruel.

Of course, Du tended to bring out the very worst in all beings.

And since their return to the mortal realm, Du had been even more distant and hollow than while married to her sister.

Colder. Meaner.

Until Cameron.

In all the centuries Marcelina had known him, she'd never seen him so . . .

Kind. And for the first time, it made her wonder what he'd been like with his sister. Could he have been someone's beloved older brother, who watched after and cared for her?

If that were true, then maybe, just maybe, he wasn't the tyrannical animal she'd always thought. . . .

Was he?

I don't want to be here!"

Devyl let out a tired sigh at the strident tone that left his ears figuratively bleeding. "Neither do I, Miss Jack. Believe me. But until we recover your brother and secure him, I can't allow you near the . . ." He paused as if biting back an obscenity. ". . . creature we just took custody of."

"Is she one of the evil beasts who captured him?"

The intensity of her tone caused him to look up from his book to see she'd stopped pacing in front of his desk to glare at him. He had to force himself not to smile at the cheeky way she postured with clenched fists as if ready to take on the world. He'd always admired courage in anyone, but especially one so tiny.

"Supposing the answer was aye, what do you plan to do?" Bleed on the bitch would be the most apropos answer, as she was hardly prepared to deal with a creature of such powers and venom.

"Depends on if the answer is aye or nay."

He laughed in spite of himself. And the sound of it shocked him thoroughly, as it was a real, unexpected laugh. Not the feigned kind he normally practiced whenever it was socially expected of him.

What the hell?

Sobering to his usual gruff demeanor, he cleared his throat. "No need in you being ruffled, lass. Calm yourself and rest. Tomorrow's a bitter day."

"Meaning?"

He turned the page in his book, and tried not to think about the Sight he'd been born with that too often fed him coming details he'd rather not know. " 'Tis nothing. We are a ship without marque, sailing through pirate waters and bearing the red jack as our only color. Trouble is forever finding us, even when we try to avoid it."

Cameron hesitated at his words. A letter of marque was what some captains carried that authorized them to prey on ships and cargos from enemy nations. Essentially legal pirating. Most pirate crews carried such letters, many of them forged. Along with flags from multiple nations, just in case.

The fact he didn't bother with a forgery or fake colors said he was a man of honor. . . .

Or completely insane.

"May I ask you something, Captain?"

He let out a sigh that said he was put upon by her question. "If you must, Miss Jack."

"How is it you came to be captain here?"

He whispered something that sounded like a curse beneath his breath before he answered. "Lady Marcelina made it so."

"Why?"

"No doubt so that she, much like your incessant inquisition, could forever torment me."

That caused one corner of her mouth to quirk up as she struggled not to smile. "*I* torment *you*?"

He glanced up. "Conversation in general annoys me."

"You sound like me brother. He used to threaten to sew me lips shut if I didn't shush around him."

Grunting at that, he returned to reading.

"So where do you intend to sleep, Captain Bane?"

With a deep growl, he slammed his book shut and set it on his desk. "Apparently, in my bed, as you seem to have no interest in using it for yourself. Am thinking one of us should get some use out of it in these wee hours. Aren't you the least bit tired?"

For some reason she couldn't even begin to fathom, an image of him in said bunk went through her mind. Followed by a thought so scandalous that it caused her entire face to heat up.

He stood slowly. "Careful where your thoughts lead you, lass." As he headed for the door, she stopped him.

"Can you hear my thoughts?"

"I can read your expressions, and they lay bare everything in your mind."

Heavens, he was astute and frightening. And still she dropped her gaze to his lips. She'd never kissed a man before. Had never wanted to.

Until now.

She didn't even know why. Bane was completely unacceptable to her. He was a beast and a terror. A man who liked to intimidate and frighten others.

And yet . . .

"What made you marry a Deruvian if you hate them so?"

Devyl winced at a question that shredded what little blackened soul he had left. He didn't intend to answer. He never answered such questions, as they offended him and were no one's business.

But his lips didn't listen. Like everything and everyone else in the universe, they betrayed him. "Vine was kind to me."

Cameron scowled deeply at such a shocking, unexpected answer. "Kind?"

"Aye, Miss Jack. When you've never been fed anything save insults, degradation, and horror, a little kindness goes a long way." And with that he left her to seek fresh air and a clear head.

That was what he intended. Unfortunately, the past was a treacherous bitch who forever sought to bring him to his knees. Tonight that whore was after him with a vengeance, churning up images he'd rather see buried for eternity.

Except for one.

It was the only comfort he'd ever known. And it'd come to him on the night he'd murdered his parents.

Or maybe "murdered" was a bit strong, given that it was self-preservation. After all, his bastard father had been trying to kill him first. And for what crime? Having the nerve to protect his sisters.

Even now, he could feel the heat of the fire on his face as his sisters had cried in the shadows.

While their mother's shrieks as she begged for mercy echoed against stone walls, they'd come running to his room, where he'd been trying to ignore his mother's pain. Not because he didn't care, but because the one time he'd tried to stand up for his mother as a boy, she'd punished him for it far worse than his father had.

"He's my husband, boy! And your father! You don't ever raise a hand to your parents!"

So while he hated to see his mother beaten, he'd learned to leave his parents alone to deal with it.

Until that night.

He hadn't known what the fight between his mother and father was about—it could have been anything from his father's dinner hadn't been salted properly to his mother had put her shoes in the wrong place.

At least not until Edyth and Elf had burst into his room to hide. Bemused by their peculiar act, he'd scowled at them. Though none of them liked the sounds of their parents fighting, they were well accustomed to the routine familiarity of it.

Like him, his sisters normally stayed in their beds and pretended to sleep through the cacophony.

Yet this night, everything was different. The fact that Edyth had come into his room was strange in and of itself. Barely a year older than him, she had never thought much of her younger brother. Other than to use him as a target for her acerbic tongue and ridicule. He couldn't remember a time in his life when they'd gotten along.

So for her to seek him out was a rare event indeed. Elf, on the other hand, had run to his bed and thrown herself against him to weep such horrendous wails that he'd feared for her health.

"Calm yourself, Elf! Breathe and . . ." His voice had trailed off the instant he'd seen the marks on her young body. The heartbeat he'd seen what their father had done to her.

Horror had filled him as he met Edyth's tormented gaze over her rumpled hair.

"I tried to stop him, Duel." Her sobs had matched Elf's. "I never thought he'd do it to her, too."

Too? That one word had hung in the air like some ghastly fiend that taunted him without mercy.

Clutching Elf against him, he'd sat there stunned and cold as his fury turned into something he couldn't even begin to describe. A rage so deep and dark and foul that it'd left him with a heightened sense of calm that terrified him. "How long?"

Shame darkened her gaze. "Since I was Elf's age." Edyth had sunk down in the shadows as if trying to blend in with them. "I-I-I tried to keep him from her, then I went to get Mum."

"And?"

"She held me in her room until he finished. Then he came for me and . . . they started fighting."

Closing his eyes, Devyl had cursed himself for being such a stupid fool as to not realize the source of Edyth's bitchtress nature. To have never known what went on between them at night. How could he have been so incredibly blind to his sister's pain and suffering?

So stupid?

But no more.

With a kiss to Elf's head, he'd stood with her in his arms and carried her to Edyth. "Stay here. Both of you."

Edyth had clutched Elf against her trembling body—like a mother with a toddler. "You can't go out there! Ta will kill you, Duel!"

"I came into this world fighting and covered in someone else's blood, Ed. I got no problem leaving it the same way. And if I must go out like that, then I plan to take the bastard with me to Caer Vandwy and hand his heart to Y Diawl meself. One way or another, I swear to the gods that he'll touch you no more!"

Still cold. Still furious, he'd walked out of his room to find his father in the Great Hall. His mother sobbed off to the side while his father sat in his chair as if all were right with the world.

At least until their gazes met and locked.

His father had snorted derisively, then poured himself more wine. "What do *you* want, boy?"

With a calmness he still couldn't fathom, Duel had walked to the wall, pulled down an axe, and smiled. "Your head . . . *both* of them."

The stupid bloody bastard had had the nerve to laugh. And then he'd sicced his hounds upon Duel with a kill command.

They'd charged him, but, too angry to care, he hadn't moved. Rather, he'd glared at the ferocious beasts and dared them to attack. "You want me? Bite me and I'll send your heads to Annwn, where you can guard for him!"

Those growled words had caused the hounds to back away in confusion, then whimper and flee.

Unlike his father, who lacked the hounds' good sense. Instead, Axe of the Dumnonii had risen slowly to his feet and unsheathed his long sword. "Well, well, the worthless tosser's finally found his spine." The fierce dark warrior had come at Devyl then, with the intent to lay him in his grave.

But too many years of frustrated abuse, hatred, and vengeance burned inside Devyl. Within a few strokes, he'd taken the bastard's head as he'd promised he'd do.

Instead of being grateful that he'd finally liberated her from his father's cruel fist, his mother had rushed him with her dirk, screaming that she'd avenge his father.

A dirk she'd sunk deep into his shoulder, then yanked out and aimed at his throat.

Devyl hadn't meant to kill her. He'd struggled with her in an attempt to wrestle the knife from her hand. But when she'd used her own powers against him, they'd ignited his. Too young to have full control yet, he was unable to stop the innate self-preservation that was deeply rooted in his blood. It lashed out without compassion or restriction and consumed his mother in one single fiery emotional blast.

Horrified by the sight of her scattered remains lying in his father's blood, Devyl had finally lost the fury inside him. And with its passing, he began to shake. To cry.

To feel.

And he'd hated every moment of it. Bitter and gutting, his grief had risen inside like an unholy serpent that was feasting on his innards. Shredding and eating away every last bit of innocence he'd ever possessed.

Not that he'd had all that much. His father's brutality and mother's weakness had seen to that. It devoured all his worth and happiness. Any sense he'd ever had of being decent or good. It left him shattered and bitter. Worthless and used up. With a sense of being hollow and lost.

Too stunned to move, he'd still been there hours later when the servants had come in for work, only to discover the carnage that surrounded him.

Since his father had been the leader of their tribe, Devyl had fully expected to be hanged for what he'd done. He'd expected no mercy whatsoever from anyone as his father's men had rushed in to check on his parents' remains.

Still coated in the blood of his father, Devyl had refused to answer any question. Refused to speak at all.

How could he explain it? He didn't want to tell anyone their family secrets. Didn't want to expose what had been done to his Elf or to Edyth. He refused to see his sisters shamed or harmed in any way. Their parents had wounded them enough. By the gods, their brother wouldn't harm them, too. It was his duty to protect them.

Let their people damn him alone. It was a secret he would take to his grave.

And as the watchmen sought to drag him from the room and

into their custody for the murders, Edyth had come forward to shove them away. "There were wandering bandits who broke in during the night! Duel fought them off by himself! You can't take him for it. He's our hero! But for him and his bravery, we'd be dead now, too. He saved our lives!"

Elf had backed her story.

It was the only time in the whole of his life that anyone had sought to protect him and keep him safe. The only time anyone had ever stood to defend him. While he'd loved his little sister before that, he'd become even more devoted to her.

And to Edyth. He would have done anything for her after that day.

When she'd died of a rare fever a year later, it'd damn near destroyed him. How cruel that they had finally become close, only to have something as pathetic as a worthless cold take her life and rob him of a very special friendship.

So he'd clung to his Elf after Edyth's passing even more and with a passion that had oft left her so frustrated at him that she'd spent endless hours playfully teasing him for it.

You're stifling me, brother! Can I not have a moment to myself? I swear it wouldn't surprise me to find you sitting atop me one day as I do my morning business in the privy, like some great mother hen! Indeed, you're so close that I eat the food and you burp for me. Words she'd spoken with humor and never with malice.

Unlike him, his Elf had never held any ill will or anger toward anyone.

God, how he missed her.

Don't think about it. . . .

Because thinking about her even now, after all these centuries, still tore him apart.

"Captain?"

He looked over his shoulder to see Belle headed his way. "Aye, milady Morte, what can I do for you?"

"Be ye aware of what it is you've taken aboard the ship, sir?"

"Indeed. Why? Is she giving you trouble?"

"You could say that."

He arched a brow at her evasiveness. "I did say that. What sayest you?"

"Well . . . she got a bit lippy with us."

Ah, dear gods. He arched a brow as she paused in her recitation of what all "lippy" entailed.

"And?" he prompted when she failed to elaborate.

"Well," she repeated, "be it all right with you if Mr. Death pins her to the wall?"

Devyl hesitated as several scenarios for those words went through his mind. William having his way with the beast in a corner.

Or Will literally daggering the hag.

Not sure which of the two would be worse for the lot of them, Devyl headed for the women's quarters, where he quickly found his quartermaster one heartbeat away from killing the bitchington.

Grabbing the sword from Will's hand, he arched a brow. "Really?"

William grimaced at him. "Begging your pardon, Captain. I should have asked. May I kill the worthless trollop?"

"Sorry, Mr. Death. I want that particular amusement myself."

Gagged by a piece of linen, Mona shrieked and struggled against the ropes William had double-knotted around her hands.

Especially when Devyl turned on her, sword held at the ready. Aye, this time, he was going to gut her.

Gate be damned.

And no one would stop him.

8

Just as Devyl would have killed the Deruvian, Mara appeared in the room and used her powers to dissolve his sword. His temper flaring, he glared at her. "Don't need a sword to destroy *your* sister."

As he started to choke Mona, a massive, invisible wave knocked him away, into a wall.

"Don't push me, Du. I'm not the scared little child you found that day in the Fforest Fawr. I've come a long way, and so have my powers."

Growling, he faced Mara with his full demonic

visage. One that caused Belle, Janice, Sancha, Valynda, and even William to pull back in fear. Even the bitchling slithered toward the shadows to hide from his wrath.

"And who gave you those powers?" he growled.

"Do *not* push me!" she repeated.

He closed the distance between them so that barely an inch separated them. "Ditto."

Her breathing ragged, she lifted her chin while her eyes blazed defiance and hatred. An unseen wind flared her pale hair around her slender form while she hovered above the boards of the ship that had been crafted from her body. "You're still just an animal, aren't you?"

Those words cut him to the quick, but he refused to let her or anyone else know it. Insults and abuse were mother's milk to his blackened soul. They were all he'd ever known, and so what if she gave them to him? "Savage and rabid from my first breath to my last."

"Then you need to leave and let me deal with this. Calmly. Without you."

It took everything he had not to retaliate. She had no idea how lucky she was that he wasn't the beast she accused him of being.

He curled his lip to sneer at her. "Deruvians forever, aren't you? It's why we hated the Vanir so. You were always so high and mighty in your arrogance. Thinking yourselves above the rest of us."

If only she knew the real truth.

"*You* dare lecture me on morality? On humanity? Seriously?"

He let out a bitter, scoffing laugh. "Nay, *lady*." He sneered the word, turning it into an insult. "I would never deign to tarnish *your* people. None of you *ever* committed a single atrocity against *anyone*. Did you, now?"

"What's that supposed to mean?"

"Think about it." With those words, he stormed from the cabin to leave them to it. Let Marcelina have it. He was done seeing condemnation in her eyes.

Damn *her* for it. Even after everything her sister had done to him . . . after the atrocities her Vanir people had committed against his, she still refused to acknowledge it. They were perfection, while the Aesir were feral barbarians. That's all she'd ever seen any of them as.

Her blind loyalty to her people over all others galled him to the core of his being.

But it hadn't begun that way. Her precious Vanir were the ones who'd started the war between them. And for what?

Futtocking selfishness of the worst kind.

Marcelina could deny it all she wanted. He knew the absolute truth of it all. This battle between their cultures and generations of hatred had started when his great-grandfather had made the mistake of asking the Vanir Deruvian princess Gullveig and her court to help their people after a plague Gullveig had deliberately sent to them had swept through their lands, laying waste to everyone.

Man and beast.

Sadly, they hadn't known the Vanir were behind the plague then. Naïve to a fault, his great-grandfather had been unable to conceive of such treachery. All he'd known was that Gullveig was a goddess of healing and her skills in that regard legendary.

So Woden had swallowed all pride and appealed to her to save the life of his son Tyrin and their people. As a goddess of healing, it should have been easy for her to do so. And that was all that had mattered to the Aesir king. Not his pride. Not his crown. His love of his son and people had led Woden to make a bitter, foolish bargain.

But that was the way of the Aesir. They were a communal race who believed in the good of all. One life was inconsequential when compared to the benefit of the whole. They were born a cog in a larger machine, and it was hard-wired into them to serve the good of their race. To put others before themselves in everything.

Not so with the Vanir. To them, the one was always greater than the whole. Petty and vain. Better to sacrifice their entire species than see one hair on their individual head harmed. The rights of one individual were forever superior to the rights of the whole.

They were selfish, through and through.

And so Gullveig had agreed, but only if she married the king and was given the whole of their gold.

Since his people didn't value gold over life, Woden agreed. After all, what good was gold to the dead? It was only a metal to be bartered for supplies. Too weak to smelt for weapons, it wasn't even used by his people for decoration. The Aesir had never placed any real value on it. In fact, they'd used iron for coin because it was the more valuable metal to their people. Far more important than gold.

So they had turned all their gold over to the greedy goddess without hesitation.

The moment Gullveig had it and was wed, she'd used her magick to poison the great king and all his heirs from his first wife. Her people had quickly moved into their lands and begun taking everything for themselves.

But Gullveig hadn't known about Woden's daughter, who'd married a fey husband long before the arrival of the Vanir goddess. A daughter who had gone to Alfheim to live there among her husband's people.

Determined to avenge her Aesirian family and save what remained of her people, Devyl's grandmother had returned to her father's home. There, Kara had stabbed the goddess and set fire to Gullveig in the hall of the murdered king.

Not once, but thrice she'd laid the goddess down in flames.

Each time, the Deruvian whore had returned to life. That had been the Aesir's first exposure to the regenerative powers of the Vanir Deruvians.

Worse? Gullveig had come back stronger after every death, and on her third incarnation from the flames, she'd emerged as the goddess Heiðr—more powerful and more evil than any creature the Aesir had ever encountered before.

A ten-year bloodbath had ensued as the Vanir gods had demanded vengeance against the Aesirians for the attacks on Gullveig. They'd wanted the life of Devyl's grandparents.

And all hell had broken loose as a result.

Yes, his people had gone more and more feral during that war. The Deruvians had forced them to it in order to survive against them and their unholy magick.

The sad truth of survival was that it seldom brought out the best in anyone. Rather, it forced people to take actions that went against every moral they held and left them bankrupt and bitter. Wondering if they'd ever be whole again.

Over a thousand years later, and Devyl was still as broken now as he'd been then by his own wars he'd led against the Deruvians for additional crimes.

And for what?

Not a damn thing, in the end.

I should have stayed in hell.

At least there he knew his place and had found a sick kind of comfort with his misery. Or at least he'd come to terms with it.

He didn't belong in this callous world where no one could be trusted. He never had. There was nothing here for him save pain and utter misery. Everything he'd ever loved had been brutally stripped from him.

Friends. Family.

Devyl had no quarter of any kind.

Suddenly, and as if to prove those very words, he felt a sharp, stinging pain to his side. Gasping, Devyl doubled over from the vicious ache.

"Captain!"

He tried to blink past the staggering agony, but even without Will and Bart, who continued to call out to him, he knew what had happened.

Marcelina was wounded. Damn her for her blindness in dealing with the other Deruvian wench!

With a fierce grimace, he bit back his groan and headed for the cabin where he'd left her. He ignored the men who tried to explain the events he had full knowledge of.

Marcelina had reached out to Mona and the Blackthorn bitch had taken advantage of it.

As was Mona's Deruvian nature. They were treacherous to the end. Why was Mara in such denial when she had to know that even better than he?

His vision blurring, he found Mara on the floor with Belle standing guard over a jubilant Mona.

Growling deep in his throat, he issued orders as fast as he could. "We've a hull breach! Death? Meers? Gather the men and find it! Sancha, head us toward land before we sink entirely. Get every man on the pumps!"

They ran to obey him.

Mona gave him a twisted smirk. "You won't make it."

"You best pray we do. Otherwise your heart is the last thing I'll be feasting on." His breathing ragged, he turned to Janice. "Guard her, and if she so much as belches in your general direction, set her ass on fire and burn her to ashes."

With those words spoken, he picked Mara up to carry her from the cabin toward her own chambers. But that was much easier said than done given the amount of pain he was in. Which told him how severely the ship was wounded.

"How much water are we taking on?" he gasped as he struggled to carry her.

Marcelina groaned as she clung to him—an action that betrayed the depths of her injuries. Otherwise she'd die afore she touched the likes of him. "I'm trying to close the gap." Tears glistened in her eyes. "Thank you, Du."

"For what?"

"Not rubbing my nose in this."

He answered with a grimace as he kicked open the door to her room and carried her to her frilly bed that looked more like a cloud than a place of rest. With a gentleness he resented, he set her down and staggered back, intending to leave. Unfortunately, he only made it to the opposite side of the small room before his own misery drove him to his knees. Damn . . . it'd been a long time since anything hurt him this much.

Glowering, he grimaced at her. "What hit us?"

"Not sure. I told William to keep Kalder from the sea, lest it kill him. Whatever it is, it's a foul beast that has ripped me asunder."

With a bitter half laugh, he met her gaze. "Well then, 'tis high time I met him and thanked him personally for this stomachache."

Mara gaped as she watched Du push himself up. "You can't be serious?"

Yet against all odds, he managed to stand. "He wants a fight . . . I'll give him one."

And with that, he was gone.

Mara shrieked in frustration as she called him back, knowing it was futile. Duel listened to no one.

Ever.

"You stubborn, stubborn fool!" What was it in him that he could never back down from a confrontation of any kind? She'd never seen anything like it.

Coughing and choking, she rolled from her bed and tried to go after him. What good would it do if he got himself killed?

Again.

He'd take her with him to the grave. Then what would become of their crew?

Of the world they were sworn to protect?

Then again, what did she expect from someone who'd been born of such a violent race? All he knew was bloodshed and killing. Mayhem. Chaos.

Yet she couldn't quite forget the gentleness of his touch as he'd carried her to her bed. Even while he'd been in pain, and though it must have galled him to come to her rescue after he'd warned her of Mona's treachery, his touch had been as gentle as a fairy's kiss.

Just as he'd been kind to Cameron even though he'd known her origins. As much as he hated the Seraphim. As much as he hated Menyara.

And why shouldn't he hate them all? He'd sold his soul to the dark forces to keep the Romans out of their lands. Had tapped forbidden power and the blackest magick to make himself king and ensure that no one could ever defeat him. He'd fought against Thorn and the Sarim for years. Had laid waste to every army they'd dared send against him. Gutted any man who'd tried to take his crown or questioned his authority in any manner.

After years of living in hell with the oafish brute, Mara had been delighted when she'd learned that Menyara had combined her forces with Thorn's and planned to move against Du in an all-out attempt to overthrow him and end his bloody reign and life. She had been sure they'd finally defeat him and free her from their godforsaken bond.

But that hadn't happened.

Instead, Du's army, at his command, had torn them asunder. He'd scattered their forces and set them ablaze with a zeal that still caused the bile to rise in her throat whenever she thought about it, or the way he'd returned home afterward. Triumphant. Jubilant.

Giddy.

He'd laughed as he recounted the carnage in gory detail. Worse? He'd mocked her for the fact that she didn't share in his merriment over such raw brutality.

"What's the matter, Mara? No stomach for it?" he'd asked while he drank warm, mulled red wine from the stained skull of the largest soldier he'd killed in battle.

That had left her retching for days.

Nay. She'd never had any stomach for the lot of it. And even less for blood and gore.

Unlike him.

But that being said, never once had he ever acted ignobly toward an innocent. Never slaughtered a child or raped a woman. Nor had he allowed his men to do such. If they killed a woman, they were punished harshly for it.

Indeed, for all his evil ways, he wasn't one for deceit of any kind. Duel came at his enemies in the open. Well announced. And usually with a great deal of fanfare.

It was virtually his only endearing quality.

But now that she thought about it, he had a number of . . . well "good" was a stretch.

Better traits?

He could be extremely tolerant of others. Where many would be put off by the flamboyant and oft-eccentric ways of his crew, Duel was practically indulgent of them all, no matter how peculiar their quirks. He never said a word about Sancha's extreme language or drinking. Or Belle's pungent spells that required some rather noxious ingredients. He guarded Sallie's soul bottle as a sacred object and made sure no one harassed Kat and Simon for their unconventional relationship. Indeed, he'd even performed a marriage ceremony for them without lifting so much as an eyebrow over it.

She was the only one he was openly rude to. And much of that was her own fault. She did bait him unnecessarily and without cessation.

Much like a nagging spouse . . .

Feeling a foreign twinge of guilt, she forced herself to stand, and followed after him.

On the upper deck, she found Duel locked in battle with a giant squidlike monster that was rising from the water, breathing fire and trying its best to engulf them all. He and Zumari, along with William, Bart, Belle, and the rest, were throwing their own fire and tar grenades at the beast. Shooting cannons.

Nothing deterred it.

With fangs as large as a man, it snapped at them, and reached with its barbed tentacles, trying to flay them where they stood. Several of their crew were lying on deck, wounded, while others tended them.

She used her own powers to keep the ship upright even though she could feel the lower deck taking on water. The sensation made her sluggish and sick. Tipsy. But if she gave in to the weakness, it could kill them all.

That she could never allow.

If Duel could find it within him to fight in the same condition, then it was the least she could do to carry on for them all, as well.

But it was so hard. The rocking wasn't helping. It left her weak and disoriented. Her stomach pitched as a wave of nausea threatened to undignify her before them all.

"Dammit, Mara!" Duel snarled as soon as he caught sight of her on deck. "Get below!"

She shook her head. "You fight. I fight."

The curse he let out rang high over the roar of battle. Impressive indeed.

But not nearly as much as the sudden explosion that sent wood, water, and pieces of the beast flying over the lot of them.

"What the hell!" Devyl ducked as the sea itself rained down on him. Along with a lot of blood and intestines.

He turned to see another ship fast approaching on their starboard side. His gunners struggled to turn their cannons into position for it and reload.

As they made ready to fire, he realized that the ship wasn't aiming at them. It'd struck its mark.

Devyl grimaced as soon as he saw who it was. "Halt! 'Tis friendly."

Sort of, anyway. Though a friend should be a little more circumspect than to be firing at them like this.

William groaned out loud as he recognized the ship. "Santiago?"

"Aye. Bugger's no doubt thinking to lend us a hand." Devyl grimaced at the slimy chunks of entrails that clung to him. "Would rather he lend me a towel, to be honest."

William laughed. "Indeed." Then he sobered as he glanced around at the number of their crew who'd been wounded or "killed."

It was a sight Devyl could have done without, as it took him back to a past he'd never been particularly proud of. Aye, he'd led his army through untold bloody conquests. Driven by reasons that seemed paltry now, he'd been ruthless as he tore his enemies asunder.

But at least this army wouldn't stay dead. In fact, their "dead" were already rising up from where they'd fallen. Griping and moaning in colorful alacrity as they returned to physical form and pulled themselves together.

Literally, in some cases.

It was the one benefit they had in serving Thorn. The only way the Deadmen could die again was for something to obliterate their bodies or souls. So long as their flesh remained intact, as well as their souls, they would reanimate.

Fire, axes, and acid, however, could still ruin their days.

Even a vat of piranha could prove a rather grisly end for them.

Hmmm . . . that gave him a thought for their guest.

He turned toward Bart. "Did we lose anyone, Mr. Meers?"

"Don't think so, Captain." He cast an eye toward one of their crew who was slowly healing from death. "Least not permanently."

Devyl continued to wipe at his face and neck. "Good. Send over some of our best rum to Santiago, with my compliments."

"Aye, aye, Captain."

With a determined stride, he headed for William. "Death? Get to our Miss Jack and keep an eye on her. Make sure she stays put and safe. Continue heading us toward land to patch our lady. Keep a weather eye for more attackers."

Bart drew up short at those words. "You think there are more?"

"I know it." And with that, he continued on to return belowdecks so that he could make sure Belle hadn't been injured in the fighting.

If she had . . .

He'd be bathing these guts off his flesh over a Blackthorn bonfire.

As soon as he entered the small cabin room and Mona saw the expression on his face, she shrank back in terror. And well she should, for he was through playing her games. Worse, he was in too much pain for them. Bile rose into his throat as he seized her wrist and yanked her forward. "Do you know what my people did with zraif?" He used the ancient name they'd given the Blackthorns.

She paled considerably. "Nay."

An insidious smile curled his lips. "'Tis said sulphur runs through you. Powerful magick is in the root of your hearts and bones. Bones we'd grind into blood potions to protect us during war and for healing any wounds we might incur. Potions we used to commune with our darker gods when we summoned them for wisdom and insight. Or make blood offerings to Mórrígan and Aeron before battle. But the most prized parts?"

She gulped audibly. "W-w-what?"

"Your hearts we'd devour for spells and eyes we'd eat for visions."

"You're a monster!"

He laughed at her. "You've no idea. Now, you will tell me where that gate resides or I will begin carving off pieces of your anatomy and adding decoration for Rosie's chest plate."

Her blood turned black in her veins as his words struck their mark. It ran down her pale skin, forming a road map over her body, marbling over the alabaster. "I told you I would give it to you."

"And then we were attacked."

"I-I had nothing to do with that."

Devyl scoffed. "I don't believe you."

She tried to pull away, but he held her fast. Cringing, she put her arm up, over her face. "Why would I betray you?"

"Because you're an idiot."

"Duel! Let her go!"

He ignored Mara as she came into the room with them. "Answer me, Mona, or else I will begin carving you into all manner of objects for my use."

"Duel!"

He glared at Mara over his shoulder. "I'm not a dog to heel at your command!"

"Yet I am your commander, am I not?"

His eyes glowed an instant before he let out a curse so foul even Thorn would have blushed had he heard it. Reluctantly, he released Mona and stepped back, but not before he passed a sullen grimace to Mara that would have made a petulant toddler proud.

Disregarding his distemper, she stepped forward to deal with their betrayer. She put herself between Mona and Devyl, and it took everything he had not to cut off both their heads. If not for the fact it would only make them stronger, he would have given in to the impulse.

With a calmness he couldn't fathom, Mara took a deep breath. "Vine sent you here, didn't she?"

"I don't know what you're talking about."

"Very well." Mara reached out then and shoved her hand straight into Mona's chest. Devyl's jaw dropped as she wrested the bitch's heart from her bosom and yanked it out, then used her powers to incinerate Mona before she could hit the floor.

Her expression one of total serenity, she turned to face him and held the bloody heart toward him. "Use it to heal us as fast as possible. I'm sure others are on their way to attack us."

Dumbfounded by an act that was completely incongruous to her nature, he stared at her as if seeing her for the first time. "I can't believe you just did that."

Still her features betrayed nothing. "In all the centuries we've been together, you've never bothered to learn the most basic thing about me. Never had a single conversation with me where you asked about my thoughts on any matter. And you know nothing of my people. When Vine killed you, she knew I would die, too. Did that thought never occur to you?"

Nay, it had not.

"In my darker hours, I've wondered which of us was the real target of her wrath. And why she did what she did. I've always assumed it was you, Du, because it was more comforting to do so. Yet what if it wasn't? Either way, she is *our* enemy now. Both of ours. Mona has proven that without a doubt. You would have left Mona alive, not knowing that Vine was able to use her as a living conduit to us. A doorway better kept closed. And now I am weak. My powers are fading. I can't heal myself. Therefore, I need you to do it for me."

He caught her as she passed out. Cradling her against his chest, he took care not to crush Mona's heart or harm Mara.

As gently as he could, he carried her to her cabin and placed her on her bed. Then he set about preparing the potion that would restore her strength and heal her injuries. All the while trying to come to terms with a side of her he'd never suspected existed.

Honestly? He liked it.

Black looked good on her.

It was why he'd do anything to heal her. Even use the darkest kind of magick he'd learned from his father. The kind his Druidic forefathers had specialized in. Unlike the rest of their breed, the Dumnonii branch of the Aesir hadn't been just counselors, teachers, and priests, they'd been warriors, too. Protectors imbued with a fierce sense of noblesse oblige to safeguard the fledgling humans from their brethren who'd sought to harm them.

Descended from the gods themselves, the Dumnonii had been the ones who'd established the Druidic orders and taught them the ways of magick and given them their wisdom and ability to commune with the gods. They had brought order to the world of man. It was why their home realm had been termed Asgard and not Asaheim. Why the world of man was known as Myddangeard or Mydgard and not Mydanheim. This wasn't just the home realm of mankind or Asgard the home of the Aesir. These two realms were where they'd brought order and discipline to the chaos of it all. They were wards set up to protect humanity.

When the primal gods and their creations had been at each other's throats and were tearing the universe apart, this was where his ancestors had drawn the battle lines and put the boundaries that protected humans from their armies that would have destroyed them. From their monstrous creations that would have preyed on the humans without mercy.

Out of all the nine known and established realms, only these two worlds bore the protective "gard" suffixes that designated them as places of human refuge. Places where order and discipline reigned supreme over animalistic, primal urges.

The rest were the home realms of horrific preternatural predators who made feasts and war on humanity. Realms where the gods and others lived and ran rampant with unchecked powers. Home dimensions that existed behind carefully crafted veils that shielded them from human knowledge and sight.

Alfheim. Myrkheim. Jotunheim. Niflheim. Muspelheim. Helheim.

Even Mara's precious Vanaheim, where her Vasir had descended from. They were all the realms of some of the most vicious creatures ever spawned by the universe. Creatures who cared nothing for humanity, who only thought of themselves and what they wanted. Creatures who saw humans as prey or tools to be used and then discarded.

Creatures such as Vine.

Creatures like me.

Devyl winced at a truth he wanted to deny and couldn't. He hated that part of his mother's blood that beat inside him. He always had. But no matter how much he tried to fight it, he couldn't deny that it was there. That selfish part that was forever tainted by a union that should never have been. It was what had made his father so weak and hate-filled in his latter years. Had Axe been an honorable Aesir, dedicated to their cause, he wouldn't have been the monster Devyl had been forced to kill that night in their hall.

I am a beast.

Like father, like son.

Like mother, like son.

He would never be able to escape it. But at least he could stop Vine from destroying the world. That was one promise he would keep, no matter what.

And sooner or later, he'd have to be put down again. Mara had been right about that. It was why he didn't expect to survive this quest. Didn't expect Thorn to free him. Not for one heartbeat. He had no delusions there whatsoever.

His kind didn't belong in this world. They were the worst sort of predators. Mara knew it as well as he did. He was barely leashed on his best day. His ancestral fury simmered just below the surface, ever a pot on a steady roiling boil that just waited to overflow the edges of its confines. All it took was one blink, and a disaster would ensue that didn't care whose hand it scalded.

No conscience. No constraint.

Nothing mattered except that he destroy whatever was nearest him, consequences be damned.

Aye, that be he.

And his explosion was coming. He could feel it deep within. His Sight was ever unerring. His mother's one gift to her son, besides the back of her hand. Dera had been an exceptionally gifted sorceress in that regard. 'Twas what had led his father to her. Why Axe had wanted to bind their bloodlines together and had sought the treaty with her tribe.

Too bad she'd failed to see what a scabbing bastard his father was. Or her own fate at the hands of the worthless son she'd birthed for him.

Don't think about it.

The past was a course that had been cast and set. Cruelty laid in by the gods to torture those who survived it. He needed all his resources and attention on the future. That was still in motion and changeable.

While he'd been unable to save his Elf and his people, he had a chance to help those on this ship. To help the Seraph and *his* sister.

His own soul was blackened and unworthy of redemption, but theirs were not. They were good and decent beings who'd lost their way. With a little prodding, they could go on and find the right path again.

That was what Thorn had seen in them. Hope. Redemption. Core goodness. And as a commander, Devyl understood that strategy. To win, certain sacrifices had to be made for the good of all.

He was the pawn that would be leveraged so that they could live on. An acceptable loss for all involved. Perhaps even a relief to them.

And as he cast the healing spell for Mara, he realized that she shouldn't be part of any of this. She should never have been. His selfish wrath had snared her and brought her into a war that was never hers to fight.

"I'm sorry, Mara," he whispered for the first time, as the guilt of his actions against her choked him.

If only he could find some way to unbind their destinies and free her, too. She deserved to have a life of her own. One that didn't involve his surly, unreasonable ass. She would have made someone a fine mother. An incredible mate to stand by the side of her husband.

Any man would have been lucky to call her his. He alone had robbed her of that.

Disgusted by his own actions, he brushed his thumb over her gentle brow. She was so incredibly beautiful. But then, she'd always been that way to him. And while in the past he'd often seen her as an annoying vexation, as an enemy to be hated, today, he saw her for what she really was. . . .

His innocent victim.

And he hated himself all the more.

"I will make this up to you." Words spoken so easily. As all vows were. The trick was in the fulfillment of them. The devil in the details.

But then, he wasn't called Devyl Bane without a reason.

He picked her delicate hand up and rubbed her limp fingers against his lips. Closing his eyes, he tried his best to access his Sight and see the future.

Like everything else in his life, it failed him utterly. It shouldn't surprise him. He'd never been able to depend on anything when he needed it. His own horse had once thrown him in battle. His sword had broken at the worst possible time.

My own wife cut my throat.

Sighing, he placed a kiss to Mara's palm and tucked her hand beneath her covers. His side still ached, but the pain had lessened, letting him know that the spell had begun to work.

What a futtocking bad day this had been.

But then he'd known going in it wasn't going to be a boring one.

Dawn would be breaking soon. He had a fledgling Seraph on board, along with a Dark-Huntress who couldn't be in daylight.

One massive hole in the side of his ship. A crew of human pirates trailing them who were being pursued by an infamous pirate hunter who wanted a piece of them all. A motley band of dead lunatics at his command and the bitch of all time out to send him back to hell.

"It's good to be the living dead," he said with a bitter laugh.

But then he'd never been one to shirk from a challenge of any kind.

He was a surly bugger that way.

And honestly? He was looking forward to the fight.

Staring up at the heavens, he smirked. "Bring it, bitches. With both fists. You want a piece of me? I'm ready for you."

Because they'd never gotten the best of him.

Even after they'd killed him, he'd still found a way to strike back from the grave.

One thing about the Devyl, he came with the heat of hell behind him and packing an army of demons in his wake. And if you knocked on his door for a fight, then you better be prepared for what you were asking.

It was a new day and the Devyl was here to get his due.

9

Mara awoke to the warmth of bright sunshine on her face and the welcomed scent of fresh salt water. Seagulls screeched from outside, along with the sounds of raucous laughter and jovial music. For a moment, she forgot where she was and thought herself a girl again. It felt and smelled just like the seaside town where she'd been born. Where she'd frolicked with her sisters in the nemeton.

But that happiness inside her heart didn't last, because she knew this wasn't ancient Cornwall.

And those weren't her people out there.

Then again . . .

Perhaps they were. At least they were the closest thing she had to a family now. The thought lightened her spirit a bit, but it didn't return the joy to her heart. Not really. Because it wasn't the same. She hadn't felt that raw, unmitigated happiness of homecoming in so long that she could barely remember the taste of it. The sensation of that long-forgotten friend.

All she recalled was loneliness.

Isolation.

Desolation.

An unending sense of despair, and unquenchable longing for family that she'd once known. Du had robbed her of so much. Not just her safety and normality, he'd taken away all semblance of belonging to a community.

His people had been so incredibly violent and callous. Animals who wore itchy wool and lived in spartan hovels. Warriors more at home on a battlefield than at a feast. Their belief had been that you were judged more on how you died than on how you lived. And warriors who died in the midst of bloody battle were rewarded far greater than those who'd lived long, honorable lives and died peacefully in their sleep, surrounded by family.

And that had never been the belief of her race.

She shuddered at her memories of having been forced into Duel's world of violence and mayhem. They had never gotten along.

Yet for reasons unknown, he'd hesitated to kill her that day he'd come to her adult nemeton. She still didn't know why. Any more than she understood why her sister had killed him.

Nothing made sense in this world.

But at least she appeared to be healed now. Grateful that Duel had kept his word, she pushed herself up and went to see where they were.

As she reached the upper deck, Mara expected them to still be at sea.

Instead, they were docked on an island, and she'd slept through most of the day. The sun hung low in the sky, casting shadows across the palms and greenery, while fishermen, merchants, sailors, and those inclined to less than legal means of support scurried about their business on the docks.

But the most curious of all had been left aboard her own ship, while the others appeared to have taken a short liberty ashore. Mara scowled at the two inseparable humans who were working on swabbing the deck. Though to be honest, they were far more engrossed in swapping insults than completing their assigned task.

Jake Devereaux and Blake Landrey. Rugged and tough, they were opposite in every way. One tall, the other short. One plump, the other emaciated. One fair and the other darker than sin. Yet they were best mates and forever fighting over every little thing. She'd never seen anything quite like them.

"Would you stop with the shifting the bucket while I be mopping, Jake? What's wrong with you, man?"

"Me? Ye be the idiot what's moving it!"

Hinder Desai, who'd also been left behind to referee the two— lucky him for *that* punishment—let out an exasperated sigh as he raked his hand across his face and met Mara's gaze. "Can I be killing them, mum? You think the captain would notice it?"

She laughed at his dire tone. "Probably. Where are we, Mr. Desai?"

He wiped at the sweat on his forehead, then pushed back his black hair before he answered. "Tortuga. We pulled in about two hours ago to make repairs. How are you feeling, mum?"

"Much better. Thank you."

"Good. Do you need me to fetch anyone for you?"

She considered it. "Are most of the crew on board or on shore?"

"Shore, mum."

As she figured, then. "Thank you, Mr. Desai."

"Pleasure, mum."

She wandered away as she considered his disclosure. It wasn't like Du to clear the ship completely. What could he have been thinking?

Lost in thought, she collided with Kalder, who came out of nowhere to catch her against his lean, hard body. She gasped in startled alarm.

"You all right?" he asked quickly as he righted her.

"Aye. Sorry. I didn't see you there."

"It's all good. Captain told me to stay behind and keep an eye on you. Not get in your way. Least I accomplished half my mission."

She laughed. "Where is he?"

"Chasing demons."

Her chest tightened. "Was he fit for it?"

"Didn't think it my place to question him, as I didn't want my throat handed to me."

She bit back a curse. "Where did he go?"

"That way." He pointed toward the gangway.

She gave him a droll, irritated glare at the obvious answer, since that was the only way to leave the ship and it gave her no clue as to which way Duel had traveled once he'd reached shore. "Really?"

He shrugged teasingly.

"You know if the captain dies, Mr. Dupree, I go with him to the grave."

"That would really be a bad day for those of us standing on the ship. Especially if we're out to sea when it happens." Screwing up his face, he scratched at his neck. "Except for me, of course. Wouldn't matter, as I breathe water. But I'd sure feel bad for the rest."

"Aye. 'Twould be bad for them, indeed."

"Shall we go find them, then?"

She wrinkled her nose. "Let's."

Clearing his throat, he allowed her to lead the way. Mara wasn't sure where to start. Tortuga wasn't the most savory of places. Rather, it was a favored haunt of the derelicts of humanity and otherworldly beings who preyed on those sordid creatures. If ever someone sought a reason as to why a zombie apocalypse should be allowed and why humanity should root for their enemies to win, this place gave them cause for it.

She pressed her hand to her nose and sought to breathe through her mouth so as not to gag on the unholy stench of it all. How anyone could stand to live here, she couldn't imagine. Yet there were many who deemed this hellhole some kind of desired paradise. Jack Rackham. Anne Bonny. Blackbeard. Jean-Luc St. Noir. Even Rafael Santiago was known to frequent these shores with giddy delight.

They were all mad, if you asked her.

But as they searched the taverns, Mara and Kalder found no sign of Du. Only a number of their crew embroiled in things she'd have rather remained ignorant of.

Especially when she found Bart in a full-on orgy with not one, or two, but *three* buxom maids.

While the man's dexterity and prowess impressed Kalder, it left her a bit piqued and embarrassed. And Bart seemed flustered as he scrambled for his pants.

"Well, then . . ." Mara paused outside in the hallway of the brothel as they left Bart in the room to finish with his doxies. "I think we've run the course of the stews on the island."

"Aye to that."

And she was honestly grateful that they'd found no sign of Du in any of them. More grateful than she'd ever admit to out loud.

But there had been no sign of Belle, William, Cameron, or Du anywhere at all. It was as if they'd vanished into thin air. She couldn't imagine where they might be. "Any idea where to look for our missing members?"

"Your guess is as good as mine, mum."

And her guess was worthless.

Although . . .

She felt a peculiar pull. The kind she hadn't felt in a long time.

Unsure about it, she allowed it to guide her down the stairs and back to the street, through the filthy town where she saw nothing redeeming about the place. Only absolute misery lived here. Along with the pox, neglected children, women in need of stern morals, men in need of lectures and decent role models, and poultry possessing some kind of feather-molting plague that ailed them.

Even the cats and dogs seemed to have questionable virtues.

She wandered aimlessly, wishing she were anywhere else.

Until she reached the outer edges of the soiled, brightly painted buildings. Here, there was a pristine little white church. Well kept and inviting, with long, opened hurricane shutters. Yet by its isolated and lonely condition, it was obvious no one in this godforsaken place sought refuge for their immortal souls. Better-kept chickens ran freely around the building, along with three stray cows that grazed in the yard and several mud-covered pigs. Dried-out palm trees twisted around the building like skeletal guardians. It was strangely eerie.

Yet it beckoned her closer.

She had no idea why. Until she entered the building and stopped dead in her tracks at the absolute *last* thing she'd ever expected to find.

Kalder was so stunned he actually slammed into her back.

Gaping, she blinked, then blinked again, unable to trust her own eyesight as she stared in total stupefaction at what was in front of her.

Du sat on the rear porch with a little girl in his lap, surrounded by a herd of children, reading a collection of Aesop's Fables to them. Nay, not just reading to them, but reenacting the stories to the children while Belle made poppets for the girls and William carved soldiers for the boys. Cameron was helping some of the children dress their toys with spare rags from a box on the floor.

Well, I'll be . . .

Du looked up and caught her gaping stare.

The little girl in his lap pulled her thumb from her lips and scowled at Mara before she leaned back to stare up at Duel. "Is she an angel, Uncle Dubu?"

"Nay, Lizzy. She's another member of our ship. That be your aunt Mara."

"Oh. She looks just like them bootiful angels Father Jeffrey talks about."

He didn't comment on that. Rather, he took a deep breath and closed his book. Then he gave a light hug to the girl in his lap. "Well, children, it appears I should be going."

They let out a loud sound of communal disappointment.

"Don't let me disturb you," Mara hastened to assure them.

"It's all right. Their dinnertime approaches."

"Will you come again?" A young boy rose from beside the chair to pull at Du's arm.

Du brushed tenderly at the boy's hair and smiled. "Of course, Robby. You know you're my only reason for coming here."

The boy threw himself against Du with a giddy yelp and hugged him before he rushed off.

Du stood with the girl in his arms and carried her to an old priest who'd come forward from a side door that had been left ajar. She reluctantly allowed the older man to take her from Du's arms while Belle and the others finished up their tasks.

The priest, who must be Father Jeffrey, thanked Du for his reading and promised the girl that Du would come again, as was apparently his habit.

Kalder moved to help Cameron while Mara went to retrieve the book from where Du had left it in the whitewashed chair. It was one she recognized from Du's private collection he kept in his cabin on board the ship.

Now that she thought about it, he'd always been strangely studious . . . as far back as she could recall. There had never been a night he didn't read at least an hour before going to sleep or a morning that didn't begin with an hour of quiet study time.

Even before Vine had joined them, he used to travel to monasteries to barter for books. Ofttimes they'd rebuffed him entirely for his pagan ways, or tried to convert him before allowing him to look through their collections. Several times he'd almost been killed by the Romans as he sought scrolls from them.

Yet it'd never deterred him from seeking their knowledge. He'd even haunted the Cornish docks where foreign merchants would come to trade, asking if they had any manuscripts or scrolls he could purchase.

It was as if knowledge and books were as much nourishment to him as food.

Suddenly, his shadow fell over her. Looking up, she caught the haunted ghosts that resided deep inside his soul, and for the first time, she was curious about them. Curious about him. "What made you love the written word so?"

"My grandfather. He always said that education is an ornament in prosperity and a refuge during adversity. And that a learned mind is the only wealth worth hoarding, as it is the sole treasure that can never be stolen."

"Yet you were a ruthless barbarian?"

"Even a scholar has to eat."

She glanced back to where the children were smiling and playing. "How is it that in all the years we've been together I missed seeing this more tender side of you?"

He shrugged nonchalantly. "People make their own realities. They paint the truth as they want it to be, regardless of fact. For those who want to believe, no proof is ever required. For those who refuse to believe, no proof is ever enough. And so you see me as nothing more than the monster you first met. I can never be anything else in your eyes. It's a fact I've long accepted."

He was a lot wiser than she'd ever given him credit for. And yet she shouldn't be surprised. Not really. It took more than sheer strength to win the wars he'd fought. He had been cunning in the face of far greater numbers. His shrewdness had been remarked upon and admired by his enemies and allies every bit as much as his stamina and sword skills.

Nay, he'd never really been the mindless animal she'd accused him of being. However, this was a role that she'd never seen him in.

Doting and kind.

And it was one that did the strangest things to her breathing. Made her feel a peculiar kind of weepiness she'd never known before.

"How long have you been coming here?"

"Since Thorn freed us and Rafe told me it existed. His mother taught here. This orphanage and church were her pet charity." He jerked his chin toward the door. "It's why it's named St. Rafael's. His father built and donated it for his mother, and she named it for her son . . . with the church's blessing."

"And you volunteer time here?"

"He gives a lot more than that." Father Jeffrey came forward with a small stack of papers for Du. "The children wanted me to make sure I handed you their thank-you letters, Captain. With what you and Captain Cross donated, we should have the girls' dormitory finished by winter."

"Glad to help." He took the letters and inclined his head to Mara. "Father Jeffrey, may I present Lady Marcelina?"

"My lady, it's an honor."

"The honor's mine, Father."

With a quick bow, he cleared his throat. "Now, if you'll excuse me, I'd best be seeing about that dinner. The wee ones get a mite frisky if they're not fed on time."

Du smirked. "Believe me, I understand. The big ones are much the same."

Laughing, the father left them.

Mara scowled at Du. "Why do you always do that?"

"Do what?"

"Introduce me as a lady?"

"Would you rather I introduce you as a trollop?"

She rolled her eyes. "Nay, but you know I'm not a lady."

"And you're not exactly common, either."

Crossing her arms over her chest, she narrowed her gaze on him. "You're avoiding the answer, Dón-Dueli."

Devyl paused to let out a long, tired breath as he considered a complicated response. "What do you want me to say, Mara? I'm a bastard beast who plucked you from your forest and your species. I know full well what you really are, and therefore I refuse to see you treated as anything less."

"And what am I?"

"A goddess."

Mara's jaw dropped as he walked nonchalantly past her after lobbing a cannonball at her.

Had that been a compliment?

From the evil Dón-Dueli?

Unable to believe it, she watched as he went to help Belle and Cameron gather their things to return to the ship.

"Are you the captain's pretty lady?"

She turned at the high-pitched voice to see a beautiful blond-haired girl behind her. "Nay, child. I'm just a friend to him."

"Oh. But he seems to like you a great deal."

"You think so?"

"Aye." The girl smiled as she rocked back and forth on her feet. "You're very beautiful, my lady."

"Thank you, child."

The girl twisted her finger in her hair as she glanced over to the others. "Might I ask a favor of you?"

"Of course."

"I lost my poppet in the woods outside. Would you please help me find her?"

"Sure."

Smiling, the girl led her toward the door.

A peculiar chill went down Devyl's spine as he stopped to look about the room for Mara. She was nowhere to be seen. "Where's Mara?"

Belle paused to glance around the church. "She was just here."

His gaze went to Cameron as a streak of white appeared in her chestnut hair. Even though Thorn had yet to return her medallion, her blood was reacting to the same thing he felt in his bones. There was something here that didn't belong in this realm.

A douen.

Shite . . .

"Fan out and find her. Belle, keep an eye on our Miss Jack."

"Aye, Captain."

While William, Kalder, and Belle began to search, he took a moment to warn the priest to secure the children within the confines of the church. If it was a douen, they were bad to go after the souls of the innocent, and children in particular. No doubt that was what had brought the demon here originally. They would normally find any child they could and lead him or her off so that they could either possess them or kill them.

Wary, he made his way into the underbrush to search. He knew better than to call out for Mara, as that would strengthen the demon's power over her. Damn them. They were crafty beasts. Some of the most dangerous. They preyed on people's kindness. Preyed on their sympathy.

And Mara held far too much of both, in spite of her Deruvian blood.

Little wonder the douen had found her. On this island, compassion was in short supply. Hers would have stood out like a beacon to draw the demon straight to her kind heart.

"Come on, you bugger." He was thirsty and in need of nourishment. It'd been a long time since he made a meal off something as powerful as a douen. It'd do his own powers good to feast on this bastard's heart.

Provided it didn't kill Mara first and end him in the process.

Where would it have taken her? Not like it could kill her in the open. Or maybe it could. These bastards were more brazen than most. It was what made them so dangerous.

Devyl went deeper into the thicket, where the overgrowth was so dense it was hard to see much. Even daylight.

Suddenly, he heard a rustle near him.

Turning, he summoned philosopher's fire into his fist. And moved in for the attack.

"Halt!"

He barely caught the release before he unleashed the flames over the newcomers. "Dammit, Alabama! Rafe! You almost lost your heads! What are you doing here?"

"Kalder said our lady had been taken. We're here to help you hunt." Alabama was one of Devyl's gunners. A large, beefy member of their crew, he'd belonged to the Choctaw nation before his death and recruitment to the Hellchasers by Thorn. Like Rosie, he wore feathers braided into his long, black hair, and a bone and beaded choker. "I take it you haven't found her?"

"Nay. Can you track them?"

Alabama shook his head.

Devyl cursed. Out of the three of them, someone should have been able to pick up something. For them to have nothing at all . . .

Then he felt it.

"This way!" He ran through the brush as fast as he could. Birds scattered at his reckless pace.

At the end of the path, the trees broke to a clearing. And not just any clearing—there appeared to be a hole in the very earth. One that dropped straight down to what seemed to be hell itself. Devyl barely caught himself before he fell into it.

"What the devil is that?" Alabama breathed.

"Eye of Mama D'Leau." Rafe crossed himself as the hole began to quickly fill with bubbling water.

Alabama scowled. "Who and what?"

"She's a goddess," Devyl explained. "She protects these lands and people. And in particular the sea. You cross her and she's capable of all manner of evil." He glanced to Rafe. "Can you get her to help us?"

"I can try." Rafe rubbed his hand gently against his necklace that his mother had made for him. "Mama! I implore your kindness and offer you my faithful heart and loyalty. My mother taught me to respect you and Papa Bois, and all your creatures of the land and sea. Now an evil jumbie—a douen—has taken a friend. Will you please help me and my friends find her? I implore you, my lady, in all grateful humility."

Biting his lip, he waited for a full minute as the water swirled more and churned angrily about, threatening to spill over the banks of the hole.

Then it went perfectly still.

Not even a single ripple. It was as if the whole thing had frozen over.

Rafe sighed regretfully. "She'd probably respond better to Belle."

That was the theory until a bright red mist blew up from the water. Shimmering and dancing, it formed the likeness of a beautiful African sea goddess. Her eyes were made of Tahitian pearls and her lips the color of vibrant coral. She smiled at Rafe.

"Son of Masika, you have been faithful. Let my light guide your way." She opened her hand and breathed across her palm. The moment she did so, a small ball of bloodred light appeared. Like a beautiful firefly, it bounced and hovered.

Mama D'Leau faded back into the waters and vanished into the waves. Waves that evaporated until nothing remained but the giant hole in the ground.

The light quickly headed for the forest.

Devyl and his companions ran after it.

Unlike them, the tiny light had no trouble whatsoever locating the douen.

The problem was? It wasn't alone. In fact, it had spawned well.

Alabama cursed as he saw the large circle of demons that surrounded Mara. Rafe gulped audibly.

And Devyl smiled at the sight. He'd be feasting well tonight. Or dying painfully.

Either way, he'd be free of Thorn.

10

Marcelina could neither move nor breathe as the stench of sulphur invaded every part of her being. It felt as if the demons around her were pulling out her life force, molecule by molecule. As if they were draining her powers with excruciating slowness to cause as much pain as they could.

They laughed while they did it. Unable to protect herself, she couldn't even cry out for help. Never had she been so helpless.

Worse? She still didn't know how she'd gotten into this position.

One moment she'd been walking with what she thought was a small child, looking for a doll, and the next—

She'd been slammed to the ground by an unseen force.

Then bound in a vortex and held up for them to feast upon. How could they do this to her? She didn't understand it. She was more powerful than this. No one, other than Du, had ever bested her in anything.

Yet they'd tricked her with nary an effort. She still reeled from the ease with which they'd worked their magick on her.

Suddenly, she heard them screaming. Heard the sound of *their* agony.

"Mara?"

Tears welled in her eyes as she heard Du's deep, resonant voice nearby. Never had his ancient accent been so welcome to her ears.

Or at all, for that matter.

Even more relief flooded her as she felt his grip on the ropes that held her bound. For the first time ever, she was grateful he was here. Grateful to feel his strong grip on her hands.

With a fierce grimace, he tore her bindings away and scooped her up into his arms.

Sobbing in relief, she clung to him and buried her face against his neck. The scent of his skin and the hardness of his body anchored her and reassured her that she was finally safe and that no one could harm her.

A beast he might be, but he would always keep her safe. That much she knew beyond doubt. If not for her own sanity, then to at least protect his own life.

He was *her* beast, and never had she been more grateful for it.

Devyl hesitated at Mara's embrace. At the warmth of her breath on his skin as she clung to him. Never once had she touched him so intimately. She sank her hand into his hair and fisted it there to hold him as if he were sacred. As if she were desperate to keep him close.

"Thank you," she breathed against his ear, causing chills to rise up along his arms and back.

And other things to rise he was best to not think upon.

He gave her a bashful grin. "You've got to quit falling into such messes, my lady. One day I might not find you and then what would happen to us?"

She laughed nervously. "Perhaps you should teach me to use a sword, then?"

He arched a brow at her teasing tone and knew better than what she suggested. "A Deruvian swordmaiden?"

"Why not? You're a Druid warrior."

She had a point. It would be no more unlikely or out of character than his own past. "Perhaps I *shall* teach you, then."

He set her down by Rafael and Alabama. "Would you mind escorting her back to the ship while I finish this?"

She hesitated at his tone. "Finish what?"

"I'm not sure you want to know my answer, given how they need to be dispatched, lest they return to prey on more hapless victims. And since their primary targets would normally be the children of Rafe's orphanage . . ."

She placed her hand on his arm. "Do whatever you must."

And with that, she headed back toward the docks with Alabama, leaving him to stand in total stupefaction after her departure.

Rafe gave him a knowing grin. "You're gaping, Devyl. And, no offense, it's scaring me."

Indeed. He was flat-out floored by her words.

Baffled beyond rational thought, he set about destroying the demons' remains while Rafe left to join the others. Yet he couldn't quite get the strangeness of the day from his mind. What had caused Mara to change so drastically where he was concerned?

To touch him when she normally couldn't look at him without sneering. Dare he even hope that . . .

Don't think it. You know better.

She hated him.

Nothing had changed. It never would. Ever since Thorn had brought them back, she'd been as frigid and vicious to him as always.

He was everything Mara despised. Everything she found repellent in the world.

Meanwhile, she was the epitome of beauty and grace to him, even though he did his best to deny and extinguish all untoward thoughts. A light that shined so brightly he didn't dare look at her for fear of going blind from the intensity of her innocent purity. Never had he met her equal in character or kindness.

If only she'd have shown some to him. Instead, they had fought worse than his parents. Any time she came into his presence, it ended in a vicious verbal altercation that left him wanting to strangle her. Left him one heartbeat away from the violence he deplored as much as she did.

Nay, there was nothing between them except centuries of hostile regret and bitter words.

"Duel?"

He froze as he moved toward one of the decapitated demons. Awake and alert, it stared up at him with eyes that were the same color and form as his ex-wife's. He smirked at it. "Well, well . . . the empress of all bitches finally speaks. How are you, Vine?"

She hissed at him. "As if you don't already know. But have no fear, Duel. I will get out of this hole where you cast me."

He gave her a tolerant smile. "Tell me where you are, love, and I will come get you. Open the door myself and let you out."

She released an evil, seductive laugh. "You'd like that, wouldn't you?"

More than she'd ever know. Thoughts of their reunion were the only thing that kept him going.

"You should have kept fighting when I told you to, you worthless bastard. But no . . . you wanted peace. Tell me, how does it taste?"

He tossed another demon onto the fire. "Wouldn't know, since you deprived me of it."

"You promised me the world!"

"And you promised me your heart. Guess we both lied." He reached for another head to add it to the pile where he'd already placed the others. "Any final words?"

"Watch your back, Duel. I won't lose again."

"Neither will I. Beat to quarters, love. Be coming for you, dead running. Above board." He tossed the head in and watched the flames consume it as he tried not to let her words get to him. It was, after all, what she wanted. Mental warfare was how she played, and he knew it well.

Besides, she couldn't possibly have a spy among his crew. No one would be so stupid. They were too afraid of him for that, and well they should be. One thing he'd learned from his father, an iron fist went a long way in limiting treachery.

Betrayal was never served from the hand of an enemy. It was a blow that by its very nature came from the fist of a friend or loved one. Hence his current stint in this lesser perdition known to his people as Myddangeard and his sentence in the greater inferno Christians called hell.

And for what?

Not giving a large enough shit about himself and his own needs. Rather, he'd been damned for trying to save his people. For his crimes in attempting to drive the Roman plague from their lands and for keeping the dark fey tribes from overrunning them.

Marcelina was right. He'd been a brutal, bloody warlord after the death of his sister. One who'd sold his soul to keep his clan safe from all who wanted them enslaved or eradicated. It'd seemed a fair enough trade at the time. There had been nothing and no one else for him to live for.

He'd lost all hope. All sense of any kind of purpose or desire. His own existence had meant absolutely nothing to him in those bleak days. Because of the brutality of Elf's death, he'd gone to war with the world and hadn't cared about anything, other than making sure no other woman or child under his protection fell victim to a similar fate.

In truth, he'd wanted death to come and spare him the agony

of living. But he'd been too good at fighting to go down in battle. Too contentious and spiteful to die to a lesser swordsman. They'd taken everything else from him. He wasn't about to let them take his reputation, too. Nay, by the gods, he wouldn't fall to a lesser barbarian.

If he was going to perish from this earth, it would only be to a greater bastard than he.

At least that was what he'd thought back in the day. . . .

Devyl blinked as the heat and flames of the pyre in front of him took his mind back to that one moment so long ago in Iron Age Tintagel when he'd stupidly slit his own throat and not known it. Unlike his parents', his death hadn't come so swiftly from his own stupidity. Oh no . . . Once set in motion, it'd taken Vine a bit longer to find the courage to end him.

But she would never have done it had he not given her the motivation.

"What do you mean you're negotiating peace with those mindless sheep?"

Still covered in the blood of the boys he'd slain in battle, Devyl had set his dented helm on the table and reached for the goblet of mead Vine had been drinking upon his arrival. "You heard me. I'm done with this, wife. 'Tis time we let peace reign in our fields for a while. Our borders are secure. The Romans have retreated. I've been at war and in battle since before I first grew whiskers on my cheeks. No more."

Draining the cup, he poured more and locked gazes with her. Damn, she was ever a great beauty. With hair as red as her fiery temper and curves that men dreamed about losing themselves in, she never failed to turn his thoughts away from anything else whenever she was near. "Besides, you promised me a son. 'Tis time we set about that family." And right then, she was the only field he wanted to plow.

She'd screwed her face up at him. "But what of the Mercians? The Saxons?"

"What of them?"

"What if they encroach? For that matter, the Romans are likely to return. You can't trust them."

Scoffing at her ridiculous concern, he passed a droll stare over her body. "Given the number of heads upon pikes on our borders, I doubt it. Am told even the Picts and Adoni Fey pissed themselves when last they saw my grisly fence."

In retrospect, he should have known by the way her eyes darkened that she was plotting his demise that night. But his thoughts had been on the fact that her gown had dipped low enough to expose the top swell of her breasts. And on the fact that her hair teased the creamy crest of it. The fact that if she leaned forward just a bit more, or sneezed, she'd most likely spill out of her gown completely. . . .

I was such a fool.

His own parents had been incapable of showing him even a modicum of affection. Why had he thought for even a heartbeat that a Deruvian bitchington would be any better?

He'd been nothing more than a tool for her. A weapon she'd used to strike back at her own enemies.

Devyl blinked as he forced himself to return to the present and to the fire, where he cut the heart from the last of the demons for his supper, taking care to save its blood, and then threw it to the fire.

That was all he'd ever been to anyone. A stupid pawn.

Even Elf, really. While he liked to pretend that his sister had loved him, in his more melancholic moments he couldn't help but wonder if perhaps she was no less self-serving than everyone else he'd known. Maybe even she'd seen him as nothing more than her mindless tool to be manipulated at her whims.

Just a rabid attack dog Elf had set loose on those she didn't like.

In her meaner moments, it had been something Edyth had frequently taunted him with when they were children. A vicious, cold insult she'd known wounded him to the core of his worthless, black soul.

And Vine. She'd taken a sick, vicious pleasure in telling him that he had no other use in the world.

You're nothing, Duel. Just a cold killer incapable of feeling anything more than the sword you hold. The only warmth you know is the blood you spill. Face it, they might proclaim you a king, but at the end of the day, you're nothing more than a servant to the blood-hunger inside you. A mindless animal forever seeking a comfort you were never born to know. You trust no one. Not even yourself.

Throwing his head back, Devyl let loose a cry of bitter agony and grief. A cry born of utter loneliness as he drank from the demonic blood he'd spilled.

Just once in his life he wanted to know what it felt like to be cherished. To be desired. To be touched by a tender hand. Not because he was a weapon or tool.

Because he was loved.

You're still a futtocking idiot.

And he was old enough to know better. Love was for women and children.

He was a creature of vengeance and hatred. It was all he'd ever been, and all he'd ever be. Vine was right. Not even friendship came to the likes of him.

I am the Devyl's Bane.

There was no need to fight destiny, because sooner or later that bitch always came and took whatever she wanted. And his destiny was darkness and pain.

Accept what you are and be done with it.

There was no need to fight destiny. Not when he was the hand it'd chosen to be its executioner.

Are you all right, child?"

Cameron jumped at the soft tone of Marcelina's voice as she walked up behind her in the galley. "Sorry. Aye." She pursed her lips and scowled. "Sort of." Blinking, she met Mara's gaze. "Are *you* all right, mum?"

Mara pulled a cup from the shelf where Cameron had taken one down just a moment before. "Like you, I'm a bit shaken by the day's occurrences. Not used to dealing with demonic children. There's something profoundly wrong with that entire concept."

"Aye, indeed. Says much for what we're up against that they'd stoop so low." She handed Mara the rum. "Your sister, is it?"

She nodded. "Not as innocent as I wanted to think." Mara took a drink, wishing she could stop remembering a few disturbing truths that she'd been trying her best to keep buried. Yet in spite of her best efforts, they wouldn't stay chained.

Rat bastard things . . .

"What devil lives in *that* grimace? And don't be saying the captain. I'm beginning to know ye better, me lady."

Mara snorted at the lass, who was a bit too astute for her own good. "I'm just thinking . . . there's a disease among my people that comes from the misuse of our magick. One that causes our hearts to shrivel and petrify into a hard stone."

With color fading from her cheeks, Cameron gasped. "You're serious?"

She nodded grimly. "We call it Heart-rot or Wintering. It's where we begin to decay from the inside out. Like what you saw with Mona. We turn pale and our blood darkens. Those of us who are strongest can mask the disease longer than those who are weaker, but sooner or later, it will show itself. And when it does, it turns us into monsters who live on the pain and blood of others."

"Is there a treatment for it?"

Shaking her head, Mara winced at the brutality of the plague-like illness. Though it wasn't common among her people anymore, she'd seen more than enough of the illness in her time to be afraid of contracting it, and to want nothing to do with any manner of Wintering.

"Because the heart no longer beats on its own, it causes a painful hunger inside the sufferer for fresh blood, to the point they will hunt others for it. Tear them apart and devour them whole to get what they need. Even their own children aren't safe around them. No one is. 'Tis said when it gets bad enough, they'll even gnaw on bones like rabid rats, trying to get every last bit of blood they can out of the very marrow of them."

"It sounds awful."

"You've no idea." Anger brought a bitter taste to her mouth as she silently seethed. "Worse? It was Du's race who first cursed us with it. His own grandmother, Kara, sentenced her stepmother Heiðr for killing Du's grandfather after they were married. A dark Disir goddess, Kara gave this disease to my people for what was done to hers, and we returned the favor to them with our own version of a similar illness. First Kara was stricken with it, then her son, and finally Du himself came down with it."

Cameron gasped as she realized what that meant and why Du was so very evil. "If there's no treatment, can it ever be healed?"

Again, she shook her head. "It's what causes his eyes to turn red whenever he becomes angry. What makes him an unreasonable beast. It's a credit to him that he contains his madness as well as he does. Most are driven so insane by it that they have to be put down like rabid animals."

"'Most' implies that some escape."

Mara sighed as she poured more drink. "There are legends—silly ones, of course—that claim they can be saved by true love's kiss. Or the hand of one who can see past the beast to love them in spite of their cruelty. But that's such hokum as to be ridiculous."

"You don't believe in love?"

How could she? She'd never seen it in her extremely long life.

And she'd seen some rather miraculous things. But never love. Never anything close to what the poets described in their ridiculous songs. "Do you, Miss Jack?"

"Aye. Me brother loves his Lettice. It's why I think we'll find him. He won't leave her. Not without a bitter fight."

"Then they are lucky, indeed."

Cameron sipped at her rum. "So you've never been in love, then?"

She shook her head. "My people didn't believe in it. Not the way humans do. And the gods know Du's definitely didn't. He'd laugh like a madman if you ever so much as hinted at it. They only believed in duty, honor, and family."

"You mock that?"

"'Tis not mockery you detect in my tone. Just pity. No matter how noble something is as a concept, when taken to extremes, anything can become corrupted and used as a vehicle for evil."

"So you think the captain is beyond all redemption?"

Mara paused at the question. A few months back, she'd have said yes unequivocally.

Now . . .

She scowled as her gaze went past Cameron's shoulder to focus on Devyl's massive form, headed for them. There was an intensity to his swagger that she hadn't seen in a long time. One he reserved for battle.

Or enemies he intended to gut.

He hadn't approached her with it since the day they first met, and it wrung the same reaction from her now as it'd done then. Her gut tightened as every part of her sanity screamed for her to run.

Unfortunately, flight wasn't in her. So she stood her ground, even though a part of her expected to wet herself at any moment.

Without a word, he took her arm in a fierce grip and hauled her from the galley to the upper deck.

"What are you doing?"

He practically carried her. Though he was insistent, he wasn't rough, per se. Still, it unsettled her. And it seriously rankled her.

But not as much as his continued silence on the matter.

"Duel! Answer me! What is this about?"

"You wanted to learn to protect yourself. I'm here to teach you."

What? Stunned and confused, she blinked at him as he finally let loose of her arm so that she stood in the center of the deck, near the mainmast. "Pardon?"

He handed her a sword. "You're going to learn to fight."

Now? Had one of the demons possessed him? She'd never seen him quite like this. And she'd been jesting earlier. Surely he'd known that. By his actions, she'd assumed he'd known it for the japing it was.

Glancing around at the crew that had paused to watch them, she shook her head. "I don't need to learn to fight." It was what she had *him* for.

"Aye, you do." He pressed the cool grip of the hilt into her hand.

She refused to take it. "What are you about?"

Pure unmitigated fury darkened his brow. It was so cold and fierce that it actually scared her—something she wouldn't have thought possible. "Take. The. Sword." Each clipped word cut even more sharply than that weapon would.

"What is wrong with you?"

His eyes flared vibrant red. "Take that sword!" he growled in that deep, demonic rumble. "Now!"

"Nay, I will not."

Du shoved her back. "Is that your answer then? To let your enemies have you? To bleed? To die? To do nothing while they rape and dismantle you?"

"Captain?"

Du shot a fire blast at William as he came forward to lend a hand to her. "Stay out of this, Mr. Death, before I make your last name a permanent condition not even Thorn can save you from." He turned back toward her. "Is it?"

Her lips trembling, she hesitated at the sight of what she saw in those red eyes. There was something a lot darker than a demon soul inside him. Something a lot worse had its claws in his heart. "Duel . . . I'm not going to get hurt."

"Don't patronize me. Not after what happened today." He grabbed her hand and forced her grip around the hilt of the sword. "Take it and learn to protect yourself!"

With a ragged breath, she shook her head. "You can't teach me to fight in one day . . . in one session. Duel, you know this! A single lesson is absolutely worthless. Do you really think you can train me to be you in one afternoon? How long did it take you to learn your craft or train an army?"

Anguish lined his brow as her sanity broke through his madness. His own breathing picked up speed. He glared at her with the worst hatred she'd ever seen on his face. It made a mockery of what he'd directed at her on the day they'd met. "I won't bury you! Do you hear me, Mara! I won't do it!"

Those words baffled her. "Then graft me and I'll return."

His nostrils flared and for the merest instant she'd have sworn she saw tears in his eyes before he stormed off toward his cabin.

Relieved, shaking, and still quite terrified, she glanced about at the stark and pale faces of the crew, all frozen in place by their captain's strange outburst.

William was the first to recover himself. "Are you all right, mum?"

She nodded. "See to the ship, Mr. Death."

"Aye, mum."

With a deep breath to attempt to settle her raw nerves, she headed after Du.

Cameron was nearest the cabin door. "Are you sure you want to go in there alone?"

Not really. But it had to be done.

"Aye. I don't think he'll harm me."

Or so Mara hoped.

Cameron arched a skeptical brow.

Not that Mara blamed her for her doubt. She wasn't so sure herself. That had been quite an explosive display Duel had given them.

Offering a smile she was certain didn't reach her eyes, she headed into the cabin to check on Duel.

He was knocking back something she was positive he shouldn't be drinking.

"Du?"

He froze instantly for a few heartbeats, then drained his goblet.

Her hand shaking, she reached out and touched his shoulder. "Talk to me."

Snorting, he poured more blood.

She caught his hand to keep him from imbibing any more, then gently took the cup and set it aside. When he started away, she fisted her hand in the billowiness of his sleeve. The size of him overwhelmed her for a moment. It was easy to forget sometimes just what a massive beast he was.

But this close . . .

He could tear her apart.

Yet he didn't move. Even though his fury reached out like a tangible force, he stayed completely still in front of her. The only movement was the tic in his whiskered cheek that kept time with his rapid breathing.

"Why are you so angry?"

He growled like a rabid predator. "Why didn't you fight them?"

"They were children."

"They were demons."

"I didn't realize that until it was too late."

Pain flickered across his brow. It darkened his eyes back to their natural black state before they flared red again. "You're just like *them*. I hate you for it."

Those words should hurt her. They should cut, but the agony beneath them said that his hatred was directed more at himself than at her. "Them who? Vine?"

A single tear fell down his cheek. So fast and unexpectedly that her jaw dropped.

He swallowed and shrugged it away on his shoulder, then stepped back and cleared his throat. "You should leave."

Like hell!

"Not until you explain this to me . . . Duel. Please."

Devyl started to tear into her. It was what he'd have normally done.

What he *wanted* to do. And yet he couldn't bring himself to hurt her. And for that, he hated himself all the more. Damn it to hell and back. And damn him, too. Why had he always been weak where she was concerned?

It was what had brought them to this place and time. What had allowed her to bind them. That one moment when he'd been so furious and bloodthirsty . . .

He'd looked down into her terrified amber eyes as she stood so bravely and defiantly against him, and lost himself to her completely.

It was why he'd slept with Vine originally. While their coloring was different, their features were not. The two women could be twins but for their hair color, and oft at night, he'd closed his eyes and imagined Vine with hair of silvery white and eyes of amber. That she smelled of feathery roses and spice.

But in the end, Vine had been a cold substitution he'd used, hoping to drive Mara out of his thoughts. Hoping to purge the unholy craving he had for her from his heart.

In spite of it all, he was forever drawn to her. Against all sanity and reason.

All common fucking sense.

Like now.

Wincing, he closed his eyes and swallowed hard. Why not tell her at this point? Why continue the farce that had driven him to more madness than the curse her people had placed on his? It seemed ludicrous.

So he took a deep breath and finally spoke the single coveted truth that had lived inside him for countless centuries. "You remind me so much of my mother and sisters."

"Pardon?"

He turned to lay his fingers against the coolness of her pale cheek. The softness of her skin reminded him of a fragile flower petal. The kind Elf used to make and line their beds with. "You're a white oak. Me mother was a dera sylph."

She let out a soft gasp as that unexpected news hit her. Her eyes widened as she stared up at him in utter disbelief. By her expression, he could tell that she didn't want to believe him. That she wasn't quite sure if he was being honest or trying to deceive. But this was one thing he'd never lie about. After all, it was the one thing he'd spent a lifetime denying and hiding with everything he had.

A dark secret he was entrusting to her alone.

"What?"

"Aye. Elm. She was designated as my father's guardian when he left Alfheim to take his place as the leader of the Dumnonii. She was supposed to keep him grounded and stable. Never were they to marry."

Because it was forbidden. A Druid-Aesir was never to touch his guardian Deruvian. They paid homage to them and set up nemetons for their honor and comfort.

Never were they to "know" or marry them.

Her breathing turned ragged as she continued to struggle with an impossible truth. Not that he blamed her. There were times when it was preposterous to him as well.

"That's the secret of your power."

He nodded. "Why no one could ever defeat me. I'm not just an Aesir, but Vanir and dark Adoni, too."

Covering her mouth, she let out a ragged sigh as she finally appeared to accept it, even though her amber eyes were still troubled. "Did Vine ever know?"

"Nay. I've never told anyone."

She arched both brows at that shocking declaration. And again, he couldn't blame her. They were enemies, after all. Had been for countless centuries. "Why tell me?"

He let out a bitter laugh at a question that surely had to be transparent. "Don't you know, Mara?" He took her hand in his and led it to his heart. His eyes faded to black.

Mara swallowed hard at the fierce beating of his heart beneath the palm of her hand. At the tender heat in his eyes as he watched her with an expectation she couldn't even begin to fathom.

She was still reeling from his news. Reeling from this new side of him that she'd never known existed.

And now *this*?

It was more than she could cope with at once. More than anyone could handle. Honestly, she'd rather battle demons out to steal her soul than deal with these strange feelings that made no sense to her. Face down the real devil than think for one second that she might have tenderness for Devyl Bane—the scourge of her people. The creature who'd torn her world apart and left her with nothing and no one.

Nay, she hated him.

Aye, she did. She must remember that. Hold to that. It was the truth.

Was it not?

Determined to stay the course, she met his gaze unflinchingly. "You know there's nothing but hatred between us, Du."

A deep, heart-wrenching sadness darkened the shade of his eyes. "Aye." Letting out a tired sigh, he lifted her hand to his lips and placed a tender kiss to her knuckles before he headed back to the main deck.

Mara didn't move as she heard him calling orders to the others. As the sea rocked against her planks and she felt the motion of the waves.

And inside her body, she was as hollow as the ship itself. Hollow because she knew who the real beast was on board.

For once, it wasn't Devyl Bane.

Remember, sister . . . you bring me Du's heart and I will see to it that you're set free to live out your life independent of the ties that bind you to his fate. I swear it.

While she wasn't sure she could trust Vine, she knew she could trust in her sister's hatred of her ex-husband. To get him in her clutches, there was nothing Vine wouldn't do. And if there was one creature in existence who could undo the spell Mara had cast that united her life to Duel's . . .

It was Vine. That was why she'd followed the demons away

from the orphanage. Vine had promised Mara through the guise of the douen that she would free her.

For too long, Mara had been bound to him. Had been forced against her will to serve him as his helpmate and guardian. To give her blood and powers for his spells. This ship was a prime example. He'd sold his servitude to Thorn, then forced her to become this vessel to carry the lot of them and watch over his crew like some warden that they cursed her for.

She was done with it. It was time to take back her life.

Even if she had to end his to do it.

It's the right thing to do and you know it in your heart.

But if that was true, then why did it hurt so much? And why did doubt plague her so?

11

Mara leaned her head against the boards as she allowed herself to merge with the wood and seek comfort there. While it wasn't the same as being in a mother's arms, it was the closest sensation she'd known since the day the winds had scattered her parents' essence to the corners of the world, and allowed them to return to the universe that had birthed them.

Wanting . . . nay, *needing* to feel connected again, she touched the locket her mother had given her so long ago and allowed herself to freeze that way as buried memories tore through her.

So easily, she saw herself as a girl on that day in their small nemeton where they'd made their home. Saw her mother as she placed the locket around her neck and placed a tender kiss to her brow. "What is this, Mam?"

"That be your harthfret, precious."

Scowling, she'd opened her locket to find the glowing and pulsating green kernel inside it. Similar to an acorn, it'd been unlike anything she'd ever seen before. The fire that held the rhythm of a heartbeat mesmerized her as it danced and glistened against her skin. With a child's enthusiasm, she'd started to bite into it, but her mother had stopped her.

"Careful, Mara! That's your life source you hold."

"P-pardon?"

Her mother had laughed and taken the kernel back to return it to its caged nest in her locket. "On the day we're born, all Deruvians carry a harthfret in their navel that falls free when they lose their umbilical cord. 'Tis said that it was from the first Deruvian and his harthfret that mankind was born to the earth. But because mankind lost their harthfrets, they lost their immortality and higher powers. It's why they're so much weaker than we are."

"But we kept ours?"

"Aye. And so long as we have it, we are virtually immortal. With it, we can call on the powers of the universe and command them. It's our connection to the higher mother. To all that runs through the vast heavens and all the worlds."

"Where's yours?"

Her mother had smiled. "I planted mine here in the nemeton beside your father's. One day, you'll meet the man you love and the two of you will plant your hearts together to put down your own roots. But be warned that when you do so, you will be forever bound to that one place. For all time. So never do so lightly, daughter. It's the same as a binding spell. You might leave, but you'll never be whole. And if gone too long from your roots, you will wither and die. For no Deruvian can exist without their life source."

"Then I shall never plant my harthfret."

Laughing, her mother had tucked her hair behind her ear. "Careful of those convictions, little one. They have an awful way of coming back to haunt us."

"I'll be careful, Mam."

"Good, and whatever you do, never let anyone steal your harthfret."

"Why?"

"Because that is the essence of who and what we are. It's the source of our power. Whoever possesses it can command us to do *anything* they want. They become our owners and we are enslaved to them, especially if they combine it with their blood. Then there is nothing we can do so long as they live. We are forever their slaves. So guard your harthfret as you would your life, for it's much more sacred. It, my precious, is your freedom."

Mara cursed herself for the day Duel had captured hers. It'd been her own arrogant stupidity that hadn't believed him capable of knowing its significance.

In all these centuries, she'd never known how it was that he'd learned the carefully guarded Deruvian secret.

Now she did.

He was one of them. Which meant he had a harthfret, too. And if she could find *it* . . .

Then he would be hers to command for all eternity.

So, you didn't lie. How ever did you manage to get one of his ilk *here*?"

Vine smiled at the dark Seraphia who stood before her. Clad in the ancient bloodred armor her species had once donned for battle, Gadreyal was a winged beauty of extreme and utter grace. Tall. Sleek. Voluptuous. It was easy to see why she was the first among those sent to tempt the army of the Kalosum to their downfall.

And as a member of that same loathsome, sanctimonious army, Paden shrank away from her approach. He cringed even more as Gadreyal reached for him. "Don't touch me!"

His Seraph form activated, turning his hair instantly white and causing his own wings to spring out of his back. The golden feathers extended out and slashed at them both.

Laughing, Gadreyal caught one of his wings and snapped it. The sound of breaking bone was harsh even to Vine.

Paden cried out and arched his back against the pain.

With a fake, sympathetic *tsk,* Gadreyal cradled his head against her shoulder, exposing his throat. "There now, little one. Don't come at your betters. I'm not one of the halflings or mickles you've been fighting." She ran her silver talon over his Adam's apple. "And I can make all this misery go away in an instant. All you have to do is give me your vow of loyalty. Fight for us and I'll free you."

Tears welled in his eyes. "Never!"

"Awww." She mocked his pain with a treble note. "Poor little Seraph. All alone in this hole. No one to care for you. To rescue you. Do you really think the Sarim will come? That my brother cares what happens to you? I promise Gabriel laughs at your suffering. Michael even more so."

"I will not turn."

"Aye, you will," Gadreyal whispered in his ear. "And you will cut the throat of your own sister to give me that medallion before all is over, too. Trust me, little man. Far greater warriors than you have fallen to my wiles." She kissed his cheek and stepped away.

Her gaze turned bright red as she closed the distance between her and Vine. "You should leave now, Deruvian. I will take it from here."

"What of my reward?"

Gadreyal smiled coldly. "I haven't forgotten. The moment I have his medallion and his soul, you will be freed. That is what we do."

Thorn felt the shift in the air around him and knew instantly what caused it. Fury spread through his veins like lava, demanding satisfaction.

And blood.

"Misery!" He summoned his demon companion from her hole. Honestly, he should have killed her long ago. She was a feckless bitch who could never be trusted for anything.

Other than sheer treachery.

Which was why he trusted her. Because he knew better, and therefore she was incapable of betraying him. His guard never laxed around her.

She appeared before him with an irritated grimace. "You shouted, my rampaging overlord?"

"What are your sisters up to?"

Shrugging, she started to leave, but he caught her wrist and jerked her back toward him.

"Don't play this game with me, Misery. Or I'll make you earn that name."

Fear replaced her smug expression as she saw the face of Forneus and realized the tenuous ground she stood upon. For all her arrogance, she was his slave and at his utter mercy.

Something he ran very short on, especially when it came to creatures like her.

She gulped before she gave up her answer. "They have the spawn of Michael."

"Tell me where he is."

Shaking her head, she pulled away from him and went to cower in a corner of his study. "I don't know."

Thorn reached for her, which caused the shadows that were concealing her to shrink away and leave her exposed to his gaze. Even they knew not to tempt him when he was in this mood. No one, other than his own father, dared his wrath when he was like this.

Squeaking, she tried to teleport out of his study, but he used his powers to trap her here.

"Don't, Misery. Just don't."

She visibly shook as she sprang to her feet and moved to put a chair between them. "I swear to the Source, I have no idea. They . . . they know I serve . . . that I'm bound to you. T-t-there's only so much they'll say in my presence."

He threw his arm out and drew her to him so that he could wrap a single hand around her throat. Not tightly, but enough to remind her of how much power and how little regard he had where her life was concerned. "I hate you for what they did to me. Do you understand?"

She nodded eagerly.

"I should never have been conceived or born. And I begrudge all of you every single breath I've ever drawn. For that alone, it's a daily struggle not to kill you." He tightened his grip to let her know how serious he was. "You will find the Seraph they hold before he's turned or I will spend the rest of eternity going to bed to the sounds of your screams for mercy. Do you understand *that*?"

"I understand, my lord."

"Good. Now go!" He cast her away from him and watched as she scrambled from his study.

Fury pounded through his veins so vehemently that it caused his own wings to jut out. His skin turned the vibrant gold he resented even more. Ever since the day he'd learned who and what he really was.

How his mother had come to spawn him . . .

Damn them all to the fiery pits!

"Forneus?"

Great. That was just the maggot-licking bastard he needed to suffer in this mood. What? Were the gods really *that* bored?

Reining in his temper as best he could, he turned to find the last creature he wanted to face.

Second only to his father.

Folding his wings down, Thorn crossed his arms over his chest. "Michael . . . been a while."

Seven feet in height, he was a massive bastard. Whereas most of the Seraphim were pretty enough to pass as women, Michael was ruggedly handsome. No one would ever mistake him for a Seraphia. And in his Seraph form, he was snow white—armor, weapons, every part of him.

Even his eyes were a stark silvery blue.

So it was always shocking to Thorn how dark the tool was whenever he donned a more human appearance. Dark hair, tanned skin. The only thing that remained the same were those celestial blue eyes that glittered like spiked icicles in front of a setting sun.

And they had the same effect today that they always did on him.

He wanted to punch the sanctimonious bastard in the face.

"What are you doing here, Mikey? Last I heard, none of you would sully yourself by crossing the boundary into this dimension."

"You have something that belongs to me."

"No. I have something that belongs to your bloodline and I promised her that I'd return it. So sod off."

Michael let out a tired sigh. "You can't help it, can you?"

"What?"

"Being a complete and utter asshole."

Thorn smirked. "What can I say? I take after my father."

"You know, throwing him in my face is a really bad idea. You weren't there that day in battle. You've no idea what it feels like to have the person beside you—the one whose back you've protected for centuries—turn their sword on you. To look into the eyes of a friend and see an enemy. It's a special level of hell I wouldn't wish even on you. And when we look at you, we see your father and remember he was one of us once. Until he got crossed up with his own siblings."

Rubbing at the bridge of his nose with his middle finger, Thorn snorted at his tirade. "Should I get my violin out? I feel this little chat of yours needs an accompanying rhapsody."

Michael rolled his eyes. "And that nasty attitude doesn't help us get past our natural distaste for you. Any more than the fact that, at the end of the day, we all know you turned on your own men and brutally slaughtered them."

Thorn arched a brow at that. "I didn't turn on my men. I gave them a choice before I declared war."

"Tomato, tomahto."

"No, arseling! Big. Futtocking. Difference. I turned on my father once I learned of his lies—same as *all* of you. There's no difference whatsoever there. Then, I gave every sword under my command an opportunity to either fight with me for a new cause or to be on the receiving end of my skills. Those stupid enough to choose my father were given a head start before I went after them. I *never* put anyone down without allowing them their chance to change, which is more than *any* of you ever offered me."

"What about your son?"

Thorn hissed as the demon inside him exploded and took over completely. For a moment, he almost went at Michael's throat— which was probably what the bastard wanted.

But he roped the dragon down and forced it into submission. His breathing ragged, he glared at him. "*Never* speak of Cadegan again, or I will slit you from asshole to appetite."

Michael held his hands up in surrender. "You've put together teams of demons. Released on parole in all corners of the world. Living side by side with unsuspecting humans. Do you really think we're all right with what you're doing?"

"I'm redeeming the damned. Giving them another chance to learn from their mistakes and make something of their lives and eternity. Is that not what we're supposed to do? Is that not what all of you have preached since the beginning of time? To protect the innocent from those who prey upon them?"

Michael scoffed at him. "It's the ones you've chosen as their guardians we take issue with. These aren't the souls of those who were borderline damned. You've chosen some of the blackest souls ever spat out from the farting abyss of hell itself. Have you any idea what you've released back into the world? Especially with this latest batch of . . . What are they calling themselves? Deadmen?"

"Jackdaw flies with jackdaw."

"More like the vultures circle together."

"Whatever. The Cimmerian Magnus has a team to tempt saints to be sinners. I figure it's only fair we have a team to tempt the sinners back to saints. Balance. If anyone in the universe should appreciate that . . . should be *you*, Mikey."

Michael stepped back with a frown. "When you put it that way, what you're doing almost makes sense." Yet after a second, he shook his head. "I can't believe we're on the same side. How is this even possible?"

Thorn snorted. "Does this mean you're going to help me now? Are we friends . . . lovers?"

"You're such a sarcastic wanker." He growled deep in his throat. "While I don't trust you, I do commend you. And I hope you don't live to regret what you're doing."

Thorn didn't comment. The only things he'd ever regretted had to do with his son and the woman who'd birthed Cadegan. To this day, they were the only ones he'd ever loved.

The only ones who'd ever gutted him.

"Just so you know . . . the reason I came? Because of what's happened with the Carian Gate and with your swift actions that helped hold back what's been unleashed so far—"

"Excuse me? I believe the correct words you're looking for are *Thank you, Thorn, for saving our asses when we got caught with our britches down.*"

Michael cleared his throat before he continued on without acknowledging Thorn's interruption. "We decided to stop being so adversarial toward you and yours. From now on, whenever your Hellchasers need backup, they can call on our earthbound Necrodemians. Either they, or we, will answer your miscreants."

"Really? Hell froze over?"

"Not yet. But one of its main gates is fractured. So long as there's no similar rebellion of your troops, we will back you in this fight."

"How magnanimous of you."

"I believe the words you're seeking are *Thank you, Michael. We could use the help and appreciate it.*"

"And you'll hear those words from me the day Lucifer's cock rots off from frostbite."

Michael let out an annoyed sigh. "I so miss these conversations with you. Like having my head drilled and skull pried open." Wrinkling his brow, he pressed his fingers to the bridge of his nose as if their exchange was giving him the same migraine currently thumping through Thorn's head. "One last thing. The gate? It's located in the Quella."

Thorn winced at the mention of the chain of notorious islands. They should have known. "Of course it is. And which fun island holds the honor? Oh wait, let me guess. It wouldn't be the one inhabited by pissed-off dragons. They'd only eat us, and there's no fun in a quick death. Or the island of demons, because that would be too routine, and half of Bane's crew would be delighted since they, including Bane himself, would consider it a buffet they could gorge on. Nor the land of the seven giants . . . because, again, death would be too quick and painless for them. Nay. This fun-filled adventure could only be found on Meropis. Am I warm?"

"Your deductive reasoning impresses me."

Thorn scoffed. "How 'bout I do you one better, then? Out of all the places they could have planted that gate, they put it squarely on that one island—bet I can actually peg the correct lost and abandoned city where it's housed . . . Anostos." So named because it literally meant *No Return*.

"Again, you astound me." His voice matched Thorn's level of sarcasm.

"I hate you so much, Michael."

The Seraph leaned forward to playfully slap at his cheeks. "Back at you, demon." And with that, he vanished.

Thorn didn't move as he considered this strange turnaround. It wasn't like the Sarim to reconsider *any*thing they did. And especially never their attitudes on a matter.

Or a person.

The Sarim were forever right in all things.

Everyone else was wrong. Always.

But in this, they'd reversed course and come around to his line of defense. More than that, they agreed with him and were willing to aid his cause.

That . . . that actually scared the flaming shit out of him.

The world really was coming to an end. He just hoped he'd chosen the right side to be on.

Maybe I ought to rethink a visit to good old Dad. . . .

HELL-HUNTER

12

Mara stretched as she resumed a human form. They were far out to sea now. Santiago still trailed after them, but, at Du's insistence, at a safe distance.

She pulled up short at the sight of food someone had left for her in her room.

Nay, not someone. Only Du ever did that. She'd never been quite certain how he knew when she'd be resuming her human skin, yet he always did.

Because he's Deruvian, too.

He must be able to sense her moods the same

way she sensed them in others of her kind. And yet, she'd never once had an inkling that he was one of them.

Of course, she hadn't looked for it either.

Still . . .

She scowled as her gaze dropped to a small box he'd left next to the tray of food. It was set upon a folded note. Scoffing at whatever he had to say, she opened the box, then sat down promptly in her chair as her legs gave way from the shock of what it contained.

Her missing harthfret that he'd taken so long ago.

With a gasp, she reached to finger the small gem and recalled the day Du had taken it from her.

"Where is it, you bastard!" she'd demanded as she rushed into his bedchambers to begin searching through his chests and belongings for it.

He'd arched that black brow in the same arrogant expression that always made her want to claw out his eyes. Dressed all in black, he'd been freshly bathed and groomed for once. Not that it mattered.

A clean beast was still a beast.

"Don't you knock?" he'd challenged before he shut the door behind her.

She'd ignored him. "What did you do with my necklace?"

Smirking, he'd pulled it from the small leather pouch on his belt and handed it to her.

The moment it touched her fingers, she knew the harthfret was gone. "You took it without asking?"

Nonchalant, he'd shrugged at her indignant tone. "You bound my life to yours without my permission, so I can't trust you with your freedom, as it is now intrinsically tied to my own. It seems only right to me that I hold both."

She'd hated him for that. And for all the centuries he'd kept it hidden from her.

Now . . .

Unable to believe he'd finally returned it, she opened the letter that he'd left so that she could see why he'd finally changed his mind after all this time.

> *I should have given this back long ago. It was an unbeliev-*
> *ably selfish thing to do and I won't keep you bound any*
> *longer. When we make our next port, I'll purchase a new*
> *ship for the crew. Santiago has agreed to take you to any*
> *port you wish. Not that you need it, as you are the ship, but*
> *I did ask because I know how much you hate to be alone.*

> *D.*

A strange weepiness possessed her as she stared at the strong, masculine script. Undeniably thoughtful, this was the kindest thing anyone had done for her.

What was more, he'd had her stone reset into a new necklace. A beautiful, delicate cage that formed the outline of an ancient oak. The glow of her harthfret silhouetted the gold to make it appear as if a moon or fairy light illuminated it. It was so beautiful and carefully constructed.

As if made by a loving hand. His own hand, no doubt, as he wouldn't have entrusted it to anyone else, since a careless smith could have accidentally destroyed it and killed them both in the process. Aye, metalworking was another of Du's gifts from his human life. Though the only thing he'd ever given such tender care to was the forging of his weapons or the carving and engraving of his ogham runes and casting sticks.

The things his life depended upon.

Cradling it in her palm, she went to find him.

Which didn't take long. He was on deck, next to Sancha, while the tall, ethereally beautiful woman straightened the collar of his shirt and jacket that had gotten rumpled from some activity.

"Best be careful, Captain. You almost fell overboard."

Du snorted. "Water's the least of what concerns me. Besides, Kalder would have fished me out."

Mara didn't miss the way Sancha's hand stayed a little longer on Duel's chest than what was necessary to fix his collar. Or the hunger in the woman's eyes as she smiled up at him and brushed her hand down his arm to smooth the jacket down more.

As if sensing her presence, Du looked up and caught her gaze, which must have betrayed her irritation. At least the questioning expression on his face said he had a good idea that she was less than happy about their exchange.

And apparently their close proximity, as he quickly stepped back from Sancha and gruffly cleared his throat. Adjusting his somber cuff, he came over to Mara.

"Is there a problem?"

Aye, but she wasn't about to give him the satisfaction of stating it out loud. He was arrogant enough already.

Worse? She had a sudden, inexplicable urge to duplicate Sancha's actions with Du's standing collar, even though there was nothing amiss with it at present. "Nay. I only wanted to thank you."

Her gratitude appeared to embarrass him. "Nothing to thank me for. If you'll excuse me . . ." He moved past her to speak with William.

Mara started to call him back, but that would be cruel given her earlier words to him when he'd offered her friendship—perhaps even more—and she'd returned it with rude enmity.

Now she mentally kicked herself for that stupidity. Why had she never noticed before just how handsome he was? How caring he *could* be whenever he chose it?

Instead, she'd focused solely on his short temper. His caustic ways with those he didn't care for, and the fact that he was extremely reclusive. But then, given his mixed heritage, she couldn't blame him for the latter. His parents had saddled him with a horrible secret. One wrong move and his Aesir brethren would have cut his throat to claim the other half of his blood.

The Deruvians would have been no better. Indeed, what had they done to him and his family? Killed his sister and slain him while his guard had been down.

Vine had slit his throat, then cut out his heart to use for spells.

Which made her curious. . . .

She rushed back to his side. "How did you die?"

Du stepped back from the rigging he was examining to scowl at her. "Pardon?"

"How did Vine kill you?"

"You were there. I'm told you lived half a day before your curse took your life along with mine."

That wasn't entirely true and they both knew it. Somehow, Duel had managed a spell that had first elongated her life and then cast her to sleep while he'd been dead. A spell he must have done long before Vine had cut his throat and never mentioned to anyone.

Not even her.

She still remembered how shocked she'd been to find out about his death and learn that she maintained her own life for those precious few hours he'd provided. To this day, she had no idea how he'd done it. What magick he possessed that had trumped hers.

Or why he'd cared enough to bother.

"Aye, but if you're . . ." She glanced around to make sure no one could overhear them. When she spoke, it was in a whispered tone. ". . . one of us, how could you die by Vine's hand?"

He leaned down to whisper back. "It was my third death. And I was reborn."

"I don't understand."

He let out a bitter laugh. "I placed you under a sleep spell to keep you from knowing that I came back. But I was reborn on the other side. It's why I changed my name. As you know, on the fourth reincarnation, if we've gained enough powers and mastered enough skills, we are transformed. In such rare cases, never do we keep the name our mothers gave us."

Her heart sank to her feet at that revelation.

Dear gods . . .

"You're a coryn," she breathed. It was the status they all prayed

to attain. The most powerful of their kind. A sorcerer of unparal-
leled strength and abilities. Wiser than wise and virtually invincible.

"Better. I'm a corymeister." His eyes turned vibrant red.

Gasping, she stepped away. "Why did you bring me back?" With
those powers, he could have kept her asleep forever.

His gaze dropped to her lips, and the hunger in those red depths
was terrifying. "I told you, Mara. I wanted you with me." He lifted
his gaze to lock onto hers. "I realize now that you're one mistake I
can't afford to have at my back. It's why I expect you to be gone in
the morning."

"Aren't you afraid I'll seek my sister?"

He laughed bitterly. "Tell her. It changes nothing, except my
feelings toward you, and since you don't care about those . . . it
affects no matter of any great import. Whether she knows or not,
the end remains the same. I will see her dead and scattered." With
those words spoken, he left her again.

Mara ground her teeth as Belle approached her.

"Trouble with the captain?"

Indeed, and yet . . . "Nothing new."

Belle jerked her chin toward him. "Except you see him now,
whereas you didn't before."

"Pardon?" she gasped.

She smiled at Mara. "You know me, mum. I see right through
you both."

"Then tell me how this ends."

Belle *tsk*ed at her. "That I can't do, Marcelina. Only you can.
Our lives are always only up to us." She glanced at the Deadman's

Cross on her wrist and ran her fingers over it. "As is our damnation." Then she cut a sideways glance toward Duel. "And sometimes our salvation. What we seek is always what we find."

Mara didn't speak as Belle went over to speak to Rosie. The wind from the sea whipped across the deck, bringing a chill with it as they sped along their way over the hostile, unforgiving black waters that hid many secrets.

Just like she did. Like all of the passengers who were currently sheltered under her boards.

Her sister had offered her much for a bit of Duel's flesh.

Nay, for his heart.

Her bargain with Vine had seemed a simple one. But now . . .

She rubbed her hand over her necklace and the warmth that came from having her harthfret again.

You hate him. You know you do.

Yet if that were true, why was she having to attempt to convince herself of it?

Devyl tried to ignore the pair of eyes he could feel on him. If only that was the part of her he wanted touching his flesh.

Damn it.

He had no one to blame for Mara's hatred and resentment of him but himself. Nor could he blame her for it. It was better than he deserved, all things considered.

Still, he couldn't keep his rampant thoughts steady to the course. The sooner he removed her from this crew, the safer they'd all be.

"Captain?"

He glanced over his shoulder to see Bart eyeing him. "What can I do for you, Mr. Meers?"

"Sallie's soul has gone missing again."

With an irritated grimace, he turned to face Bart. "Am I captain or the nursemaid of small children?"

"Apparently, you'd be both." He flashed a sarcastic smile at Devyl.

Growling at the aggravation, he handed his spyglass to Bart. "Batten down, Mr. Meers. There's a storm headed in. Secure the deck and sails. It'll be a heavy squall."

Bart looked up at the sky. "You sure? It's as clear as it can be."

"Won't be within the hour. Trust me."

"Aye, aye, Captain."

As Devyl neared his cabin before he dealt with Sallie's soul, he felt Thorn's presence there. Or at least the remnants of it. Curious about the visit, he stepped inside to find a map pinned to his desk with four very specific kinds of daggers. The kind that would have angered him had a fifth one not held a note pinned to a set of islands north of San Juan.

Your ex-bitch and her pack of demons can be found here. Guard your back, my brother. They will be gunning for you.

The Sarim send their best to you. Claim they'll come should you call. Wouldn't bet on that, but you can always try.

You know where I am.

TTUYA

Devyl actually laughed at the signature, which stood for "The Thorn Up Your Arse." He'd give the demon credit. Thorn was even more antagonistic than he was.

He strangely liked that in a person. Liked it even more in a demon.

Prying the dagger loose, he glanced over the map. Then cursed and rolled his eyes as he saw where they'd be heading.

Meropis. He should have guessed that on his own. What better place to put a gate to a hell dimension?

Perfect. Just futtocking perfect.

A chill went up his spine. Not from the location, rather, there was a breach he felt. Cocking his head, he listened carefully.

He'd just about convinced himself that he was being paranoid when all of a sudden he caught the scent of the beasts that had crept on board, under their collective Sights.

Water sprites.

Shit! Grabbing a dagger, he rushed to let the others know before they were sent to the bottom of the ocean, compliments of Vine.

13

Cameron was talking to Kalder when a bit of the sea came up over the side of the ship. At first, she thought it nothing more than the usual spray.

Until the water took on the form of a muscled man. Then it quickly formed armor over his aquatic skin. . . .

Her jaw slack, she felt the blood heat up in her veins. Kalder turned, then called to the others as he dove for the creature. The moment he touched it, his body changed over to his merman features.

William, Rosie, and Kat unsheathed their swords to lend a hand. But before they could, more creatures came over the side in slick tidal waves.

Valynda grabbed her arm. "We need to get belowdecks. Fast!"

"What are those?"

"Water sprites."

Cameron had never heard of such. "And how do you fight them?"

"With a great deal of skill . . . there's a split instant when they solidify into flesh to attack. It's a blink of an eye and the only time they're vulnerable."

Cameron saw what she meant when one went after Kalder. It rose up for him and just as Valynda described, it became flesh for only the merest heartbeat. Kalder quickly jabbed his sword into its chest right as it turned solid. With a fierce, ear-piercing shriek, it exploded into a gory mess and rolled across the deck.

She started forward to help, until another wave manifested in front of her. It rose up like a skeletal monster and turned toward her with fangs bared.

It reached out with a clawed hand.

Too petrified to move, she froze as it reached for her.

Just as it would have seized her, a sword went through its middle. Like the other, it exploded into a bloody mess to show her the captain who'd speared it. "You all right, Miss Jack?"

"Aye, sir."

"Then you'd best be getting below." He turned to fight another.

Mesmerized, she watched him as he took down two more with expert skill—one right before it would have killed Kat.

He was amazing. At least until one of the masts came free and slammed into him, an instant before two of the sprites sank their fangs into his flesh.

Kalder and William rushed to his side to fight the sprites off. Time seemed suspended as she expected the captain to be swept over the deck by the waves of attackers. Yet a heartbeat before he would have been taken into the sea, the side of the ship rose up to cradle him and hold him fast from their grasp. It took her a moment to realize that it was Marcelina as the ship who was now fighting off the sprites and protecting the crew.

But why had she waited to stop them?

Belle let out a chant. One that was taken up by Janice. Then Rosie. Together, their voices caused a shield to go up over the ship to protect it and block the sprites from accessing their decks.

Only then did Bart and William lift the captain from the deck and carry him between them toward his cabin.

Cameron and Valynda followed, intending to help. Though to be honest, Cameron didn't know much about medicine or doctoring. A bloody nose or black eye were the worst injuries either she or Paden had ever suffered at home.

"The captain can't die, right?" she asked them.

Valynda screwed her face up at Cameron's question. "Technically true."

"Technically?"

"While we can't be killed the way a person can, we can be deported back to where we came from."

"Meaning?"

"Remember what we told you about Thorn? How he could revoke our pass and return us to the hells he saved us from?"

"Aye."

Valynda drew her brows together into a deep fret. "He's not the only one who can do that. Other creatures have that ability, too. Problem is, we don't always know which ones we're fighting against what can do it. Until it's too late for us."

William sighed as he pulled the covers over Captain Bane. "And sometimes the process of being pulled back looks an awful lot like this." He jerked his chin toward Devyl.

Bart nodded in silent agreement.

"Is there anything we can do?" Cameron asked them.

"Pray," they said in unison.

Marcelina entered the cabin and quickly shooed them out.

Cameron hesitated in the doorway. She wasn't sure why, but something inside her was unsettled. "Mum? Why did you wait so long to help the captain fight against the water sprites?"

"I thought he had the matter well handled."

She narrowed her gaze on the older woman. For reasons she couldn't quite name, she wasn't sure if she could believe a word of that.

Mara arched her brow as she sensed a change in Cameron. A darkness inside her that hadn't been there before. A sudden mistrust. "You have something more to say?"

"Why do you hate him so?"

"For reasons you'd best be glad you can't fathom. I've seen a side of him that is inconceivable to one of your inexperience."

"I'm not near as naïve as you be thinking, mum." Cameron glanced back to the bed and frowned. "None is perfect. 'Tis what me mum always said. When first she met me da, he was hiding from the law. 'Twas what brought us to America, after years of living in terror of being found, and their fear of what would become of me and Paden should the law find me da over there. They'd have hung him in England as sure as I'm standing here. So they changed their names and left all they knew to protect him so that we could start fresh."

"Is there a point to this story?"

"Aye," she said sharply. "He got his own brother and me mum's killed during a robbery what went bad in London. For that, she hated him. Yet she knew her brother had loved him as his friend and so she didn't turn him in when he came wounded to her to hide."

Cameron paused a moment before she continued. "As me dear father used to say, we can easily forgive a child who is afraid of the dark, but the real tragedy of life is when men are afraid of the light. When we refuse to see the truth that lies before us because facing it is too hard and scary for us. Because when we acknowledge that light, then we see the monsters the dark no longer hides and we are honor bound to do something to stop them. It's easy to lock your heart with hatred. But only when it's free will you be able to move forward without pain anchoring you to a past that's holding you back."

Grief filled her eyes. "Like you, mum, I've lost many what were dear to me. But were I ever lucky enough to find one who could love me, one who looked at me the way the captain stares after you whenever he thinks no one's watching him . . . that I'd hold on to with a white-knuckled grip."

And with those words, Cameron left her alone with her Bane.

How Mara wished it were as simple as the girl thought it to be. Unfortunately, Duel had a way of complicating the simplest of matters. He always had.

Her heart heavy, she went to the bed to inspect his injuries. The good news was that he'd heal. But he was rather battered.

And it was her fault. As Cameron had said, she'd let her indecision go on far too long and delayed helping him when she shouldn't have.

He would never have withheld his protection of her. No matter their quarrel.

Grimacing at the bruises and cuts, she gently pulled his shirt over his head, then used her powers to manifest a towel so that she could dry him off.

Yet as she began to clean and dress his wounds, she became aware of the scars that marred his perfect physique. The roadmap of battles he'd fought for his people.

And for his sisters.

Every part of his body was covered with them. And in her mind, she didn't see the captain. She saw the barbarian warlord in his black armor who'd ridden at the head of his army.

The bastard leader of the Dumnonii.

As she touched his hand and saw his ring, those thoughts scattered.

Was that . . .

Her heart stopped. It was a harthfret! How had she missed it? In all the years they'd been together, she'd never really looked at his ring. Never once noticed what the vibrant red stone was.

Biting her lip, she reached for it, then hesitated. *He'll kill you. Deader than even dead itself!*

In fact, he'll bring you back just to kill you again.

Aye, he would. But if she had control of him, he wouldn't be able to harm her. She'd own him completely.

Scared and trembling, she forced herself to pry the ring loose from his finger.

Yet the moment it came free, it shot a light through the room. One that blinded her. More than that, it ripped a hole through her emotions as she realized too late that it wasn't his harthfret, after all.

It was his sister's.

Suddenly, she was in the past. In the Great Hall of Tintagel where Dón-Dueli's family had ruled with an iron fist.

"Elf!" he roared as he came through the doors in all his massive glory and sent the hounds and servants scattering for cover. Even the watchmen seemed a bit nervous and in want of shelter from even so much as his passing glance.

The only one who wasn't afraid was a tiny wisp of a teen girl who sat in a wooden chair near the window, doing needlework. "Would you stop calling me that already? My name is Elyzabel."

He'd snorted dismissively. "Why weren't you in the list to train?"

"I told you why. I've no intention of learning swordplay. It's what I have you for, Duey."

The growl he let out succeeded in causing the watchmen to withdraw from the room. They scurried away like rats fleeing a fire.

She laughed. "You're scaring the guards again, brother."

"Too bad I can't scare *you*."

Sighing, she tied off her thread, then bit it in twain. "Well, you need the frustration of dealing with me. Everyone else gives you your way."

With a grimace that would have caused a sane person to wet herself, he knelt by the girl's chair and handed her the cup from the floor so that she could sip at it. "Why won't you train?"

She reached to toy with the braid that fell down from his temple. "I've no wish to take a life."

When he opened his mouth to speak, she placed her finger to his lips to stop his argument.

"That is no judgment against you, Duey. I love you more than anything in this life and I always will. But as you know no peace, I want to know no war. Ta gave you no choice in your life or your fate. He forced a sword into your hand as soon as you could walk, and saddled you with responsibility for me and Edyth and our people. Never once have you ever complained of it. I've watched you all these years as you've grown from a beautiful boy to a handsome man. I couldn't be prouder of you. And I thank you for the fact that you've given me a choice as to my future here with you and with our people. Please don't take it from me now."

He lifted her hand into both of his and kissed it. "I want you safe, Elf. You've no idea what horrors I've seen. What happens to the women when their men fail to protect them. The Romans keep advancing on us. I've held them off thus far. As well as the Adoni, but should I fall—"

"You will *not* fall," she said with a chiding smile. "No one can defeat my brother."

He brushed his hand tenderly over her scarred knuckles. "What happened to my little Elf who used to climb trees and beat any boy who said she couldn't run as fast or shoot as well?"

Sadness darkened her eyes before she blinked it away. "Childhood scuffles are vastly different from what you do."

"You blame me for our parents." He started to stand.

She held him fast by her side. "I never said that. 'Tis your guilt driving you, not me. I want to see you happy, Du. You never speak of family or peace. 'Tis as if you don't think yourself worthy of either."

He let out a bitter laugh. "How can I marry and have children when every woman, save you, cringes at my approach?"

"Not true. I've seen the ones what vie for a place in your bed."

"And flee the moment we're done as if terrified I'll strangle them come morning."

"Then let them see the side of you that you show to me."

He glowered at her. "What side is this?"

"Well, not *that* expression. Dagda's toes, Duey, you'd scare grown warriors to their graves." She used both hands to smooth out the furrows on his brow until she had him smiling. Something that betrayed a set of deep dimples in his cheeks. "There now! That's what would melt the coldest heart. No woman could ever resist a smile so sweet."

"Sweet? You've gone completely daft." Standing, he tugged playfully at her braids. It was an action so out of character for Du and yet so completely normal for an older brother that it warmed her heart.

"In spite of what you think, Duey, you are a kind man. A *good* man. And a fair one, to boot. Never let anyone tell you otherwise."

He didn't speak, but the expression on his face was unlike anything Mara had ever seen. It was one of pure affection. "So what do you want?" There was a teasing note beneath those gruff words.

"Pardon?"

"I know you, Elf. You never compliment me unless there's something you've got your heart set upon."

A blush stained her cheeks. "Who says I want anything?"

He gestured toward her face. "*That* does. So tell me already."

Clearing her throat, she reached for more thread and refused to meet his gaze. "I want to marry."

His eyes flared red.

As if sensing it, she glanced up and *tsk*ed at him. "Nay, you cannot disembowel him, brother. He has not laid a finger to me for fear of what you'll do to him. He's barely spoken to me."

"Then how do you know he wishes to marry you?"

She arched a brow. "Am I that intolerable?"

"You know what I mean."

Smiling, she wrinkled her nose at him. "I do, and we have spoken. He's merely a quiet man. Like you. He wishes to ask you himself, but is terrified of how you'll react. So I told him I'd approach you first to keep you from lashing out and gutting him before you've had a chance to acclimate to the idea of it."

His nose twitched as if he were holding back a deluge of curses or an outburst. But after a few heartbeats, it settled down to a fierce tic in his jaw. "It's what you want?"

"It is."

"I suppose if you change your mind later, I can always kill him then."

"Du!"

"What?" he asked innocently. "I'm king here. Can do as I please."

Shaking her head, she laughed. "You're incorrigible." Then she sobered and met his gaze. "Have we your permission?"

"Only if he asks me himself. Then I shall give it."

"Without a gutting?"

"Aye."

She arched one brow.

Making a sound of supreme annoyance, he flung his hands out. "Fine! No denutting, either. Though that's being unfairly cruel to me, just so you know."

She laughed again. "You'll survive."

"And he'd best be good to you or else I'll tear him to pieces." Duel went over so that he could lean down and kiss the top of her head.

"Love you, Du."

He growled in response, then stepped away. "Don't you dare think for one minute that I'll allow you to move away from here. He's to move in with us. Final word on that."

"Whatever you say, dearest."

"Mean it, Elf. No planting of any rocks will be done. I won't have it. You keep you-know-what caged and around your neck or else I will have his nuts planted at my feet."

"Aye, brother."

Mara blinked as the scene faded. She wasn't sure why Elyzabel's harthfret had taken her there.

Not until it flashed again and she saw the image that had driven Duel to madness.

Against Du's words and threats, and at the insistence of her fiancé, his sister had planted her stone in the nemeton where Mara had been born.

"Why here, my love?"

Mercyn smiled at Elyzabel. "I was born in this forest. While my father's hall may be gone now, he told me that this would always be my home. That the trees here would shelter me and mine. So I wanted a piece of you placed here so that they can watch over you, too."

But it was a trick. He didn't want Elyzabel as his wife. He wanted vengeance against Du for his own family, who'd been slaughtered during a raid that had been led by Du's father. The same raid that had destroyed that hall.

A vengeance Mercyn had known he couldn't take until Elyzabel was separated from her harthfret and brother.

That was how they'd managed to kill her—especially since she wasn't fully Deruvian, but rather half. Separated from her stone, she'd been unable to regenerate. They'd raped and slain her as a human woman.

And left her floating in the lake where they knew Du went in the mornings to read. It was the cruelest thing they could have done.

Mara gasped out loud as she saw his sister's brutalized, naked body as Duel had found her. Tears blinded her at their cruelty.

No wonder he'd gone insane. Through his sister's harthfret, she could feel his anguished shouts as he sprang from his horse and called her name. Feel his heart shattering the moment he gathered her frail body into his arms and held her like a baby against his chest, willing her to open her eyes and live again.

But they'd seen to it that she couldn't.

Never in her life had Mara seen anyone so heartbroken. Heard more sorrow as he shouted his misery to the heavens and demanded the gods spare his sister and take his life in her stead.

No one had answered him.

That was the Duel she'd met as he'd torn her nemeton apart in an effort to find the ones who'd taken from him the only person who had ever given him kindness without cruelty or condition. The sole heart he'd held sacred above all others.

The only person or family he'd had in the entire world.

"Oh, Du," Mara breathed as she finally saw the truth of him. All he'd ever known was pain and loneliness. Heartbreak. Betrayal.

No one had held him when he'd ached. Or grieved. No one. He'd gone through it all alone. Without friend or family.

With her cursing and damning him every step of the way.

That was why he'd hesitated that day in the forest. Even after everything they'd done to his sister, he'd refused to harm her. Because deep down, in spite of Mara's Deruvian magick and his desperate need for vengeance and blood to assuage his sister's death and his own guilt for not protecting Elf, he'd known that Mara was weaker than him. That she couldn't defend herself against him any more than his sister had been able to fight off her attackers.

And rather than see her harmed or lay another innocent in her grave, he would have walked away and left her alone. Because, in spite of his ferocity, it wasn't in him to harm anyone who couldn't fight back against him.

Du was not the savage beast she'd proclaim him.

It's all my fault.

All these centuries, she'd blamed him for something she'd done to herself.

The truth slapped Mara hard and furiously. Duel wouldn't have gone after her sisters. He hadn't been burning the women. It'd been the men he'd attacked. They alone had been the ones he'd wanted to slaughter. Because they had been the ones who'd attacked his Elf.

He'd been in so much pain. And no one had reached out to help him through it. So he'd lashed out, needing relief, and had sought it through the only means he knew. Violence and vengeance.

Why didn't I see that before? Why hadn't she seen him before this?

Because she'd been angry and afraid.

Her heart pounding, she sat down on the bunk beside him and returned the ring to his finger. The last thing she'd ever do was separate him from this most precious piece of his sister. It was all he had left to treasure.

No sooner had she settled it back in place than he took a deep breath and groaned. When he started to thrash about, she placed her hands against his chest. "Easy, Duel. You're injured. Do you remember what happened?"

With a fierce grimace, he glared at her. "You smacked me in the head with the mast and knocked me to the sprites."

Leave it to him to remember *that* part.

"I also saved you from them."

"You hit me first." He rubbed his hand across his stomach and winced. "Are you here to finish me off?"

"Nay. I've been tending you."

He scoffed rudely. "Really, why are you here?"

She'd be more offended and outraged by his doubt had she not earned his suspicion. "Answer me one thing first. Had I not bound our lives together, what would you have done with me that day we met in my nemeton?"

Devyl looked away, but she caught his cheek in a gentle grip that seared him all the way to his soul. How cruel it was that the only thing he'd ever craved was a tender touch from her.

And it was the last thing she'd ever give the likes of him.

Against his will, she turned his head until he was forced to meet her gaze. "I want the truth."

"I wanted to kill you. Truth. When I first saw you, my only thought was that you'd be the perfect revenge for what they'd done. What they'd taken. To give back to them exactly what they'd done to my sister, in full brutal measure. But when I looked into your eyes and saw your fear, I knew I couldn't do that to you. For I saw no enemy that day. Only a frightened girl who was brave enough to stand when she knew she had no way to defend herself. And it infuriated me that your own had left you there alone to face me while they ran to save their own arses, like the very cowardly dogs they all were. That was the renewed fury you saw inside me. First, they'd violated and desecrated my blood, then they'd cast you out for what they thought to be the same fate. I wanted them all for that. None of them deserved your loyalty. Or your noble sacrifice."

Tears welled in her eyes. "And my sister? Why did you choose her for wife?"

Devyl ground his teeth at a question that burned even deeper. He didn't want to open himself up for her rejection. She'd cut him enough and he was done with it. He was too old to play these games.

So he started to rise.

Mara held him fast. "Truth, Dón-Dueli . . . please? I want to know why you married Vine."

That simple, innocuous question wrung the most excruciating wave of pain from deep inside his soul. He'd had mortal sword wounds to his gut that hurt less. He had no intention of ever speaking about such anguish. To anyone. Not for any reason whatsoever.

And yet the truth spilled out of his treacherous lips before he could stop it. "I wanted you and you wouldn't have me. So I let her seduce me with words I knew were false. I felt her coldness every time she touched me."

"Then why marry her?"

"She told me she was pregnant. I've never wanted anything more than the babe I thought she carried."

Mara winced as she realized the lie. "She was never pregnant."

"Something I suspected, but couldn't prove. She played her hand well and then told me that she lost the child not long after we married. Then promised me that there would be others. A home filled with them. Even at the time, I doubted her words, but you loved her and so I let her stay."

She laid her hand against his cheek as she stared into the torment that haunted those dark eyes. All he'd ever wanted was for someone to love him. To have the very thing that others took for granted. And her people and family had robbed him completely. "I'm so sorry, Du. Sorry for the lies my sister told. And sorry for what my people did to yours. For what they took from you, personally."

"I don't want your pity."

"Good, because I don't offer you any." She toughened her voice with him, knowing he couldn't abide insincerity or patronization. He was too strong for that. Physically, mentally, and emotionally.

"Then why this elaborate show?"

She snorted at him as she sank her hand in his tangled hair and balled her fist in the silken dark strands. "For such an incredibly smart man, you're such an idiot." And with those words, she pulled his lips to hers.

Devyl couldn't breathe as he tasted the passion she offered. Tasted a desire that he'd never known before.

What fresh hell was this?

But he couldn't think straight. Not while her tongue swept against his and she clutched at him with a hunger he'd never expected from her. Growling deep in his throat, he fisted his hand in her dress and pressed her body closer to his as he lost himself to a dream he didn't want to end. How many times had he fantasized about holding her in his arms and having her in his bed? He'd tortured himself with this. Lain awake for hours on end, knowing he could force the issue, and yet refusing to ever hurt her because her heart meant so much more to him than his own base needs. Indeed, he would bleed just to see her smile.

A part of him hated that she had so much power over him. Hated that he couldn't stop himself from caring. He'd tried so many times to purge her from his thoughts and heart. Nothing had ever worked. The more he attempted to carve her out, the deeper she seemed to sink into his soul. A never-ending madness.

Now this . . .

He was lost. And only she could anchor him.

Mara closed her eyes as she drank in the scent and taste of her irritating nemesis. And yet right now, she felt something so very different. Not an enemy, but rather a missing piece.

It made no sense. She should hate him. Despise every breath he drew.

And yet, for the first time ever, she didn't hate him at all. Not even a little. This wasn't a beast she held. He was a wounded man. One who'd been abandoned and betrayed by everyone he'd ever dared to let near him.

And when he pulled away, she saw vulnerability in his eyes. Never before had he shown that to anyone. He'd always been so steadfast and strong. Incredibly cocksure. No weakness of any kind.

He brushed his thumb against her lips. An action that sent chills down her spine. "What do you want from me, Mara?"

"I don't know, Duel. Right now, I'm as confused as you are. I've spent so many centuries hating you that this concept of not . . . it leaves me at a loss. But I don't want to hate you anymore. If you can find it inside yourself to forgive me, I should like to try for a new label."

"And that is?"

She bit her lip as she considered it. If they weren't enemies, then what were they? What was left?

"I'm not sure. Friends?"

He snorted. "I want more than that, Mara. Much more."

In truth, so did she. "I know. But I'm not sure how to give you that."

He scowled at her.

She smiled at his consternation. "I was scarce more than a girl when you plucked me from my nemeton. You're the only man I've ever been around, Du. Think about it."

And with that she faded from the room to return to her nestling.

Devyl felt his jaw go slack as he finally understood why her blood had always held so much power for his spells.

So much power for *him*.

She was virgin still.

"How could I have been so stupid?"

She was right. He *was* an idiot. Raking his hands over his face, he cursed himself for the fool he'd been. Normally, he could sense such things. Had no problem, point of fact.

Marcelina had always been different. She was his weakness, through and through.

Today, she'd almost been his death.

I have to get rid of her. It didn't matter how much he might love her. She'd forever been his one blind spot. The one vulnerability in an otherwise impenetrable fortress.

He rubbed his finger over his ring as he finally admitted the one truth that he couldn't escape. Mara didn't need his harthfret to control him. He'd been her hopeless slave since the moment he first gazed into those amber eyes. She owned him, body and soul.

His only salvation was the fact that she'd been as blind to him as he was to her—that she'd never once realized he wasn't the one in control of their relationship.

She was.

For her, there was nothing he wouldn't do at her simplest command. That was why he'd brought her back to be their ship. He didn't want to be here without her. Even if it meant enduring her hatred and scorching condemnation. So long as she spoke to him in any manner, he'd take it.

But no more. It was time that he severed their tattered past and let her go.

All things came to an eventual end.

It was time he cast away his heart and made sure that nothing stopped him from what was to come. He was the one who'd given Vine her powers. Who'd enabled her to become the threat she was.

Thorn had charged him with protecting the world and that was his duty now. He couldn't let anything else get in the way.

Not even Mara.

And certainly not himself.

Nay, he would give his life to this cause. That was the way of it. There was no other outcome to be had, and he knew it.

MICHAEL'S
KEY

14

Mara groaned as the tumultuous sea crashed against her sides and battered every part of her. For hours now, the storm had surged violently as if trying its best to send them to the bottom of the ocean.

All of the crew had taken cover belowdecks.

Meanwhile, she lay in her bunk, sick to her stomach, wishing for any reprieve from this misery. It was so bad, she couldn't even change forms for it. The last thing any Deruvian wanted was to regurgitate in their wooden form.

That was a sight and sensation no one needed. Ever.

And just when she didn't think she could take another minute of it, strong arms pulled her against an equally hard chest.

"Drink this."

"I'm too sick, Du."

He brushed the hair back from her cheek. "I know, love. This will help." He lifted the cup to her lips.

Convinced she'd return it within a few seconds of swallowing, she obeyed. But as she got a bit of it down, it did indeed ease her nausea. After a few minutes, her headache began to lessen, too, and it was only then that she realized Duel was in the bed with her, holding her against his warmth while he rocked her in time to the sea.

He set the empty cup on her nightstand. But due to the storm, it didn't stay there. Rather, it was thrown to the floor and rolled across the boards to land in a corner.

"What was in that?"

"Ginger root. Peppermint. A little honey . . ."

When he didn't continue, she arched her brow at him. "And?"

The corner of his lips lifted into a teasing half smile as he smoothed her hair around her face. "Best you don't know."

Laughing, she let out a small groan as another wave went through her. "How much longer till the storm passes?"

"The worst of it is over. The sea should settle within a few hours."

"A few hours?" she moaned. "I shan't make it."

He snorted at her misery. "Sure you will. Just think about something else."

"Like what?"

The teasing light remained in those dark eyes and for once, she caught a glimpse of the dimples she'd never known he had until very recently. "How much you hate me."

Impishly, she placed her hand over one of those beckoning deep indentations in his cheeks. "I told you, I don't hate you."

"Anymore."

Grimacing at his continued torment, she glared at him. "I'm too ill for this, Duel. Please don't harass me." She dropped her gaze down to the bruise on his arm from his fight earlier that day. "How are you feeling?"

"Honestly? I'm in agony."

"You handle it well." Much better than she did.

" 'Cause I'm used to it." As he started to withdraw from her bed, Mara stopped him.

"Stay with me and hold me. I've no wish to be alone when I feel like this." Rolling to give him her back, she snuggled up against him and rested her head against his muscled arm. "I haven't had any comfort in so long. . . . I miss it terribly."

Devyl winced as guilt stabbed him hard at those whispered words. He was the sole reason for that. Had he not removed her from her home, she would have been with her family and friends. Not locked in his hell where she sought to avoid all contact with him and his people.

Or worse, kept in stasis because of his magick.

Wanting to make it up to her, he settled down behind her and pulled her back against his chest so that he could hold her in the dim light. Before he could stop himself, or think better of it, he caressed the softness of her silken cheek. Thoughts of what could have been haunted him and tortured him.

If only he could go back in time. . . .

Closing her eyes, she let out a contented sigh. But he was far from satisfied with this small bit. Rather, his body was rock hard and aching for the one thing he knew she'd never give him. And now that he knew she'd never been touched by another . . .

That was out of the question. He'd purposely avoided virgins. They were a complication no man needed. He preferred women who knew their own minds and bodies. Those well experienced who didn't get their hearts entangled needlessly.

Yet therein was the problem. Her heart was something he'd wanted since the first day they met. And for once it wasn't to feast upon it out of vexed frustration.

Squeezing his eyes shut, he tried to banish the part of him he hated most. That weak, insipid, useless piece that continued to crave frumpish things he knew he couldn't have.

Home. Family.

Love.

Those were for better men. Never were they meant for the likes of him.

And as he lay there, harder than hell, the unthinkable happened. She trailed her hand down his forearm until she laced her tiny fingers with his. Then she brought his hand up to rest between her breasts so that she could snuggle against it.

"Why do you tremble so?" she breathed.

Because her gentle touch humbled him. It wrought a foreign tenderness inside him that wanted to protect and hold her forever.

But he would never admit that out loud. "I'm trying to respect you, my lady."

Mara rolled slightly so that she could meet his gaze, which swam with emotions she'd never seen there before. The moment she did, she felt his erection against her hip and saw the vibrant red color of his eyes. "Are you angry?"

"Nay. Too hungry to feel any other emotion."

"Then you should eat."

He gave her that handsome, adorable, crooked grin of his. "It's not food I be craving."

Her heartbeat picked up speed. "Would it take my mind off the storm?"

Again, he tried to pull away. But since he didn't use his powers, she knew that he didn't really want to go.

"Duel?"

"You have to leave, Mara. So long as you're here, I can't do what I need to."

"And what's that?"

"Stay focused on closing the Carian Gate."

"If I go, a regular ship can't protect you or the crew the same way I can. You know that. It's why you awakened me from hibernation."

"I'm a Deruvian, too. I can do it."

She arched a skeptical brow. "Have you ever?"

He looked away.

"Nay, you have not," she chided gently. "You've spent the whole of your life hiding those powers, haven't you? And you'll find it's not as easy as you think. You learning to bend the laws of nature to make and run a ship would be the same as my trying to learn swordplay. You can't just pick up and run until you've mastered crawling. And you have yet to stand on your own with those powers."

Refusing to release her grip on his hand, she pulled him back into her arms. "We have been together far longer than we lived as single beings, Dón-Dueli. By Deruvian law, we would be considered married."

Devyl swallowed. What she said was true. Deruvians considered marriage to be any communal arrangement where two of them took care of each other and cohabitated. Where two unrelated by blood were dependent upon each other. As much as he wanted to deny it, he needed her with him. He always had. "And what about your sister?"

"She's a widow by her own hand. You're free to marry another."

Dagda's hairy toes, how he wanted to believe that.

Nay, he needed to believe it, but . . .

"Is this a trick?"

She pulled her necklace over her head and placed her harthfret into his palm, then closed his fingers around it. "No trick, Du. The more I think it through, the more sense this makes. I've known no man save you. I can't imagine my life without you aggravating me."

He laughed bitterly at those words. "I aggravate *you*?"

"'Deed you do. All the time."

Sinking his hands into her hair, he kissed her playfully. This was all kinds of madness. To even contemplate it . . .

But as she said, he couldn't imagine his life without her in it. And if she would have him, then he had all the more reason to fight

Vine and win. All the more reason to see this through to the end and come out of it alive.

If Mara truly meant what she said, then he would see his soul redeemed. Her words gave him hope for the first time in his life. A reason for living past the closing of the gate.

And he was desperate for *that* future. For any future that didn't leave him alone.

She pulled his shirt off.

Devyl froze, half expecting her to change her mind and order him from her room.

Instead, she ran her hand over the scar across his ribs where he'd been stabbed centuries ago in battle, and then to the jagged remains of where Vine had cut out his heart. That gentle touch set fire to his blood, but not half as much as when she dipped her head and replaced her fingers with her lips.

The chills and desire awoken by her breath on his flesh wrung a fierce groan from him. Never in his life had he experienced anything like this.

Unable to stand it, he lifted her across his chest and rolled so that she rested on top of him.

Mara smiled before she nipped at his whiskered chin. This was a miracle and she knew it. For the first time, she didn't see his mistakes or shortcomings when she thought of him. She saw only all the thoughtful things he'd done for her over the centuries. Such as making sure she was cared for. That she had her own small nemeton in the courtyard grounds of his hall when they'd lived in Tintagel.

Small matters, really, and yet he'd taken great care of them all, to ensure that she had everything she needed.

Closing her eyes, she held him close as she remembered the way he'd looked just a few months ago when he'd awakened her from her slumber. She'd been so angry to find him in the shadows of an abandoned abbey. So terrified of the foreign landscape that had seemed eerily familiar and completely alien. "What is this? Where am I?"

"You swore an oath to protect the Myrce." It was, after all, what her name, Marcelina, meant. "They're being threatened and I need your help to banish their threat back before it eradicates the last of the people you guard."

Stunned, she'd stared up at him in total disbelief. "I saw you dead. How are you here?" Dumbfounded, she'd glanced around the overgrown courtyard. "How am I?"

"I was returned to life to fight the threat. Because I'm back, so are you. Are you with me for this?"

She'd nodded without full understanding of what he was proposing. Without knowing about Thorn or his Hellchasers, or the fact that it was her sister they'd be up against.

While her people weren't warriors like Duel's, they did use their magick to control the elements and to shield those who came under their protection. Their idea of battle and war was vastly different than his.

And his people had no concept of love.

At least that was what she'd always been told. But as she met his gaze and saw his tender expression and felt the hesitancy of his touch, she finally knew better. He did know what love was. It showed in everything he did for her. All those little things that he'd gone out of his way to ensure were done to make it easier for her, such as having food ready, or lodgings. To guarantee that she was always respected.

Seeing him clearly now for the first time, she lifted her hips as he slid her nightdress up so that he could skim his hand over her thigh, to her waist. A moment of panic went through her at the shocking contact, but she forced it away. There was nothing to fear with Duel. Of all beings, he wouldn't hurt her. Not intentionally. She knew that without a doubt.

He left her lips so that he could kiss his way down her body, to her exposed belly. Hissing, Mara sank her hand into his wavy mass of soft black hair and held him closer to her as his hot breath caressed her skin.

Devyl took his time sampling every inch of her skin, and especially her breasts. He still couldn't believe he was here and that this wasn't a dream. That she was finally allowing him to have her.

How many times had he imagined being with her like this? Dreamt of her touching him with something other than scorn or hatred? And the reality was so much better than anything he'd ever concocted in his fantasies.

Licking his lips, he pulled her gown over her head, then rolled to trap her under him. "Are you feeling better?"

She touched her nose playfully to his before she answered. "You were right. My mind is completely off my misery."

Too bad his wasn't. The pain of wanting to be inside her was excruciating. And it took every bit of his will not to rush, but this was her first time and the last thing he wanted was to ruin it for her.

Or worse, cause her pain.

A smile tugged at the edges of his lips as she bashfully reached for the waistband of his breeches, then hesitated. He kissed her again. "You can touch me, Mara. I promise you, I won't mind at all."

A bright red blush crept over her cheeks.

*Tsk*ing at her, he took her hand into his and slowly guided her toward his cock, then showed her how to stroke him.

Mara bit her lip as she watched the pleasure play across Duel's face. He was so hard and soft at the same time. Like velvet stretched over steel.

That familiar tic returned to his cheek as he growled deep in his throat.

It made her feel powerful to hold him like this. To know she controlled his pleasure.

At least until he returned the favor and began stroking her intimately. Arching her back, she cried out at the most incredible pleasure she'd ever felt. What was he doing to her?

But even more incredible was the unexpected surge it gave her powers. They sizzled through her body. "Can you feel that?" she whispered.

"I feel it."

Mara gasped as she realized that his eyes were no longer red or dark. They now glowed a vibrant amber . . . the color of a Deruvian magus's eyes. She trembled at that significance. "How much power do you wield?"

"My grandfather was the king of the Adoni, and my mother a daughter of Yggdrasill."

Mara's head swam at that confession. A daughter of Yggdrasill would have held unbelievable powers. No wonder he could predict the weather. Which made her wonder . . .

"Can you control the elements?"

"I can summon storms, but not banish them. And I can command lightning, but the control of the sea is beyond my abilities."

That sent a shiver over her. "And from the Adoni?"

He nuzzled her neck as his hand sent ribbons of pleasure through her. "Is this really the conversation you wish to hold right now?"

She blushed again at his question. "I'm just trying to understand you."

Devyl nibbled her collarbone. There was nothing for her to understand. Not really. He was terribly uncomplicated. Just a broken man who was bent on vengeance.

Of course that was a little more complicated given the fact he doubted Mara would stand by while he took her sister's head. The one thing about Mara, she was loyal to a fault. There was nothing she wouldn't do for her sister.

Worse, he held a secret that, if she ever learned it, would guarantee her enmity for all eternity.

But he didn't want to think about that right now. Not when her warm, supple body was beneath his.

His heart pounding, he pulled away long enough to remove his boots and stockings.

Mara traced the scars on his back with her nails, sending chills over him. "Are all these from battle?"

"Nay," he said gruffly. "My father was a firm believer in the lash. As was my mother."

"I'm sorry, Duel."

"It doesn't bother me." That was the truth. Perhaps there had been a time in his childhood when it had, yet he couldn't recall it. "Better me than either of my sisters."

She rose up to gently kiss his scars. He sucked his breath in sharply. And when she wrapped her arms around him, he lost himself to her completely. Dagda help him. He wanted to die in this moment. To end eternity right here and now on this one perfect feeling of being wanted. Desired.

He could almost believe that she loved him, and that was the worst of all. Because he wanted it to be real. He wanted this fantasy.

Craved it with everything he wasn't worth.

But it was bullshit. He had no doubt.

And yet . . .

His hand trembling, he undid his breeches and slid them from his body.

Mara froze as she saw him completely bared. Not that she hadn't seen him that way before.

Many times. He'd never been a particularly modest person. Point of fact, he'd seemed to delight in embarrassing her. But this was *very* different.

"Are you all right?"

She nodded. "I haven't changed my mind."

"Good." A tiny smile played at the edges of his lips before he leaned her back on the bed and covered her with his warmth.

She sighed at the pleasant weight of him, reveling in it and in the massive size and hardness of every inch of his flesh. His body felt incredible against hers. And when he slid himself inside, she cried out and clutched him as pain overrode her kinder thoughts where he was concerned. She sank her nails into his back.

He held himself completely still while he kissed and nuzzled her. "Breathe, *blodwen*. I'll never hurt you. I swear. It'll pass in just a moment."

Mara choked on a sob at his endearment and kindness. *Blessed flower*. For their people, that was reserved only for those who resided deep within your heart.

And it wasn't an endearment bandied about idly. No one used it unless they meant it. To a Deruvian, it was as sacred as saying *I love you*.

Pressing her cheek to his, she cradled him with her body. "I love you, too, Duel."

He rose on his elbows to stare down at her in disbelief. "What?"

"You don't have to look so stunned. Is it so hard to believe that I feel the same?"

"A little bit. Aye."

She snorted at him and his continued suspicion as she brushed at his long hair that fell forward to frame his face. How strange that such a simple thing could make so ferocious a beast appear boyish and vulnerable when she knew full well he was neither of those things. "Not exactly the reaction I was wanting, Captain."

This time, he gave her his full dimpled smile and charmed her completely. "You've stunned me past all rational thought, my lady. Therefore, you'll have to have a bit of leniency with me while I acclimate to hell freezing over."

Laughing, she kissed his lips.

Until he started to thrust against her. She bit her lip against the pain, but as he'd promised her, it quickly subsided into the most incredible pleasure she'd ever felt. And to a deep intimacy that overwhelmed her. He locked gazes with her as he stroked her with his entire body.

Honestly, she didn't think anything could feel better or more personal. Not until he quickened his strokes and thrust so deep inside her that it splintered her.

The moment she came, her powers shot out and echoed around the room in a vibrant ricochet similar to lightning. Duel caught them with his powers and laughed as he absorbed them to keep her blasts from doing harm to the ship or the lanterns. But his own laughter died a moment later when he found his own release.

And with it came a new charge to her Deruvian abilities. It was unlike anything she'd ever encountered.

Colors exploded through the room, raining down over them like a spring shower. She not only felt and heard the aether. She saw it. Nay, she saw the very fabric of the universe that bound together every creature that was both living and gone.

Her breathing labored, she struggled to get a handle on it and understand what was happening and why.

"Duel?"

"It's all right, my love." Rolling over, he pulled her across his chest to cradle her there and comfort her rising panic. "It's a by-product of what we are. There's nothing to fear. It'll pass in a moment, but you will be stronger."

He was right. With every heartbeat, she could feel the charge inside her.

"No wonder Vine sought you out so much."

He took her hand in his and placed it against the center of his chest, over the scar where her sister had cut out his heart. "I never did this with Vine. I wouldn't allow it to happen."

Those words baffled her. "What do you mean?"

"We had sex. But it never charged our powers. I never gave that part of myself to her, as I knew what she'd do with it. And I'm a fool for letting you have it now, but I couldn't stop it from happening. My feelings for you run too deep. There was no way for me to pull it back before it happened. I'm afraid I have no control where you're concerned."

"How do you mean?"

That familiar dark shadow returned to his gaze and saddened his eyes. "I know about your bargain with Vine, Mara. I'm well aware of the fact that you're planning to hand me over to her to get yourself free."

15

"Thank you, Miss Jack."

Cameron smiled up at Kalder as she knotted the bandage on his arm. "My pleasure. You should be more careful while you climb about the rigging in a storm. You could have been killed."

He snorted as he reached for his mead on the galley table. "Not really at the moment. Just would have injured me pride more than me head. Oh, wait! It did. Teach me to not pay attention in a tempest,

272

but then to have such a beautiful lass tend me wounds, it was worth a little flesh off the bones and lost dignity, I think."

Blushing at his unexpected compliment, Cameron paused her hand over the marks on his skin that appeared as tattoos. She knew now they were his *fins*. How strange that they lay so flat whenever his skin was dry as to be indistinguishable from his flesh. Indeed, there was no difference whatsoever. He appeared completely human. What a strange thing to have happen. "Does it hurt when your body changes?"

He screwed his face up as he kept his arm completely still in her lap. "No more than you with yours. Just a mild sensation really. I barely notice it."

Realizing that she was holding on to him a lot longer than she should be, she quickly released his arm and put more space between them. Even though she didn't want to. There was something about Kalder that drew her to him a lot more than it should. He was a very handsome man . . . for a mermaid.

And that thought made her smile. "What are your people really called? I don't think 'mermaid' quite fits you."

Nay, it definitely did not, as he was more masculine and handsome than most of the men on the ship. There was something innately deadly and fierce about him. Something that made the Seraph blood in her quite literally hum whenever he drew close.

Kalder laughed at her words. "For the record, Miss Jack, I hate to be called a mermaid. It sticks in me fins a bit, but don't let the others know or there will never be any peace from the bloody bastards for it, as they'll assume it to be a personal challenge to make me life hell. Especially Bart." He winked at her. "We're correctly called Myrcians."

"Like the medieval kingdom?"

"Aye. Those were some of us originally. Till they mingled with humans and lost the ability to breathe water. They kept the name, for reasons only they know. However, they were only one group of many of our tribes. At one time, we were found all over the world, in great numbers, but war and angry gods have thinned us down to only a small handful these days."

"I'm sorry."

He shrugged nonchalantly. "It doesn't help that we're a belligerent bunch, by and large. Sooner fight than do anything else." He passed a teasing grin over her body. "Some of us, that is. I meself have that tendency. But I can be persuaded to other, much more pleasurable endeavors . . . if the company be right."

This time, her cheeks heated to a volcanic level. What disturbed her most was the fact that she wasn't offended or even all that adverse to what he was suggesting.

Indeed, she was nowhere near as mortified as she should be. And definitely *not* insulted. Rather, she was drawn to him against all sanity.

"I find it hard to believe you'd be belligerent, Mr. Dupree. You seem exceptionally kind and sweet."

He slapped his hand over his heart. "Ah, lass, you wound me to me core. And call me Kalder, please. 'Mr. Dupree' sounds like I ought to be in some posh coat and hat, issuing orders. Me people don't run on such formality."

She shook her head at his cheerful play. While "surly" definitely described a certain large proportion of their crew, Kalder most assuredly was one of their more jovial members. "You seem rather easygoing to me."

He sobered at that. "Looks are deceiving. Let's just say there's a good reason I was gutted."

"Aye to that," Rosie chimed in as he walked by and handed off his rum bottle to Kalder. "You're on his good side, Miss Jack. Trust those of us who are permanently engraved on the bad end—you'd gut him, too. Especially in the morning. He's a beast of a fish, then."

She didn't believe it for a minute.

Kalder laughed, and took a drink.

"Hey there! What's that sound?" William cocked his head.

Cameron didn't hear anything other than the storm—which was concurred by the others as they responded to William's question. They heard nothing either.

Not until Simon suddenly lifted his head from where he'd been resting in the corner. "I hear it now. It sounds like . . . takarum!"

Bart cursed as he shot to his feet. Kalder and the rest did the same.

"Takarum?" Cameron scowled at the unfamiliar term. Since she had no idea what it was, she was much slower to rise to a battle station.

"Souls of those who've died at sea." Belle and Valynda moved to stand by Zumari. "They're here to find bodies so that they can possess them."

"Or those they can take down to the locker to replace themselves so that they can go free and live again." Simon crossed himself and spit.

Cameron's hair went white. Her back began to burn as if her wings were trying to break through the surface of her skin.

They were right. Whatever was here wasn't human.

And it was here for prey.

"Where's Janny?" Belle glanced about for the Dark-Huntress who'd been playing cards with Sallie, Kat, and Roach a few minutes ago.

Valynda's eyes widened. "She went to the privy."

Unsheathing his cutlass, Simon cursed. "She'd be the one they'd want most. We have to get to her afore they do."

Cameron was confused by that. "Why would they be after her more than anyone else?"

"Janny's soulless already." Belle pulled a torch from the wall and lit it. "They wouldn't have to struggle to take her over. Nor take her to the locker. They could move right into her body and make themselves at home." She ran for the door.

Cameron rushed after her with the men following closely behind them. She was just about to ask what she should be looking for when she saw a shadow move off to her right.

And not the way they normally did. Rather it came toward her like a vicious predator. More than that, it appeared to have dreadlocks and a skeletal form. One that developed fangs and bony fingers.

With a whispering rattle, it reached for her.

Kat grabbed her and pulled her back, out of its reach. "Don't let them swarm you. That's how they claim their victims and drag them down. If they pull you from the light, you're done for!"

"Stay to the light!" William warned.

Rosie used a torch to scatter the takarum back into the crevices of the ship. They made a peculiar scurrying sound that was similar to that of bat wings and rushing rodents, and yet unique to the beasts. "Aye to that! They fear light and fire. It's the only thing we have to fight them with."

Yet a takaru doubled back through the shadows, and grabbed another sailor who was at their rear.

With a scream, he was pulled into the shadows and then vanished as if he'd never existed at all.

Only a faint image of his screaming face was left behind as an impression in the dark wooden walls, and the faintest of outlines of his body.

Cameron froze as she realized he really was gone. Completely. Those . . . those *things* had dragged him away quicker than she could blink.

The others scrambled to light the corner, but it was too late. "Is there any way to get him back?"

Belle shook her head. "It's done. Whatever you do, lass, don't let them sink their claws into you."

"Janice!" Simon shouted, rushing past them. "Can you hear me?"

More of the takarum crept across the boards, reaching out for them like insidious puffs of smoke that only the light could disperse.

Valynda handed Cameron a torch. Cameron swung it as one of the shadows reached for her. She twisted out of its reach.

Bart tried to open the door, then cursed. "We're sealed in with them."

William scowled at those words. "What do you mean?"

"I mean we're locked down here." He kicked at the door as

hard as he could. It rattled on the hinges, but didn't give at all. "Someone's latched it from the other side."

William tried the handle. "What the hell?"

Zumari shoved them aside so that he could try it, but as when they'd attempted it, it didn't budge. The anger in his eyes said that he was about to have a fit to make a toddler proud.

Cameron felt her cheeks growing warm as she tried to think of a way out of this mess. The room grew darker and darker as more shadows closed in on them.

The torches began to dim.

What new hell was this?

Suddenly, she heard her brother screaming outside, in the hallway.

Her jaw went slack. "Paden?" She headed for the sound.

Simon caught her by the arm.

Fighting against him, she tried to get free. "It's me brother!"

"It's a trick."

"Nay! I know his voice!"

He picked her up and tossed her over his shoulder, refusing to let her go. " 'Tis their cruelty, lass. Trust me. Your brother's not there. It's a lure they're using."

It didn't feel that way.

Nay, she even smelled his cologne. "Paddy!" she called. "Is it you?"

"Cammy-belle? Where are you? Help! I need you!"

"It's him!" Cameron fought with renewed vigor against Simon's hold.

And she'd almost succeeded in gaining her freedom when something struck the ship so hard, it knocked it off keel, tipping it dangerously to the starboard side. They all stumbled, fell, and rolled to the starboard wall.

Everyone paled as objects skittered across the boards and slammed into them. Several sailors screamed out as the takarum reached from the shadows and claimed them.

Valynda and Belle combined forces to form a shield wall while Bart and William were forced to extinguish their torches or risk setting the ship on fire.

"Where's the captain?"

No sooner had Roach asked the question than a booming voice answered. "On deck! Now! All of ye! Move your sorry arses!"

There was no missing the fury in Captain Bane's tone as he ripped open the door that was no longer locked.

He and Marcelina came into the room and helped them up, and then one by one they left the room until they were outside in the rainstorm.

The ship finally began to right itself so that they could stand on deck and not risk being swept overboard.

"Stay out of the shadows," the captain ordered them. "Sancha, head us due north toward the Quella."

"Aye, aye, Captain!" She ran to obey him.

As he started below again, Cameron stopped him from his descent. "They have me brother, Captain."

He paused to meet her gaze. "Nay, lass. I fear something a lot worse than the takarum has your brother. Now stay here and let me clear them." He gave her a gentle push back toward Marcelina before he vanished through the hatch.

She turned toward Mara and scowled. "I don't understand."

Marcelina handed Cameron the medallion she'd loaned to Thorn. "Paden's been seduced by the darkness, child. He's no longer the man you knew him to be. Rather, he's someone else entirely."

Nay, Paden wouldn't have done that. She knew better. "I don't believe you."

Thorn came up on deck, not far from them. "Believe it. I did everything I could. I'm sorry, Cameron."

Nay . . .

Nay! This wasn't right. Cameron could feel it deep in her soul.

But she didn't know how wrong things were until a moment later when William and Belle swung about.

"Cameron! Avast! Them ain't Thorn and Mara!"

"They be shifters!" Belle warned. "Duck, lass!"

Before Cameron could move they seized her and swept her overboard.

16

"Duel . . . it's not what you're thinking."

He arched a brow at Mara's whispered, guilt-ridden words. "Then you're not intending to hand me over to your sister as soon as we reach the gate?"

She cringed as she realized that he did indeed have an exact handle on her original plan. Pity, that, for her, anyway. "It *was* the plan. . . . But things have changed."

"I'm sure of that." Sarcasm dripped from his tone.

A sarcasm Mara didn't understand given all that had transpired this day. "Meaning what?"

No sooner had she asked the question than she understood exactly where his thoughts had gone.

And why.

Her jaw went slack. "You can't honestly think that I'd have seduced you for *that*! Can you?"

"To make me more pliable for your wiles and an easier fool to manipulate? Aye. It's the exact kind of treachery Vine specialized in. So why not you? As her sister, it makes complete sense."

"How dare you!" She raked a furious grimace over him as she felt an urge to do him bodily harm. Pushing herself up, she wrapped the sheet around her body to glare down at him. "And if you truly thought that and slept with me anyway . . . you're . . . you're despicable!" It took everything she had not to reach out and slap him for such an insult.

Relief filled his eyes as he reached for her and pulled her back to the bunk. "Don't be angry at me, Mara. 'Tis glad I am that you're not that treacherous. But can you blame me for being a mite suspicious after learning you'd made such a pact with her behind me back when you know how she did me?"

When he put it that way . . .

She still wanted to punch him on her basest level.

However . . .

"Don't you dare be reasonable in this, Dón-Dueli. Not when I want to be mad at you for that insult you just dealt."

He snorted at her agitated tone. "Well, far be it from me to deprive you of anything, love. If you want to beat me arse, I'll even get naked for it. . . ." He lifted his bare leg out from beneath the covers to wiggle his toes at her. "Oh, wait, I already am." The teasing finally returned to his eyes.

Yet even so, the hurt beneath those words wrung her heart and she hated that she'd caused him even an instant of pain or doubt, because she knew how much treachery had been served so coldly to him in his lifetime.

It was the last thing she'd ever do to him now. As he said, it was her sister's specialty.

Never hers. And she hated herself for ever having conspired with her sister to do him harm. Surely, there was a special corner of Annwn reserved for her punishment.

"I won't betray you, Duel. I swear it."

He cupped her cheek in his warm palm. "Then I shall put forth all my meager faith in you."

But she saw the shadow of doubt that remained in his eyes and it made her ache all the more. Not because he felt it, but because she knew that she honestly deserved it. That she had earned his mistrust.

I swear I will make you believe in me.

She had no idea how, but she'd find some way to erase that doubt. Come the devil or the sea, she would prove it to him. Beyond any reason. Du would know that she was sincere, and that in her he had at least one person in his life that he'd never again have to fear betrayal from.

Suddenly, they heard a loud clamor, on the top deck outside.

"I thought everyone was below for the storm?"

Duel scowled. "As did I. I told them not to risk it." Getting up, he quickly dressed and went to see what the noise was about.

She dressed and followed suit, only to find the crew scrambling to retrieve Kalder from the raging sea, where he must have fallen overboard. Yet how strange. It wasn't like him to ever lose his footing for anything.

Even in a storm.

He only did that whenever he was trying for the attention of a maid—and usually then, only on land. A ploy Devyl and the others had oft chided him over. But surely, Kalder wouldn't have tried that in this storm. . . .

Especially not with the women onboard. He'd respectfully kept his distance from them all, since they lived in such close proximity. And, in spite of Kat's and Simon's rather untraditional marriage, it was forbidden by Thorn for them to fraternize. A rule Devyl had just broken with Mara, but he'd deal with that later.

Mara hesitated on deck as she took in the frenetic madness.

Rushing past the shouting crew trying to pull Kalder from the sea, Duel didn't hesitate to dive in after him and be swallowed by the black, crashing waves that sought to drown them both. She ran to the side, wanting to yell and curse him for his reckless stupidity that never failed to frustrate her. Terrified of the way the giant surf surged and ebbed like mountains, Mara choked on a scream and watched with her heart in her throat until she finally saw Duel break the surface to bob and float above the dangerous mess.

Against all odds, he quickly made his way to Kalder and somehow, in spite of the furious waves, he helped the Myrcian back to the ship. She used her powers to lengthen the wood and scoop them both out, taking extra care to cradle Duel.

Coughing and wheezing, Kalder crawled up her planks to lie on deck while Belle swept her jacket off to lay it over him. Mara carefully placed Duel at her feet and checked on his condition, but he'd have none of her coddling.

With an irritated grimace at her fretting over him that was softened by a peeking dimple in his cheek, he rose and squeezed her hand gently in his, then pressed past her to examine Kalder.

"What happened?" Duel demanded, kneeling beside the merman.

"Bastard shifters took our Miss Jack." Bart added his jacket to Kalder's shivering body so that he could use it to blot the water off his skin and hair. "We were trying to stop them from fleeing when lackwit Kalder jumped in after them in an effort to save her. Sadly, didn't work."

Duel cursed. "Anyone else go over?"

William shook his head. "They be the only two, Captain. Miss Jack and Shite for Brains. But we did lose a couple below earlier to the takarum."

Ignoring the epithets he agreed with, Devyl met Mara's fretful gaze and bit back what he really wanted to say. Instead, he let out a long, tired sigh. Damn it all. He hated to lose any member of this crew. For anything.

Things were getting bad.

Worse?

He was getting desperate.

Devyl ground his teeth. "You know, when I become the sole voice of reason in any given affair, we're in a sad, sorry state, mates."

William laughed, until he met Devyl's sinister grimace. That quelled his mirth. "What are your orders, Captain?"

He glanced over his shoulder to where Belle and Janice stood, both soaked as much as Kalder.

And that gave him an idea. . . .

"We need to raise a water witch."

Sancha laughed out loud. "I'm not *that* drunk, Captain."

"Then you need to grab yourself some more rum, Miss Dolorosa, for that be the next step. We're going in for a long, deadly haul."

Belle paled considerably. As did Janice and Kat. "Have you ever raised a witch of that magnitude, sir?"

"Aye." But it'd been a while and hadn't gone very well. They tended to be cantankerous bitches, hence the boo-hag moniker they'd earned.

With no better plan, he locked gazes with Mara and waited for her to join the others in calling him a fool.

"Are you sure about this, Du?"

Not even a little bit, but he couldn't let the others know how much he doubted his own intelligence in this.

Or his abilities.

"We can't leave Miss Jack with them. Signal to Santiago, and we can transfer the bulk of our crew to his ship. I'll need a few volunteers to—"

The sound of their protests drowned him out. But none were louder than Mara, Bart, and William.

"We're in this together, Devyl," Will said. "To the end. Come what may. Ain't a man-jack or molly here what's going to leave the others to burn."

"Aye!" they shouted in unison.

"We burn together!"

"But I'd rather we try other means, first." Valynda cleared her throat as she spoke over their raucous voices. "Not that I'm afraid, mind you. Just, being made of straw, would rather we think about it first. And set fire to our enemies before we give up our ghosts so cavalierly."

"Hear, hear!" Zumari agreed. "Died once. Not eager for a repeat."

Sallie snorted. "Bugger that. I say we set the whole of the world on fire. Damned be he who cannot fight and get out of our way!"

"*Oui!*" Roach clapped Sallie on his back. "Make the black-guards rue that which birthed them and the very air we breathe!"

William grimaced. "You mean *they breathe*?"

"*Non!* They should regret that we breathe, for we will make them weep at all the wounds we give unto them. I piss down the throats of the swine!"

Laughing, William clapped him on the back.

"Thieves, drunkards, lunatics, wastrels, and whores we might all be, but there ain't a coward among us." Sancha crossed her arms over her chest as she dared Devyl with her gaze to try and move her from the ship.

Devyl wasn't sure what to make of this camaraderie. Honestly? It scared the shite out of him. He'd never known it before. Not even his own army had been that loyal. Rather, they'd been too scared to raise arms against him for fear they wouldn't kill him. Only anger him so that he'd disembowel them for the affront.

But that being said, he was all about going after Miss Jack and her brother and seeing this made right. Whatever the cost.

Even if they did have to set the world on fire as Sallie wanted.

Bart handed him a towel. "The shifters pretended to be you, Captain. They told us to head toward the Quella."

"Well then, let's not disappoint them. Full speed. Storm be damned, me hearties. In the meantime, let's see about conjuring us up a hag, shall we?"

Mara groaned out loud, finally giving voice to the doubt he expected from her. "By all means, open the door to hell and unleash someone even more terrifying than Vine. Why not?" She rolled her eyes and shook her head, then narrowed her gaze at Devyl. "Are you sure we need to? Shouldn't we call for Necrodemians instead? Thorn said we could."

Devyl snorted at the thought. 'Twas the last thing he'd ever do. "I'd sooner trust Vine. At least I know where I stand with her. Problem with good men . . . you never know when they're going to do something evil in an attempt to make something right. Personally, I like stability in battle." He pulled his flintlocks from his belt and handed them to Bart who, in turn, scowled at him.

"Should I ask, Captain?"

"You never want a water witch to lay her hands on gunpowder, Mr. Meers. Even if it be damp. Disarm yourselves, everyone. It's not worth what could happen."

"He's right." Mara glanced about. "Make sure all the powder's put away before he embarks on this next round of idiocy he's set himself to."

Devyl smirked at her recitation of his idea, but didn't bother to correct her words. Mostly because she wasn't wrong.

It was just irritating to have her undermine him out loud before their crew.

Belle paused beside Devyl to stare up at him with a knowing grimace that melted into a smile. "Feeling better now, Captain?"

He bit back a groan at her silent insinuation. "Don't be getting cheeky with me, Miss Morte. Me humor's still not restored fully."

Her gaze slid to Mara. "I'd wager otherwise."

"You know, I ate the last crewman who annoyed me."

She laughed at that. "I'm not worth the indigestion, Captain." And with that, she flounced off to clap Mara on the shoulder and kiss her cheek.

Trying not to think about the fact that he was actually embarrassed, Devyl waited until all the weapons and powder were secured before he and Janice began the conjuring necessary to summon the witch up from the ocean.

And not just any hag.

The handmaiden of Tiamat herself. Some said she'd been banished to the bowels of the ocean as punishment by a jealous goddess who envied her for her beauty. Others claimed it was a coven of other witches who'd been commissioned to chain her there by women who were sick of her preying on them and their men at night while they slept—that she'd visit them in the form of a cat and suck away years of their life so that she could maintain her beauty and immortality.

The latter being what they attributed sudden sea storms to in this region. It was the old sea hag needing souls to maintain her longevity, and the only way she could get them to her prison. None ever returned from her watery home.

He turned to Mara. "Can you hold her after I summon her?"

She arched a brow. "Did you mean to insult me?"

"Nay, love." He winked at her with a laugh. "I'd never do such . . . out loud. Besides, I'm about to put my life in your hands. But I didn't want to put *your* life in danger. If you need reinforcement, I'd rather get it now than summon her and find out too late that she's more powerful than we thought. Last thing I want is to have to cut me own throat for allowing you to be harmed."

Mara choked on a joyous sob at those words. Words that Dón-Dueli wouldn't say lightly, which made them all the more valuable. While he might be protective, he never spoke publicly about such things.

To say it for others to overhear . . .

I love you, too, my surly beast.

He left her side to instruct Simon to signal to Rafael and his crew what they were about while they brought the ship around to head for the area where Strixa was known to prey on unsuspecting vessels.

Kat watched Rosie, then Devyl, as the sea kept the ship rocking while the storm continued to rage. "And do we know for a fact that this be where the boo-hag haunts?"

"The she-bitch takes the form of a giant black owl with glowing red eyes whenever she spies for victims. And an owl at sea tends to stand out."

Simon crossed himself. "What are we summoning her for, Captain?"

He hesitated on giving up the entire reason. There were some things he didn't want the others to know. So he settled on a smaller, more logical one they wouldn't argue with. "It'll behoove us to pay homage to her, as the gate lies in the midst of her perching range, and we'll be passing by it. Anyone who doesn't give her her due regrets it immensely. Not to mention, nothing goes on in this area that Strixa doesn't know about it."

"Sound reasons." William called for them to set anchor and steady the ship as best they could, given the storm.

Belle returned with her oils and salts to help him, and Janice cast the circle for it. "Be ready whenever you are, Captain."

While Belle set about beginning the ritual with Janice, Devyl took a moment to make sure that Rafael was far enough away from them to be protected should something go amiss—which, given his luck, was highly probable. No need in putting both their crews at risk. Besides, the Deadmen would need to be fished out of the sea if things didn't go to plan.

Devyl turned to the man who was the closest thing he'd ever had to a friend. "Should this go afoul, Mr. Death, I want you to save as many as you can."

"No fears, Captain. Me arse'll be the first one I'll be rescuing."

He scoffed at the surly tone, knowing Will better than that. William would never see to himself over the life of another. It was, after all, what had caused him to be hanged.

And that had been over someone William knew had betrayed

him, yet he took the noose for the man anyway. Because, aye, Will was just that loyal.

Once they had the ship as stable as they could, Devyl turned to Mara. He saw the concern in her eyes and it warmed him a lot more than he wanted to own up to. "It'll be fine, my lady. I've done worse."

"Indeed. That's what scares me most. For I have witnessed some of your more stellar moments of gross recklessness . . . *and* stupidity. I shudder at the thought of you repeating them."

With worry haunting her eyes, she stepped back and melted into the ship so that she could better control it and form a cage around Strixa once she manifested.

Devyl took the small iron pot from Belle's hand, where she'd already begun the mixture they needed to bind the powerful creature they were evoking and not invoking. A dangerous thing that, especially when dealing with gods and those most powerful.

The fumes from the pot were pungent enough to make his eyes water and to catch in his throat.

Sancha rubbed at her nose as he began to make sigils on the deck. "Doesn't she prey on children?"

"She can. Why?"

"I'm trying to think if there's an easier way to lure her. Mentally, Kalder should draw her in."

Kalder gave a loud, fake laugh at her insult. "I've heard she prefers to drink the nectar of loose women, meself."

"Well then, we get a double dose of it with you." Sancha grinned at him.

Kalder laughed good-naturedly, taking her insults in stride. At least until a fierce, harsh, screaming wind began.

Devyl grimaced at the banshee-like sound. "Relax. It's her. She's protesting our interference with her free will."

"Is she going to—" Bart's voice broke off as a massive swell of water came over the starboard side and sent the ship careening.

Several members almost fell overboard, but Mara caught them in a basket and held fast.

Devyl cursed as more waves pummeled them and uprooted their anchors. "Hold tight!"

Easier said than done. Strixa was after their blood and their lives for this. And not just to take a few years off.

She wanted them entirely.

As a result, a wave lifted the ship out of the water and sent it crashing down with a force that rattled their bones and sent them all to the deck. It was so fierce, it shattered the cage Mara had created to hold her.

"Mara?" Devyl shouted, terrified she might have been injured.

"I'm fine." But her tone was stressed. "Don't worry over me. You be careful."

He pressed his cheek against the plank, wishing she was in her body. "Do not get harmed in this," he breathed before pressing his lips to her wood. "Above all, do not risk yourself."

The planks warmed beneath him. "Above all, Du, do not be harmed."

Devyl caressed the boards before he pushed himself to his feet. "Strixa!" He shouted for the witch as he began to evoke her, chanting in the ancient language of his people in an effort to calm her fury and save his crew.

It didn't work.

She came out of the sea like a phoenix on fire, trailing a stream of water in her wake. Her black wings flapped with the force of a hurricane, sending their ship plunging beneath the waves. Only Belle's shield, Janice's chant, and Mara's determination kept them from being ripped apart and sunk.

The crew lashed themselves to whatever wood they could and many prayed as it seemed the ship was trying to buck them all off into the sea to be drowned.

"This was a stupendously bad idea," William said as he wrapped rope around his waist and the mainmast.

Devyl growled as he pulled himself up and stood to the side. "No bitching, Mr. Death. I tried to get you to leave."

"Deeth! And I regret me decision, Captain. Seriously. Should have done it when you told me to."

Bart caught Zumari as he went skittering past and helped him to anchor himself to the deck. "Am thinking . . . she's an owl. They like insects. I vote we feed her Roach and run for it."

Roach let loose a long string of French obscenities.

Ignoring them, Devyl used his powers to summon Deruvian fire so that he could shoot it at the ancient being to get her attention off his men and onto him, where it belonged.

With a loud screech, she ducked his blast and came for him. He expected her to fight.

Especially as she angled her talons at him. Instead, she flapped her wings as the sea and storm settled down into an eerie, fog-laden stillness that was far more terrifying than the storm they'd just been in. It was so quiet now, he could hear his heartbeat and the creaking of the ship boards around him. The clanking of winches against wood and the slapping of ropes against the side.

A single cannon ball rolled across the deck.

In one bright flash, the great black owl turned into a woman dressed in a long, flowing ebony gown and a cloak covered with iridescent owl feathers. An ornate red crown held back her black hair from a face that was perfectly sculpted and beautiful beyond description. Features that could easily belong to a goddess. Her dark skin glistened from the drizzle as those red eyes focused on him while she held her cloak back from her body with graceful fingers that were tipped by the same red metal as her crown. Only these formed filigree talons for each of her phalanges, including her thumbs.

Nearing Devyl, she cocked her head in a very fowl-like manner as if she were studying him from one eye only. She reached to cup his chin with her taloned hand. The chains that connected each digit hung down, making her hand appear as a flower. "Well, well. You're a fair one, aren't you? Are you my offering?"

Before he could draw in a single breath to respond, Mara manifested beside her and socked her one. "Get your hands off my husband, she-bitch!"

Devyl wasn't sure who was the most stunned by her unexpected declaration.

And explosion.

Basically, they were all gaping. So much for Mara not being born of violence. That had been a spectacular show of Aesiran anger that he'd have never attributed to a full-blooded Vanir.

Furious over Mara's actions, Strixa came around to return the blow with her own.

Devyl quickly caught her arm before she could deliver it. "None of that, now. I promise you, you lay hands to my lady and you'll be meeting a side of the devil you never want to."

"You think not?" She leaned in to whisper in Devyl's ear. "I know what you are, and I know who you serve. And you cannot cage me. Neither of you have those powers."

He smiled at her. "Perhaps not, but there's no blood here for you to feast upon. No souls for you to claim. Yet you've shown us your true form. . . ."

She gasped as she realized what she'd inadvertently done.

Bound herself to him, as her curse forbade her to ever show her real face to anyone, save her victims. And since she had no victims on this ship, she was now enslaved to him.

Screeching, she tried to change forms to flee. But it didn't work.

More than that, she wasn't the first of her kind that Devyl had bound in such a manner. "Mara?"

She manifested his spirit scepter and handed it to him so that the wolf skull at the top of the yard-long staff faced the sky. Crowned in gold and feathers and encrusted with radiant jewels, the scepter had been the most sacred object at Tintagel. For many, many reasons, and not just because his ancestors had embedded it in their battle shields and thrones.

With this totem, generations of Tintagel kings had bound, held, and commanded countless demons, spirits, and ghouls. It was said to be even more powerful than Solomon's key and seal combined.

And it was deep in the jaws of the skull that the holder of the scepter placed his harthfret on the day ownership passed to him or her.

Something they never spoke of until the heir of the scepter was old enough to understand the repercussions of allowing anyone else to know exactly what the staff was and how powerful a talisman they would inherit. This had been the symbol of the Dumnonii people.

Every generation of his family, from the beginning, had offered their own blood sacrifice to the wand, and with it, they had become one of the most powerful families of the British Isles.

Until Vine had viciously slain him. Thinking his harthfret was a piece of jewelry and not knowing he was strong enough to regenerate without it, she'd stolen his mother's necklace he'd worn and cast his scepter away, never knowing what it really was. Any more than Mara knew now as she handed it over to him.

But this . . .

This was the key to his soul and power.

With that in mind, he snatched one of Strixa's black owl feathers from her cloak and placed it in the brightly colored crown that haloed the skull.

"You are mine until I free you."

She let loose a venomous hiss of fire, yet because he controlled her, it couldn't harm him. He held the scepter up to catch the fire and be charged by her anger.

It glowed like a second sun.

Baring her fangs, she raised her arms and shrank away from it as if it burned her. "Do you really think that paltry stick's magic can protect you?"

"Not really, but I find it to be a most apt bludgeoning weapon should the occasion call for it." He raked a meaningful sneer down her body. "Shall we test it?"

That succeeded in calming her a bit, as she wasn't sure whether or not he meant that threat. While he didn't relish the thought of doing battle with a woman, he wasn't about to lie down and let another cut his throat. He liked to think that he learned from his experiences, and that was one particular event even he was definitely not eager to repeat.

She curled her lip. "What do you want of me?"

"Calm seas. Cessation of the water sprites, and a few more of your feathers."

"Feathers?" She drew her brows together into a perfect baffled expression. "Why?"

"For me to know and you to give. Do we have an accord?"

Her gaze slid from him to Santiago's ship in the distance before a slow smile spread across her face.

"Don't think it. 'Tis too late for you to seek their blood for your freedom. You're bound already." That was the beauty of his people. The ability to control her kind and bind them was instinctive. It was what had allowed Mara to combine her life force to his on the day they met. Unfortunately, she'd been too young and inexperienced with her powers at the time to do it properly.

He wasn't so foolish.

And the water witch belonged to him now.

Baring her fangs again, she showed him the sight of her true hideous form. "You will regret this."

"I do most things I choose." He smiled coldly in her face. "Now give me your word or I'll bind you to something very uncomfortable for a long, long time."

"You wouldn't dare!"

"Care to try me?"

She finally backed down as she lifted up a corner of her cloak and the weather instantly calmed. "I will see you to the bottom of this ocean before all is said and done."

"And I'll make sure to take your heart along with me." He plucked the feathers his spell required and handed them off to Mara.

When Strixa opened her mouth to speak again, he used his powers to transform her back into her black owl form. "How 'bout you remain like this for a bit. Safer for us all, I think."

She let out a fierce shriek as she flew to land on the ship's railing so that she could glare at him with her glowing red eyes.

William cleared his throat to get Devyl's attention. "Beg pardon, Captain. Can't help wondering if taunting her isn't a bit foolish? Most especially given our current situation?"

"Of course it is, Mr. Death. Why else would I be about it? Where would be the fun of practicing caution and intelligence? If we're bound for hell again, let it be with full sail and flagrant disregard of all sanity, I say."

William let out a nervous laugh as he turned toward the crew. "Who is with me for a mutiny, eh?"

Bart clapped him on the back. "I'd say aye, but the captain scares me too much."

"Aye to that," Zumari agreed. "Besides, he'd take too much pleasure in eating our entrails. Methinks he's the only captain alive—or dead—who craves a mutiny."

"Would definitely explain some of his more peculiar actions," Bart muttered before he cast an exaggerated grin toward Devyl. "Don't know why I said that, Captain. Must be the witch a'witching my tongue."

Devyl rolled his eyes at the sorry lot of them. "Sure of that." His tone carried the full weight of his sarcasm.

"So what's with the feathers?" Kalder picked one up from the deck to hand it to Devyl. "Not sure why it was worth the risk of attracting the witch's notice for so paltry a thing."

Before Devyl could answer, it was Belle who stepped forward and volunteered it. "Why, Mr. Dupree, ye might be able to swim with the fishes, but with what you have in your hand, the rest of us can fly with the birds."

"Pardon?"

Devyl nodded. "With those . . . we can cast a spell that will grant us flight. Forget relying on the winds to find your Miss Jack. We're going airborne to get to her. And this time, they won't be able to stop us from taking her back."

17

"He doesn't love you. You have to know that his kind is incapable of comprehending what you think of as love. It's beyond their ability."

Mara ignored Strixa's words as she went over the map in Du's room while waiting on him to join her there. "You know nothing about him."

Still in her owl form, she pinned those creepy red eyes on Mara. "I know his kind. As do you. They only value the goal and their people. You are a pawn to get what he wants. Worse? You're his enemy."

"And you are a troublemaker." Mara picked up Du's baldric from where he'd left it, draped across his chair. Hand-carved with intricate Celtic scrollwork, it was a piece of exquisite beauty. And a lot heavier than it appeared. Gracious! No wonder the man was so muscular, wearing things that weighed so much. "I won't allow you to come between us."

Strixa shook her fowl head. "I'm not the one who will come between you. He doesn't need my help in that. You two have broken a cardinal rule. Think you you'll be left alone to live in peace?"

That was honestly what she feared most. But she refused to show it to the creature. "I know what you're about and it's not working."

Yet in spite of her denials, it was, and she suspected the witch knew it as well as she did. Returning the baldric to the chair, Mara swallowed hard. Even if Du's flying spell worked, they still had a ways to go to get to the islands that made up the Quella.

Antillia shouldn't be that hard to get past . . . especially if they weren't in the water. It was policed by a group of fairymaids who were known to lure sailors to their deaths. They haunted the shoreline caves and rocks where they would call out for help, and when the unwary tried to lend a hand, the fey creatures would drown them. But so long as they didn't wreck the ship or find themselves forced to land near Antillia, nothing would happen. The fairymaids shouldn't come near them.

Of course, if they were flying it would put them directly in the path of the dragon clans who called Jesirat al-Tennyn home. In fact, that was what the island's name translated to—Dragon's Isle. Those vicious, bloodthirsty clans were highly territorial and wouldn't take kindly to anyone venturing near their lands. They barely tolerated one another.

Humans were seen as nothing more than snack food.

Then they'd have to get past Satanazes—the demon island that was nestled close enough they'd have to approach it from the sea. Some twenty leagues west of Antillia, it would be directly in their path and would be tricky, as demons always were. A mist covered the island and shielded their presence. Some claimed the mist itself was a demon.

The only ones who knew for certain were the unfortunate victims who'd been eaten or enslaved by the island's inhabitants. And none of them ever escaped to tell others what happened there.

As for the Meropis island, rumors claimed it was inhabited by flesh-eating, soul-sucking creatures who preyed on any dumb enough to venture there. They were worse than even the demons, and were said to be far more unholy.

Crueler.

Those vanishing islands were directly responsible for many of the legends that made up the Caribbean. The monsters and mysterious disappearances. It would be hypocritical of her to not believe in them, given that her own race could turn into and live as trees.

Still . . .

She knew how humans could also twist, turn, and expound on reality. So what was told and what actually existed could be radically different. A little truth went a long way in an overactive imagination and the overblown legends people told for attention.

Suddenly, she felt the air behind her stirring. A smile spread across her lips at the rich masculine scent that warmed her an instant before Du wrapped his arms around her and pressed his cheek to hers.

"Sorry it took so long to get away. Janice took more convincing than I thought to get her to leave for Santiago's crew. But she'll be safer there for the time being."

Closing her eyes, she savored the sensation of being engulfed by him. And a part of her wanted to kick herself at the centuries she'd deprived them of that could have been spent like this. And for what?

Vanity? Stupidity? Stubbornness?

Things that no longer seemed to matter.

"Is anything amiss?"

He glanced to Strixa. "Nay. Not where I'm concerned. What treachery has the she-bitch wrought?"

"Pardon?"

He stepped back. "If she's anything like Vine, I shudder at what lies, doubts, or half-truths she's filled your head with in my absence."

Strixa squawked indignantly at his words.

Mara laughed. "Fear not. I didn't listen."

"Good. Because the only one to hear is me."

But as he leaned against his desk to study the map, her gaze went to his battle-scarred hand that toyed with the hilt of the dagger that held the parchment in place. In spite of her bold words otherwise, doubt played in her head.

Worse? It played in her heart.

Strixa was right. Du was a creature of extreme and utter violence. Love didn't come easily or naturally to him. It was an alien concept. As foreign to him as generational war was to her. While she knew it existed, she wanted no part of it and didn't really understand those who partook of it or why they did so.

And in that moment, she didn't see the loyal pirate captain in front of her. She saw the ancient warlord, covered in blood and dressed in his black armor. Saw his black braids and beard. The arrogance of his swagger as he returned from war and strode through their hall to claim Vine while his bloodlust still colored his cheeks.

Reveling in his war and conquest, he'd been terrifying. His ferocity such that even the trained war hounds had fled, yelping, at his approach.

Indeed, the air around him now, as then, sizzled with his unholy power and raw determination. It reached out like a living, breathing entity to cause the hair on the back of her arms to rise. The mere fact that he could effortlessly hold a witch as powerful as Strixa . . .

I'm a corymeister. Du's words went through her head. He was the strongest sorcerer of his kind. No one could touch him when it came to the ability to bend the natural laws.

Mara went ramrod stiff as that brought a new, horrifying thought in its wake. What if her feelings were nothing more than another spell he'd cast? How would she ever know the difference?

Was any of this real?

He glanced up and caught her gaze. "Mara?"

She offered a smile and prayed he couldn't sense it was false. "Aye, sorry. Was lost in my thoughts. Did you ask something?"

Suspicion clouded his gaze, as if he knew she was lying, but wasn't quite sure about what.

"Are you all right?"

"Fine. Worried about that coming conflict."

That seemed to placate him. He glanced toward Strixa. "No fears, my lady. So long as you put your faith where it belongs, all shall be well."

Mara wanted to believe that. Desperately. Yet she couldn't shake the ill feeling inside her that warned things were not what they seemed.

And that Vine had something in store for them that neither of them could predict.

Thorn cursed as he pulled back with his men before he lost another one to the demonic horde that was pouring through the breach from their realm into that of mankind.

Thankfully, this rupture was in the desert where no human was around to witness it. But it didn't make the dusk-lit battle any less bloody or intense.

"Gabriel!"

The Seraph general ducked barely before he would have lost his head to a sword stroke. Slightly taller than Michael, Gabriel was a huge bastard himself. In Seraph form, his darker complexion looked almost ashen, but his hair was every bit as white as the others', as were his wings and weapons. His gold armor was blinding in the dim light—a tactical advantage when battling demons whose eyes were sensitive from living in flame-lit darkness for so long.

And a damn annoyance for Thorn, who was one of them and yet on Gabriel's side for this conflict. Lifting his hand, he squinted to see past the brightness that sent waves of agony through his skull.

"They're slipping through to the right," he called out, warning Gabriel's soldiers to shore up the area where Thorn's men were growing thin.

Thorn cursed again as he realized how right Michael had been. This was far worse than he'd imagined. It wasn't just the Carian Gate that had failed.

Three had gone down.

The Cimmerian forces were stronger now than they'd been in centuries.

Thorn drove his blessed sword through the demon closest to him and took an unnatural pleasure at the sounds of its screaming. Normally, he'd only banish them back to their prisons. But today, he wasn't feeling merciful.

Today, he wanted blood and soul.

Most of all, he wanted to hear their cries of agony.

"What happened to cause this surge?" he asked Gabriel.

"The Malachai killed his son and absorbed new powers. When he did so, he broke the seals on the gates."

Growling, Thorn renewed his fight. That would do it. "Who was the mother?"

"A demon whore who wanted to get back into Noir's good graces. After the Malachai attacked her, she sought to barter the boy and Adarian's soul for her own freedom. Sad for the child when he tried to kill his father and learned firsthand that Adarian didn't let his fatherly devotion get in the way of his self-preservation."

Thorn rolled his eyes at that bit of common knowledge about the Malachai, and at the clichéd ploy too many she-demons had used throughout the centuries to try and bring Adarian down. It was what had made the Malachai demon so incredibly powerful and dangerous. Because the Malachai alone took on the memories and powers of all his predecessors whenever he came of age and assumed his role as head badass, he became stronger with each generation. The current Malachai, Adarian, had lasted longer than any before him.

Lucky for humanity, Adarian hated Noir and Azura—the two primal gods he served and was bound to—and had escaped them to hide in the mortal realm. So long as Adarian remained free and apart from them here in the human plane, the world wouldn't end. But if he were to ever make amends with them, or a she-demon ever mothered a Malachai son who could take down Adarian and assume his father's powers and those of the previous Malachai . . .

Thorn would definitely kiss up to his father and sell out the world. It would be the only way to survive the ensuing holocaust.

That was what they all feared. The one Malachai who was prophesied to end the world and bring about the eternal reign of the demons.

Still, with that being said, the thought of Adarian absorbing new powers was even more terrifying to Thorn. Because sooner or later, whenever Adarian thought he had enough strength to pull off a coup, he'd go after Noir and Azura to get his complete freedom from the two of them, and that battle wouldn't be any better for the world.

Might even be worse, given Adarian's inherent sense of entitlement and hatred.

Worse still, his bloodlust.

And Thorn ought to know. He'd been caught up in the previous such war that had almost ended all existence as humanity knew it. Because win, lose, or draw, the Malachai would not go back into his box, and Noir and Azura lacked the powers to kill him. They could only enslave their favorite pet.

Which was also part of the prophecy.

One day, the Malachai would slay the gods of old and replace them all. And once they were gone, and their curse with them, their Malachai demon would reign as the supreme power of the universe and rebuild his bloodline.

Another army of Malachai would rise and no one would be able to stand against them.

Neither god, nor man. Nor any preternatural creature.

They would all burn and kowtow to him.

The only hope was an obscure legend of the Excambiare Malachai. Like the firstborn Malachai, known as Monakribos, this one would be conceived from an equal share of the light and dark powers. Whereas Monakribos held a father of light and a mother of dark, the Excambiare would have a mother of light and a Malachai father of utter darkness.

The Excambiare's birth would complete the Malachai cycle and restore the balance that had been shifted by the thousands of Malachai who'd come along after Monakribos. It would break the curse that had been placed on the Malachai bloodline by the primal gods, and shatter the Malachai's Cimmerian bonds. He would be free to serve himself, and no longer be bound solely to evil.

After all these centuries, the Malachai would exist as a fully balanced creature.

Regression to the mean. It was, after all, what the universe ever endeavored to achieve. And as one of those chosen tools it used to maintain such a balance, Thorn was well used to the games the universe played.

But no one really believed in the legend. Mostly because of how a Malachai was conceived.

They were born from acts of extreme and utter violence. It was why their mothers were almost always demons. Humans rarely survived sex with their hated breed, and the Malachai avoided the gods because divinity tended to heap even more curses upon their already damned bloodline.

So the concept of a birth mother born on the side of light, loving her Malachai child, was inconceivable and about as likely as Thorn embracing his father and having a beer with the beast.

Of course, it didn't help that as soon as any child of Adarian's reached the age of puberty and showed any signs of holding a Malachai's powers, Adarian slaughtered him and ate the boy's abilities whole.

The last time that had happened, it'd been bloody enough.

Now . . .

"How is Adarian so strong if he's not living with Noir and Azura?"

Gabriel grimaced as he killed the demon in front of him and swung around to face Thorn. "Like the parasite he is, he feeds on human hatred and violence. God knows, there's plenty of that to go 'round. He's found a way to channel it to his own powers, so when he slaughtered this most recent child, some of the gates crashed."

"And his generals?"

"So far, none of them have escaped their prisons to rush to his side. Let us pray it remains so."

Definitely. That was the last thing they needed on top of this mess—the release of the Riders of the Apocalypse.

Yeah, he'd like to avoid dealing with those pissed-off bitches for a bit longer.

"I have to warn Bane and the others."

Gabriel caught Thorn's arm as he started to withdraw. "You know the rules. You interfere now and you'll end their parole."

Thorn's jaw went slack. "What of Michael's medallion?"

"You can return it later. But for now . . ." Gabriel swept his gaze over the desert battlefield where they were slowly losing more ground. "We need you here."

Thorn scoffed. "Sarim asking for *my* help? Seriously?"

Yet this was what he'd always wanted. For them to accept him as one of them. Still, he knew not to put any faith in this day or their truce that wouldn't last. This was nothing more than necessity. There was no true camaraderie here. No love.

He wasn't one of them and they all knew it. But it was a chance to prove to them that he wasn't the backbiting piece of his shit his father had been.

So he'd stay and fight.

However, as stated, he wasn't the backbiting piece of shit his father had been. And he wasn't about to leave the Deadmen out to hang either. Not with what was coming through this gate, or with the Carian. Not while they were depending on him to keep them notified and safe. He would never abandon his own men. In spite of his genes and what others thought of him.

Rules and codes be damned. They were his friends.

More than that, his Hellchasers were the closest thing to a family he'd ever known and he'd die before he let any of them down.

Falling back into the shadows of a palm tree, he used his powers to summon his sharoc companion. "Sorza!"

As dark as the sorrow she was named for, she appeared by his side. A mere wisp only he could see.

Thorn pulled the medallion from his pocket and handed it to her. "I need you to take this to Devyl. He'll know what to do with it. And tell him that I haven't abandoned him. I'll be in touch as soon as I can."

She scowled. "You're bidding me to do good?"

"I am."

That only baffled her more. But she faded away and left him to continue his fight.

Thorn lifted his shield and chased after a demon that was flying for Adidiron's back. He didn't get far before the demon turned to face him with a snide grin that was all too familiar.

Paimon.

Damn him.

"Hello, my son."

Thorn shuddered at his "friendly" greeting. "Don't call me that."

"Why? It's what you are, aren't you?"

Thorn curled his lip. "Just because you carried my father's sperm doesn't make us related. Really, Paimon . . . you're just a two-bit pimp doing whatever you're told."

"That makes your mother a whore, does it not?"

Thorn dodged the sword strike that would have severed his head had it made contact. "Your words are as clumsy as your fighting skills. My mother sold her soul to conceive me. That's an undeniable fact. Call her what you will. Makes no never mind where I'm concerned."

Mostly because his mother had hated him the moment he'd been born over said bargain. And Thorn hated everyone who'd had a hand in his conception—his mother, father, Jaden, Paimon, and Lucifer. End of the day, they'd all taken turns screwing him.

Which was nothing compared to what his stepfather had done the day he'd learned of their bargain. And the fact that his "beloved son and heir" wasn't really his, but rather a cruel hoax played on his gullible stupidity by a conniving bitch and her demon lover so that she could maintain her position and her lover could connive to steal his throne.

Aye, Thorn still had those scars.

Outside and in.

It was why he fought so hard now. No one should be used by others for their own gain. Damned because someone else was selfish and had sold them out without any regard for what it would mean to them once the truth became known. He'd had no choice in what had been done to him.

That anger and hatred had turned him into a monster at a time in his human existence when he should have been carefree and looking forward to a life well spent. Instead, he'd become the very thing his stepfather had wanted him to be—had trained him to be.

The fiercest warlord to ever lead his army over blood-saturated fields. And his stepfather's head had been one of the first Thorn had claimed as a trophy—payback for the betrayal of casting him aside so very brutally over something he couldn't help.

There, for a time, Thorn had been content and happy to play the beast, and slaughter everything he came into contact with.

Until the day he'd seen himself for what he really was. And that sight still haunted him in a way no demon or monster ever could. For he knew the truth.

He was the scary thing that gave grown men and ruthless demons nightmares.

But never again.

Thorn raked a sneer over Paimon's horned, ghastly form. "Crawl home, you fetid bastard. Slither into your pit and stay there until you find some semblance of decency."

Paimon laughed in his face. "You've been corrupted by humanity. How can you put faith in something so pathetic and weak?"

He smirked. "We live by faith. Not by sight or proof."

"How can you have faith after the way they've turned on you and done you?"

Shrugging, Thorn answered with the simple truth. "The testing of faith produces perseverance, and faith without action is worthless."

Paimon shrieked in his face. "And so are you!"

I'm not so sure about this spell of yours, Du." Mara's eyes widened as she saw the size of the raven he'd convinced to lift them up and carry them. "When you said we'd fly, I thought you meant without additional aid."

He smiled at her. "Nay, my precious *blodwen*. But fret never. It's not what you're thinking. We couldn't be in better talons. Trust me."

Famous last words, that. She wasn't sure if anyone could control something *this* large. And he refused to tell her exactly how he'd conjured this giant beast of a bird.

Even Belle appeared skeptical as they all gathered on deck to stare up at the fowl above them. With massive talons, it gripped the railings and lifted them through a sky as dark as the bird itself. Her heart pounding in fear, she clutched at the rope nearest her and gulped.

The wind from its wings whipped against them. Cool and pleasant over the heat, yet disturbing in that it was so unnatural.

William glanced over to Bart. "Thinking of feeding Roach to this beast as well?"

"How'd you guess it?"

"The expression on your face. You're quite transparent."

Roach passed a less than amused glare at the pair of them that forced Mara to press her lips together to keep from laughing. But she deeply appreciated their humor, given the severity of this, and her trepidation over it.

Only Duel seemed at ease. Damn him for that confidence. But then nothing ever seemed to rattle the beast.

Her heart in her throat, she tightened her grip. As if sensing her unease, Du moved to stand behind her. "It'll be fine. I trust our raven."

Problem was, she didn't. How could she? She knew nothing of the creature or where it came from.

Worried, she turned toward Duel and the comfort he offered. Honestly, what she wanted most was to walk into his arms and have him hold her again. To bury her face against his chest and let the scent of his skin soothe her until it drove away the last bit of her fear and turmoil.

And still a part of her was scared to be so close to him, for he was every bit as dangerous to both her sanity and reason.

He met her gaze and frowned. "What?" The word was more a bark than a question, and that, right there, was part of her fear about this. He was ever unpredictable.

Swallowing, she glanced up at the bird, then down to the man who controlled it. "Have you ever been afraid?"

He reached to touch her hair, and hesitated as if he realized suddenly what he was doing and how many stood near enough to see. "Aye. Many times."

She couldn't imagine it. Not Duel. He was always so confident and in charge of himself. She'd never really seen true fear from him. Not like what other men showed. "Name me one time."

"Every time I reach for you," he whispered against her ear. "I'm terrified you'll rebuff me."

She started to scoff at his answer, until she caught the sincerity in those dark eyes. "How could you ever fear me?"

"I don't fear you, Mara. I fear the power you hold that reduces me to your mindless servant."

"You flatter me."

"I only speak the truth. Had you ever once looked at me, you would have seen it plainly. Vine knew it, and it's why I never held her full loyalty or her heart." And with that, he stepped away to check on the others.

Tears welled in her eyes as she choked on the pain in her throat that his own anguished words had wrought. She wanted to call it a lie. To say he was playing her falsely and trying to weaken her.

She couldn't.

Because in the back of her mind, she saw him as he'd been. The times their gazes had met over the years when they'd lived in Tintagel and he'd sobered as if someone had punched him. More than that, she remembered the way he'd rush to her side if she ever felt ill or needed something. Even leaving her sister during such instances.

Aye, it had infuriated Vine whenever he did such. Many times, she'd gone into a fetid rage at them both. Du had ignored her tirades and Mara had dismissed them as part of her sister's unreasonable jealousy. It was ever part of Vine's personality that she could become incensed over the smallest of things. So she'd thought nothing of it then.

But now . . .

Mara remembered the first time she'd appeared in Duel's court after he'd brought her home with him. . . .

"She's a Deruvian whore! I say we should get some entertainment from the wench for the trouble they've put us through! Let us all have a turn at the bitch! We've earned it for the blood we've lost."

Duel had ruthlessly gutted the soldier faster than she could blink. Faster than anyone, even said gutted man, could anticipate. Indeed, he'd been in the midst of his next sentence when Duel had struck without warning.

His sword coated with the man's blood while the poor man had gasped his last breath, Duel had glared at the gathered nobles and warriors inside his dark, somber hall. "Anyone else takes issue with the lady, they take issue with me. You will respect her and speak to her as if she were one of our own. And a queen, no less. Never let me catch anyone near her, for *any* reason, or else I'll make you wish your own mother had gutted you the moment she made the mistake of whelping you."

Mara had assumed those growled words were motivated by the fact she'd bound their lives together and he feared them killing her out of ignorance and spite, and ending his life in the process.

Now . . .

She winced as she realized how stupid she'd been. How unkind and selfish. But how could she have known he felt anything more than hatred for her, given what she'd done? That his protection of her had stemmed from something far more tender than his own self-preservation?

I'm such a fool.

Belle came up and touched her shoulder. "Let the past go, mum. 'Tis a fleeting shadow that can never be captured."

"I'm so mad at myself, Lady Belle."

"I feel that pain that lives in your heart, Mara. Think you there's not a one here who isn't a refugee from that monster called Past? On the surface, it appears we bartered our souls for another chance at freedom, but the truth is we're all hoping to find something we can hold on to that will kill that beast inside us. Something to quell our guilt and conscience. *That* is what we're hoping to salvage. Not our souls. Just our sanity."

She squeezed Belle's hand. "You're a good friend. Much better than I deserve."

"Nay. You never want to know what caused me to be damned, mum. Suffice it to say, I'm grateful the captain approved me pardon when Thorn offered him my service. Not many what would, given my crimes." She glanced around to the others. "He sees more than you credit him with."

"How do you mean?"

"Think about it. Thorn gave him the ability to veto any member of this crew for any reason, no questions asked. Makes you wonder what Captain Bane saw in this sorry lot that he thought us worth redeeming, doesn't it?" She jerked her chin toward the wheel. "And Sancha, you know why she drinks?"

Mara shook her head.

"She left her daughter alone with the man what fathered her, but he didn't want to be a father. Truth was, back then Sancha didn't want to be a mother, either. Not until she got home from carousing with friends only to find her daughter dead by the unfeeling hand of the blackguard she'd entrusted with her care. Too late, she realized how much she did love her girl, and that she didn't really mind the responsibility of motherhood, after all."

Her eyes filling with tears, Mara gasped at the horror poor Sancha must have faced that night. No wonder she was so harsh now. "What did she do?"

"Without a single word, she calmly picked up his flintlock and shot him where he sat. They say they found her sitting in her daughter's nursery, holding the babe while still coated in her husband's blood. Don't think she's been sober since. Because whenever she is, she sees her daughter's face and blames herself solely for what happened. And she can't bear the guilt of it. It's why she took on the name Sancha Delarosa—holy lady of sorrow. Her real name was Maria Esmeralda de la Vega y Tarancón. Or more to the point, *Donna* Maria Esmeralda de la Vega y Tarancón."

"She was a noblewoman?"

Nodding, Belle pressed her hand against the amulet she never removed from her neck. "And Kalder . . . he was mixed up in all kinds of evil in his day. Because of who and what he is, he thought himself above all human law."

"They caught him?"

Belle shook her head. "Those he'd cheated mistook his honest brother for him. Beat the poor lad to death in his stead."

Wincing, Mara ground her teeth at the sheer misery that must haunt the poor merman. "Did they find him, too, after they took his brother? Is that how he died?"

"Nay. Unlike his brother, he was a brawler, through and through. They'd have never taken him in a fight. Was his own mother what did it, when Kalder came home to pay respects. She said it was only right he join his brother in death, as he was the reason his brother had been on the docks that day. Apparently, Kalder had been wanting to meet with him for some scheme he had planned, and had gotten distracted by a buxom maid. So while his brother lay dying from the beating he should never have had, unable to get help, Kalder was occupied with baser needs."

Mara felt sick to her stomach. It explained much about the Myrcian. "That's why he's been celibate."

Belle nodded. "Because of the guilt, he's not wanted to go near another woman. Not until our Miss Jack. So while he might be flirting with one, he never sees the deed through."

"Now he blames himself for what happened to her."

"Aye."

Mara glanced around as a shiver went down her spine. "Why are you telling me all of this?"

"I wanted you to remember that the cross each of us bears isn't truly the one that be on our wrists. 'Tis the one of guilt we carry inside our hearts. And while those two cut to the bone, they are nothing compared to the double-crosses of our trusted friends and family that scorch us soul deep. That is what the red jack we fly truly stands for, Mara. A fanged skull to remind us of the eternal bite that comes from such nasty treachery. And the ribbon 'round it is the captain's eternal promise that he will never betray us. No matter what, he will keep faith and be at our backs through whatever nightmarish hell comes our way."

"Captain!" Kat's voice rang out from the crow's nest high above her head, interrupting Belle's words. "Incoming!"

So accustomed to the sea holding all their incoming threats, it took Mara a moment to realize that wasn't what he was warning them about.

Nay, this threat came from the skies.

There was a group of dragons, and they were headed straight for them.

18

"Paden?" Cameron crawled toward her brother on trembling arms and knees that threatened to give way at any moment. He was so battered and bruised that she barely recognized him. Yet even through the misshapenness of his features and his strangely pale hair, she'd know him anywhere.

Or so she thought.

No sooner had she reached him than he looked up with coal black eyes that were shot through with bloodred veins. He hissed at her, baring fangs.

Shrieking, she pulled back. "What have they done to you!"

He let out an inhuman growl as he slid across the floor after her like a rabid dog intent upon her utter destruction.

Terrified and unwilling to hurt him, she shrank into the corner and held her arms up to protect herself as best she could. Tears welled in her eyes. She whispered a prayer of protection. "In the name of St. Michael, dear God, deliver me from evil. Preserve me from violence and set Your shield around my body. In the name of the Father. The Son. And the Holy Spirit! Please, Paden, please! Mercy!"

His breathing ragged, he paused an instant before he would have ripped out her throat. Drool dripped from his fangs to her neck while he hovered so close that his rancid breath scorched her flesh. "Cammy?" Her name was an anguished whisper.

"Aye, brother."

He let out a sob so deep that it seemed to come from the very bowels of his soul. His body shaking, he gathered her into his arms and clutched her tight against him while he wept tears of blood.

"Ah, how precious and sweet."

Paden tightened his grip on her to the point of pain. A heartbeat later, his wings sprang from his back. When he tried to rise, the demons grabbed his chains and dragged him away from her, then slammed him to the ground.

She tried to help, but the voluptuous woman in bloodred armor used her powers to drive her back against the wall. And held her there with an ease that infuriated Cameron.

*Tsk*ing, she smirked. "Now, now, little spawns of Michael, we can't be having any of this."

"Let her go, Gadreyal!" Paden growled. "This has nothing to do with her!"

"Oh, but it does. And had you wanted her left alone, you should have cooperated. Now . . ." She let out an evil, insidious laugh. "We shall play a little game called Plant the Seed. One of you will carry it, but neither of you will know who it is. At least not until it takes root and grows to such a beast that it can't be defeated and it's too late to be stopped." Her laugh echoed in the room. "Aye. I'll have the head of Dón-Dueli, and the spawn of Michael will be the one who brings it to me."

Her laughter died an instant later when a demon manifested behind her and whispered in her ear. "What?" she growled.

"Aye, my lady. They've broken through and are approaching the gate."

Her features turned to stone. "Gather my army. 'Tis time we returned Thorn's Deadmen to the hell that spawned them."

Using his thoughts, Devyl commanded the raven to set them down on the sea barely a heartbeat before the dragons began their vicious attacks. Their incendiary breath lit the sky as they sought to sink the ship. Fireballs exploded all around.

In a bright flash of light, the raven transformed back into Simon Dewing, which startled the rest of the crew, as they realized Devyl had used the witch's feathers for a spell to enlarge their striker's alternate incarnation. As a shapeshifter, Simon had come in handy a number of times for certain tasks. But never more so than today.

Mara smirked at him. "You could have told us who the bird was, you know."

Winking, he cracked a rare smile at her. "And miss the look upon all your faces? What be the fun in that, love? Got to have some enjoyment in me death."

With a deep laugh, Simon moved to stand ready with Kat and Roach. He draped his arm around Kat, who shook his head at him and rolled his eyes.

"I should have known it was you."

"Aye, you should have. You'll never be hearing the end of it now. Didn't even miss me or ask after me. . . . And I saw the way you were eyeing Bart in me absence. Don't think I didn't. There'll be the devil to pay later over that, mark me words."

Kat jerked his head toward Bane. " 'Tis the other Devyl we have to pay right now that be worrying me most, me love."

Simon wrapped his arm around Kat's shoulders and pulled him close so that he could kiss the side of his head. "No worries. Ain't no one getting their hands on you but me. They'll have to come through me first." He unsheathed his sword and used his powers to ignite the blade.

Devyl and Bart took the first wave of dragons that flew in to attack the ship as William went to stand beside Mara so that he could protect her. Bart and Devyl deflected the dragons' fiery goo before it could land on deck or set the sails ablaze. Thank the gods that Bart and Will were as skilled with their magick as he was.

Their being Simeon Magi was one of the main reasons Devyl had approved Will and Bart as first mate and quartermaster for his crew. They were old school. Highly trained and deadly in just such encounters. While their astral hands were tied whenever they were around baretos, or uninitiated humans who knew nothing of the real preternatural threats that surrounded them, out here on the open water, among their own . . .

Bart and Will were every bit as lethal as he was, which was good, as he'd need them all to survive this day.

"Roll the long nines!" Devyl shouted to his gunners while he reviewed the best way to defend the ship and crew against their incoming threats.

Those would be their best *regular* defense. A demi-cannon wouldn't be accurate enough at the distance the dragons were flying and the culverins didn't shoot a heavy enough ball to penetrate dragon scales.

Aye, that load would only piss them off.

Same for their philosopher's fire. Since dragons breathed fire, it wasn't the most optimal weapon against them as they were heat-shielded for it. Their hides were thick and hard to pierce. Worse than trying to harpoon a whale with a sword. While it wasn't impossible to take down a dragon, it was a specialized skill and none on board were dragonslayers by trade.

Damn me for that oversight. He should have thought ahead on that.

But that was all right. Their gunners were all Aru Mages—courtesy of a most defiant Thorn. Normally, such demonic creatures were reserved by the Sarim only for Necrodemians. And they would be all kinds of furious to find them on board the *Sea Witch* at Devyl's command.

Why? Because they were a secret weapon the Hell-Hunters

didn't want to fall into the hands of their enemies under any circumstance. A special breed of demon, an Aru Mage was capable of assuming any metallic shape or object a Necrodemian might need for battle against the Cimmerian horde.

And it was an advantage that might allow them to emerge victorious this day.

Throwing his fire, Devyl brought down one dragon, which only angered another.

Just how had the beasts seen the ship, anyway? They had all been using their powers to conceal their presence as they headed into the dragons' territory. It made no sense. None of them should have seen a single thread of sail. His answer came a few seconds later when bloodred clouds parted and he saw the other winged creatures flying beside their enemies. . . .

I should have known.

"Iri!" he shouted to warn his men so that they could prepare.

These were the Seraphim who'd turned against their brethren—or the children of those betrayers who'd chosen to fight with their fathers and mothers against Gabriel and his Kalosum warriors—they were what the Necrodemians had been created specifically to fight.

And they were a lot more powerful than the demons Devyl's crew had been recruited to return to their respective dimensions. These were the top-level commanders. The most powerful of their kind.

More than that, they'd once been Devyl's allies.

He cursed as he saw Gadreyal leading them. She was a nasty piece of work. The kind of demonic creature no man wanted to meet alone.

Except for Devyl. He relished a good fight with an equal opponent.

In particular, he wanted a piece of her highly attractive ass to mount to his wall for what she'd done to him. Right next to his ex-wife's head.

"Gadreyal!" he called, summoning her away from his men as the cannons turned from firing on the dragons to aim at the new threat.

The moment she saw him, her eyes lit up to a vibrant red and she dove for him straight away. While he'd been damned, she'd been his primary torturer. They had centuries of mutual hatred they'd nursed against each other.

She bypassed his men and left her dragons and soldiers behind to deal with the rest and the cannon fire so that she could take Devyl on personally.

Good thing, that. It was enough to make him smile.

"Well, well," she sneered, flapping her wings. "If it isn't my favorite toy." She unsheathed her sword. "Ready to give me what I want now?"

"I'm not imprisoned here, Gaddy." He blasted her.

Shrieking, she landed before him and attacked.

Devyl caught and deflected her thrust with his own sword and advanced with the skill that had won him countless battles. He wasn't bound by chains now, nor weakened by all-out starvation. While he might not still be up to full strength, he was a lot stronger than he'd been in centuries.

She was in for a full-on battle and he was ready to give it to her with everything he had—mage fire, fangs, and swordplay.

From the corner of his eye, he checked his men, who were

locked in similar fights with the rest of her forces while cannon blasts rocked the ship beneath their feet and deafened him. Luckily, his crew seemed to be holding their own.

Good. He didn't want any distractions. He only wanted her head on a pike.

Gadreyal *tsk*ed at him. "Be a good boy, Duel. Surrender and we'll make it easy on all of you. Surely you want to be on the right side of the conflict again?"

"You planning to give me Vine's throat for it?"

"You know better. I can't do that."

Well, that ended that discussion then. And any thoughts he had of ever switching sides.

Not that it'd really crossed his mind. He'd given his loyalty to Thorn. And unlike the others, he never went back on his word.

He swung for her head and blasted her with his fire.

Sadly, she ducked and returned with a shot of her own.

He went skidding across the deck on his shoulder. Damn, that hurt. Rolling to his feet, he shook the pain off and ignored the sight of the smeared blood he'd left behind on the boards. By God, he wasn't about to let any sort of agony get in the way of his fight.

Or his victory.

Gadreyal laughed as she launched herself to flight and landed before him. "You haven't asked me about your little Seraph. Have you forgotten her so soon?"

His blood ran cold at the mention of Cameron. "What have you done?"

Throwing her head back, she laughed. "*I've* done nothing. But she lacked your fortitude. Then again, most do."

Rage clouded his sight. "If you've harmed her—"

"Harmed?" She interrupted him. "I made her more powerful and reunited her with her precious brother. How is that a harm? It's what she wanted and better than you gave her."

Bellowing in rage, he advanced on her with a renewed vigor, even though he knew it was all kinds of stupid. It was what she wanted. Only calm rationale won a fight. But he couldn't stop the fury inside him that wanted to feast on her entrails.

Not when he was the one who'd brought Cameron into this. She wouldn't have been near this she-bitch but for him. He was directly responsible for her.

Gadreyal *tsk*ed in his face. "Poor Duel. You can't even sell your soul to right this. Tell me? Was your bargain worth it?"

"Release Miss Jack!" he growled between gritted teeth.

"You don't have the power to command me."

"Mayhap not, but I do have the power to crush you." He blasted her and sent her reeling.

Now *that* made him smile.

Until she rose up in her serpent form and gathered a group of her companions to her. In a giant cloud like swarming bees, they arched before him, then tumbled down to kill him in one massive wave.

Mara fell to her knees as she struggled to keep the ship upright under the fierce assault. William stood by her side, driving away the Irin who was attacking them.

We're not going to make it. She didn't say the words out loud, but she felt them deep inside.

And it terrified her. What were they going to do? She didn't see any way to drive the beasts back. There were just too many of them. Every heartbeat, they appeared to multiply.

While the Deadmen couldn't, in theory, die, they could be overrun, and that was quickly happening.

"Get Mara below! Protect her!" Du's voice was a fierce, stabilizing growl above the sounds of war.

And his words caused a surge of tenderness to rush through her as she rolled with the ship. Even now when his thoughts should be on his own survival, they were on her welfare.

In that moment, she saw him the day they'd met. Saw the look on his face as he hesitated to harm her. His dark eyes haunted and furious.

For the first time, she fully understood what Belle had told her. What the Deadman's Cross on their arms really meant.

Blood and bone, Devyl Bane would give it all to see them safe and their souls returned so that they could have their lives back. So long as there was breath inside his body, he would fight for them.

He would fight for her.

Her gaze went to him and his battle with the one Irin who hated him most. Long before Vine had killed Du, Gadreyal had wanted Duel's head for the simple fact that he'd shown her up and won favor in the war against Thorn and his army. Until Duel, Gadreyal had been the premier Cimmerian general in Britain. The chosen one of the ancient dark gods, and they'd doted on her for it. Yet in no time, he'd surpassed her success rate.

No one could match Duel's ferocity.

But as Mara watched them, she saw that he was still weak from his earlier attack. Because of the conditions of his release that forbade him from consuming human blood or the hearts of his enemies, he hadn't been feeding properly and therefore couldn't heal as fast as he should. His Aesir lineage held certain dietary necessities that were deemed rather gory to those unfamiliar with their race. Things she'd judged him for over the centuries.

And Gadreyal knew it too. She was taking no mercy on him as she drove him back against the railing.

If they didn't do something, Gadreyal would defeat him and return him to the hell Thorn had spared him from.

"Help him, William!"

He hesitated. "No offense, mum, but he'll have me head if I leave your side. And he's a mite big blighter with an awful temper. I'd rather not test it right when he's already upset, if you know what I mean. And I'm rather fond of me bullocks. I'd like to be keeping them a bit longer, if you don't mind."

Biting her lip, she debated what to do. To attack Gadreyal would be all manner of stupid. Unlike her, the Irin had been born to battle. She had even more experience than Duel did.

With no better idea, Mara lowered her chin and used her powers to smack Gadreyal with the mast.

It worked. Tucking her wings down, she stumbled away from Duel with a foul curse.

Proud of herself, Mara headed for Du, intending to check on him. She didn't make it.

Something grabbed her from behind and sent her sprawling. . . .

Devyl ran as he saw the demon tackle Mara. His heart pounding in fear for her safety, he leapt for them and, while airborne, took the bastard's head with one stroke of his sword for daring to touch her. He landed on the deck and rolled, making sure to grab Mara and pull her with him out of harm's way.

They came to rest at the side of the ship, with her on top of him.

"Are you all right?" he breathed.

"Aye. You?"

He nodded. "Why aren't you below like I said?"

"You know I don't follow your orders worth a damn."

Her teasing tone made him smile in spite of the danger they were in and undermined the anger he wanted to feel. He dropped his gaze to her parted lips and wished fervently they weren't in battle.

No sooner had that thought gone through his mind than Gadreyal's troops pulled back.

Shite! This can't be good. Dreading the sudden turn of events, he rose gently with Mara in his arms to face whatever hell-storm was coming for them. He kept one arm on her waist while he braced himself.

In spite of the continued cannon fire, the dragons circled above, spewing fire down at them that Bart and William deflected. Fierce waves rocked against the ship.

A screeching shriek came out from beneath the waves, letting him know that the Carian Gate wasn't the one that had broken. Nay, something far, far worse had happened.

There were three major gates that led to Gehyne, or Azmodea as it was originally known. The land most of his crew would call hell. One was located in the desert. One in Jerusalem.

The third in the sea.

Because of the evil they held back from the world—because mankind could *never* protect themselves from the vile creatures who called that place home—the portals had been set and locked so that they couldn't be broken.

Or so they thought.

And to secure them even more, no one had ever known their exact locations.

Until now.

That was what was coming up from below.

Devyl cursed as he understood what was happening. Through Paden and Cameron, they had access to Michael's blood. With it, the Cimmerian forces would have had the means to open any portal in any realm. Even those most sacred, secured gates.

And to think, I handed it to the futtocking bastards. . . .

If the world ended, he was the moron to blame.

Worse, the *Sea Witch* was currently taking on water and listing to port. The boards creaked around them, letting him know that she was in mortal danger. Afraid for Mara, who wouldn't be able to stand much more assault, he turned toward her. "Separate yourself."

"What?"

"You heard me, woman. For once in your stubborn life, do as I say and be about it quickly. Pull out of the ship completely. Let the bastards have it before they use it to destroy you."

To his utter amazement, she did so without any further argument. Which told him exactly how much pain she was in and holding back from him.

And he knew the moment she pulled her consciousness from the wood. Color returned to her cheeks as her strength flooded back into her body.

Grateful that at least one of them was recovering from this searing assault, he kissed her forehead. "Thank you."

"What are you planning to do?"

His gaze went past her, to the very visage of all futtocking hell realms that was rising from the sea and headed straight for them. Mara hadn't seen it yet, and for that he was truly grateful.

So he gave her a cocky grin. "Best you not be asking me questions that have answers guaranteed to upset you, me *blodwen*."

"Meaning?"

"Duel!"

Mara's cheeks paled again as she heard Vine's low growl.

The ship tilted more, sending half the crew to the edge and some over, into the water.

"Enough of this." Devyl felt his eyes change over as he summoned up every last bit of his powers and did the one thing he'd sworn he'd never do.

But drastic times called for drastic measures. If Vine wanted a battle, let it be on solid ground where they couldn't drown his men.

Stepping around Mara, he sent a blast toward Vine and hated that he missed her as she ducked it. "Och now, Vine, you always wanted to be me queen." He gave her a cold smile. "See you in Alfheim, if you dare it."

And with that, he ruptured the very membrane of the human world and opened the door that was guaranteed to get him into all manner of shite later.

So be it.

The only thing that mattered to him was keeping everyone safe. He'd gotten his crew into this. By the gods, he'd get them out, whatever it took.

And if the dragons wanted to follow . . .

The Adoni Fey had their own special breed there that would be waiting to swallow them whole.

Screams filled his ears as his men were sucked through the swirling darkness and carried away from the realm they'd known and into that of his grandfather's people.

God help us all.

Devyl had no idea what kind of reception they'd receive upon arrival. What they would find waiting on the other side. It was forbidden to do what he'd done. He wasn't technically one of his grandfather's people anymore, and his mother had brought them all into a war that had caused every one of them to be cursed.

Aye, this most likely wasn't going to end well for him. . . .

He just hoped he was the only one who suffered for his rash decision.

Suddenly, he stopped falling and landed hard against a solid surface. With a fierce groan, he opened his eyes to find himself in a strange meadow. All around them was purple wheat that seemed as if it had a mind of its own.

He glanced about to make sure everyone was here. While most of them had regained their feet, there were a couple who'd been wounded and had decided that sprawled flat upon the ground was more their suited style at present. Their repose was punctuated by unctuous moans and complaints—mainly against him and their concerns about his current mental state. Even more about the state of his parents' marriage at the time of his birth.

Not that he blamed them. First, he was beginning to doubt his own reasoning skills. Because, face it, he was the one what brought them here.

Secondly, he'd like to stretch out himself. Damn for being captain and having to set an example. Times like this, he was tempted to promote Death or Meers to his position.

If only he could follow orders.

And speaking of those incapable of listening to others, Mara approached him with a stern countenance he was sure had terrified lesser men. It was so fierce, it even shriveled a bit of his own personal anatomy. "You've brought us to Alfheim? Are you mad? Answer me honestly, is there any semblance of sanity left inside you at all? Or did that knock on the head from Gadreyal spill it all out?"

"I thought it the safest place from your sister."

"And what about the ship?"

No doubt it was at the bottom of the ocean by now. He just hoped Santiago and his crew didn't follow it down to the locker. Hopefully, they'd seen enough to know to stay back, and as far away as possible. Since Devyl hadn't seen even so much as a sail from them during the fighting, he was praying it meant that Rafe's mother's magick had kept his crew shielded from all the hell that had rained down on them.

"Warned you to separate yourself from it."

"Aye," she said with a note of hysteria in her voice. "That you did. Had I known it was for this bit of lunacy, however, I'd have refrained. Just to . . ."

Her voice trailed off as she glanced over his shoulder to see something in the distance. The color washed out of her face as her eyes widened.

What the bloody hell now?

More than a bit irritated, Devyl turned to face whatever fresh pandemonium was heading for them. And it was pandemonium indeed.

He winced the moment he saw the approaching horsemen and the standards that adorned them. Though in theory they weren't demons, there wasn't much difference between the two breeds. In fact, he'd rather deal with a demon than these particular cod dangles.

The irony that they still used his mother's family symbol of a tree and bird, white on black, wasn't lost on him.

With hair as white as snow and darker skin that fair glistened in the mystical sunlight of the realm, they were more beautiful than any creature ever spat out of the universal abyss.

And more loathsome and corrupt.

These were the Adoni. Known as fair elves to much of the world, they were the bane of Devyl's existence, as was evidenced by the male's name, which said it all about not only the Adoni, but the character of this particular bastard's family. . . .

Flaithrí Álfljótrsson.

Álfljótr, meaning "ugly elf" or "horrible" or "treacherous." That had been his father's name, hence the "-sson" added to the end of it. The mere fact a mother had given such a moniker to her child also spoke volumes about their family dynamics and why Devyl was such a bastard himself, given that the same blood flowed through his veins.

Devyl stepped past Mara to greet them away from his men. They slowed the instant they saw him. At first, he wasn't sure he was recognized.

Not until Flaithrí's gaze swept over his body and his eyes widened. He held his gloved hand up to stay the ten Adoni warriors who were with him.

William and Bart moved to stand at Devyl's back.

"Friend or foe, Captain?" William asked.

Devyl scratched at his chin as he considered how to answer. "Not sure." He narrowed his gaze on the riders. "So what's it to be, cousin Flowery? Are we friends?"

His nostrils flared. "Flah-ree," he ground out between clenched teeth in the lyrical accent that marked all of their race.

"As I said, Florian—"

"FLAH-ree!" he growled even louder.

William laughed. "Well then, nice to know I'm not the only one you antagonize in such a manner."

Devyl cut a menacing glare to him.

He held his hands up in surrender. "I'm not questioning your cantankerous nature, Captain. Far be it from me."

Crossing his arms, he returned his attention to the matter at hand. "So, cousin Flowery, what's it to be? Blood or wine?"

"I hate you, Dón-Dueli. Your mother should have drowned you the moment she went to wash the afterbirth from you."

"And yours should have fed you to her hounds."

Bart cleared his throat suddenly. "Um, Captain? Not questioning you in any way, sir. But is it wise to antagonize them so, given what's likely to show any second and renew what we just left?"

He passed an irritated smirk at Bart. "Given that I be the rightful king of the throne Flowery's father currently parks his arse upon, aye. I dare them to question me." He turned back to his cousin. "That not right, Flowery? Or have you finally found the bullocks to behead your father and come for me?"

He stiffened visibly in his saddle. "What would you have of me . . . Majesty?" The word was more insult than title of honor.

Ignoring the slight, Devyl glanced over his shoulder as he felt the hairs on the back of his neck rise.

Gadreyal was about to pierce the veil and come after them. He could feel it like a tangible touch on his skin.

"You might want to gather up some troops."

Flaithrí arched his brow. "Might I inquire as to why?"

No sooner had he asked the question than Devyl's enemies brought down the shield and found their way into his grandfather's realm.

Devyl smiled coldly at Flaithrí. "No particular reason, other than if you don't, you're going to have something a lot worse than me to worry about."

19

Devyl's men scrambled to their positions as the Iri broke through and spilled into the meadow behind them.

"Bloody hell," Flaithrí cursed as he stood in his stirrups to get a better look. Then he cast a hate-filled grimace down to Devyl. "Did you bring the whole lot of those fetid mongrels here?"

Unsheathing his sword, Devyl shrugged. "Left a few of the smaller ones behind. No need in being greedy."

Flaithrí began a rush of epithets for Devyl as he used his powers to summon his enchanted armor. He turned to his companion on the right. "Get to my father and summon the watch force. Tell him what we've got. Let's send these bastards back to where they crawled from."

His companion's dappling horse stretched out wings from its side. He backed the horse up and launched him into flight.

Devyl summoned his own armor. Now that they were out of the human realm, the rules of engagement were entirely different.

And they were entirely his.

"All right, me hearties! Let's show these futtocking bastards what we Deadmen be made of." He added fire to his own sword and made ready for battle.

Time for holding back was gone. They were on dry land and in the realm of his grandfather's people. If Vine and Gadreyal wanted a fight, he was more than ready to give it. . . .

With the full ferocity of his entire lineage burning deep within his heart and gullet. One thing about the Aesir, they caved to none, and nothing lit their fuses brighter than the promise of a good, coming brawl.

Mara grasped his arm as he started past her. "Duel?"

Pausing by her side, he waited for her to take him to task for his warring ways.

Instead, she offered him a winsome smile. "Kick their tossling arses. Don't get hurt."

He lifted the visor of his helm so that he could give her a quick kiss. He should probably show restraint before the others, especially given the amount of shocked gasps he heard, but in the event this was his last moment with her, he didn't want to die again with another regret.

Let his men know that he and Mara had finally put the past behind them and come to terms that were agreeable to them both.

Nay, they were better than agreeable. Better than anything he'd ever hoped to have.

And if he must die this day, he wanted to go back to his hell with the taste and feel of her lips fresh in his memory. Aye, with that, he could die in peace and be all right.

Mara fisted her hand in Duel's hauberk. It took everything she had to make herself let go, knowing he was about to face the Cimmerian army again. How strange that she'd once hated that enchanted black armor—had thought it the ugliest, most vile thing she'd ever laid eyes to. Now, she wished it were thicker and even more enchanted. Anything to keep him safe from harm.

So she added her own spell to it.

Please come back to me. Keeping herself together right now was the hardest thing she'd ever had to do. Especially when what she really wanted was to take on her tree form and wrap herself around him until she was an impenetrable cage that no one would break to get to him.

If only he'd allow it. . . .

His gaze scorched her as he pulled away and gently kissed her hand, then let go. It felt as if he ripped her heart out and carried it with him. Never had anything burned so badly.

Or cut so deep.

Without a word, he went toward Sallie.

"Ready to free your fighting soul, Mr. Lucas?"

"Be it safe here, Captain?"

"Indeed. If it wreaks havoc in this realm before, during, or after the battle, more's the merrier."

Sallie cracked a happy grin. "All right, then. Here's to me blessed mum and to all things what come of good rum!" He uncorked his bottle, and when he did, a fierce, shrieking wind tore out of it. One that quelled and captivated every Deadman near them.

Better still, it spooked Flaithrí's and his companions' horses and dumped an arrogant Flaithrí straight on his arse. And when he rose, he came up cursing everything about Devyl.

And his men.

In virtual unison, their jaws dropped as the wind encircled Sallie, transforming him like a jinn into a huge, muscled berserker— complete with long braids and a double-headed axe. One he flexed over his head as he growled in grave invitation of the blood he planned to feed to his weapon this day.

"God's pointed bodikin . . ." Bart turned to Devyl. "You knew about this, Captain?"

Devyl flashed a wicked grin. "'Course. Captain knows everything about his ship and crew. It's why I kept telling the lot of you to leave the man's soul alone afore one of you foolishly let loose the beast in the bottle."

Bart choked as he watched Sallie grow to stand even taller than he, and take on the youth that had cruelly been stripped from him when his soul had been savagely severed from his body without his permission.

Zumari scowled. "I don't understand."

With a knowing grin, Devyl shrugged. "'Twas a curse placed

upon him when he came up short a sorcerer years ago. He can only let his soul out when he's on the battlefield. You don't want to know what happens when it's released during peace."

"Let them learn it once, Captain," Sallie said with his own grin. "They'll never forget it thereafter."

"Duly noted." Bart cleared his throat as he respectfully gave Sallie a bit more room to maneuver. "One more thing, Captain . . . any pointers on how we're to win this?"

"Don't die. Be the last man standing."

"Good to know. Pointers on how to kill them, then?"

"Cut off the head. If that doesn't work? Run like hell, preferably faster than the poor bloke beside you. Might want to consider tripping him if he proves to be faster."

"Beautiful. I so look forward to these deep, meaningful discussions and motivational speeches from you that leave me bullocks completely shrunk and shriveled."

Laughing, Devyl lowered his visor for battle. "Better the bullocks than the brains. And better both than your courage."

Bart snorted. "Not sure about that. Especially given what's coming at us." He saluted Devyl with his sword. "In case I go down and forget to say it . . . been an honor serving with you, sir."

"And with you, Mr. Meers. Here's to taking them before they take us, and if they do, making sure they join us for the descent into hell."

"Amen, coz. Amen." And with that, he left Devyl to head straight into the fray.

As Devyl started forward, a foreign chill went up his spine. He turned to see if it was Zumari, but the man was already embroiled in a fierce fight. For a moment, he thought it might be Vine.

Until a shadow on his left moved.

Now *that* was all kinds of peculiar. Scowling, he braced himself for an assault.

Instead, the shadow came to wrap around him and whisper in his ear with a soft, feminine lilt. "Thorn has sent me with a gift for you. He wants you to know that he hasn't abandoned you, but will be here as soon as he's able." With those words spoken, she pressed something into his palm.

Then, as suddenly as she'd appeared, she was gone with nothing more than a mere breezy kiss across his flesh that was fully covered by his armor.

His scowl deepened the instant he opened his hand and saw what she'd given him.

Michael's Seraph medallion. The very one Cameron had entrusted to Thorn.

So there it was. . . .

He wasn't sure how he felt about that, what without Miss Jack being here and all. It didn't seem right for it to be returned now. And with that thought came the deluge of everything they had failed to accomplish. They hadn't found the bodies from the Fleet disaster. The plat-eyes still had control of those poor bastards. He'd allowed Vine to escape her prison by not stopping it. Gadreyal had captured both Cameron and her brother—two mortals born with Michael's blood.

And another gate had fractured. . . .

I seriously reek at my job.

Why Thorn had chosen him for this, he did not know. Perhaps the beast was a masochist. Or he'd taken so many blows to the head in battle that they'd finally addled him.

Devyl hadn't felt this low or incompetent since the day he'd found his sister. Despair threatened to overwhelm him.

Until he glanced to Mara, who watched on with terrified fretting. *I haven't lost anything yet.* Other than a little dignity, and that he could take. Honestly, he didn't mourn its loss at all.

Just don't let Mara get hurt. Losing her was the one thing he'd never come back from, and he knew it.

Determined to see this through, he let out a fierce war cry and ran straight to Gadreyal.

Marcelina?"

Mara went cold at the sound of her sister's voice. Prepared to give nothing away as to her thoughts or feelings, she turned toward her and was immediately taken aback by her sister's incredible beauty. Strange how she'd forgotten just what a graceful, seductive creature Vine was. Why Duel would prefer her over Vine's confident femme-fatale persona, she couldn't imagine.

The man must be insane.

"Vine." She was proud of herself for keeping her voice so steady and calm.

"You didn't free me as you said you would, sister."

It was only then that Mara realized Vine had used her powers to completely freeze William beside her. He couldn't move at all.

Wanting to check on him, but terrified her sister would kill him if she did, she diverted Vine's attention as best she could. "I was trying. Your friends sank my boat before I could get near your island."

Vine *tsk*ed at her. "Think you I believe that lie?"

"We had a bargain, did we not?"

"Aye, we did." Vine's gaze went to Duel as he fought against the Cimmerian army. "But it seems you've been distracted. Not that I blame you. He is a fine specimen of manhood. Well formed and skilled in all the right ways."

Mara barely caught the urge to slap her sister, and that wave of unexpected violence shocked her. She stilled her breathing and gathered her composure before it betrayed her and got them all killed. "You've never spoken so highly of him before."

And then Mara saw it. Only a flash, but Vine's perfect, porcelain complexion was lined with the black veins that exposed her sister's illness.

"Are you Wintering?"

The veins flashed again. This time, the black twined over her flesh like a living creature, slithering its way to her lips and eyes to turn them jet black. Even her Titian hair and the sclera of her eyes turned.

Mara wasn't sure what stunned her most about that. The fact that her sister was that far gone and she'd missed it, or the fact that Vine could be so beautiful even while disease-ridden.

Unaware of her physical transformation, Vine glared at her. "What lies has he told you about me that you believe?"

Mara wanted to laugh at the thought of Duel gossiping about anyone, but Vine was being serious. *Dead* serious.

The Wintering had taken the deepest root imaginable. Was any part of this rotted creature the sister she'd once known? "What happened to you?"

"What happened to me?" She laughed bitterly. "I was locked in a hole for hundreds of years! You . . . *you*"—she stabbed Mara in the chest with a long black fingernail—"my husband coddled and sent into a sleeping trance to protect. Meanwhile, he made sure I was to be tortured! Held so that I couldn't escape!"

"You *murdered* him, Vine."

She sneered at Mara. "Have you any idea what he had planned?"

"Nay."

"He was going to hand us over to our enemies."

Mara froze at the mere thought. Surely Duel would never have done such a thing. . . .

"Pardon?"

"Aye. He wanted to put down his sword and start a family! Can you imagine? Dón-Dueli of the Dumnonii . . . the Dark One . . . the World-King wanted *peace*." She spat the word to make it sound like the worst sort of insult.

Wincing, Mara hated herself for ever doubting Duel. "We are Deruvian Vanir. 'Tis what we dream of. You should have encouraged it."

"As I did my first husband? A true Deruvian!" Her sneer lengthened, contorting her face into that of a hideous crone. "Let me tell you what such peace brought my first husband, *child*. A grave! And it's what would have become of us all!" She grabbed Mara's hand. "Now give me what I need to bury him, once and for all, or I'll make sure you die in a way you won't come back from!"

Mara sucked her breath in sharply at the threat. She wanted to deny that this was her sister. But as those words rang in her ears, others followed.

Duel was right. Vine had never loved him. She'd never really been capable of love. Even when they were children, her sister had been petty. Mara had overlooked Vine's faults, especially after so many of their family had been slaughtered and burned. Their charred ashes scattered to the winds so that they couldn't regenerate.

She'd convinced herself that Duel and his kind were the real evil in the world.

But evil didn't pick and choose who to corrupt. It took root like an insidious weed that sought to destroy whatever garden it could find succor in, no matter who, what, or where that garden originated from. Evil was never picky about its host. That was why it was so important to rip it out and toss it off before it could spread and rot the garden from the inside out.

Take over and destroy the beauty that made the garden whole and healthy.

Tears choked her. Mayhap had she seen it sooner, she could have saved her sister. Too late now. Vine didn't want to be saved. Unlike Duel, Vine didn't fight against the darkness or even try to tamp it down.

Rather, she reveled in it.

And Mara refused to sit back and watch Duel go down for such a worthless trifle as Vine. To see him die again while he fought so hard for others. Fought so hard against the evil that wanted him. She might not have seen the truth of him in Tintagel, but she saw him now.

More than that, he was hers, and the one thing about Deruvians . . . they protected their own from any threat.

Perhaps there's a little Aesir in me, after all.

She was not going to protect herself or her sister. Not anymore. And not when she had someone else who now meant more to her.

Summoning her own armor, she faced a startled Vine.

"What is this?" Vine asked incredulously.

"Me choosing to oppose you and your desires. I will give you nothing, except my contempt and disdain for your behavior. Shame on you, sister. Shame on you!"

Vine arched a black brow. "You do this and I'll never separate your life force from Duel's."

"Good. It will save me the trouble of having to bind it again later."

Shrieking, Vine summoned her own armor. While Mara had chosen a light blue, silver, and white for hers, Vine's was a startling green that glowed with its unnatural power. The aura around it hummed and shimmered like a living, breathing membrane to protect her.

But nothing was going to stop Mara from keeping Duel safe. Not today.

Regretting her decision not to accept Duel's offer to teach her swordplay when she'd had the chance, she summoned the only weapon she'd ever used.

Wind and Fire wheels. Though she was a bit out of practice with them, they were the weapons her people were known for. Two half circles very similar to a chakram, they had curved spikes protruding from the blades that were made to look like sunrays or fire.

And they cut through flesh, both human and demon, as easily as they cut through the wind.

Vine's eyes widened. "You truly plan to fight me?"

"To keep Duel safe? Indeed."

"What happened to you, big sister, that you'd dare choose an Aesir over family?"

"He's been more family to me than you ever were."

That caused Vine to attack, full force. With an ear-splitting scream, she manifested her spear and went for Mara's throat.

Mara caught the tip against the edge of her right-hand wheel and twisted so that the protruding spike would lock to the blade. It seemed like a good idea until Vine twisted her weapon and almost wrenched Mara's arm out of its socket.

Crying out, Mara struggled to remain standing. She couldn't let her sister kill her in this fight. If she did, Duel would die, too.

Vine gave a cruel, sinister laugh. "Nay, he will not," she said as if she'd heard Mara's thoughts. She jerked Mara closer with her spear so that she could whisper in her ear. "News to you, big sister . . . I killed the bastard the day I realized he loved you so much that he sold his soul to give you your freedom so that you could live without him. He was going to tell you when I sliced his throat and then cut out his treacherous heart! That was why you lived on after he died. Why *I* put you into a sleeping spell."

"You're lying!" Distracted by the thought, Mara turned to look out at Duel.

The moment she did, Vine stabbed her through her stomach.

Crying out in pain, she tried to hold her breath to keep the vicious, biting agony at bay. But it was no use. Every heartbeat drove more pain through her. Worse, Vine kept her upright and on her feet by holding on to the spear. "Half of it was a lie, dearest. I would tell you to figure out which, but you won't live long enough for that."

Vine pinned Mara to the ground with her spear, then called for Strixa to join her. She flew in as an owl, then transformed into her human body.

With a smile, Vine checked to make sure Mara was dead. Once assured, she ripped the harthfret from her throat. "Good death to you, sister."

Strixa arched a brow as if she disapproved and wanted to say something, but didn't speak while Vine made her way over to Duel's henchman. How Duel had always been able to inspire such loyalty from those around him, Vine had never understood. And this particular little tossling pet of Duel's . . . he'd been a nuisance almost as much as her ex-husband, so it was time she put the bastard to use.

Touching him on the brow, she cast her spell. "I think I shall let Duel kill you for me."

Devyl staggered as he felt something go through him like a hot poker. It sliced through his middle and left him in agony. For a moment, he thought Gadreyal had gotten through his defenses.

Until he realized it was something far, far worse.

Mara was dying.

Kicking Gadreyal away from him, he ran to find her and cursed himself for not using his powers to send her away from here, her protests be damned. As he reached Mara and William's position, he started to yell at William for failing to keep her safe, then noticed that he was bespelled and had no way of assisting anyone.

Not even himself.

So he sank to his knees by her side and gathered Mara's cold, limp body into his arms and tried to wake her.

She didn't move. Her skin was icy and cold. Her body completely unresponsive.

Unable to breathe, Devyl cupped her precious cheek in his hand and pressed his forehead to hers as grief tore him asunder. In that moment, he felt shattered. Lost.

Desolate.

"Nay!" His eyes changed over an instant before he blasted William free from the spell holding him. "What happened!"

"She gave Vine your harthfret? I know not what that is, but it sounded important."

That only confused him more as he glanced down to his sword that was comprised of his wand—the same sword that held his stone. No one had taken his harthfret. It was intact. He could feel the power emanating from it. Mara would have known she didn't have his harthfret to give . . .

Yet no sooner had that thought gone through his mind than he realized Mara's necklace was missing from her throat. "What did you do, Mara?" Tears stung his eyes.

Had she given it over to her sister as a dupe to protect him? He went cold at the thought.

If Vine had her harthfret, she could kill Mara forever. There would be no way to bring her back.

Unable to stand it, he rose with Mara's body in his arms and handed her to William. "You better not get caught again. And you'd best make damn sure no one touches her. Do you hear me?"

"Aye, Captain."

Grinding his teeth against the grief and agony inside him, he balled his hand in her precious hair and bit back his tears, then teleported William and Mara to Santiago's ship, where they'd be safe. At least he prayed for that to be so.

That bastard had better not have gone down during their fight.

More than that, Santiago had best keep Mara safe from all harm until this was over and Devyl could get to her.

Furious and terrified that he wouldn't be able to save her in spite of his magick, Devyl headed toward Gadreyal with only one thing on his mind.

Saving the only person in this world who mattered to him. The world and all else be damned.

"Where's Vine?"

"Vine who?"

"Don't play that game, she-bitch. I'm in no mood for it." He raked a glare over her blood-colored armor, wanting to add more red to it. And some brain matter as well. There was nothing left inside him now except a fury so raw and potent it would not be appeased until he tasted someone's heart and soul.

He wasn't selective as to whose it had to be, either. The beast within was awake and it was salivating.

Gadreyal threw a bolt at him.

He absorbed it and shot it back to her, with interest. Then he added another. And another. He summoned the lightning and shot it at her.

She shrank away in terror.

You better run, trollop! He was done with them all.

There was no Aesir left in him now. None whatsoever.

Devyl swept his gaze over the battle, seeking Vine. It was an even split as to who was winning. His Deadmen were holding their own. But the demons were fierce.

As one of Gadreyal's men ran at him, he shot a mage blast at the moron and disintegrated him.

"Vine!" he snarled, wanting her head.

"She is here."

He hesitated at the feminine voice in his head. "Strixa?"

"Aye. And it's not a trap."

"Why would you help me?"

Strixa hesitated before she answered. "Vine has broken the code of sisterhood. I will not tolerate that. She has the harthfret and is planning to plant it to kill your Marcelina."

Devyl let out a curse as she pierced his brain with an image of where Vine was. Damn, that hurt.

But he was grateful beyond measure.

And it was too bad the stupid twitling didn't have his stone instead of Mara's. Where she was burying it would have fed his powers even more. But he had no idea what it would do to Mara.

Tiveden, or Tyr's Wood, was said to be some of the most fertile land here. It's where the god had once planted his own seeds to grow his warriors. Those preternatural soldiers who'd been born of Tyr's brook now comprised the bulk of his uncle's Royal Guard.

That gave him an idea. Pulling the Seraph medallion out, he placed it in the same cage as his own harthfret. The moment the two touched, it sent a jolt through his entire body. One that left him breathless and warm.

Heat spread throughout his body, and for a moment, he heard more than just the aether around him. He could taste it, even.

It also brought him to Gadreyal's full attention as she felt the awakening of the Seraph blood mixing with his. That caused every member of her horde to disengage from their opponent and head toward him.

Which was great for his men.

For him? Not so much.

Belle wiped the blood from her sword before she and Sancha came to take up positions by his side. "What's it to be, Captain?"

"All-out bloodletting. No prey, no pay."

With that, Bart threw out his hand and raised his own army of soldiers made of blackthorns. They twisted up from the ground and into monstrous beasts, complete with thorny swords, standing ready to fight to the end.

Valynda summoned Ghede Nibo—the Vodou loa. He was the leader of the spirits of the dead, and the one Thorn had bargained with for Valynda's parole.

They were also *close* friends. How close, Devyl wasn't sure. But he'd heard Valynda speaking to him whenever she thought no one else was around. And obviously, Nibo thought enough of her that he'd negotiated with Baron Samedi to bring her back to life so that she could join their crew. It wasn't something either of them did lightly. Or anything they were known for.

Dressed in a black coat with a bright purple sash and shirt, Nibo was in his human form—ethereally beautiful, with dark curly hair and chiseled features. As usual, he was accompanied by his "twin" companions, Masaka and Oussou. Yet for being called twins, they were complete opposites of each other. Masaka a tall, androgynous woman who wore a small white tricorne emblazoned with skulls that matched her jacket and breeches, and a black ruffled shirt. Her skin was as dark as Oussou's was pale. And while her hair was black, Oussou's matched her bone-colored coat. Dressed in a black gravedigger's jacket that held a white cross on each sleeve, he had his pale braids covered with a black tricorne that was festooned with mauve feathers.

A smile spread across Oussou's handsome face that said he was savoring the coming battle as he handed Nibo his skull cane. In turn, Nibo passed to Oussou his bottle of white rum that held medicinal herbs. Oussou took a deep drink of the rum while Nibo pulled the head of the cane to reveal the sharp saber inside it. He handed the scabbard to Masaka. She held it up and bent it in the center. It immediately broke apart and crawled down her sleeves like twin snakes to form a thorny set of knives along her forearms.

Though they were members of the Ghede loa nanchon, they had much more in common with their warring Petro cousins. Fiery to their bones. There was nothing the three of them liked more than to raise hell and brawl.

Well, there was *one* thing they liked better. But the fury in their eyes said that their passion right now wasn't carnal. They craved the same blood Devyl could taste.

And their combined presence here made Gadreyal shrink back.

She hovered over the ground with a jaundiced eye at the increase in their number.

"You can't wield Michael's blood," she snarled at Devyl. "It's more likely to kill you than serve you."

"Then why are you so afraid all of a sudden?"

She threw her axe at him. Devyl caught it in his hand, kissed it, and hurled it back.

His reward was another shrill shriek. And he knew this was a ruse to buy Vine more time. Every second that passed was critical for Mara.

They all knew it.

While his cousin led in his own attack, Devyl gave the signal to his crew to renew their battle with everything they had. He hated to leave them, but he had no choice.

For the first time ever, he understood the Deruvian code—that one life was indeed far more precious than all others combined. Aye, it was that very selfishness he'd once hated Vine and her entire Vanir race over.

Maybe he was more Vanir than he wanted to admit. But right now, nothing mattered to him.

Nothing except Mara.

The world could burn for all he cared. Without Mara, it didn't deserve to be here.

He could hear his heartbeat thrumming in his ears as he left the field of battle to teleport to Tiveden.

No sooner had he materialized on the side of the tallest hill than he drew up short to find his ex-wife in all her fiery glory. Right down to the orange and red dress that appeared to move like living flames in the fading sun.

"You're too late," Vine gloated the moment she saw him. "I've planted you here and here you will stay."

His knees went weak at her declaration. "You didn't plant me here—'twas Mara's harthfret you stole."

She paled. For a moment, the black veins left her skin as confusion lined her brow. It was obvious she was trying to discern whether or not he was lying. "What?"

"Had you asked, I'd have gladly given you mine to keep her safe. You should have known that, Vine. I always protected Mara over anyone."

That had the desired effect on her. She let loose an insane cry before she started toward him.

Yet before she could reach him, the ground on the hill began to tremble and boil. Like a living, starving beastie, it rose and fell, and percolated with such force that Vine squealed and danced away from it.

Half expecting something foul to emerge out of the chaos, Devyl stumbled and barely caught himself before he went sprawling.

"What have you done?" Vine gasped accusingly.

He shook his head as he struggled to comprehend it. Never had he seen the like. "Nothing. That is *not* me."

Smoke billowed up in sharp, inky black spirals. They danced in an invisible breeze until they began to slowly twine about and take the shape and form of a woman.

Devyl held his breath, praying silently for a miracle.

But to his utter disappointment it wasn't Mara they formed.

The shape was too short and flat about the bosom to be his better half. Yet there was something vaguely familiar to that outline. Something that wiggled in the back of his mind.

Suddenly, he knew exactly why.

Nay . . . this could *not* be.

It's not possible.

His breath catching in his throat, Devyl froze as shock claimed him fully. And still there was no denying the woman who manifested in front of them.

"Elf?" His voice shook with uncertainty. "Is it really you, lass?"

Like a newborn fawn, she worked her face as if trying to remember how to speak. How to see. She stared down at her hands and wiggled her fingers, then scowled at Vine.

Color flooded into his sister's pale cheeks. The air began to stir to a fierce level. It whipped at Elf's hair, spiraling it into tendrils and plastering her burgundy dress against her lithe body.

"You sought to harm my brother?" she finally spoke.

Her features pale, Vine stumbled back. She glanced at Strixa and then Devyl. "What is this?" Her mouth worked soundlessly before she choked out, "*How* is this?"

He wasn't sure, except for one thing. . . .

"You must have buried Elf's harthfret instead of Mara's." Though how it could regenerate her after all these centuries, he had no idea. He'd never heard of such.

It wasn't possible.

On furious impulse, he'd reclaimed Elf's harthfret that day when he'd gone into Mara's nemeton. Like a frenzied beast, he'd dug through the wood and earth until he found it at the base of the tree where she'd planted it.

For years, he'd tried to regenerate her.

Nothing had ever worked. Never had it taken root, and so he'd set it into a signet ring to keep it forever with him.

So aye, he was with Vine in one way only . . . how the futtocking hell was this possible?

Vine started to leave, but something held her in place.

Elf's breathing turned ragged as she stalked toward his ex-wife like a vicious predator with cornered prey. "You do not escape here. You do not escape *me*." Her voice was no longer the sweet lilt he'd known from his younger sister. It was demonic and fierce. "You wanted war?" Elf blasted her. "By all means, have some!"

Vine screamed as fire consumed her. Holding her hands up, she tried to save herself, but it was useless. The fire spread quick and fast, and engulfed her entirely.

Then Elf turned to him.

Devyl braced himself for her attack, especially when she came running toward him, full speed. But instead of attacking, she threw herself into his arms and held him close, as she'd done when they were young.

"I should have listened to you!" She sobbed in his arms.

Dumbfounded, he held her in an awkward embrace, still not completely convinced this was his sister. It was just the sort of cruel trick Vine specialized in.

Among many others.

Not until Strixa moved closer to them and reached out to touch his arm in a comforting gesture of solidarity did he begin to have some belief that this might not be a massively cruel jape. "Mara stole the harthfret from you. She was working to see if there was some way she could bring your sister back. While I may not think much of you, demonspawn, the Lady Marcelina loves you."

"This is real then?" His voice trembled.

Strixa nodded. "It would never have worked had Vine not planted Elyzabel here, where Tyr's blood saturated the fields, and had your sister not died unjustly before her time."

"Because Tyr's a god of justice."

She nodded. "And is part of your family. His blood is her blood. It rejuvenated her. Yet even so, it wouldn't have been enough had Nibo not come here with his magick."

Because regenerating the dead was one of his specialties.

And that gave him another thought. "Where's Mara's stone?"

Strixa *tsk*ed at him and lifted the hand he had on Elf's shoulder. "She left her heart with you."

It took him a second to realize that Mara had swapped her stone with Elf's in his ring. He'd worn the ring for so long, but because it reminded him of his failings, he seldom looked at it.

Until now.

Now he let the warmth of Mara's life force heat his entire body.

"Elf?" he breathed, kissing the top of her head. "There's something I must do."

"Save Mara?"

He scowled at her. "How do you know about Mara?"

"Once you carried my stone with you, I could hear everything you said."

Heat scalded his cheeks as he realized some of the other things she might have overheard.

In that familiar teasing way, she tugged at his whiskers. "Aye, my brother. Even *that*."

He groaned out loud. "I'm so sorry."

"For what? Not abandoning me? You did nothing wrong, Duey. Now let's go save your wife."

Devyl drew up short as he reappeared on the battlefield where he'd left his men. He had to give the Deadmen credit—they didn't withdraw from conflict.

Ever.

And this was a bloodbath. Gadreyal and her forces weren't going down easily. Lightning flashed. The sound of battle rang in his ears.

This was what he'd grown up on.

And as he took his sister's hand, he hesitated for the first time in his life.

"I failed to protect you."

"Nay," Elf breathed, reaching up to cup his face in her hand. "My fiancé failed me. At *their* behest." She jerked her chin toward Gadreyal. "She was the one who set me up, and you. She wanted you out of the way."

He felt his fangs elongate at her words as the demonic beast inside came to the forefront.

Elf stepped back and inclined her head, then turned herself into a small sprite. She flew to kiss his cheek and whisper in his ear. "None shall see me, big brother. Do what you do best and worry not this time. I'll be right here." She pressed herself against his jugular and became a part of his skin.

Knowing she was safe so long as he didn't take a blow there, he lowered his visor and headed straight for Gadreyal.

This time when he caught her with his sword, it knocked her reeling. But he gave her no quarter. Not now.

Not ever again.

"Where is Cameron?" he growled. "Her life is all that will spare yours."

Gadreyal staggered back from his blows. She tried to fly away, but he sliced her hard across the wings, almost completely severing one.

His time for mercy had passed. Her time for living was growing perilously short.

"Release my men and give us back our Miss Jack! I shan't say it again."

Gadreyal hissed and twisted, then blasted him. But he didn't feel it. He was too angry. "Thorn can't save you!"

"I'm not looking for him to." Devyl kicked her back.

"Captain!"

He hesitated at Hinder's and Belle's shouts. Glancing to them, he saw that his cousin had opened a gate and allowed Thorn and a group of Sarim inside this realm.

The moment Gadreyal saw them, she gathered her warriors and vanished.

"Nay!" Devyl started after her, but Thorn caught him and prevented it.

"We have Cameron and her brother."

Those words barely registered. "What? How?"

Thorn tightened his grip on Devyl's arm. "We've found them, but we need the blood of a Deruvian or Myrcian to unlock the gate that holds them. It's why we're here." He glanced around the field. "Where's Mara?"

Devyl choked on the answer, then forced himself to speak past the agony that seized him. "Vine killed her."

Thorn's eyes widened. Because he knew what Devyl did. Deruvians didn't always come back from their graves.

"You gave me your word, Leucious. Can I hold you to it?"

Thorn nodded glumly. "What of Cameron?"

Devyl handed him the sword. "Her medallion's inside. I will take her place and let them out, but you have to finish this."

Before Thorn could take him up on it, Kalder came forward. "Nay, let me go, Captain. My life for Miss Jack and her brother."

"Kal—"

"No argument, Bane." Kalder glanced around at the Deadmen. "I'm the most expendable here. But you and the Lady Ship . . . the crew needs you both."

"We're pirates," Sancha said as she wiped at the blood on her cheek. "We vote."

William grimaced. "I vote we lose no one."

Thorn scoffed at his suggestion. "It doesn't work that way. One of you has to go. There's no other way for it."

Kalder nodded. "Matter's settled, then. We need our ship and our captain. We don't need a mermaid."

It still sat ill with Devyl. And for once, he was coming around to the way the Vanir saw things. He didn't like the thought of sacrificing the one to save the many. "I'll find a way to get you back."

"God, I hope so, Bane." Kalder winked at him. " 'Cause one way or another, I plan to return for Miss Jack. Please tell her I said that."

Devyl held his tongue as he watched Michael and Gabriel take Kalder. He didn't have the heart to warn the merman of the truth.

Either way, he was dead.

Most likely, they both were.

His heart heavy, he locked gazes with Thorn. "Well?"

Thorn grimaced at the question. "Well, what?"

"We have to get Mara back."

"I can't do anything. You know that. She's beyond my reach."

When Devyl started forward, Valynda stopped him from grabbing Thorn and ripping out his throat. "It's not final, Captain." She turned to Nibo. "You can help her, can you not?"

Eyes wide, he exchanged a nervous grimace with his twin companions. "Is not so easy, *ma petite ange*."

"But not impossible. Especially for you, Papa." She reached up and caressed his cheek. "You can do this for me, can't you?"

Nibo practically melted at her touch. "*Oui.* I will try."

"Nay, love. You will succeed."

In every culture, crossroads were significant. As an Aesir, Devyl had been taught to be wary of them, as they were oft haunted by the cŵn annwn, cyhyraeth, Adoni, or Gwrach y Rhibyn, who preyed on unwary travelers, seeking souls or victims for nefarious ends. Nothing good ever happened in such places.

And this evening was no exception. For it was here in his grandfather's kingdom that he was being returned to the hell Thorn had saved him from.

Nibo let out a tired sigh as he finished his chant. "You're sure about this?"

Devyl nodded. "She doesn't belong there. Are you sure this will work?"

"Aye. The parties have agreed. They would rather torture you, as you have earned damnation, while she has not." He gestured toward his companion. "Masaka will lead you in and then return with Marcelina."

Devyl narrowed his gaze on the loa. "No tricks?"

Nibo quirked an amused grin. "You are wise to be suspicious. But on this, I gave me word to Valynda. I assure you that I won't break her heart."

"Nor will he cross me." Thorn cleared his throat abruptly.

The laugh Nibo let out contradicted Thorn's arrogance. But that was all the loa had to say on the matter. "If you're ready?"

Almost.

Devyl swallowed hard against the painful knot in his throat as he met the tear-filled gaze of his sister. "I'm sorry to be leaving you alone in this world, Elf."

Sniffing, she nodded. "I understand. I just hate to lose you again."

He kissed her hand and held it for a moment longer. "Tell Mara that I've always loved her. And that she's never to feel guilty for this. I would rather she think of me fondly, if she's able. And only smile whenever she does so."

A tear slid down her cheek as she nodded. "I love you, Duey."

"My precious Elf." He kissed her forehead. "Take care." And with that, he stepped back and glared at Thorn. "Let no harm come to my girls."

"On my honor, Dón-Dueli. It's been a privilege."

"I wouldn't go that far. You're still a thorn in my arse."

Thorn laughed, but his eyes were as sad as the others' as Masaka placed her hand on Devyl's shoulder and they faded back into the hell Devyl knew he'd be forced to endure for all eternity.

Think of Mara. This was for her. She was safe now. She had her life back. Free of him.

But that didn't help. Not really.

Because in the end, the greatest hell wasn't the physical agony he knew awaited him. It was the mental and emotional torment that came from knowing that she finally loved him and that now he would be forced to live without her.

Forever.

Kalder hesitated as he saw the dense crystal wall that kept Paden and Cameron imprisoned. They were frozen in a sheet so thick, they barely looked human. But the worst part of all was the expressions of horror frozen upon their faces—as if they were caught in the midst of a nightmare only they could see.

"What have they done to them?"

Rage darkened Thorn's eyes to a vibrant green glow. "It's not what's there that's terrifying, Myrcian. It's what's not."

"How do you do mean?"

Thorn placed his hand on Kalder's shoulder. The instant he did so, pain tore through Kalder's head and ripped back the layer of this world so that he could see the reality where Cameron and Paden currently lived. The realm where their souls had been cast by Vine's evilness.

Gasping, he felt a fiery chill that was so cold it burned. Felt Cameron's despair and her brother's terror that he was going to kill his own sister, and that Paden would be powerless to stop the hunger inside him that demanded her innocent blood.

Thorn let go and stepped away from him.

Kalder staggered as his vision cleared and he returned to this reality. His breathing ragged, he blinked rapidly, looking from Thorn to Michael and finally Gabriel. "Can you always see like that?"

They nodded in turn.

"Not fun, is it?" Thorn said bitterly. "To know what lies behind the human veil and not be able to interfere. It's its own form of hell."

Kalder wiped at the tears as he struggled to even out his breathing. "Is that why you came for us?"

Thorn passed a sullen glare to the other two. "Aye. Unlike some, I can't abide injustice."

Michael turned on him with a vicious hiss, exposing a set of fangs that Kalder hadn't noticed before. "Never speak to me of injustice, demon! You've no right! You know nothing of me or mine."

Thorn held his hands up. "Point being, I believe in second chances."

Michael curled his lip. "Most demons do, as the second strike usually cuts even deeper than the first."

Now it was Thorn's turn to go for Michael, but Gabriel caught him and forced him back.

"Enough! Both of you! We're not here to fight each other." He jerked his chin toward Paden and Cameron. "Every second you bicker, we risk losing them forever."

"If we haven't already," Michael said under his breath.

Kalder winced as he pressed his hand against the cold rock that kept him from Cameron's warmth. How strange that he barely knew her and yet she'd sparked something inside him that he'd never known he possessed.

A heart.

He hadn't even kissed her and yet here he was willing to die to save her. It made no sense whatsoever. But then life seldom did.

Perhaps it was that innocent optimism she held in spite of all the shite life had heaped upon her that had restarted the dead organ in his chest. Or the loving light in those hazel eyes that sparked whenever she spoke of her brother. The way she kept faith even when it seemed there was no hope whatsoever.

No one had ever held such regard for him.

He'd never wanted them to.

Until now. By all that was holy and not, he wanted her to look at him like that. To see her eyes light up and twinkle for him in the same manner as they did for Paden.

Nay, that was a lie and he knew it. He wanted much more from her than that. He wanted to have one woman, just once, see him the way she saw her brother.

As a noble hero.

As *her* noble hero and champion.

One she was willing to sacrifice her life for.

He wanted someone to love him like that. Completely and without question. With total loyalty and devotion. To love him the way his mother had loved his brother. To have someone mourn his passing and regret that he was no longer part of her life. No one had even shown up for his burial after his mother had gutted him.

Not even a priest. The watchmen had taken him out and dumped his body in a common grave like garbage. No pomp. No last rites. Nothing. Not a single kind word.

After all the years he'd lived, he'd meant nothing to anyone.

Only Cameron had ever teased him like a friend and made him feel noble or welcome. Damn him for craving it. Because now that he knew the taste of it, he couldn't go back to his ignorance. It was a raw, fetid hunger that wouldn't leave him in peace. He couldn't return to the way he'd been. Numb and oblivious.

She'd opened his eyes and awakened him.

And if he had to die to bring her back, so be it. Unlike him, she was a vibrant soul who brought happiness to the world, and to those around her. As did her brother. He had a woman waiting for him, and a child who needed a father to claim it. They were rare lights that shone brightly in this dim, awful world.

No one will ever miss you, Kal.

"Let's do this," he said to the Sarim. "I don't want her to suffer another moment."

SHERRILYN KENYON

Thorn inclined his head to Kalder, then passed a harsh, condemning glare to the Sarim. "Tell me again how the damned are beyond redemption?"

They looked away sheepishly.

He clapped Kalder on the back. "Know that it sickens me to do this to you. If there's any way to save you, we will find it."

Kalder nodded. "Tell Cameron that it was my honor to spare her." He pulled the necklace off that had belonged to his brother and handed it to Thorn. "And give her this from me. Ask her to pray for my brother's soul."

"Not yours?"

He let out a bitter laugh. "We both know where mine belongs and where it be headed."

Thorn took the necklace and tucked it into his pocket. What he had to do sickened him to the core of his worthless soul. But he had no choice. The two bitches with him weren't about to spare him this, and he knew it. They would never spare him any nightmare.

Cursing his father and himself, he pulled out his dagger and as quickly and painlessly as possible, he sliced Kalder's artery so that his blood coated the floor.

The Myrcian staggered, but Thorn caught him and kept him from falling to the cold ground like garbage. He held him in his arms as his life faded.

"Sleep in peace, little brother," he whispered against his ear. "I won't let you die alone this time. And you will be mourned and missed. You are a good man, Kalder. Let no one ever tell you otherwise. Not even you."

Sinking to the ground, Thorn cradled him in his arms and held him there until he bled out and was gone. Tears filled his eyes as he hated everything about himself and the choices he was forced to make. Choices they were all forced to make.

Michael didn't say a word as he gathered Kalder's blood and used it for the incantations he needed to free his progeny.

Gabriel knelt by his side. "Thorn?"

He blinked slowly, unable to answer for the pain inside him that churned and ached so deep that it left him hollow and numb.

"You need to let him go."

Yet he couldn't bring himself to do it. Not when he knew the horrors that had haunted Kalder. "He's not garbage."

"I know."

Nay, he didn't know. Not really. Closing his eyes, Thorn clutched at Kalder's head and swore to them both that he would find some miracle to free the Myrcian. Even if he had to unravel the universe to do it.

"Kalder?"

Blinking, Thorn looked up as Cameron came out of the wall to see them on the floor, saturated in blood.

With a fierce sob, she rushed to them. Her hands trembled as she sobbed and clutched at Kalder's jacket. "Nay! Nay! I can't lose him! Not like this!"

Thorn pulled her against him to comfort her. "Shh, child. He only sleeps."

She stared at him as if he were crazy. And he was, indeed. For only a crazy person would have defied the powers that be to create the Hellchasers as Thorn had done.

He felt his eyes turn bright red before he offered her a determined grin. "I brought him back when he had absolutely nothing to live for. Do you really think he'll stay down now that he has so much to lose?"

Mara came awake to the most peculiar warmth. Until she remembered her sister's treachery.

Furious, she sat up and . . .

What the devil?

She was on board a ship, but it wasn't *her* body that made up this vessel. "Du?" she called, glancing around the small, unfamiliar cabin.

Instead of Duel, Thorn came in to stand beside her bunk.

"How are you feeling?"

"Very confused. Where's Du?" How had she gotten here? She couldn't remember anything. Not really.

Everything was so vague. Like a strange, flimsy dream.

Thorn didn't answer. Rather, he stepped aside for another woman to enter the room through the door behind him. "I don't think the two of you have ever met."

Nay, she'd never seen the . . .

Her heart stopped beating as she realized who this was. It was a face she'd only seen in her visions. "Elyzabel?"

She inclined her head to Mara. "Aye, my lady. How are you?"

"Where's your brother?"

Elf glanced nervously to Thorn.

When they didn't answer right away, a bad, horrible dread went through her. She tried to leave the bed, but Thorn prevented it. "You're still weak."

"Tell me where Duel is!"

Thorn continued to hedge. "Well . . . you know where you were."

"Aye." She was finally beginning to remember the hellish hole where Vine had cast her. She couldn't imagine how Duel had stood it for so long.

"To get you out, we had to have someone sacrifice their life and harthfret for yours."

Oh dear God, no!

The blood faded from her cheeks as tears welled in her eyes. Surely Thorn wasn't telling her what she feared he was saying. Nay, Du wouldn't be so stupid.

You know better!

Of course, he'd be that *stupid!*

Agony and grief wrapped around her heart and set it to pounding. "Tell me he didn't," she breathed as dread washed over her and brought tears to her eyes.

Elf nodded. "He wouldn't be swayed. For you, he was willing to do anything. Sacrifice all his crew. He wanted me to tell you that he's always loved you and that you are not to feel guilty. That you are to remember him fondly and only smile when you think of him."

Silent tears streamed down her face. "Nay!" She struggled to breathe past the pain that choked her. "We must get to him." Rising to her feet, she shoved Thorn out of her way. "I . . . I . . ." Her legs gave way and sent her to the floor, where she broke down into fierce, racking sobs. The agony of his loss was unlike anything she'd ever known.

Du! Oh gods . . . She couldn't do this. She couldn't make it without him. Especially knowing that it was her fault he was gone. That he'd done this to spare her.

Suddenly, strong arms surrounded her and held her against a hard, muscular chest. She started to struggle for release until the scent of this man's skin hit her.

That sweet sea musk scent wasn't Thorn's.

Shocked and stunned even more, she looked up into a pair of angry red eyes. "Thorn! You rank futtocking bastard! What did you do?"

"Du?" She reached to touch his face, then sobbed even harder.

"Shh," he breathed, rocking her in his arms. "All's well, my love."

Her breathing ragged, she glared at Thorn. "What cruelty was this?"

Crossing his arms over his chest, Thorn smirked. "No cruelty. All of it was the honest truth. Devyl took your place in order to set you free."

Elf nodded. "He said to tell you every word I spoke."

Mara scowled at them. "I don't understand."

Du wiped at the tears on her cheeks, then offered her a crooked grin. "I'm such a cantankerous bastard, they refused to keep me. Apparently, my face is not nearly as sweet as yours."

Thorn scoffed. "Not entirely true. When I signed Devyl on, it was with one understanding."

"You were never to be harmed, Mara." Devyl brushed the hair back from her face.

"Aye." Thorn sobered. "He gave his soul to unbind your lives and by doing that and then sacrificing his life so that you could live again. . . ."

Du held up his wrist for her to see that his Deadman's Cross was gone. "I bought my freedom."

Thorn nodded and smiled. "He made his sacrifice. His slate is wiped completely clean. And rather than flee and start his mortal life anew, he chose to stay on with his crew and to wait and see what you wanted to do with your freedom."

Gasping, she ran her fingers over his arm where his brand had been. "You're free?"

"Aye, thanks to you."

Thorn and Elf gave them the cabin.

Aghast, Mara stared up at him. "And Vine?"

"Dead. I killed her. We're on Santiago's ship and—"

She interrupted his words with a kiss. And then another. "I will make our ship again with my body as soon as I'm strong enough."

Devyl nipped her lips, then brushed his nose against hers. "Our?"

Laughing, she nodded. "Aye, Captain Bane. You don't think I'm about to let you sail without me, do you?"

"You're sure?"

"Absolutely."

His eyes turning even darker, he reached for the laces on her gown.

Mara's breath caught as he gave her a kiss so hot it scorched her. His hunger was absolute and it matched her own. More than that, it inflamed hers. She still couldn't believe this was real.

That she was back from the dead and that he was here in her arms.

"What were you thinking when you switched places with me?"

"That you had no business there." His tongue teased her earlobe, sending chills over her as he laid her back against the bunk. "And that I couldn't live knowing you had died because of me."

"You are a fool, Dón-Dueli."

He pulled back to flash his dimples at her. "Aye, but only for you."

That was true. Her breath caught as he swept her gown off her body and the cool air hit her skin. Desperate to feel his flesh against hers, she pulled his shirt over his head. And leaned against him so that she could savor his embrace. "We've much to do, you know."

"True." He nipped her chin with his teeth while he held her gently in his arms and cradled her body with his. "Santiago has signed on to be our backup until we see this finished."

"And Thorn agreed?"

"Free will. Agreeing's got nothing to do with it. He can't stop him."

She shook her head at the poor pirate who had no idea what he and his crew were in for. "What else have I missed?"

A boyish grin played along the edges of his lips while he drew small circles around her breasts and nibbled the outline of her jaw. "Much bickering. A lot of soul-searching as we tried to put Sallie's soul back in its bottle and Strixa decided to stay on with us as well."

She arched a brow at that. "Really?"

He pulled back with an irritable grimace. "Aye, but is this truly what you want to be focusing on right now, love?"

She dropped her hand down the waistband of his breeches and noted the way he held his breath. And the instant softening of his glower. "Not really."

His breathing turned ragged the moment she dipped her hand inside to gently stroke him. His features relaxed and turned gentle and sweet.

Biting her lip, Mara took pleasure at the power she had over her captain. A dark and fearsome sorcerer corymeister he might be, but it was a Deruvian magelyn who owned his heart and could change his mood at her merest whim. "I will always fight for you, Du. Come the morrow, I want you to teach me how to wield a sword."

He arched a brow at that. "You're sure?"

She nodded. "You were right. We're only as strong as our weakest link, and I will not be the means to defeat you."

Devyl cupped her cheek before he kissed her. "You are never my weakness, Mara. You are my strength. And I will teach you to be the best swordsman in all the world."

"Good." She slid his pants from his hips. "Now come here, husband, and show me some of your finer, most skilled moves."

Laughing, he laid her back against the bunk and gently slid himself home.

Mara sucked her breath in sharply at the sensation of Duel deep inside her as she cradled him with her body. She should be afraid of the future. The gates were still cracked. And they'd lost a number of their crew. Paden's unborn child carried with it the blood of Michael that could open all the gates and unleash the worst of all evils upon the earth.

And yet in Duel's arms, she felt completely safe. Because she knew her Devyl would never allow any harm to befall her.

Nay—so long as this Devyl and his Deadmen were on the side of right, evil didn't stand a chance.

EPILOGUE

Gadreyal hesitated as she neared the only creature she answered to . . . the one being even more corrupt and dangerous than she was.

Papa Noir. Dark and sinister, he sat on his throne with his sister Azura by his side, glaring at her. "You failed."

"Not yet. I merely positioned my pieces."

Noir rolled his eyes. "You failed," he repeated.

Gadreyal could have handled it a lot better had Jaden not picked that moment to enter the room.

He was a handsome beast, except for those unnerving eyes. One a bright, bright green and the other a deep earth brown. Like Noir and Azura, he was a primal power who would have been invincible—

Had Jaden not sold himself to them to protect one of Gadreyal's greatest enemies.

"Is it done?" Noir demanded of Jaden.

He took a long minute to glare at his owner until he finally nodded. "I wasn't given dominion over trees for nothing." He snapped his fingers.

After a few tense moments, Vine slowly unfurled from the floor until she blossomed back into the great beauty she'd been.

Her eyes were dark and deadly as she glanced around them.

But Noir was unimpressed. "You two know your target. Do not fail again."

Gadreyal inclined her head to him before she took Vine's hand and led her from his study.

Vine didn't speak until they were alone. "I can't believe I live again."

"It's temporary. And if we don't succeed this time—"

Vine interrupted her with a laugh. "Don't worry. We have the element of surprise on our side. More than that . . ." She held up the medallion she'd traded out.

The medallion that gave them complete control of Cameron Jack and her bastard Seraph brother.

This wasn't over.

It was just beginning.